Rugged Mountain Ink

Filthy, Dirty, Small-Town Love

Khloe Summers

Summer to Winter Publishing

Contents

OBSESSED

Chapter One

Raven

I lean against the wall, sighing softly as the brick cools my bare back. I'm not usually this free with my body, but after countless conversations with my cousin Addie, I'm convinced that I've made a mockery of my college experience. I didn't go out drinking, I didn't club, and I didn't date a single soul. In fact, most every day of the last four years I spent locked away in my dorm room studying and drawing. My hours with a pad of paper and pencil made up my life. It didn't much bother me until I really got to thinking about how this was the last chance I had to be wild. After graduation, my get of jail free card expires. No one feels sorry for a college graduate who's making mistakes. That excuse is only good for those still enrolled. So then, here you have it. My attempt at wild and crazy... posing naked for the students in my art class. It doesn't have the same spice that a sorority party would have, but it's too late for that. Now, I work with what I've got.

A woman peeks from behind her canvas to study me. I think she's staring at the sheet, to be honest, examining how my hand grips the fabric and holds it loosely at my chest. Okay, so I'm not fully nude. I'm working up to it.

I try to relax my muscles, but there's an endless worry in my head that won't subside. *What if he comes back? What if he sees me exposed like this? When he left the room, I was still a fully clothed shy girl sitting in the back of the classroom like I have been all semester.* Now, apparently, I'm some exhibitionist who's wild and free.

My eyes trail from the door and back to center at least a thousand times in a series of two minutes. The professor instructed us to choose a muse and work on our final project. I volunteered *after* he left the room. I could never do something like this with him here. He makes me nervous. The way he looks, the way he talks, the air of confidence and sexuality that swings around him like a pendulum, it's all so overwhelming. If I had to describe him to someone, I would go with something more along the lines of intoxicating. He's like a drug. A drug I've taken a shot of every day now for months.

"Most are using graphite," a smooth, deep voice says from behind me. "Though I did see a few with oil."

My hair stands on end and my heart thumps against my chest like a hammer. It's him. Tall, dark, and handsome beyond any realm of reality, with a wide stance and the burly appearance of a man from the woods. He doesn't belong in this space, in a plain white button down. He's too big, too wide, his arms too tattooed, his beard too wild. He's an animal. An educated, well dressed, *wild* animal.

"Graphite," I nod, clearing my throat. "Yeah."

Oh my God. I'm such an idiot. If I could be cool for just one second, I would really appreciate it. I grip the sheet tighter at my chest and let out a weird cascading laugh that draws attention to me as students spy from behind their canvas to see what all the racket is about.

"Capture the essence of the subject," Professor Hill says. "Her shy laugh, and the way her dark hair falls over her shoulder. Memorize her." He looks toward me. "Drink her in."

My heart pounds nearly as quickly as my clit, as he stares back at me in the light of the mid-afternoon sun that streams through the skylight above.

Who am I? Who is this girl? And why is she naked?

I suck in a deep breath and let it out slowly. I try not to notice the scent of spice and soap that's on him, but I can't help myself. I want to know what he smells like; it will help me later when I'm fantasizing him to life around midnight.

God. I'm fucked in the head. This isn't normal. All this time here and the one man that I find interest in is my professor? Maybe I should have a visit with the school psychologist. I'm sure she could talk some sense into me. Then again, maybe they'd have me kicked out for even thinking such things about my teacher.

My throat tightens as his gaze stays fixed on me. "You should get dressed now, Raven. Class is just about over."

I hold my breath as he says the words. Part of me wishes he'd dismiss the rest of the class, lay me out here, and have his way with me. Or at the very least, tell me I'm too beautiful to take his eyes off. Then again, the attention from him would only dizzy me further and I'm not sure I need that kind of distraction so close to graduating.

Nodding, I stand from the stool and hold the sheet tight, making sure it's covering me fully before making my way to the storage room to change.

When the door closes, I hear Bethany's voice rise two pitches higher than normal as she talks. She's in her junior year, and she's the one that should've been posing. She's tall, thin, and everything about her is perfectly symmetrical. Art wise, she's perfection. Her boobs are small and perky, her waist is tapered and tight, and her face looks like one of those faces that belongs on a magazine cover somewhere.

I shake my head and I flick on the light as reality sets in. I'm panting over this grown man who barely knows I exist. Not to mention the fact that he seemed less than amused by my nudity. At this rate, I'm not sure I'd want him to be. I mean, it would be nice if he was, but he's not, and that's perfectly appropriate.

Shifting my weight, I slide back into the sundress I wore to class, then tuck into my cardigan. It's a warm reminder of the reality I should be living in. The one where I'm completely covered and *not* on display for the rest of the class. The one where I don't take unnecessary risks and do crazy things just to prove I'm not boring.

My hand grips the door handle, but I hold it in place, hoping the bell will ring before I come out of the room. I'm not sure what kind of dream state I went into in order to get naked and pose for the class, but that's clearly dissipated now and it's just me. Me and all my anxiety, hoping to avoid all the eyes that were just staring before I sneak out of the room.

Thankfully, the bell rings before my head gets too far into some alternate reality of what happened and I crack the door open slowly and sneak sideways out of the room, keeping my head down so that no one will notice me. But a shrieking voice does, and my toes curl.

"Raven," Bethany says, shuffling up to me on her way to the door. "You're so brave to do what you did today." At first, I think she's complimenting me, then I realize she's mocking. "I mean, I'm not brave enough, and I'm fit as a fiddle. I have to take lessons from you on how to be more confident."

My stomach tightens and my blood boils, mostly out of anger, but I think a little embarrassment is in there too.

"Have a nice day, Bethany," a deep voice says from behind me.

Bethany smiles wide and does this little hair flip blinking thing that makes my stomach turn. She's flirting with him, like she always does. If he was into anyone, it would be her. *God, can I please disappear? How about right now and forever?*

"Raven," Professor Hill says, "can we talk for a second?"

Technically, we could talk for the rest of the day. I'm free as of three minutes ago.

"Yes," I say, turning back. "Hopefully, I didn't do anything wrong."

A warm, genuine smile lifts onto his face as he strokes his hand over the top of his beard. "I have to know what made you pose today. You've been so quiet all semester."

Quiet is probably an understatement. I've worn the same color as the wall some days, just hoping I blend into the background enough not to be noticed.

"I think I lost my mind. My cousin called me last night and got in my head about my college experiences and I realized I'm graduating this month and I've had zero." I exhale as nerves tighten my throat. "It's dumb. I shouldn't have listened. She's much wilder than me. She loves dancing and bonfires. I love horses and books. Well... and drawing."

"I'm proud of you," he says, turning to busy himself with cleaning the space. He folds a few easels and stacks some sketchbooks in the corner of the room. "It takes a lot to come out of your shell like that."

I follow behind him, helping gather pencils and supplies to wrap into a cloth that we set on the edge of the table.

"I don't mean it the way Bethany said it," he says. "You make a much nicer subject than she does." He clears his throat. "If it's any consolation."

My heart squeezes. It *is* a consolation, and I'm not sure what I'm hearing, but I'm immediately reading into it. "She's beautiful," I finally say. "Her lines are sharp and pronounced. Mine are—"

"If I may," he says, dragging his finger along the lines of a canvas that's been left behind. It's hard to look at... me... in my natural state. It's funny what you think you look like and what other people see. "Someone like Bethany is all straight lines. Sure, they're sharp, but they're... boring. You, on the other hand..." he drags his finger along the outer rim of the drawing. "You're curvy. Your body tells a story. It's more enticing," he pauses, and his gaze meets mine, "to draw or paint, I mean."

My heart races as I look toward him. This is the part where I should excuse myself for the afternoon. Class is over. It has been for twenty minutes now and being next to Professor Hill has my body wanting to do things it shouldn't want to do. My mind isn't much help either. The longer we're alone, the more he says, and the more confused I get.

I shuffle forward, ready to run back to my dorm, and twist on the vibrator I've kept tucked under my pillow.

"Raven," he calls, smooth and even. God, I'm a mess. I'm officially a complete and utter mess.

I twist back, studying his oversized frame again with a hitch in my breath. He's perfect in this light. The late afternoon shadows and a bit of darkness on the left highlight his tattoos, though I can't see clearly what any of them are.

"Tomorrow, you'll finish your pose."

"Oh, no. Thank you, though. That was a once in a lifetime kind of mistake."

He grins. "I have a class of half drawn Ravens that need to be finished for final grades."

I'm not sure what to tell him. I'm definitely not in the headspace to strip down again and let the whole class see me naked for a second time, but I did start something. Something I should've thought through better. I mean, of course this would be a two-day event, if not more. I have no idea how long it takes to sketch a person.

"I'll think about it," I say, heading to the door in a hurry. "I'll see you tomorrow."

The second I'm in the hall, air finally filters through my lungs with ease. An ease it hadn't since Professor Hill walked in on me posing for the class.

I swallow the lump down in my throat and walk toward the campus center. Maybe mom was right about the city. It changes people. Maybe I've changed. Maybe I'm one of *those* girls. The girls that do risqué things with older men like the books I read. I'm not usually into student-teacher stuff, but the thought of Professor Hill telling me my curves were nicer than Bethany's straight lines is probably going to make my year... maybe my life.

It's just three more weeks. Three weeks until graduation and then I'm free. Free of his drug, free of this addiction, free of the intoxication of Professor Hill.

Trouble is, I'm not sure that freedom is all it's cracked up to be.

Chapter Two

Gage

I take a swig of beer and settle the glass bottle onto the table as I stare at the sketchbook in front of me. I've drawn what I could from memory, but my view was brief and fleeting. If I'd known she was posing, I'd have made my way back to the art room sooner. Then again, I left the class alone today just to give myself some distance from her after a dream I had last night. *A dream.* Reality is much more... real.

Shaking my head, I dig my palms into my eyes and groan. "*Fuck.*"

I'm crossing lines even thinking about her. I knew it the second I saw her. She's so quiet in the back of the classroom, so timid. She's unlike the other girls, who flirt needlessly and require endless amounts of attention. Raven doesn't want that. I'm not even sure she'd know how to flirt, or what to do with the attention once she got it. She's too innocent, too sweet.

My eyes close and I imagine her the way she was in the studio today. Her pale white skin was nearly translucent against the light as her long, dark hair swept against her bare back. Her pink lips pouted naturally and parted slightly as she bent forward, grasping the sheet like her life depended on it. Oh, and the small nuances of her face, like her scar above her left eye, and the freckle right beside it. And those dark eyes, *fuck*. She's gorgeous. Gorgeous and natural, with an eye for composition and shading that makes even the dullest of objects appealing.

I could watch her draw forever. I could watch the tip of her pencil slide between her full pink lips as she decides where to put the next line and where to shade.

My cock straightens, but reasoning kicks in before my mind goes further with the fantasy. I've never thought about a student like this before. Hell, it's been ages since I've thought about anyone like this. Thank God this is my last year of teaching. Maybe I can... no! I can't. Even if she's not my student, she's still fifteen years younger than me. I have no business messing around with a young girl.

I take another sip of beer and grab my sketchbook off the table, pulling the pencil I keep tucked in the metal rings. If anyone ever saw this book, I'd be mortified. Page after page of drawings, all of them her. A clear and visual documentation of every part of her. Her lips, her big, marbled eyes—so expressive and longing.

Touching the pencil to the paper, I relax as the rough scrape of lead moves along the textured white, my mind frantically trying to remember more of what I saw today. Her soft shoulders, her timid expression, her round breasts tucked out of sight. My skin turns hot and my cock presses against the zipper of my slacks. She's an obsession that's possessed me in the most delightful of ways. I can't get enough. The pencil moves back and forth as I shade in the curve of her collarbone and the twist of the sheet at her waist. I'm lost in a world of my own, living inside a fantasy I have no business in, until the phone rings, startling me back into the light.

"Gage here," I say, pulling back another sip of beer.

"Hey, Gage. This is Maddox down at Rugged Mountain Ink. How are you?" Maddox co-owns a tattoo shop with another guy named Henry in a place called Rugged Mountain. I met Maddox a month or so back when I was interviewing for an artist position at the shop.

"Pretty good. I wasn't expecting to hear from you all for another week or so."

"Yeah, I hope it's not a bother calling early, but we've been getting requests for you based on your drawings. We were curious if you'd be interested in starting sooner rather than later."

The thought of separating from Raven at the end of the semester is hard enough, let alone knowing I'll be far away, but I knew I needed a change from teaching the second I met her. And a lifetime ago, I used to draw tattoos in a shop right here in town. The work helped me pay for college. I never thought I'd go back, but there's something about using ink as a medium that connects you to a community that I admire. That, and this shop specifically, has offered me a large compensation package.

"The soonest I can start is three weeks from Friday, and I'll need a day or two to get moved into my cabin. Does that work?"

"That's perfect," Maddox says. "I'll have Henry send you all the paperwork you need to get started."

Pleasantries finish the call and I hang up, excited about the new path. I grew up in the mountains of Alaska, so I know what it's like to live in a small-town community. Most of the time, I miss it. Then, there're nights like tonight, where I'm lost in sketching, thinking about a girl I know I'll never have. Maybe this is for the best. She's young, she's sweet, she's talented, she's got her whole life ahead of her without a guy like me dragging her down. *This is for the best.* I tell myself again as I stare down at the outline of her pretty face.

In three weeks, school is over. In three weeks, I'm free of temptation, the pull, the obsession I have with Raven Baxter... whether I like it or not.

Chapter Three

Raven

My parents have been calling all week and I know deep down, I need to call them back. But ever since I left Rugged Mountain, there's been distance between us. I know they didn't like that I came to the city. When you grow up in a small mountain town, everything outside of the forest is like glitter. Shiny, sparkly glitter. Some people like the bright gleam of new things, others despise it. Glitter is the unknown. Glitter is the torrent that drives people to do bad things. Things they'd never do if they'd only stayed in their small town. I thought they were full of it until this semester when I met Professor Hill, and his keen ability to soak my panties a room away.

I pick up the phone and dial my parents' number, holding my breath as my heart slams against my chest. We're close, so they're going to pick up on my weirdness. They're going to know I'm having indecent thoughts about a man much too old for me.

"Raven Elizabeth," my mother, Cami, announces. She's got a tone of aggravation in her speech. I've been familiar with this voice since I was a kid. Usually, it was because I'd forgotten to take the clothes off the line before the rain came in, or I let my siblings get away with an extra cookie after dinner. I know she's not really mad, but the tone is obligatory for mothers to deter bad habits.

"Hey, Mom. Sorry it took so long to get back to you. Life has been crazy with school."

"Your dad is here too, honey."

"Hi, Dad."

I expect him to lecture me on timeliness, but he doesn't. He sounds happy to hear from me as he says, "Hey, kiddo. How's school? We miss you here."

"I know. I miss you guys, too."

"Your sister and your cousin both said they talked to you last week, so we knew you were fine. Enjoying your college life, I assume. Tell us what's new?"

Considering the most intriguing thing I currently have going on is posing naked for my art class, and the torrid affair I want to have with the professor, I decide to make something up.

"Oh, I'm just excited to graduate." I guess that's not a lie. "I have an interview lined up for a job in the city next week. It's something that—"

My father audibly huffs. "You're really going to stay in the city? Why don't you come work at the shop? I need good artists. You've always been exceptional. You didn't need college to prove that." My father is a firm believer in talent being inherent. You either have it, or you don't. To him, college is a waste of time and money.

I don't love the thought of being away from home. I do miss the country, my family, friends, the horses, the quiet, and really everything about Rugged Mountain.

"Ink isn't my medium, Dad. I'm a pencil girl, and there's a big calling for freelance work in the city. People love wedding sketches and there's a studio downtown that hires artists full time to sketch buildings for major companies. I have an interview this week."

Awkward silence burns my ears until I change the subject. "How are things there? Addie said that Uncle Maddox is having surgery next week?"

"Knee surgery. He tripped on a misplaced saddle down at the ranch and needs to have it reset. He'll be off his feet for the next eight weeks or so. Which means I'll be doing everything at the shop. How is Addie? I ran into her the other day at the diner, and she said she was coming up to visit you soon?"

Addie is my cousin and we're the closest in age compared to the rest of the kids in the family, so we've always been the best of friends, but I can't imagine if she came to visit right now. She's loud and isn't nearly as shy as me. In fact, she's the opposite of shy... she's uninhibited. I should call her and see what her plans are. The last thing I need is her showing up unexpectedly... which she's a fan of doing. Normally, I don't mind. But lately, I've been in my head and I think I want to stay that way for the time being until I get whatever hormones are raging under control. I can't imagine what would happen if it got out that I was having the hots for my professor.

"I'm not sure," I say. "I'm calling her after this. I should probably get going. I have to get started on my English paper. It's the last one of the semester and I haven't started yet."

"Okay, honey," my mom says, angling her voice up an octave so I know she's disappointed. "Are you still planning on coming for your birthday at the end of the month?"

"Your mother has spent a lot of time planning," my dad adds, reminding me that I don't have a choice. Though, I'd have come either way.

"Of course, I'm coming. I can't wait to see you guys."

"We're excited too, honey," Mom says. "Good luck on your paper. We love you!"

"I love you guys, too," I say, holding on the line a second longer before disconnecting. My family really is the best. They're supportive and loving, and they have the biggest hearts.

My dad was born and raised country folk. My mom worked in the city for a while before they met, but she's only known the mountain for the last twenty years. That and the work she did in the city didn't work out well for her, so she doesn't have the best taste in her mouth for Colorado Springs.

I check the time. It's eleven already. My art class starts in less than an hour. I can't help but wonder what's going to come of today. I'm nervous about going back. I started something I can't finish. Thankfully, today is darker, which means the light will be more forgiving.

Biting the inside of my cheek, I gather up my things, check myself in the mirror, and dial Addie. She picks up on the first ring with the perkiest hello I've heard since the last time we spoke.

"Raven! Why do I have to hunt you down every time I want to talk? I left you three messages, and I sent an email. Did you do anything wild and crazy like we talked about, or do I need to come and take you to some sketchy bar on the outskirts of town?"

"No," I say, cutting her off before she tries to talk me into some outlandish idea she has. "I did something crazy. I posed for my art class."

"That's not crazy," she says. I can feel her head shake in disapproval through the phone.

"I was naked."

"You were naked? Why were you naked? Maybe you went above and beyond the protocol. You're a nasty girl!" I hear her grin and I get a sense of sick pride.

"It was for an art class. I was the muse."

She gasps. "Lord, that's next level. Good for you! I had no idea you were such an exhibitionist."

"Well, not completely nude. I was in a sheet, but close enough."

"I'd say that counts. What's next? Apparently, art class has no boundaries, so I'm imagining for your encore you'll be fucking the professor?" She laughs, but my heart constricts.

"No! That's crazy! I would never ever even think about doing something so insane. I mean, God, they'd probably take my degree or something. Besides, Professor Hill isn't my type. He's rugged, big, and strong. You know I'm more into—"

"Oh, damn!" she says. "You *are* fucking your professor. Tell me everything!"

"What? No. I just said I'm not. I said he's not my type."

Her voice drops an octave as she says, "Girl, I've known you since the second I took a breath in this universe, and I know when you're acting shady. So, tell me now or I'm going to have to deploy a proper Baxter shakedown."

"A shakedown? Please... not a shakedown."

"Yup. I'll come up there with every cousin, aunt, uncle, and grandparent we have when you least expect it. I'll have everyone bring homemade recipes and—"

"Fine!" I say, already smelling Aunt Julie's homemade spinach and hot pepper dip. I love her and I love her cooking... but not at the dorms.

"I'm not sleeping with him. He barely notices me. I just have a little schoolgirl crush is all."

"And so you got nude in his class to show him?" There's sarcasm in her tone.

"He had gone back to his office for the remainder of class. I thought volunteering to be a subject for the canvas art we were doing would be freeing. So, I—"

"But you secretly were hoping he'd come back, that he'd see you, and that he'd *want you*." She says it like she's reading one of her dirty books, and I realize she might be right. When I thought of doing something torrid with my final days, I immediately gravitated to his class. Maybe I wanted him to ravage me right then and there like some romance novel where I inspired so much passion in a man that he couldn't help himself.

"Maybe," I confess, biting my lower lip as I head down the back stairwell toward the campus greens, "but it doesn't matter. If I was holding out hope that he would pounce on my naked body like an animal, he didn't. And if he did, it would have caused more trouble than one night is probably worth."

"So it's a sex thing, then? You just want to fuck him? Aren't you still a virgin?"

I roll my eyes and suck in a deep breath of freshly cut grass as I step out into the breezeway. "You're really hitting hard today. Yes... still a virgin. Are we good now?"

"Sorry," she laughs. "I am too. It's nothing to be ashamed of."

"You're also two years younger." I let out a heavy sigh. "I don't think it's only sex. I can see a real future with him if he gives me a chance."

My heart does this crushing feeling as I talk, realizing that I can like him all I want, but reality says I'll never have him, or hold him, or touch him.

"Oh, God," Addie gasps. "You *like him*, like him? Like you're into his *personality?*"

"Yeah. There's this way he talks that's so smooth and comforting. He's not just book smart. He's traveled the world. He's studied art at the Vatican. He's touched Greek statues. At the same time, he looks like one of those guys that would have a beer with you on the back porch swing on a Saturday night while he invited you to dance along to some country song."

She laughs. "Wow! You've really taken your time with these fantasies. Also, your roots show through even though you're in the city. I like that. You're still a country girl at heart. Maybe that means you'll come home to me someday." She spits out a fake cry, then shifts gears. "Why don't you talk to him then? The semester is over in a couple of weeks. Surely you can pursue something when he's not directly tied to your degree, right?"

"Yeah, well, he'd still say no. Like I said, he's shown no interest. And even if he had, I'm sure my parents would lose it if I came home with a guy twenty years older than me."

"*Twenty years?* Tell me he's got tattoos. What was the thing your mom always used to get worked up about back in the day? She went to see that psychic up on the hill who told her a man with a shipwreck tattoo would become obsessed with you. Maybe this is your shipwreck guy." She laughs.

"Okay, now I remember why I left the mountains. Y'all are crazy."

"Yeah right! Don't go hating on us. You know you're not too far removed from mud on your boots."

"I miss you guys, and I miss Rugged Mountain. I'll be home for my birthday. Be good, okay?"

She makes a kissing noise. "Good luck getting naked today. And if you ask me, the professor asking to see you strip down again is kind of a come on."

"Yeah, in a world where I'm not his student, and I didn't ask for this already."

"Whatever you say." She disconnects the line with a laugh, and I'm left standing outside the art room with a lump in my throat and a racing heart. I'm not sure I can do this again. I'm not sure I should've done it to begin with. Then again, I'm not sure my heart can take the disappointment when Professor Hill inevitably ignores me in favor of his office. Addie is right. I want his eyes focused on every last inch of me.

Chapter Four

Gage

Raven walks into the room with her sketchbook and pencil box tucked close to her chest. Her long dark hair drapes down over her shoulder and onto her back, across the top of a pretty purple dress that dots with white flowers. She settles into her usual spot at the back of the room and stares down at her phone, scrolling through as though she's trying to distract herself until the bell rings.

I should encourage her not to model today, or at the very least, leave the room to give myself some sense of distance from her. I'm not sure I could handle knowing she was nude in front of me for the next ninety minutes.

When the classroom is full, I start class, and Bethany is already running her mouth. "Professor Hill," she exclaims, "Raven is modeling today, correct?"

Everyone in the room glances back at Raven, whose eyes have gone wide. I know she's nervous. She didn't sign up for multiple days of modeling, and I don't want her to feel pressured or uncomfortable.

I glance toward her, softening my gaze. "Are you interested in continuing today, Raven? If not, we can work off memory."

"*Memory?*" Bethany chokes. "I barely remember what happened twenty minutes ago. I can't work off memory."

"Me either," another voice joins.

"Same," says another. "This is our final project. She volunteered to—"

"I'm good with modeling again," she says, standing from her desk to make her way toward the storage room to change.

Fuck.

I need to bail. I need to escape to my office, tuck myself behind my desk, and work on the paperwork I need to finish for leaving the college. I sure as hell can't stand here and torture myself with whatever comes out that door. But before I've gathered my things to leave, the storage room door opens, and Raven steps out, her gaze on me as she holds the white sheet tight around her chest.

"Do you mind if we play some low music? I have a playlist on my phone that's relaxing." Her voice is soft and sweet and there's a delicate scent to her that I hadn't noticed before. It's light and soft like a field of wildflowers picked after a rain.

"Of course," I manage, feeling myself unravel in front of her. "Yes, hook up to the Bluetooth and play whatever you want."

She smiles and my teeth grind together. I should leave. I need to leave. She settles herself in the soft velvet chair at the top of the stairs, where the light filters in just right from the window above. This art room was custom built for the way the skylights have been positioned. Her leg lifts and drapes over one arm of the chair as she leans onto the opposite arm. The class hums behind me, as the chorus of supplies being readied begins its symphony. I stand like a fool, studying her every move. So, when the sheet drops just slightly and her dusky pink nipples spear in the cool room of the studio, my mouth salivates.

Fuck.

I know I should look away. I know I should run. I know I can't control myself around her. She's too damn perfect. I imagine dismissing the class and stalking up toward her, sailing my tongue across her chest.

Fuck, I need her.

Restless energy spreads under my skin like a virus, infecting my mind and my soul until my fists clench and I storm from the room, leaving heat behind me as I head toward my office, locking the door after entering.

I sit back in my chair and unzip my pants, pulling out my hard, swollen cock.

This is wrong. I know it's wrong, but I can't help myself. I grip my dick hard and jerk fast, trying not to think of what an asshole I am.

She's young. She's innocent. I can see it in her eyes. Yet here I am, jerking off to the sight of her nipple. *What the hell is wrong with me?*

Her nipple. That hard, speared, pink, flesh that was desperate to be warmed. More devious thoughts ravage my mind as I pull at my cock. The thought of burying my face between her thighs, making her cry out in pleasure is too much.

My dick tightens and my balls draw up, as my muscles tense. Soon I'm warming my own hand with what I'd hoped to be painting her insides with.

I'm sick. I need help. Who does this?

I slink up from the chair and button my slacks, wiping my hand on a Clorox wipe from my desk. The chemicals burn my skin, but I deserve it. I'm not making good choices. Maybe it's good I'm leaving the college. I'm not sure I'll ever be able to scrub this shame off me.

I contemplate going back into the room, hoping that my release will be enough to quell the urges I'm having, but I decide to stay put. It's better for me and it's better for her. I can feel myself on the edge of saying something dumb and I don't want to mess with her head, especially not this close to graduation.

So instead, I file through paperwork and distract myself with words and numbers until the bell rings and I'm safe from all that haunts me.

****

A wave of relaxation presses over me as class ends. I know Raven will be heading back to her dorm and I have another class of students mooring in soon. This one, I may be able to stand in front of. Thank God, because I'm pretty sure I'm being paid to teach, not sit in my office, and jerk off.

Standing from the chair, I unlock the door and grab a file off my desk that I need to deliver to the front office.

"Professor Hill," a soft voice says from next to the door. My heart pauses all essential functioning, and my mouth goes dry. *How long has she been here? She's dressed again. I'm thankful for that, or maybe unthankful depending on how you look at it. Either way, she's standing there, with those big doe eyes and amazing breasts, staring up at me like she's feeling bad about something.*

"Raven... is everything okay?"

She nods. "Oh, yeah. Everything is fine. I just..." Her eyes twist down toward the ground. "I worried that I'd upset you somehow. You rushed out of the room so quickly after I undressed. I thought maybe I'd gone too far with the sheet. I pulled it back up after you left."

"You didn't do anything wrong. I'm sure the class appreciates your willingness to," I swallow hard, thinking of everyone's eyes on her and I'm uncomfortable all over again, "be free with your body."

Her gaze rolls to the side. "I'm hardly free with my body. I was," she draws in a sharp breath and wraps her arms tight around her books, "just pretending to be, for a few minutes. This is the crazy thing I'm doing before college is over. And now that I've done it, I'm pretty sure it was not worth the twelve canvases with my nipple drawn all over them." Her eyes trail to the side and downward as though she's embarrassed. God, if I made her feel embarrassed or unworthy of an audience, I should get on my knees right now and repent because that's not what's happening.

"Well, you did good at pretending. I had no clue you were feeling shy."

She looks up at me, those big round eyes like globes of innocence. "Why did you leave then?"

I look toward my desk. "I had work to do."

She nods. "Are you sure I didn't—" She stops mid-sentence and twists her hair for a moment before clutching the books tight again.

She's picked up on something and I need to give her more than the breadcrumbs I'm throwing, but it can't be so much that she thinks I'm interested or coming onto her in some way. I've built a nearly twenty-year career. I can't go out in some dumpster fire and take an innocent, hardworking student with me. This is my darkness, my burden to bear.

"It was uncomfortable," I finally say, arranging my face to some new expression that's somewhere between a half smile and worry. I'm not sure it's been named yet.

"Oh, God." She looks away. "It's my body, isn't it? You're embarrassed for me. I made a fool of myself." She spins in a full circle as though looking for an exit, then pauses long enough to stare at me in the eye. Damn it! That wasn't the right thing to say.

"That's not it at all," I say, focusing on her so she knows I'm serious. I reach my hand out and brush her forearm. I've probably just crossed my first boundary. Her skin is soft, like silk. "It made me uncomfortable to stay in the room because," I clear my throat, "you're—"

She sways closer to me unintentionally as though she's desperate for what I'm about to say next and for a brief second, I wonder if maybe she wants me to tell her I want her. Her lips part and her gaze meets mine, then drops to my mouth for a second before lifting again.

Am I reading this all wrong? Does it matter? I need to stop, either way. But my brain has just jumped on a train straight to hell and I'm pretty sure my cock is the conductor.

"What?" she says, almost begging. "I'm what?"

My heart clenches as I watch the thick vein in her throat beat. I want to run my tongue over it and kiss her slow until the rhythm eases.

"I..." I bite my lip and turn away. This is it, Gage. It's the last call before the train leaves the station.

A growl dislodges from my throat and I'm suddenly helpless to the words flying from my lips. "I think you're beautiful."

She hides a smile and looks down again, wetting her bottom lip before looking up.

"You're beautiful," I say, "and seeing you naked was doing things to me that aren't right."

She stares back at me with a hunger I'm sure I've never seen. A hunger I'm desperate to rescue her from.

I'm an educated man and I've spent most of my life building a career based on integrity and trust. But at this moment, none of that matters. She's awoken a reckless beast, a carnal desire, a primal instinct so overwhelming that before I have another rational thought, a growl bubbles up my throat and I tangle my hands in her hair, pulling her into my office as I grip her close and press my lips to hers.

A long aching sigh leaves her lips as she returns the touch and her books drop to the floor. Her hands plunge into my hair and pull gently as we touch, kissing one another as though life depends on our breathless survival.

My cock hardens and presses forward, poking at her stomach as she twists and moans in my arms.

Fuck. It's happening. I suck the lobe of her ear and groan out in pleasure as I hold her close. "You tell me to slow down, and I'll slow down."

"Don't stop," she moans, quietly. There's discretion in her voice, like she knows this isn't right as well. The sounds of people passing in the hall beside my office door is ever present. Anyone could be on the other side of that two-inch door from other students all the way up to the dean. If they knew what was going on behind this locked space, I'd be fired. The thought is almost enough for me to stop, but I don't. Doors slam and the bell rings for the next period to begin, and I grip Raven tighter. I hold her against my body as her curves melt into me and I lean her against my desk.

"I need to come," she begs. "I've been dreaming about you making me come all semester."

She's been dreaming of *me?*

"Oh, fuck. I had to escape to this room just an hour ago. I left to jerk off. I can't even look at you without my cock going rock fucking hard."

Our gaze meets as my words complete. Part of me expects her to be repulsed. I've shared too much. But she isn't. Her eyes light with a new kind of excitement.

"I want you, Professor Hill."

"Gage, call me Gage."

"I want you, Gage, but I've never um..." She looks away again, that nervous look back. "I've never done this... any of this before."

A long second goes by before I realize she means she's a virgin. Fuck. A virgin. Blood rushes in my ears as I try to calm myself, but it's no use. I'm not sure what to do or say, other than, "We should stop. You have your whole life ahead of you. You don't want your first memory of sex to be some dirty fling with an old professor in some windowless office."

"I do. I mean, not that you're old. But I mean... you're older than me, but you're not old and I really want you to touch me. I just thought you should know that I don't really know what I'm doing." Her hips rock against me as she speaks, threatening my cock with a tight little virgin pussy.

Fuck.

"If you don't want this, I need you to stop, because I'm about to lose control."

Her lips press into mine with an eagerness that somehow swells me further as she lies back onto my desk and looks up at me with desperate anticipation.

My hands graze up her smooth thighs and against the lace of her panties. *Fuck. How am I touching her panties?* Twenty minutes ago, I was going to carry my darkness alone. Now, I'm about to paint her walls with it.

I pull the lace down her legs, then palm her soaking wet core.

Her scent is soft and sweet, making me hungry. She rocks her hips and sways as I dip into her entrance. She's so fucking wet. Soaked, like silk and chaos against my fingers. I thrust inside of her, feeling the tight walls of her core stretch ever so slightly.

She moans as my thumb rounds her clit.

"How does it feel, sweetheart?"

She sighs and thrusts up into me with a groan searching for my cock, but I take my time with her, pulling my fingers from within to taste her sweet nectar before diving in myself.

Her breath catches at the touch of my lips to her core, and her body responds with lifted hips against my face.

She grips the side of the desk and my button down, thrusting upward in small circles as she squeezes her thighs against my ears.

"Don't stop," she begs, reaching for my zipper. She pulls it down slowly, as a strangled moan leaves her lips. My mouth suctions over her clit and I move my tongue in circles around her, striking two fingers inside as I work her body over.

Her thighs tense on my face and her fingers thread through my hair. Her moans are loud, unbridled, and riddled with relief as she spills her sweet pleasure onto my face.

I lap her up, kissing, licking, touching, admiring her in every way possible as she unzips my pants and grips my cock in her hand.

My eyes close and my head hangs back with the scent of her on my beard.

"You're huge," she says, her voice cracking. "How are you ever going to fit?"

A loud bang hits at the door and I jump. "Professor Hill. It's Dean Marshalls. We have an issue." What the hell would the Dean be knocking on my door for? I can't remember the last time she requested a personal conversation.

Then again, I'm currently fucking a student in my office, so the meeting might be warranted.

Raven looks toward me, biting her lip and scurrying off the desk to fix her clothes and hair. "I got you fired, didn't I?" she whispers, panting. "Where do I go?"

I point toward a chair in the corner as I zip my pants and beg my cock to hide itself. "It's okay. Have a seat in that chair. I'll fix this."

"One second, Dean Marshalls. I'm wrapping up a meeting with a student."

The deans voice goes stern. "This can't wait, Professor. Please open your door."

My jaw tenses as I look toward the locked door. There's no reason I should be locked in my office with a student. That's going to raise some flags. Then again, I guess that's what darkness does to a man. But I'm one hundred percent sure I would do it again... which may cause trouble with the dean.

Chapter Five

Raven

"You did what?" Addie gasps. I pull the phone away from my ear to save on the subsequent screaming that follows. "Well, you win. Turns out you're way crazier than I thought."

"Yeah, but I think he's in trouble now. The dean broke up our... session, and she looked pissed."

"Were you guys loud? How much did she hear?"

"Not much... I don't think. I mean, nothing. We were being quiet. I just... I'm sure she thinks it's weird that he was locked in his office with me and then I scurried away like I did something wrong. I'm sure she saw through it." I sigh. "I should've stayed and made up some story, but I panicked."

"How long has it been since you heard from him?"

"Forty-five minutes, but it feels like three days." I go silent, waiting for her to give me some advice, but she doesn't. She takes a big breath as she readies to probe me for more information. I should've known who I was talking to.

"Tell me everything! I need to know. How was it? Did he do all the things? Did you... come?"

"Okay, this is weird."

"Oh please. Don't get all tight lipped on me now. You're out in the big city, making big city decisions, sleeping with professors. You owe me the details."

I sigh. "Okay, well... it was great." I can't help but smile. "We were in his office, and he was touching me and his hands... they're so big, and rough. And he's just so strong when he's taking me over like this animal that needs to fill a void and I'm there like prey while he eats me and then I come... so hard. Like... Addie..." I pinch my lips behind my teeth as a rush takes over my body at the memory of my orgasm. "It was incredible."

"Okay," Addie sighs, "that sounds like some book fantasy. So now what?"

I sigh, unsure of what happens next. "Enough about me. What about you? What have you been up to?"

"Oh," she laughs. "Does something really come after your story? I mean, you clearly win the *'what have you been up to'* talk."

"Really, though," I beg, "I want to talk about something else."

"Well... this nice guy came into the diner yesterday and I'm entertaining the thought that maybe he'll circle back and want a date."

"*A guy?* What guy? What's his name?"

I almost hear her shrug. "No clue. I've never seen him before. He says he owns a series of clubs and he's looking to bring a branch here to Rugged Mountain. I guess he's getting push back from some people, but I think it's a great idea."

"What kind of club is it?"

"Not sure. Guess you'll have to come back to get the details. But I guess that's never happening now that you're dating your big city professor."

I grin and shake my head. "It wasn't happening, anyway. I told you I have job prospects here. Besides, we're not dating. We messed around once. I'd love to meet the big stranger when I'm back in town for my party, though. You should invite him."

"I don't know if he'll even be here. He seems like the drifter type."

"Oh my God! I just got a text," I say, glancing down at my phone. My heart pounds against my ribs. Seeing his name on my phone screen shoots an unexpected jolt into my groin. It's wrong that he's texting me. He must have gotten my number from the school directory. My clit thumps again at the thought of my body against his earlier, but Addie interrupts the memory.

"From the professor?"

"He asked me to meet him at the coffee shop off campus that's a mile away. Should I go?"

"Should you go?" she scoffs. "Yes, you should go! Call me right after. I need to know everything!"

******

The fact that we're meeting off campus tells me one of two things. Either he got into trouble, or he's afraid he's going to get caught. Either way, it's bad news. Bad news that I'm not sure I can bear. I want him. I wanted him the second I walked into that classroom. And though a part of me hoped having him physically would starve off the need, it's only seemed to make me want him more.

I'm selfish. His job is probably in the balance. We only have three weeks left of school, but I'm desperate to fuck him like my life depends on it. What the hell is wrong with me? And why does the risk of being caught send a pulsing straight to my clit?

I'm ten minutes early, so I order a half caff and sit at the table in the back of the shop, staring out at the scene of college kids rolling grocery carts to their cars. I don't know why I think of myself as separate from *them*, but I do. They're out partying and living it up. I'm tucked into bed by nine p.m. every night with my cup of chamomile cut fresh from my mom's garden with a romance novel in hand. We're not the same. So when I watch them shop, it's interesting, like I'm peering into the lives of the creatures around me that live the same but completely different lives. I'm surprised to see how healthy everyone is buying. Their bags are filled with organic soups and weird vegetables. I thought college kids were notoriously junk eaters. I know I haven't been shopping for ethically sourced kale for four years. I've been eating hot pockets delivered by a grocery service.

"Sorry to keep you waiting," Gage's deep, smooth voice interrupts my social study.

"You didn't," I say. "I was early. Is everything okay? I've been worried all afternoon that I'd gotten you in trouble."

He sits across from me, facing the back window. "No. It had nothing to do with you, but it was a close call. She knew something wasn't right when she left my office. Not only that, but I'm sure she could smell you all over me. In another second, she'd have smelled *me* all over *you*."

His words strike against me like a match, igniting me like a blaze of fire desperate to burn.

"I'm leaving at the end of the semester, Raven. It was in the works a while ago. I know we just started our journey but... I'd like for you to come with me when the semester is over. If we can wait these three weeks out, you can graduate, I can finish work, and we can meet again afterward." He laughs. "Even as I'm saying it, I don't think it's possible. The second I saw you again, I wanted back in between those legs." He bites his bottom lip and growls low, sending a shiver through my groin that's nearly unbearable.

I squeeze my thighs together to quell the urges, but it's no use. How will I manage seeing him every day for three more weeks and not touch him? My clit is already on overdrive.

"Where are you going? After the university, I mean. What about family and friends? You've lived here your whole life, right?"

He clears his throat, and fidgets with a straw wrapper on the table. "I used to be a tattoo artist when I was younger. I transitioned into teaching because I had a love for all kinds of mediums, but the love for ink never went away. I've, already taken a position." He looks down at the table, then back up again. "My parents passed when I was a freshman in college... car accident. From there, I've been on my own. The university was the first real family I had since Alaska, but even that has changed over the years. I guess I'm looking for that small-town feel I grew up knowing, but I couldn't go back to Barrow. That's too far off grid."

The tattoo shop thing confuses me a little. You'd think a professor would make a much better living, but my dad tattoos and has a really successful shop. I guess that's what matters. Alaska, though, makes a lot of sense. As a child of the mountains, it's easy to recognize it when you see it on someone else.

"I'm sorry about your parents," I say, reaching my hand out for him. Even the slight touch has my panties damp again. "Where's the tattoo shop you're going to work for? I hear there are tons of places here in the city. I grew up around a lot of artists. My dad owns a shop."

Gage looks toward me, his big brown eyes like warmth and security all wrapped into one, but I fear something dark is coming. "It's not in The Springs," he says, letting out a sigh. "It's a little place out in the country. The town is small, but the shop has a ton of press. These brothers are gold when it comes to advertising. They've had television shows showcasing the place, do celebrity work, and they only hire the best artists."

I'm curious to know what this place is, considering my dad's shop is the only place within five hundred miles that touts that kind of reception.

"What's the name of the place," I ask, gulping hard as I wait for his response. I already told my parents I was staying in the city for a job. That's only two hours away from home. I'm not sure I could tell them I'm chasing some professor to Wyoming or wherever this place is, especially for a rival tattoo shop. That would hit too close to home. Aside from that, it's crazy to think I'm chasing him anywhere. We've only known each other for four months. I have to think about me... my future... my degree.

"Rugged Mountain Ink," he says. "It's about two hours from here. The place is gorgeous. You could draw the mountains and I'm sure people in town would love portraits. Or you could stay in the city, and I could look for something else local. I just want you to know that I'm leaving the college and you're graduating, so if we want this to be something... it can."

A bolt of heat rockets through me and I break out into some kind of cold sweat.

"Are you okay?" He reaches across the table, gripping my hand in his. "Your face is flushing." He calls to the waitress for some water, but my ears are rushing blood like I'm drowning.

I look toward him. "Yeah, I'm good. I should probably head home, though. I'm feeling kind of sick."

His forehead wrinkles, but he doesn't question me. He stands from the table and helps me outside. "I can't let you drive like this. I'll take you back to campus. Or better yet, come back to my place tonight. I can keep an eye on you... nothing else."

We both know that's a lie. Given the time and space alone, I'd be touching him everywhere, ripping at his clothes, dipping onto his cock like some desperate tramp, hungry for professor's attention.

I smile, my stomach still turning as I scan his arms, studying his tattoos. I haven't been this steady and close before. "You really think we're that well behaved?"

He leans in slow and kisses my forehead. "Probably not. I can't let you leave like this, though. I said something wrong, didn't I? I can stay in town. I don't have to go."

"No. Rugged Mountain Ink is a good opportunity for any artist. The guys win awards over there for their work. One guy was asked to give a presentation in England on his shading and subsequently did tattoos for royalty. If that's what you love, they're lucky to have you."

His face brightens. "You know the place then?"

I swallow hard and look up at him with a knot in my stomach, noticing now, the tattoo on his arm that explains a lifetime of worry my mother's had. The man with the shipwreck tattoo. The man that's she believes will be *obsessed* with me. The man I have only now studied close enough to see the details of his sleeve. "Yeah," I sigh. "It's my father's shop."

Chapter Six

Gage

An agonizing week has gone by since I've seen Raven. She won't answer my calls, my texts, and she hasn't shown up for classes. I'm not sure what to do. Reason tells me to reach out to the guys at Rugged Mountain Ink and ask to speak to her father. I'm sure he'd understand the strange serious of events that led Raven and I to this place. Then again, I'm twenty years older than her, I was in a position of power when we met, and he's about to be my boss. I don't know as if he's going to be in an understanding mood.

Truth be told, I don't care about any job. I just want Raven, and I know how close she is to her family. I have to make this right.

I flick my pencil against my sketchpad and stare down the office desk where I had everything I needed just a week before. *Everything.* How did I fuck it all up in less than twenty-four hours time?

I could quit the tattoo job, but what good does that do? Her father already knows who I am. I've already spoken to the guy twice. The last thing I want is for him to think I'm some asshole who wasted his time and messed around with his young daughter.

I glance up at the clock. It's nearly six p.m. and the lights are going down. They'll lock the side doors soon, and the halls have emptied to a dull roar. I should go home, but I like it here, where the scent of Raven still lingers.

Twirling the pencil in my fingers, I flip to a blank page in the sketchbook from my bag. Drawing from memory wasn't a strong suit until I met her. Now, it's second nature. I can memorize a flower and recreate it on paper like it's right there in front of me. Likewise, I find myself drawing a desk, this desk, with Raven draped over the top of it, her thick thighs spread, her untouched flower open and willing, as her hair falls gently over the edge like a waterfall. This might be the only thing I have left of that memory. I could be staring at this sketchbook for years with only my thoughts to warm me at night.

"So you're still thinking of me," a soft voice says from the hall.

The sound of Raven is like being electrocuted. I'm alive again. I push the notebook away and stand, unsure if I'm having some kind of sanity break. Maybe I'm imagining her there. "*Fuck,*" I groan. "Where the hell have you been?"

"I had a lot of soul searching to do as I thought about what I wanted my future to be. I knew seeing you wouldn't help any of that. Plus, I had a job interview at one of those sketching companies downtown. Apparently, they advertise full time, but they're not full time at all. They're commission based and guess what... newbies don't get first dibs. So, I'm not sure that's going to pay the bills."

"I'm sorry to hear that," I say, desperate to reach out for her and press her against me until we're one. "Does that mean you're on the hunt for something else?"

"Sort of. You're going to think this is weird, so brace yourself," she says, reaching out for my arm to point to a shipwreck on my left forearm. "My mom went to see a psychic when I was thirteen and she said that I'd meet a man with a shipwreck tattoo. That he'd be obsessed with me." She smiles. "But I know now that it can't be true, because I'm obsessed with *you*."

She presses forward into my arms and kisses my lips. "I don't want to know what it's like to be with anyone else. I only want you."

I'm sure now, more than ever that I'm going straight to hell because having this woman in my arms again is like nothing I've ever experienced, and I'm not letting go. Not for this job, not for my integrity as a professor, not for her father, not for anything.

"I only want you, Raven, and that psychic was right. I'm obsessed with you. I can't stop thinking about you. The way you look, the way you feel, the way you talk, the way your sweet innocent smile curves so gently. You're perfect." I thumb over the top of her lips, brushing them lightly as a primal growl beats upward in my throat.

"I want you too, Gage. Do you know how hard it was to stay away this week?" She's panting as she speaks. "I talked to my father. I told him that I'd bring you home for my birthday. If... you're willing."

"I'm willing," I say, gripping her tighter.

"Truthfully, I think he's happiest that I'll be living at home again."

"Is that what you want, Raven? I can look for something in the city. I just want *you* to be happy."

She bites her bottom lip and stares up at me. "Actually, I thought of a really great idea this week. My dad has been hounding me forever to work at the shop with him, but it's not my thing. Then, this week when I was telling him about you, he mentioned opening my own shop. Not a tattoo parlor, but an art studio that gives lessons and does drawings for people in town. I thought it was a great idea." She smiles. "In his desperation to have me home, he's working on the details right now. Believe me, they're going to love you. My mom and dad have an age gap too. I'd forgotten about that until I talked to them. I think they just want to see you're a good guy." She clears her throat. "I did leave out the part where you are my professor, though. I just said we met on campus. So that might be our little secret... at least until they love you like I do." She looks away, then narrows her brows. "Love wasn't what I—"

"I love you too, Raven." I kiss her forehead. "My body knew I loved you the second I saw you."

She kicks the door to the office closed with her foot and kisses my lips, dragging her hand through my hair with an energy like she's hit her limit.

"I need you," she begs, "right now."

I know what she's feeling. It's an urge so strong that it strangles every other thought until all that's left is the thumping deep in my stomach that spreads to my groin and feeds my brain with the torturous hunger to claim her.

She kisses my lips again, panting wildly. "But maybe we should wait. I tried to stay away until graduation, but I couldn't. I know I need to hand in my final project, and I saw Dean Marshalls on the way in, but she didn't see me. I think she was leaving for the day, but—"

I mute her words with my lips, sliding my tongue across hers in a decadent sweep of desire and desperation. "I couldn't wait another second if you said the Dean was standing in the hallway watching us." I lift her onto my desk as my teeth grind closed, my jaw so tight it hurts. I know it's my body's way of trying to resist, but it's too hard. I want her too badly. There's no one left in the building but for a few straggling students and the janitors. We're safe for now.

I kiss her neck, then the lobe of her ear, heating her body with my rough beard as I trail down over her collarbone and onto her shoulders. Slowly, I drag each strap down and kiss the path where the fabric has shifted.

Her eyes study mine and hold firm as she unzips my pants and once again, reaches for my cock.

A bolt of heat rivets through me as I unclasp her bra and her large breasts fall onto her chest. She's a sight to behold as I strip off my pants and pull at her panties.

She stands from the desk and lets the sundress fall to the floor, every curve of her body displayed to me like a fine statue.

I catalog every freckle and crease, committing her to memory for a sketch later. Slowly, she unbuttons my shirt, and runs her hands through the tuft of hair on my chest.

"Last chance to stop me," I growl, my cock stretched as far as it will go.

She leans forward, resting her elbows on the desk as she swings her ass back and forth, tempting me. From here, I clearly see the roundness of her hips and her swollen pink center, opening like a flower for me.

My throat grows thick with anticipation as my skin heats. She's wrecked me, and I'm about to snap. I hold my body against hers, the scrape of my cock against her skin enticing me to break, but I hold firm and go slowly, cupping her heavy breasts in my hands. Her nipples are tight and beaded in the cool air of the room. I need to lick them. I need to suck those perfect, little nipples until they're warm again.

I turn her toward me and bend down, holding her gaze as my tongue hovers over her breasts.

She sucks in a sharp breath as I pull her nipple between my teeth. "Please, professor," she begs, more breathless than before, "fuck me. Fuck me hard. I need to be spread. Make the ache go away."

Chapter Seven

Raven

A week ago, I was harboring ill feelings about my college experience not being adventurous enough. Now, I'm bent over the professor's desk naked, begging him to fuck me. It's funny how time has progressed.

Gage's hand travels down from my breasts toward my core. He studies me close with a doleful smile that reminds me of a depraved animal who knows what he's doing is wrong, but he can't help himself. It's a look I've been craving. A look that makes my clit throb with an ache so deep I'm afraid nothing will satisfy it.

Dipping a single finger through my seam, he frolics in the wet pleasure already brewing, pulling his digit back once he's gathered a satisfying dollop. With a smile, he licks his finger clean and stares down at me, still leaned against his desk. "I think that tight little pussy is ready for me."

I lean up off the desk and stroke his cock in my hand before bending to my knees. Without warning, I slide him inside the warmth of my mouth and lick. I'm not sure if I'm doing it right, but when he groans and spreads his thick fingers through my hair, I figure I can't be too far off.

"Raven," he groans with desperation as he thumps into my mouth and holds the back of my head. A few long thrusts and he's ragged with misery. "Stand up. I have to fuck you, sweetheart. Now!" I love the way he talks. So needy, so anxious to have me, that common civilities go out the window.

I pull off his cock with a popping noise and follow his lead as he bends me forward again, holding the back of my neck with is large hand as he inches his way inside of me with a groan.

"You're tight," he pants, pooling warmth on the lobe my hear as he bends forward. "So, fucking tight." He works himself in slow, giving me time to adjust to his width, but I've anticipated him so long that my body is ready to take him.

He's large, spreading me wide, and the sting is harsh, but it dissipates in seconds, and the pleasure outweighs the pain. His weight pounds against me from behind, slamming the desk into the wall over and over again in a rhythmic series of thumps that are easily distinguished.

My nipples scrape against the cold, metal rings of his sketchpad on his desk as he gathers my hair in his hand and thrusts in deeper. I'm frantic for more and moan out my needs, "Right there, don't stop." He's hit a spot I didn't know existed. Until now, I'd only ever had a clitoral orgasm with my vibrator, but this... whatever he's hitting... is better than anything I've ever felt and I never want it to end. I grip tight to the side edge of the desk and hold on for dear life as he thumps in harder.

"Are you going to come for me, sweetheart?"

I mumble out some kind of incoherent reply as I reach back and grip his forearm for stability. He's hooked one arm onto my hip and that's the one I aim for.

"That's right," he groans. "Come for me. Give me all that tight little pussy has."

I love that I'm giving myself to him. I love that he appreciates how tight I am, how wound I am, how much I need him.

My breath quickens and a scream I've been holding echoes out louder than I'd planned.

Gage grips me tighter and thumps into me hard as I begin to tip over the edge. He leans into the back of my neck and kisses the soft flesh behind my ear. He's coming undone. His thrusting is more erratic, more brutal than it had been.

"Fuck. I'm going to come," he groans. "I don't know if I can pull out."

"Don't pull out," I pant. "I want your come. I want all of you."

He grips me tighter and leans into my ear again. "You could get pregnant. I should pull out."

"I want whatever you give me, professor. Just fuck me the way I'm meant to be fucked."

With that, a growl slips his lips, and he drives into me harder, until a knock at the door slows us.

Damn it. What the hell is going on? I can't take another stop and play. I need him.

"Professor Hill?" It's the dean, and the door is unlocked. "What's going on in there?"

Gage starts to pull out, but I hold him in place, and reach toward the door to lock it. The clicking of the lock screams in my ear as I hold Gage's arm tighter.

"Keep going," I whisper. "I need you're come."

He hesitates for a second. I hear the rumble of indecision in his throat. Then suddenly, he snaps. With rough need, he slams into me with a desire that's brutal and unforgiving.

I explode.

Showers of electricity wave throughout my body, setting me ablaze with heat and warmth until Gage too is coming, biting gently at the back of my neck as he thrusts.

"I should've been stronger," he whispers, peppering kisses down over my back as he pulls out, twisting toward me for a long kiss. "She knows what we're doing in here."

"It's not your fault. I came here. I begged you to fuck me. I made you finish. This is on me."

He shakes his head and holds me against his chest. "Maybe I can catch her before she leaves. She didn't see anything. We could blame the banging on a lodged door. Hell, she didn't even know you were in my office."

"She could know if she wanted to. There're cameras everywhere."

"Right," he says, exhaling. "The cameras."

The door knocks again. "You two can open the door. I hear everything you're saying." The dean's voice is stern and unrelenting. *How long has she been listening? Did she stay unmoving while we orgasmed? Seems to me she's the real perv here.*

When we've both dressed, Gage grips either side of my shoulders, and looks toward me. "Whatever happens here, I'm going to take care of us. This isn't your fault."

I hum a reply, but my stomach tightens as he opens the door, and we stare back at the dean who doesn't look as forgiving.

"Explanations are in order, I would guess," she demands, standing in the doorway in a dark blue blazer and heels. This is the first I've really looked at her—she's beautiful with short blonde hair and perfectly white teeth.

"It's my fault." Gage says. "I... I seduced her. I—"

"He didn't seduce me. I wanted him. I still want him. This was mutual, so whatever trouble he's in, I should be in too."

The dean shakes her head and looks to the right of the hall with a superfluous grin that's unsettling. "Was this really worth risking your degree for, Ms. Baxter?"

"It wasn't her fault," Gage growls. "It's me!"

"And was it worth risking your last two weeks of an otherwise perfect career, Professor?"

"Yes!" he blurts. "I'd do it again and again and again. I couldn't stop myself. And I know if I had to turn back time, I'd make the same mistake a thousand times over. She's worth the risk, every time."

My heart swells.

Dean Marshalls drags in a deep breath and gives us both a half-hooded expression. "I could take your degree, Raven. And Professor Hill, I could revoke your teaching license. What then?" She stares back at us long and hard.

I bite the inside of my cheek. This is it. This is four years of work down the drain. This is Gage's entire career ruined... and it's all my fault. I should've stayed away. I knew it! That's why I hadn't answered his calls. It's why I'd avoided class. I knew the second we saw each other this would happen.

Gage looks toward the dean. "You can't take her degree. I'll do whatever you need. Punish me... but Raven's worked hard. She deserves a second chance."

Dean Marshalls crosses her arms over her chest and looks toward us both, measuring her glance like an animal out for a kill. "You could've stopped fucking. I was standing right outside the door."

So she did hear us. Now, it seems stupid that I wouldn't let Gage stop, but at the time, the need was so strong it was impossible to think any other way.

"That was me," I say. "I—"

"None of this was Raven. Just do what you have to. I'll take the punishment," Professor Hill says, his voice rumbling as his face contorts to frustration. Even now, I want to relieve it again.

I need help.

Dean Marshalls shakes her head and bites the inside of her cheek. "You're in no place to be making demands, professor." She sighs. "That said, considering you're leaving anyway, and I think the only person that would be punished is Raven, who has until now," she diverts her gaze to me, "has been an exemplary student, I'm going to let you both go on two conditions. One, you two keep your fucking off school grounds. Two," she turns toward Gage, "you never teach again. There's an expectation of trust in the institution when people attend college. It's great and all that you've found someone special, but I can't allow anyone to exploit the authority they've been given. If you are both telling me this is love, I believe you. But, if I see you take another job as a professor, I'll release the tapes and end your career. Is that understood?"

We nod in unison, and the tension in the room relaxes as the dean turns down the hall, leaving an echo of clicking heels behind her as she walks. For a long moment we stand in silence, as though each of us is comprehending what's just happened. Finally, Gage looks toward me.

"I guess there's no looking back," he says with a smile.

"Are you sure you're okay with all of this?"

"I think the harder stipulation will not be fucking on the school grounds," he chuckles.

"I think you're right."

"Do you know what this means, though?"

I bite my bottom lip and shake my head, hoping for something dirty. "No... what does it mean?"

"It means your mine, no matter what. Now and forever. Mine to sketch, mine to touch, mine to hold... whenever I want."

I bury myself against his chest as my heart swells. "That's fine by me, Professor Hill. I'm yours."

Chapter Eight

- -

Gage

Two Weeks Later

A long narrow driveway leads down to a cabin tucked away in the woods. Pine and cedar surround the exterior and there's a bundle of balloons tied to a fencepost just outside the front door. We followed friends of Raven's here, but they seem to have parked somewhere else. I lost track of them when Raven was talking about her memories of the mountain, which only got more intense the closer we got to the house.

I want to know every detail of her past like I was there. I want to know how she became who she is.

"Should I go back up to the street?" I ask, resting my hand on Raven's knee as I take note of the driveway crammed with trucks.

She shakes her head. "I think we're good. You can park between the white truck and the red one. Uncle Maddox won't mind that we're double parking him. I *am* the guest of honor, after all. Besides..." She nods toward the door, noticing her dad as he steps out onto the porch.

Fuck. Maddox is her uncle. Henry, the more serious and imposing brother, is her dad. Even though we've met in passing before, I didn't realize how big he was until his eyes are locked directly on me. He's not just tall, but something about this light makes the man look like a tank with a neck like a tree trunk and limbs to match.

I swallow hard and wave. Raven said he acted excited on the phone, but I'm not naïve enough to think that he wouldn't have things he wanted to say to me. Things I'm sure aren't going to be pleasant.

"Are you okay?" Raven smiles, squeezing my thigh. I nod, glancing toward her as her father stands wide in front of the truck... just waiting.

"He's a lot bigger than I remember."

She laughs. "What are you talking about? You're just as tall as he is."

"Yeah... but look at the man. I'm not sure if you know this, but he's a beast."

"He's not going to hurt you if that's what you're worried about," she smiles. "I wouldn't let that happen. Besides, he's a teddy bear."

My throat tightens, as I watch her jump from the truck and wrap into his arms. "Daddy! I missed you!"

He holds her close, but his eyes never leave mine... and they're intense.

Yeah, real teddy bear.

Fuck. In forty years, I should've done the *'meet the parents'* thing before, but I've never been close enough to anyone. I see why it's nerve-racking.

I step from the truck and hold out my hand. "Great to see you again, sir. I—"

"Didn't expect the next time I saw you to be with my daughter. Care to tell me how that happened?"

"Oh, Dad," Raven says. "I already told you... we met at school."

"Right... and had you thought through how I could just check his resume? He's an art professor. You're an art student." Henry's gaze locks with mine and his jaw tightens.

"I was her professor, sir." I glance toward Raven before meeting Henry's stare once again. "I didn't mean for it to happen. She's electric, talented, beautiful, and I should've been stronger."

Henry folds his arms over his chest and widens his stance as he looks toward Raven. "What were you thinking dating a professor? You're lucky you didn't get kicked out of school."

"I know, Daddy." She twists her dark hair at her shoulder, and I hope I haven't overstepped what she was comfortable telling him, but I didn't want to start the relationship off with lies. "But don't blame Gage. It's all me. I was the one that started this thing and—"

A shorter woman with Raven's eyes steps out from inside the house with open arms. "You must be the shipwreck guy."

"Shipwreck guy?"

Henry shakes his head and smiles before wrapping the woman in his arms. "Darling, I think you just made a new best friend. You may have just given a man a stay of execution," Henry says with a sneer. "My wife saw a psychic a few years back. She was told a man with a shipwreck tattoo would be obsessed with our daughter. We're hoping that's a good obsessed." He laughs. "Either way, she's invited a psychic back, so get ready for a fun night."

"I'm Cami," the woman says with a smile. "Everyone picks on me, but I'm just looking out for my girl." She reaches out for Raven's hand.

"We're in love," Raven says, her voice low. "You guys didn't have a conventional meeting. We don't either, but when I'm in his arms... everything feels right."

Fuck, I love this woman. I grip her hip and pull her into my orbit, then look toward her parents with heartfelt authenticity. "I promise you, I'm going to take care of your daughter. I'm going to love her with everything I have. I'm going to build her a cabin just like this, and we're going to live out our days here on this mountain. I plan to marry her, make babies with her, shelter her, guide her, hold her, and never stop loving her." I look toward Raven and thumb away a tear on her cheek, then turn back toward her parents. I now notice the Raven tattoo peeking out behind her dad's shirt. The black beaked bird sits on his shoulder. I wonder if it came before or after Raven.

"Tattoos mean a lot to me too," I say, looking toward Cami. "I got this one eight years ago in memory of my parents. At the time I felt wrecked, like a ship lost at sea." My gaze twists back to my love. "But now... I guess your psychic was right. *I'm obsessed.* I'm obsessed with your daughter and I'm never letting her go."

Henry and Cami look toward each other and smile before looking back at me.

"I like your honesty," Henry says, hugging me. "But if you ever hurt her, I'll be the one *obsessed...* with dragging you behind my truck."

"Dad!" Raven shouts.

"What?" Henry smiles. "He's a big boy. He's come here telling us he wants to be with you forever and become a member of our family. So, these are my terms."

"I accept," I say, squeezing Raven's shoulder. "No one will ever harm Raven ever again."

"So, this is the man everyone's talking about," a young, curvy girl says stepping out of the house. "He's hot! Are you guys coming in or is the party moving out here? Everyone is inside dying to meet your date!" She leans toward me and holds out her hand. "I'm Addie by the way. Raven's cousin and very best friend... so you might want to get used to me."

I smile and hold her hand in mine. She's spunky and I like it.

"I hope you like families," Henry says, leading the way for us all to head inside, "because this one is about a mountain wide."

I hold Raven's hand as we step into the cabin and greet the room of people all looking back at us. I don't know their names yet, but the light on Raven's face when she sees them all is everything I need to know. This is her home. These are her people... and I can't wait to be a part of it.

Epilogue

‑‑

Gage

One Year Later

Raven lays out on the couch with her hand resting on her forehead. She wears one of my flannel shirts with the top button fastened while the rest of the top flies open, making room for her perfectly round belly that protrudes from her abdomen. We're seven months along today.

"I think the party went well, don't you?"

She nods. "I think I'm the only girl in the world that still gets full blown birthday parties courtesy of mom and dad. I hope it never stops."

"I'm just glad your mom gave up on the tattoo hunt."

"Well, to be fair, she did make you talk to that psychic for a full thirty minutes last year to get a vibe before she trusted you."

I laugh. "I don't blame her. Hell, I'll probably be doing the same with *our* daughter." I place my hand over her stomach, moving in circles as I wait for Sienna to kick, but she doesn't until Raven's phone rings.

"It's Addie," she says. "I'll put it on speaker."

I nod my head and continue on with my rubbing. Addie is a huge part of Raven's life and has subsequently become a part of *my* life.

"Hey, girl," Raven says, setting the phone on her swollen breasts as she talks. "What's up? Did you hear back from that guy you were talking to?"

"Sort of. He's coming back to town this week for the opening of that club. I'm going to see what trouble I can stir."

Raven laughs and darts me a look of worry. "You are good at starting trouble, aren't you?"

"What does that mean? You're the one that rolled back here a year ago with all the secrets."

Raven laughs. "And now I hear about it constantly."

"Just promise me that when I make the same bad decisions with Mr. Dirty Talk, you'll cover for me the same way I did for you."

"Mr. Dirty Talk? Who's that?"

"The guy," her voice strains. "The club guy. He's got this way about him that's like," she sighs, "we were having a donut down at Josie's bake shop when he was here last, and he didn't just eat it. He told me all the things he loved about it. The creamy center, the sugary icing, the way it melted in his mouth. You have no idea how hot it was."

My brows raise as I look toward Raven.

"Well then," Raven says, "let's hope he takes an apply all approach... for your sake."

"Yes," Addie sighs, "I agree. Anyway, I just wanted to call and see how you're feeling after the party today. Your mom acted like you were dying, not pregnant."

Raven smiles. "She did, but I'm her first born and I don't know... I get it. She wants to protect me."

"Well look at you," Addie chirps. "Your motherly instincts are already kicking in. You're a savant. Must be all that Professor fucking." She laughs harder than she should. "Sorry... sorry... you know me, always keeping it real."

Raven and I smile as well. "I love your realness... and I can't wait to hear about your dirty talking club owner. People say it's going to bring a lot of tourism into the area. It'll be good for the tattoo shop, and for my art studio."

"I'll let you go. I'm sure you have to pee or eat a pickle or something." She laughs again. "Love you, girl."

"Love you more," Raven says, disconnecting the line.

It's interesting, watching your partner connect with other people. You appreciate them for one thing, but watching them be a friend, a mother, or a daughter deepens that emotional attachment. Raven's good at all those things. Everyone loves her, though I beg to say I love her most of all.

"The light is really good right now," I say, reaching out for her hand. "Would you come out onto the back porch with me, Mrs. Hill? I want to finish my sketch."

She nods and rests her hand in mine, giving her weight to me as I help her off the couch. I'm going to miss this shape of her when the baby's born. She's my muse. And right now, she's glowing.

I lay her back on the wicker couch in the late afternoon sun, admiring her beauty as rouge slivers of light fight their way through the clouds and land perfectly on Raven's pale skin.

Her eyes flicker up to mine as her pulse races behind the thick vein in her throat and I'm brought back to the first time I saw her. She was so innocent and needing at the back of that classroom. My cock roars upward just thinking about it.

She grins sheepishly. "I thought we were out here to draw?"

My hand runs over her smooth inner thigh. "I was, but that pregnant body of yours is killing me."

"Killing you?" She opens herself to me.

I graze my fingers over her panties, watching as her hips rock against my touch. What is it about this woman that cages me without regret? My hard length presses against her as I nudge her panties aside and dip into her sweet juices.

She sighs at my touch and handles her swollen breasts with care as I work my lips between her thighs.

"Fuck, you taste like honey." I lick her up gently before sucking onto her inner thigh. Then I kiss her pretty slit once more before pulling off her jeans.

I like her like this, swollen and curved, aching and helpless, whining and panting. "Do you want my cock?"

Her gaze meets mine with heat and she nods, biting her bottom lip. "I do. I want you."

I sit on the couch next to her, my cock straight in the air, hungry for her hips, and her wet, creamy, center.

She sits up from the couch and stretches a leg over me before sitting slowly on my dick. She's slower now than she was a few months ago, but I like it better this way. The moments last longer, and there's a build-up that's more rhythmic. Her hips rock and spin as her head tips and her hair falls down over her back, tangling with my fingers as I hold her in place. Her swollen breasts bounce slowly, her nipples a darker shade of purple with her pregnancy. She's a scene to be memorized and drawn later. Her mouth hangs open and a simple sigh releases as she looks toward me.

Fuck. I'm sitting and my legs are wobbly. She's too much.

With one hand still entwined in her hair, I use the other to circle her clit, licking on her sensitive nipples as she continues to ride.

Raven grinds harder, leaning forward until our foreheads are pressed together. "I'm going to come, Gage. I'm going to come so hard." She's breathless as she speaks. Her thighs tighten around me, and I sense my own nearing.

My cock throbs and my balls tighten, as the walls of her mound close in on me when she bears down.

"Yes," she pants. "Now... right there."

Her sweet sounds take me over the edge and I lose myself in a blinding moment of ecstasy that empties my soul into hers.

She grinds a second longer, coming over my sensitive cock as I hold her against me.

"Fuck," I growl, kissing her lips before trailing down to the lobe of her ear. She loves it when we end in this sensitive pile of nerve endings.

A shiver runs through her. "I love you, Professor Hill."

Her words have my hair standing on end. I lean into her ear again. "You know I love it when you call me professor."

I feel her smile against my face. "I know you do. I should probably stop after the baby's born. I don't want her getting the wrong idea about her teachers."

I bite the inside of my cheek. She might be onto something there. "Okay then, I'll keep you my dirty little secret."

She kisses my lips gently and presses her forehead against mine. "I wouldn't have it any other way."

Dirty Talker

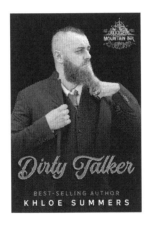

Chapter One

Addie

M ost of my best memories come from some old dirt road at twilight. Which is why I can't explain my bliss balancing a tray on my palm as I walk through the biggest country club Colorado has ever seen. It's even more complicated that it's a new addition to my childhood home, Rugged Mountain. A place where generations of my family grew and raised families of their own. Now, The Barnyard caters to people not looking for that small town life, but rather a crazy nighttime atmosphere. Thankfully, I can keep my two worlds separate on opposite sides of the mountain.

When I get to the table I'm delivering drinks to, I smile and settle long necks in front of the couple. I've never seen them before. Between my day job at the diner and this one, I feel like I've met everyone that comes up on this mountain. This place is completely different from the diner, though. For one, it's set off away from the main part of town. I'm not sure if it was intentional to give some distance to our small community or no one would sell space to a club. Second, this place is trendy. There's a mahogany wood bar, big string lights, a wood pine dance floor, a mechanical bull, a stage with a band playing country music, and big, wide beams that hang above that make the place seem like a big old barn. Plus, the tips are better than the diner. Sure, I have to wear this super short skirt and I unbutton my shirt a few more notches, but it's worth it. I make triple the cash in two hours less, and I get to look at Declan Myers.

Granted, he's a supreme tyrant with a grandiose complex that I'm sure rivals Stalin, but his shoulders are wide and his biceps flex through the white button down he wears, threatening the fabric with each bend of his elbow. Even with silver threads running through his black hair, he's more attractive than any man I've ever seen.

The hard work mentality that he has doesn't end at work. He carries it into his personal life as well. He's disciplined and tenacious. It makes me wonder what else he'd be tenacious with.

I set my tray back onto the bar and rattle off an order to Violet, who's been bartending here since her twenty-first birthday six months ago.

She runs her hand back through her short black hair and grabs a bottle of vodka off the shelf behind her. "Has your dad found out you're here yet?"

I bite the inside of my cheek and sigh. "Not yet. I need to tell him before someone in town recognizes me and mentions it. You know how fast news spreads around here."

Her dark eyes widen, and she nods, mixing grapefruit juice into the shaker. "You're telling me! Ever since I quit college, I've been getting the third degree daily. Apparently, no one thinks I can make a career from that hiking guide thing, but I've had like three calls already this week from tourists looking for a guide. Plus, I meet people here daily that want to take a walk alone in the woods." She laughs. "You know what I mean." Before she says another word, her eyes gaze up and away from me. It's then that heat grows behind me that wasn't there before. I see it in her eyes that it's *him*. His big, strong body is heaving behind me.

"What are we doing, ladies?" Declan's voice is so deep he's almost growling when he talks.

My stomach turns and my eyes meet Violet's.

"Just finishing up a drink, Declan," Violet chirps, busying herself again with my salty dog.

"What about you, Addie?" Even when he's angry, the way he says my name is enticing.

God, what's wrong with me? I shouldn't like the way my boss says my name. I shouldn't think about the way he looks.

I grip the edge of the bar and spin toward him with a smile, hiding every bit of tragic yearning I have for him. At least I'm trying to, anyway. Today, that white shirt seems tighter somehow.

"I was just waiting for my drink, sir." Sir, I'd like to say that name again and again, but in different faculties. "It's a busy night."

A faint smile lifts his face. "I like to keep it that way. Do you know how we do that?"

"Fast service?"

He nods. "You're quick. And how do we ensure fast service, Ms. Baxter?"

I bite my bottom lip and stare up at him. I don't like getting ordered around, but somehow with him, it's... different. His voice is smooth, and the words are somehow warm despite their cold intent.

"Actually," I say, staring up into his dark eyes, "the customers like it when they see us smiling and interacting. It makes them feel at home."

"But they aren't at home. They're at a bar. They want their drinks fast."

I grin. "Also, this is a small town. People expect this kind of comradery between employees." My heart is set on rabbit, thumping wildly against my rib cage. I'm not sure why I'm defending my actions, but I like watching him think.

He looks away, then swipes his thumb over his beard. "You use this small-town excuse with everything. You realize that, right? Last week, you told me that inviting the delivery man in for a free beer was customary small-town behavior."

I nod. "Because it's true. That man was working hard! He deserved a break." I stare up at him, unsure of what he's going to say next. I've questioned him, and I know he doesn't like to be questioned.

His strong hand wraps around my wrist. I knew he was big, but having his hand on me is alarming. He's a giant. And though I'm not a small girl, next to him, I feel dainty. His eyes fix with mine and his thumb brushes over the top of my wrist.

My clit throbs. It shouldn't be throbbing. I should be appalled that my boss is touching me. That he grabbed me so harshly that he's holding me in place. I should kick him and disentangle myself from his touch. But my body knows better, and I swear, I lean in closer just to get a deeper sniff of the cedar and spice in his scent. Ugh, he's heaven.

"You're going to be the fucking death of me, Ms. Baxter." His stare sits on mine before a sly grin creeps onto his face.

Dizziness washes over me. What does he mean by that? He's saying it with a tone of both desperation and anxiety. And I swear there was a twinge of longing in his glance.

Is he as desperate for stolen touches as I am?

In a second, he releases my arm and I suck in the cold, staggered breath of reality before I swipe my salty dog from the bar.

"I'll be more cognizant of my actions, sir." I try not to look at him again when I talk, but it's impossible. He's massive... solid... a titan.

"Actually," he says, brushing my arm again as I walk past him, "I was hoping you'd help me with something."

Help him with something? What would I ever help him with? He's got money dripping off of him. If he wants help, I'm sure he could hire just about anyone, or he could ask any of the twenty thirsty women staring at him tonight. I don't say any of that, though. Instead, I ignore him and carry my drinks to the waiting table, then turn back, tucking my tray under my arm.

"Sorry, my boss is a real asshole."

He rolls his eyes up and shakes his head. "Is this a country girl thing, too? That you always having to be right?"

"I'm glad you've noticed," I grin. "I do like to be right. So, what do you need my help with?"

His dark eyes flicker to mine again. "Getting the word out about the party here next week. I figure you're still at the diner all day, right?"

I nod, my stomach turning at what I guess is coming next.

"You can tell everyone about the hoedown I'm throwing." He winks. "Tell them their favorite waitress will be serving all the drinks they can handle. I'm sure that will get them over."

My body is desperate to take the flattery, but my brain goes to panic. "My family doesn't know I work here."

His forehead wrinkles. "So tell them."

I shake my head. "No way! My father, for one, hates that you're open to begin with and everyone else in my family would die if they saw me in a short skirt serving drinks like this."

He stays quiet for a long while, then stands straight. "You're a Baxter. *Fuck*. What's your father's name? Why didn't I put this together sooner?"

A lump grows in my throat where there hadn't been one before and my fantasy of locking myself away with my big sexy boss grows less and less likely in my head.

"It doesn't matter who my father is. I'm twenty-three. I can serve drinks—"

"Your dad is Maddox, isn't he? I should've figured as much when I hired you. There's just so many of you Baxter's on this mountain."

"We're not *on* this mountain. We *own* this mountain."

"Yet you're working for me," Declan says, standing taller. "You need to tell your father what's going on, or we'll have to cut this off."

"Cut what off?" I balk. "*My employment?* You can't do that! I haven't done anything wrong."

He looks down at me, grazing his hand across my lower back as he walks away. "Your father is the one person in town opposed to this bar. And you said it yourself, he owns most of this mountain. He needs to know you're here, Addie." His gaze tracks back to me with heat, and I swear a bit of pent-up desire. "For both our benefit."

My clit throbs again, though I don't know why. Well, I do kind of know why. Declan Myers, the tyrant of The Barnyard just stole enough glances and soft touches to leave my panties soaked and my heart racing. And for the life of me, I can't figure why my *dad* needs to know.

Chapter Two

Declan

I'll buy Addie a longer skirt if that means she stays. I hate the way men stare at her, anyway. She's curved and shapely, with an ass that rounds out, breasts that bounce, and a waist that sturdies the two. Most men don't get to admire her face. They get stuck on her ass, or the six inches of cleavage that gets her those big tips. While I enjoy her body, my fixation is with her face. She's gorgeous. Perfection. Flawless. Long dark hair, pixie nose, a tiny freckle next to her big blue eyes, and full lips that don't stop running. Not only that, but she challenges me. *No one else does.*

A knock on my office door interrupts my thoughts. I look up to see Violet in the doorway, cowering.

"Can I help you?"

She nods. "Sort of. I'm worried I got Addie in trouble yesterday. It was my fault she was talking, and I—"

"She's not in trouble," I say. "Get back to your station."

Violet ducks her chin. She's afraid of me. Everyone is. To them, I may as well be a demon. I'm not sure I completely understand. I give them all sufficient breaks, make sure they get time off, and I pay top dollar above anyone else in this town. For that, I expect the work to be done right.

Does that make me a monster?

Violet doesn't question me; she rushes back downstairs, and I'm sure takes over her station within seconds of me asking her to. She's an honest worker with determined dreams of her own. That's something I can admire, but the girl needs to toughen up.

I glance down at the laptop and watch the security cameras as Addie walks in. She's worked all day at the diner, and she still strides with energy in a tight blue jean skirt and a button-down plaid that's popped to nearly mid breast. When I chose the uniforms, I didn't expect anyone to wear them the way she does. The dark red in the top strikes against her smooth pale skin with a beauty I didn't know existed. I follow her on the screen, watching as she moves between each room and up the stairs toward the employee office. It's only a room away. I should walk past, say hello, and see if she's told her father about her job, but before I get a chance to stand, she slams her locker closed and makes her way to my office door.

My heart crushes when she stands in the doorway. She's so beautiful. God, I shouldn't look at her the way I do. She's young. She's the daughter of the guy who owns the whole damn mountain. He detested my arrival. He detested me opening the club. He thinks my club will corrupt the youth. A slight chuckle escapes. Maybe he was right.

"What can I help you with?" My tone is darker than I'd planned.

"I didn't like your ultimatum yesterday. I just thought you should know." She spins to leave the room, but I stand to meet her in the hall.

I regret it, but it's already been said. I can't go back now. "It wasn't an ultimatum. It was an order. Your father needs to know what you're doing here."

She folds her arms over her chest, squishing them upward as her face distorts. "And what does this have to do with my job?"

I could tell her that I don't want bad blood with her family because I plan to sweep her away to my cabin later and have my way with her, but I doubt that would go over as well as, "I don't want enemies. It's not required of your job, but it would mean a great deal to me. Your father has a lot of pull here. If I piss him off, the business could pay." It's all a load of shit, but it sounds more professional, then the former thoughts I've been having.

She rolls her eyes. "My father is a cinnamon roll. A crunchy one, but still... he wouldn't hurt anyone. Besides, the townspeople voted on this place. You're here because they wanted you here, and you purchased the land. So, my father can't do much about it."

"He could start digging up dirt on me," I groan. "And with a little dirt, these nice, small-town folk aren't going to want anything to do with me."

She narrows her gaze and shakes her head before folding her arms in front of her chest again. "What? No. We aren't like that here."

I'm surprised she hasn't asked what dirt there is to be dug. Instead, she looks away and bites at her bottom lip. I know I should focus on the conversation, but there's a hunger that brews inside me when she's around. A heightened awareness that's nearly impossible to control.

"You know what I think would help you make friends and gain patrons for your hoedown?"

I shake my head with reluctance, but her eyes light.

"You should talk to the townspeople," she pauses, "*nicely.* You should talk to them like you would family, not your employees."

"I'm nice. Why does no one think I'm nice?"

She laughs, then stops, staring back at me when I don't laugh along. "Oh, you're serious. Sorry, I thought you were... anyway... I think no one thinks you're nice because you never act... *nice.*"

"I just reassured Violet like twenty minutes ago."

Her face widens. "*You reassured her?* She texted me that you were pissed."

"What?" I shake my head, with a strained tone. I want to be better. I want Addie to see me as kind. "That's the problem with people. They're all so sensitive."

I'm such a fucker.

"You should do something for the community." Addie looks away, like she's thinking, then glances back with excitement. "Oh! There's this animal shelter downtown that's—"

"No. No animals."

Her forehead wrinkles. "*Okay...* what about the community center? They could use help with cleaning and—"

"No."

"You know this is why people think you're a dick, right? What's wrong with the suggestions I gave?"

"Nothing. I just can't see myself doing them. What else do you have?"

She bites the inside of her cheek and shrugs, sending a drum into my chest. There's something about that motion... so innocent and sweet. A sharp need slices through me, but I try and ignore it.

"Oh, there's a pie-eating contest at the diner on Sunday. They're looking for a judge after Mr. Richardson got sick. I could text Josie and let her know you're interested."

"How is that going to help me with the community?"

"You're annoying," she says, turning away. "I've got tables waiting."

I grip her arm and she turns back, looking down at my hand as I hold her loosely. Touching her again is enough to have my nerves soaring. I'm not sure what I'm doing. I need to stop. It's wrong. I shouldn't touch her at all. I definitely shouldn't grab her.

Her eyes flicker with a desire I haven't seen in years. "I thought you didn't like making your customers wait."

I glance down the hall, checking for other employees. There's no one. I could tug her into me, I could kiss her, I could seal our bodies together and press her against the wall. The thoughts run through my head quickly, and soon they're insatiable. I'm an animal, operating on instinct alone.

I act on my urges.

I reach out and pull her close to me, our bodies against one another as heat brews between us. I expected relief, but instead a new, more intense feeling arises. The need to claim her. The need to devour her body and make her mine.

Our eyes stay on one another as we pant against the recycled air pushing between us. She's so close I could kiss her. My thumb grazes over the top of her lower lip and I hold her gaze.

"What's happening?" Addie whispers. Her words are ragged and breathless, her eyes wide as she rests her hand on my bicep. She looks confused.

Fuck. What am I doing? What have I done?

I back away from her touch and shake my head, staring down at the ground, disgusted with myself for acting like a barbarian. *What the hell is wrong with me?*

"I'm sorry," I say, twisting away from her. "You should get to work. I'll be down in a bit to check on everyone." I don't want to push her away, but I need to clear my head. I need to get myself together.

She doesn't do as she's told. No surprise there.

"No. What was that all about? Were you going to kiss me?"

I want to tell her that I'd planned to do more than kiss her. I want to tell her that I want to put that tight little pussy in my grip and bounce her on my cock all night. But, again, that's wrong. So instead, I snap. "No one's kissing anyone. Your tables are waiting, though."

My stomach turns as she moves away, scowling as she works back down the stairway. I've hurt her. It wasn't my intention. My intention was to make her feel better than she'd ever felt. My intention was to hold her and make her mine. Instead, I've pushed more distance between us. Hell, I've probably just confirmed every suspicion the people in Rugged Mountain have about me. I'm the weirdo on the other side of the mountain that can't be trusted.

Chapter Three

Addie

There aren't enough pages in my diary to write all the things I feel about Declan. He's annoying, pompous, full of himself, and hot as hell. My entire body tingled all night as I thought of him touching me again. I'm pretty sure now I know he wants me. I can't imagine why else he'd have reacted the way he did. Though, he didn't talk to me the rest of the night, and he didn't bother doing rounds like he usually does.

Maybe he touched me and hated it. He's way out of my league. He's got to be twenty years older than me and could be a dancer for Chippendales or some other male strip show. I'm not sure what he'd ever want with a twenty-three-year-old girl whose ass is too wide. Then again, his body felt so right against me that it feels wrong to be away from him.

"Where are you?" Violet asks the second I pick up the phone. I'm running late for work. I never run late for work.

"I'm stuck behind elk on the pass. I've been honking for ten minutes. They don't care."

She laughs. "Well, Declan is looking for you and he's furious."

I want to tell her everything that happened yesterday with him, but the whole thing feels like a blur. One second he's touching me, about to do everything I've fantasized about. The next, he's pushing me away and demanding I get back to work.

"Let him be furious. I'm only a few minutes late."

She laughs. "In Declan's eyes, you're an hour late. Did you tell your dad yet?"

I drive closer to the oversized deer, hoping that they'll get the hint, but they don't budge. "No. I haven't told him anything. I'm starting to think it's best if he just finds out through the grapevine. By then, maybe my cabin will be finished and I can ignore his calls."

"You won't, though. You'll cry. You've always been a daddy's girl." I know she's right, which is why he's the hardest to talk to. As a kid, I spent nearly every fall fishing or hunting with my dad, and every summer on the ranch, training horses, mucking stalls, and feeding chickens. In his mind, even the diner was temporary because he knew I belonged on the ranch. Granted, a part of me wants to be there.

Someday. Someday I want my own ranch. That's what I'm building the cabin for.

Right now, though, I want to do something different. I want to experience something other than the diner, and the ranch, and the people I've known since I was born. At The Barnyard, I get to meet people from all over the country. Heck, there was even a couple in from England a few weeks ago! To someone from the city, that might not be a big deal, but to me, it was like eating fish and chips with the King himself.

"Dad will get over it," I say, knowing full well it's a lie. I'm not sure what my father has against Declan, but I know without a shadow of a doubt that if he found out things were heating up between us, he'd have Declan for breakfast.

Violet laughs. "Keep telling yourself that. I actually put my notice in today. My last day is Friday."

"What? Why?"

"I saved up enough to start my hiking guide thing. I'm going to take a week or two to scout out some spots, then I'll open up shop."

"What? No! You can't leave me there alone. I don't talk to anyone else."

"You might be out of a job anyway," she chides. "Declan is coming. I gotta go."

"Is that Addie?" I hear Declan's voice in the background. Further, then closer, until he's taken Violet's phone and talking to me.

"Are you okay?" His voice is dark, raspy, and concerned.

"Yes," I say, my heart racing. Even hearing his voice sends a shock of excitement through to my groin.

"I'm fine. I got stuck behind some wildlife. They're moving. I should be there soon."

He groans into the phone. "I thought something had happened to you. You're never late. I tried calling twice. Why didn't you answer?"

"I lose reception when I hit the bend. You must have called at a bad time. The elk are starting to move. I shouldn't be long." My mouth dries. Declan was angry, but not because I'm late... but because he was worried.

"Come up to my office when you get here. I need to talk to you about something." His tone is gruff before the line goes dead.

Meet him in his office? This man is living in *The Twilight Zone*. These days, you can't tell a woman to meet you in your office, especially not after you touched her inappropriately. Then again, I *want* him to touch me inappropriately. This time, though, I want him to finish the job. I thought about what his arms would feel like around my body, holding me close. I thought about his deep breath in my ear, and the way he'd feel pressed against me, thrusting inside of me.

God. I need to get a grip. He probably wants to give me a lecture about tardiness and... maybe bend me over his desk.

A horn honks behind me and my gaze refocuses to the road, which is now cleared of the elk. *Thank God!*

My foot hits the gas, and I take off, trying not to think about the conversation I'm about to have, but I can't help myself. There's something about him that wakes up a part of me that's never been woken before... and I like it.

Chapter Four

Declan

Addie's small hand raps on the door of my office. "Can I come in?" Her face is flushed, her cheeks are pink, and she wears her uniform as always... tight.

"Of course," I say. "Close the door behind you."

The words sound wrong as they leave my lips, but we need privacy.

She does as she's told and sits on the chair in front of my desk, her chest rising and falling slightly. "I'm sorry I'm late. You know I do my best to be—"

"This isn't about that."

"Okay," she squeaks. "What's it about?" Her silky thighs shift in the seat as she leans forward slightly.

"I have inventory coming up and I'll be busy the next couple of weeks. I'd like you to take over operations downstairs until—"

"You don't have inventory. I saw all the trucks come in two weeks ago."

"There are more trucks," I bite, staring at her pouted lips like a lion ready to pounce.

She looks away and bites the inside of her cheek. "So, you're going to be busy for weeks with an inventory for a hoedown that you have *this weekend*? That makes no sense."

Okay, I should've thought of something more legitimate. I didn't realize she was paying such close attention to my deliveries. "It's going to keep me busy for a while. That's all I'm saying. In the meantime, I need you to keep an eye on the floor during your shift."

She narrows her gaze, then turns toward me. "You're full of it."

"Excuse me?" I growl, really enjoying the way she bites back.

"I said you're full of it."

My skin lights with tiny nerves of both aggravation and delight. It's like playing with your food.

"You like me, don't you?" She cocks her head to the side and stares at me, waiting for an answer. Fuck, I love those fearless lips of hers.

"Is it your youth that makes you so forward?"

"Is it your age that makes you so angry?"

I stalk toward her and pull her up from the chair, landing my hand on her thigh, and running it up the side of her skirt.

Fuck. I'm about to make bad decisions again. I need to hold back, but every nerve ending in my body just zeroed, and I don't have the strength to stop it.

She turns toward me, landing her hand on my bicep again, her gaze on me as she says, "If we weren't here, what would you do to me?"

Fuck, fuck, fuck. I can't stop myself. Reasoning is gone. It's lost somewhere I've never been and don't care to visit.

Fire burns behind my eyes and my cock presses rock hard against the inside of my slacks. I lick my lower lip and look toward her, gripping my hand on her chin. "I'd lay you back and strip you naked, admiring every inch of your body, before I tasted that sweet little cunt," I growl, looking into her innocent eyes as I talk. "And when you've come for me, and I've devoured your pleasure, I'd bury myself deep inside until your pussy clenches closed around me and my come drips from your walls. Then, I'd hold you in my arms and remind where you belong, because after that there's no way I'd be letting you go. You'd be mine... for good."

I half expect her to pull a recorder from her pocket and kick me in the groin, but she doesn't.

Heat and intensity stirs between us until she says, "What if I want all that, too?"

"Do you?" I groan.

She looks up at me with wide eyes and nods. Silently her lips fall open and I lean into them, kissing her hard as my fingers tangle in the back of her hair, then linger down onto her throat. I can't get her close enough.

Fuck. I should stop this. Any reasonable person would stop this. She's too young, too vulnerable, and from a small town of people that will probably murder me for touching her. But the pull is too strong, and we continue to kiss until our foreheads press against one another.

"Do you know how bad I want you?" I growl. "How much I think about that thick body pressed against me?"

She shakes her head, her eyes glassy. "I think about you, too."

A growl bubbles up my throat, and my stomach tightens as my cock presses harder against my zipper. "Which is why we should stop. I'm acting like an animal. You deserve a man."

Her eyebrows crinkle. "No. I like the animal."

Of course, she does. Of course, she likes it. I'm about to burst. I tip my finger onto her nose and drag it off gently. "The things I could do to an innocent woman like you... keeps me up at night."

Her hand runs over my chest, and she looks up at me with the big doe eyes that have been captivating me for months. I want to satisfy her. I want to spread her open.

I ball my fist and growl into her ear. "This isn't what I want, but it's for the best. Now get back to work."

She stares back at me long and hard, as though she's trying to decipher a code, as though she's confused by my abrupt change in demeanor. Hell, I'm confused. If I were being authentic, I'd have her laid out by now.

"The people are right," she finally says. "What they say about you..."

I deserve whatever's coming next. "How so?" I say, ready to retract every boundary I've set.

"You're mean. Mean for the hell of it. Consider this my last day."

My stomach falls and my heart follows. I didn't think I'd lose her. I didn't think she'd leave. I didn't think there was ever a possibility where I didn't see her again.

She slides from against the wall and strides toward the door, flinging it open before heading down the stairwell.

"I'm trying to do the right thing, Addie."

She turns back. "The right thing, would've been never touching me to begin with."

And to that, I have no response, because that girl is one hundred percent right.

Chapter Five

Addie

My last night at the club goes by quietly, and I spend the next two days playing things back in my head.

The kiss.

His hands.

The way he whispered low in my ear.

The way he disappeared.

The way I know he wanted more but wouldn't let himself go there.

I want to find him, release his demons, ride him, and relax his mind. I laugh to myself as I toss another bail of hay into the horse pasture. Maybe then he'll be nicer.

"Strange to see you here," my dad says, riding up beside me in his pickup truck. It's nearly sunset. He always does rounds just before he packs in for the night with a bag full of cookies my mom baked him. He shakes the plastic bag toward me. "Chocolate Chip. Your mom made them fresh when she saw you pull in earlier."

I dip my hand into the bag the way I did when I was a kid and pull out a gooey, chocolate treat. Biting into it tastes like home.

"You look stressed," Dad says, hopping out of his truck. It's been a while since we've had a heart to heart, and I feel one coming. "This wouldn't have anything to do with you working down at that club on the other side of the mountain, would it?"

My stomach turns to stone. "What?"

"Come on, Adelaide. This is a small town. You think I haven't heard about you over there? What's going on?"

I shake my head. "It doesn't matter anymore. It's over. I quit."

My dad shakes my mom's cookie bag at me again. I relent and grab another. What is it about childhood treats that taste so reassuring? And why isn't he angry?

"Why'd you quit?"

Considering I'm not about to tell him that I threw a hissy fit because the guy started me like an engine then left me running with no intent to drive. I go with something more wholesome.

"It just wasn't for me." I look down and bite into my cookie, savoring the sweet flavors of chocolate and vanilla. My mom makes her cookies with vanilla pudding mix. It makes them softer and chewier.

"Well, it's probably better this way. I told you that man and his club are bad news. You know if you do things right down at the diner, you'll own the place in the next few years."

I know he means well, and I love this town and the diner, but working there for the rest of my life sounds awful.

"Maybe," I say, brushing him off. I don't do it on purpose, but having a conversation with my dad right now about how I want to shack up with some guy, build my own cabin off grid, have a ranch of our own, and raise a family isn't what I think he's looking to hear.

"Well, you'll figure it out," he says, leaning in for a squeeze. "Just stay away from that bar."

I twist my lips to the side and climb back over the fence, waving him goodbye as he takes off toward the house. I didn't give him enough credit. I figured he'd storm the bar and beat Declan up for hiring me. Instead, he just minded his own business. I guess I am twenty-three. I can make my own decisions.

My shoulders straighten as I stride back to my truck, then shrink again when I see my father pull off the side of the road to talk to a guy who's sitting in another truck a hundred feet away.

No one ever comes down this road. It's private.

My heart stalls as I move closer and see who's sitting inside. It's the broad-shouldered man who played with my heart three days ago. The one who's had it ever since.

Suddenly, nothing else is happening. The wind isn't blowing, the trees aren't rustling, and the dog isn't barking in the distance. There's only the meeting of two trucks like a western showdown. Declan steps from his truck, standing taller than my dad, which isn't a common occurrence. My father is a big guy, and he stays in shape doing ranch work. He too is dwarfed next to Declan.

Oh god, why is Declan here? The look on my father's face as he listens to Declan's words, says it all. He's disgusted. Repulsed.

What is Declan saying?

"Hey," I say, interrupting the conversation with a lump in my throat and a hard stomach, "what's going on here?"

Declan looks toward me. He looks exhausted with dark rings under his eyes. Has he not been sleeping? "I needed to clear the air."

I shake my head. "About what?"

"*About you.*"

My heart tightens and my thighs rub together. I'm not sure which side of the fence I'm on. On one hand, it's hot as hell that Declan has shown up to say anything to my father. On the other, how dare he just show up like this after ignoring me for days.

Then again, I guess I was the one who quit.

"What's going on?" my father barks. My stomach clenches and acid burns my throat.

Declan steps forward and reaches out his hand, but my father ignores the gesture.

"What are you here for?" my father repeats, impatience in his tone.

"I know you don't like me. I know you hate that the bar is on this mountain, but—"

"I've already told him I quit working for you," I say, beating him to the chase. "There's nothing to tell him."

Declan's gaze meets mine with more intensity. "Are you sure there's *nothing* to tell him?"

I can only surmise what *nothing to tell him* means, but if Declan is talking about telling my father that we have a thing for each other, then I can't support that... not now.

I nod. "I'm sure."

"Alright then," Declan says, turning back toward his truck. "I'm sorry to have bothered you all tonight."

My father grabs the handle of his door. "You didn't come out here to tell me that you'd hired my daughter. What did you come to say? Adelaide, what did he come to say?"

The lump in my throat only grows thicker and my father's eyes blaze toward me.

I shrug.

Declan looks toward me, and then toward my father. "I came to ask for your permission to see your daughter, sir. But I see she's not interested and I'm—"

"You what?" My father's face turns red and my heart sinks.

"I'm trying to do the right thing. I know this is a small town and you value things like this, so I'm—"

"So, you, her ex-boss, *a man twenty years her senior*, is coming to me to ask to date my twenty-three-year-old daughter." My father repeats the words like it's nothing, then says, "No," sternly and laughs. "Have a good night, man. Let's go, Addie. You don't need him."

Declan stands in the dirt gazing toward me with a look that's more desperate than he wore the night we met. Every inch of me is aching to jump into his arms, tell him that I want him, tell my father that he has no choice in the matter, but the shock of the moment keeps me from acting. Instead, I walk toward the truck with my dad and climb up into the seat, looking back at Declan who stands unmoving. His wide shoulders. His thick waist. His dark features. They're all calling out to me, begging me to return.

"Daddy," I croak, "I don't think I can let you drive away."

My father looks toward me, and for the first time in my life, I see his disappointment. "What?"

"I need to talk to Declan. I need to."

"You don't need to do anything with that man. You need to go back home. This guy is bad news, Addie."

I crack open the passenger door and step out, looking back at my father whose face has turned cold with a disappointment deeper than any I've ever seen from him. "I'm sorry."

He narrows his eyes and steps from the truck.

I move toward Declan, drinking in his large body. "We should talk."

"There's no talking," my father barks. "You're not seeing him. I was understanding about you needing room to grow, Addie. I know you're an adult, but I'm not going to stand here and let you make a terrible mistake. You're not thinking clearly."

Declan steps between my father and I. "She asked for a second to talk to me."

"It's okay, Declan. He—"

My father straightens his back and balls his fists. "You come onto my mountain, you open your shit club, and you fuck around with my baby girl?" Dad laughs. "That's not how this goes. You see what happens now is you get in your fucking truck, you go back to your hole in the wall, and you leave little girls alone."

"Dad, I'm not a little girl. You and mom are like twenty years apart in age. You can't really talk."

He turns his head. "That's different, Addie, and we aren't talking about your mother and I. We're talking about you and this dead-beat piece of shit."

"He's not a piece of shit, Dad. I like him, a lot."

Declan wraps his arm around me and pulls me into his chest then looks up at my father. "My top priority is keeping Addie safe, sir. I won't let anything happen to her. But she's an adult, and I won't let you talk to her the way you're talking any longer."

Heat lights my skin until I'm sweating. *Did he really just say that?* I'm not sure whether to turn and hug him or kick him in the shin. My father isn't a bad man. He's the best guy I know. He just hasn't learned how to manage my adult boundaries yet. Though, by the sounds of things, Declan is going to help with that.

"*Or what?*" My father steps forward, sandwiching me between the two enormous men.

"Or you'll ruin your relationship with your daughter," Declan rumbles. "The sooner you see that she's an adult with her own mind, the better off you'll be."

My father has never been one for unsolicited advice... not from anyone. He's a mountain man, country folk, who prioritizes family above all else. He doesn't go against that code for a second, and to him, Declan and the club threatens all of that. They threaten his way of life.

"Dad," I suck in a deep breath and let it out slowly, "I need some space."

My father's brows narrow, and his chest visibly tightens as he steps back, holding up his hands before scowling toward Declan. "You leave my daughter be, or I'll make your life a living hell. Do you hear me?" Dad's gaze switches toward me as I climb up into Declan's truck. "I need to know you're safe, Adelaide. You can't be with him."

Declan runs his hand back through his hair and looks toward me. "Addie, the last two days have been a sleepless hell, and I came out here tonight hoping to make some kind of gesture that would make up for everything, but I don't want to come between you and your family. I want to see you happy and thriving. If your life is easier without me in it, then it's worth me walking away."

I stare back at him as a light rain starts to fall. "Could you do that? Could you stay away from me that easily?"

He smiles and looks away then back again. "Considering the past two days have been a sleepless hell, I don't think so, but I'd be willing to try for you."

My forehead crinkles. "And what if despite all these obstacles, the only thing that makes me happy is you?" I lace my fingers with his. "Your hands. Your touch."

He looks at me long and hard. "Well then, I reckon we're going to hurt some people getting there. We just have to hope they turn around once they see what we have." He runs his large palm over the side of my face and looks down at me. "But we can take our time with this. I'm not going anywhere. I promise."

Maybe that's what I need... *time*. Time to let some of this heat wear off. Time to decide if what I feel for Declan is real or just my hormones going crazy.

Chapter Six

Declan

It's my fault she's in pain and I want nothing more than to make it better. Looking back, it was stupid as hell coming out here without talking to her first.

This is why I don't do relationships. They're confusing, and everyone ends up hurt in the end.

"You can drop me off at the hotel on Main Street," she says. "I stay there some nights when I need space from my family."

"The hotel? You don't have your own place?"

"It's being built. The early snow slowed everything down."

"I'm sorry," I say, glancing toward her before turning my attention back to the winding roads away from her father's ranch. "Feelings and emotions... they aren't my primary function."

She twists toward me. "Yeah, I can tell. You touch me, then you push me away. You touch me again, then you push me away again. You kiss me, then you say all these dirty, filthy things to me and make me want you, and then you push me away for a third time. To top it all off, you show up at my *family* farm and ask my dad to date me without even talking to me about it first?" She huffs loudly. "I know you're a businessman with a big businessman brain, but being with you would never work. Especially if you can't see the basics."

I pull the truck onto a dirt road just off the main highway and turn toward her, noticing the setting sun. "Can I dance with you?"

"What? No! Read the room! We're nowhere near dancing in the headlights."

I slide from the truck and make my way around to her side, reaching out for her again. "I want to apologize. Can I do it while we dance?"

She looks forward for a long, hard moment, then finally glances toward me. "I'm not dancing with you in the rain so you can push me away again."

Her statement is fair. I take her hand in mine. "Can I be vulnerable with you?"

She climbs down from the truck and looks up at me, taking in my gaze. "Yes."

"You scare me."

She balks. "*I* scare *you*? *You* scare everyone in this town. How do *I* scare you?"

"Do you know how many people talk to me the way you do?" I pause, running my palm over her cheek. "None. No one questions me. No one challenges me. No one, but you... and your father," I laugh. "Seriously, though, the second I saw you in that diner, I knew you were going to be mine. And every day since then has been torture. Torture with myself for touching you, knowing how young you are. Torture for touching you, knowing you worked for me. Torture for touching you because I know deep down, I wasn't made for this. I'm not an emotional guy. But Addie," I look into her eyes, and hold her close to me, desperate to say what I can't find words for, "I want you. I want you with an urgency that's unnamed. You have to see that."

I'm thankful for every second she doesn't flinch away from my grip. My pulse pounds this close to her. My palms ache to wander her skin.

"Come back to work. I know you loved being at the club, and everyone loved having you there."

She looks toward me, her eyes downturned. "I just want to go to the hotel and sleep this off."

I've never been good at respecting boundaries, mostly because I don't see them coming, but this one is loud and clear. Addie needs more space, and if I have any shot at making her mine, I'm going to need to respect that.

Chapter Seven

Addie

Space. It always sounds good when you're asking for it. Your head feels like a jumbled mess and the only reprieve from any of it, sounds like a nice long, night alone in a hotel room to gather your thoughts. Besides, I like Wind Canyon. It has expansive views of the mountains and this time of year there is wildlife everywhere.

The trouble is reality is never that clear and last night was absolute hell. Not only was I dodging calls from my parents, despite my text to let them know I was safe, I was also dodging thoughts about Declan.

What is it about this man that gets me so worked up? He's aggressive and kind of mean... but I like it. I like the way he reserves his sense of kindness for me, the way he fumbles with romance and emotions, the way he pushes me to be my best, the way his hand feels on my throat and his breath lingers against my neck with an intensity in his stare.

I glare out the front windshield of my truck into the rainy afternoon. I had Violet drive it over, so I didn't have to run into my dad. But now that I'm parked in front of the club, it's probably the last place in the world I should be.

Declan's offer to return is kind of what I needed. It's an excuse to be around him again, and a distraction from sitting alone overthinking everything. Now, though, I'm not sure what I'm doing here. It's pouring rain, the parking lot is nearly empty, and I know without a shadow of a doubt, Declan and I will get into some weird emotional conversation that's only going to confuse me more. That said, I must love being confused because without more thought, I'm bending forward to grab the umbrella I keep tucked under the seat of my truck.

As I sit up, I crack the door open and step from the truck, popping open the black cover before I'm met by a wall of a man.

"I wasn't sure you were coming," Declan groans. I wish there were some sort of kryptonite for his voice. Then maybe my body wouldn't be so drawn to him again already.

I'm lying. Even if there were, I would be helpless.

I sigh. "I wasn't sure either."

He looks toward me, intensity in his gaze. "I missed you last night. It was hell leaving you." His free hand grazes my face as the other holds the umbrella over the top of us. "I realize now that I'm a fucking asshole for inviting you back here."

Rain pours down around us, but there's so much heat between our bodies that I swear I see steam.

I shake my head. "You're not an asshole, Declan."

"*Really?* Because I invited you back here, knowing full well that if I spend one more second alone with you," his thumb rests on my bottom lip as he stares at me, "I wouldn't be able to control myself."

My thighs squeeze together without thought as I stare up at him. I clear my throat, trying to stop my heart from swallowing me whole.

He's looking at me like he could devour my entire being. And I know the next words to come from my mouth are going to be fevered, rushed, and with very little thought, but I'm not sure I care. I want him.

"What if you don't control yourself," I say, staring up into his dark eyes. "What if we just do this? What if we throw caution to the wind and let fate take over?"

Declan goes still as the rain pounds around us. He stands perfectly frozen, his eyes locked on mine. His breath is even, but torrid, and there's a glint in his eye that I've never seen before. It's almost like I've awoken a beast. A beast that I'm desperate to take me.

He sucks in a deep breath and the umbrella tumbles from over the top of us onto the ground.

Buckets of water fall from the sky, soaking me as he presses one hand against my neck, the other around my waist. I lean up against my truck as his lips touch mine, hard and unbridled. His kiss isn't like before. Before, he'd been careful. Now, it's as though the chains have been cut. It's as though he's free to touch me, free to take me as he needs.

He lifts my thigh against his hip and spreads me toward him, pressing his hard cock into my stomach as we kiss in the storm pounding down around us.

Even in my wildest dreams, I never imagined him taking me like this. We're so exposed, so open to the world and to anyone who could see.

I rock against him unintentionally, grinding my hips in circles as he moves his lips down over my neck and onto my chest.

I force air into my lungs as he presses against me. I'm desperate for him, for his touch, for every inch of him on me, inside of me, against me.

"You want my cock, don't you?" His breath is hot on my ear, despite the cool rain.

My clit throbs and I'm panting. "Yes! I want it so bad."

He groans, still against my ear as his big, hot hand slides between my legs and presses against my mound.

My heart races and my body goes limp as his fingers find their way behind my panties and into my slick wet folds.

He's heaving against me. Wet, hot, hard... heat.

"I'm going to fuck you, Addie, and I'm not going to let you go. You're going to be mine." His voice is deep and wraps me in a world of desire that I've never experienced before.

My breathing goes ragged as he holds me close.

My mind is blank, an empty page to be written on, a story I haven't yet experienced, a world of touch and passion that I'm feeling now for the first time. I wonder if this is something I should share, if it's important that he knows I'm a virgin.

He kisses me harder, and I kiss him back, his thick fingers so deep inside of me that I rock against him in pleasure.

He groans. "Your tight little pussy is begging for my cock." His fingers pull from my core, and he slides them into his mouth, licking my juice clean from his hand. "You taste even better than I thought you would. Sweet, with a whisper of spice."

"I'm going to take you upstairs through the back," he says, almost commanding. "And you're going to lay out so I can eat you right. Do you understand?"

It's probably fifty degrees outside, and rain is pouring down like buckets, but I'm hotter than I've ever been.

The funny thing is, when we're apart, I'm confused. But when we're together... everything feels right, and I don't want it to stop.

Chapter Eight

Declan

Addie's hand is small in mine... delicate. Everything about her is. The way her body curves. The shy way she breathes and moves. I can't help but wonder if this is the first time she's done this. Part of me wants to ask, but another part can't stop whatever animalistic thing that's happening. I don't think I've ever been this unchained, this unbridled. I want her with a passion that I've never felt before. It's a desire that's both crushing and all consuming.

She runs behind me as we make our way across the rainy parking lot, the cool night air permeating her sweet, curvy body so her dime sized nipples poke through.

Fuck, I can't wait to get her against me. Months of stolen glances, sleepless nights, wicked fantasies, all led up to this moment, and I'm going to make it worth it.

"Get your filthy hands off of her!" a man growls from the shadows. I know who it is without looking. It's Addie's father. The big, inked, mountain man who's looking toward me with the eyes of a devil has a distinctive voice, especially when he's growling.

"Daddy?" Addie gasps. "What are you doing here?"

He clears his throat. "I'm here to get you away from this asshole! Do you know what this man did?"

Addie shakes her head. "I know him, Daddy. I know the real him."

"I love you, Adelaide, but you're not thinking clearly," her dad says. "Get in the truck."

Addie shakes her head. "No, I won't go. You don't know Declan! He's more than the guy you think he is."

I'm not sure what her dad thinks he knows, but there are some things I've been sitting on telling Addie since we met. I tried to tell her in our very first meeting, but the conversation went a different direction, and everything has been a whirlwind since.

Rain continues to pound down over us, the roar of thunder in the air. "Maybe we should all go talk," I say, gripping Addie's waist close to me. I don't want to lose her again.

"There's nothing to talk about," her father growls. "Let's go, Addie!"

I stiffen and turn toward her. I knew things weren't over with her father, but I didn't think he'd show up here.

"Addie," he says, "I was patient with you, but I'm not going to stand by while you start a relationship with a criminal."

Addie shakes her head. "A criminal? He's not a criminal, Dad." She turns toward me, those big blue eyes staring toward me like the sweet princess she is. "Tell him you're not a criminal, Declan."

I suck in a deep breath, my smile hidden. I know she can see it coming.

"Your father isn't wrong," I say, letting go of the breath that I've been holding onto since he showed up. "I *was* a criminal."

She stands in front of me, her forehead wrinkled, her arms now crossed in the pouring rain. This look on her face is the one I've been trying to avoid.

"What do you mean?" She's nearly breathless as she speaks. "I trusted you! I... I gave you everything. I was going to have sex with you!"

I reach toward her. "I would never hurt you, Addie."

"You have!" she screams. "You've made a complete fool of me. Everyone told me you were bad news, but I believed something different. I thought you were broken. I thought I could fix you. I thought..." She pauses and sucks in a deep breath. "I was wrong," she whispers. "I'm always wrong."

Her father reaches out for her, but she pulls away. "I need some space."

And with that, every bit of happiness I ever had walks away into the night.

Chapter Nine

Addie

W hen I was young, I dreamed of a man. He was tall, big, and handsome. He was inked with black and gray tattoos, and he had this attitude that made me feel safe. He quieted my mind with his strength and security, and he talked to me in a way that was different from the way he talked to everyone else.

I met that man when I met Declan, but even he was a figment of my imagination.

My phone rings as I stare out into the flooded parking lot. Streetlamps reflect in the puddles and a ripple moves the water as the wind blows.

"Hey, girl." It's Violet. She sounds somber like she's already heard what's happened. "I just talked to your sister. She said she's been trying to call you."

"Consider yourself special," I say. "I haven't been answering calls."

"She told me what happened. I'm so sorry."

I stare out the window blankly. "I feel so dumb."

"You're not dumb. You liked him. I get it. There's an energy about him. It's enigmatic." She pauses. "Plus, he's hot," she laughs. "Do you know what he did?"

I sigh. "Does it matter? He's a criminal. He hid it. Now I look like an idiot!"

"You don't look like an idiot. No one knew who he was. Your sister said your dad had some guy do a background check on him last night after he showed up at the ranch. That had to be awkward."

I bite the inside of my cheek and wonder if I should call my father and ask what Declan's done, but I can't stomach the call. I love my dad, but the sense of pride he gets when he is right about something is nauseating. And right now, I can't handle it. I can't handle the *I told you so's* or the *thank god your safe* lines right now.

"What's new with you?" I ask. "Distract me. Please!"

She chuckles then lets out a heavy sigh. "I scouted out a new trail. I couldn't go all the way to the end because of the rain we've been getting, but I think it's perfect for a guided walk."

"How long does it take to finish?"

"Two days, three if we're going slow. It goes past the ridge line, and you get an awesome view of the mountains. Plus," she drags out the words as though something good is coming next, "I have a hottie of my own that's signed up."

"A hottie? What kind of hottie?" Hearing about her happiness perks my mood. She deserves to find love. She's been dreaming of her knight in shining armor just as long as I have.

"He's been kind of secretive about who he is exactly, but we met up yesterday, and he said he's looking for a guide to take him out for a photo shoot near the highest point of the river."

I bite the inside of my cheek. I'm afraid for Violet. Hiking alone with another guy you barely know sounds terrifying. There's no cell reception in the mountains and no one will expect her back for days. Besides that, she hasn't told any family that she's doing this, so if something happens, the only people looking for her will be the rangers and I. But, I can't judge considering I'm making my own slew of mistakes lately.

"Just be careful," I sigh. "Do you plan to take any weapons with you?"

"I take bear spray."

"Maybe take a gun."

She laughs. "A gun? You know most people who have guns get killed by their own weapon."

Now I laugh. "You were raised here, right?"

"Stop. You know I was."

"Then you know how to use your gun. Probably better than some guy who came from... where's this guy from?"

"Alaska."

My stomach twists. I hate that the guy isn't a local. "Alaska? Do you know anything else about him?"

"Stop!" She laughs. "He's just a guy. A big, hot, inked guy who's photographing the world. And if I'm lucky... he'll take a shot at me."

"Wow, I had no idea you were such a seductress."

"Oh, I'm not. This is on the phone with my bestie talk. In reality, you know I'm a total dork. I'll probably spend half the time tripping up the mountain and making a total fool of myself until this super-hot man wonders why he ever hired me to begin with."

I'm tempted to ask how much he's paying, or if she's getting the money in advance, or remind her again that at the very least, a taser would come in handy, but I don't want to be that girl. She's excited. I want to be excited for her.

"You'll figure this out with Declan. Why don't you call him and talk? Maybe the criminal thing isn't that big a deal. Maybe he just stole someone's skateboard?"

I laugh, and lean my head against the windowpane. "I think the sooner I let the idea of him go, the better off I'll be."

She stays silent for a long moment, then sighs. "I'm here for you... always."

"I know," I say. "Thanks for calling. I love you."

"I love you, too. I'll check on you tomorrow."

When the line is dead, I stare back out the window, studying every detail of the dark landscape. It's funny how the night transforms the land. How a bright mountain view turns to only shadows and shapes.

Headlights pull into the hotel, blinding me for a moment, but I struggle through the pain and watch as the truck parks and a man climbs out. He's tall, built, muscular, and he wears a short beard and tight blue jeans.

I wonder what he's here for. We get a lot of people coming to see the mountains or to get a tattoo at my Dad's shop. Then again, there are some that are just passing through. I've always loved this spot at the motel for that reason. Whenever I'm stressed, I can come down here, sit in the window, and create little stories for every person and family checking in. By the looks of this guy, I'd guess he's on a business trip, probably passing through on his way to Colorado Springs.

The man steps into the light, and the shadows illuminate the ink on his arms, and then his face.

It's Declan.

He looks both ways and I can't imagine what he's here for.

Did he remember that I come here when I need to think? Is he here to talk to me or is this where he does his crimes?

I suck in a deep breath and watch him walk past me, his enormous body like a ship as he passes. He then backs up and stares me in the eye. I should've backed away from the window. I didn't realize people could see me from outside.

Damn it! He's stopping. He's turning toward my door. He's knocking.

I should move. I should tell him to leave. There shouldn't be feelings left. He lied to me. But as I stare at him knocking on my door, my heart plummets and my body reacts. I can't stop myself.

I slide the lock and open the door, staring up at his massive frame with anticipation. Anticipation to know who he really is. Anticipation to get over it. Anticipation for him to take me, love me, touch me, and finish what he started earlier.

I might have a mental illness.

"I used to sell drugs," he says, closing the door behind him. "It's not what you think. I would pick up the shipments from the docks in Miami and I'd move the product all over the US. When I found out that the guy at the top was targeting children, I contacted the police. I worked out a deal with them for a lesser sentence." He sighs. "I spent a year in jail for my involvement, over the ten that was coming to me, but I had to turn in one of the biggest drug lords in the US."

My brows narrow and my throat clenches. I'm not sure what to say. No wonder my dad feared this guy coming to town. We've worked hard to keep Rugged Mountain clean from drama.

"The guy I turned in has a lifetime in jail for various crimes he's committed. There's no threat to anyone." Declan looks down at me, his gaze soft. "I'm harsh because that's how I survived for most of my life. I didn't have a mountain family that had my back. My parents died when I was young, and I did what I had to in order to survive. When I was in prison, I spent that year planning my life. I knew I wanted to take the little bit of money I had and move to a quiet place like this. I wanted to start over. When I was released, I petitioned the town, and the people of Rugged Mountain voted and approved my permit for The Barnyard. Your father was the only one that stood against it." He looks down and away. "I guess that was for good reason."

I blink toward him, unsure of what to say, but I watch the color red climb up his throat and onto his face. I guess that he's feeling shame and embarrassment for what he's done.

"I never imagined I'd meet anyone I liked as much as you, Adelaide, and I should've told you every part of who I was sooner. I guess a part of me was terrified to lose what little I was holding onto."

So many parts of Declan make sense now. His harsh life has forced him to be aggressive, and the loss of his parents has made it hard for him to process his emotions. But he's more than those two things. He's a man that would fight for me. A man that will stand by me at all cost. And the truth is, my family may never see the good in Declan Myers... but I do.

The fog I was feeling clears, and the moment blares out in front of me in high definition. The scent of his cedar cologne, the sound of the water dripping outside, the aching desperation between my legs, the deep yearning for his hands on my throat again, for his barking orders and dirty talk.

"What if I forgive you?" I croak. "What if I understand who you are? What if I'm desperate for you to touch my body and make me yours?"

He stills, staring toward me with a visible lump in his throat.

"Then I'd ask you one last time, how sure you are. Because you know who I am Addie, I'm not a soft guy."

I run my hand over his chest and stare up into his eyes. "I don't want it soft, Declan. I want it hard. And I want you... just the way you are."

Chapter Ten

Declan

She lowers herself to her knees and unbuckles my belt, tugging my jeans to the floor, but I can't have it. I can't have her kneeling for me.

I hold her elbows and lift her from the ground, staring into her eyes. "You don't kneel for anyone, princess. Do you hear me?"

She nods and the spark I'd felt the first time we'd met turns to fire. A raging, uncontrollable fire that's desperate with the urge to light her forever.

Her breath comes in shallow puffs as I hold her against me. "Do you want me? Do you want me to touch you? Do you want me to claim you?"

She nods and I run my hand down over her pussy, my pulse pounding in my ears.

"Then lay back on the bed," I growl.

She does as she's told, and I vibrate with tension until I'm settled between her thick thighs, pulling her pretty, pink panties aside to dip in, and taste her luxurious scent. I've thought of this thousands of times. I've dreamt of her body nightly.

Her hair falls in waves on the bed and her thighs grip tightly beside my face, squeezing intermittently as I eat her out.

The stolen glances, the innocuous touches, the yearning for her body, for her presence, all culminating in this moment as I taste her sweetness.

She gasps as I pull up a suction on her clit, then she thrusts against my face.

I grip her hips and tighten my mouth to her slit. I need her from a place that's more than desire. It's deeper than skin or blood. It's in my bones. It's an ache in my bones so deep that only she can rescue me from.

Her feet rest on my back and she hitches up closer. She's spread open for me, shamelessly willing as the rain falls outside. Her pussy is soaked, and her hips flex intermittently against my grip.

"Do you like it when I kiss you there?"

She moans and my cock hardens even more as she bucks her hips toward me, gripping my forearms as I hold her down.

"Come for me, and I'll let you up."

"I need your cock," she whines. "I need it now."

My tongue flicks her faster and she groans. "Not until you come for me... hard. Do it! Give me your juices."

Her body responds to my orders like the sweet princess she is and within seconds, her thighs tighten around my face, and she's moaning out in ecstasy as her come spreads across my tongue.

I groan in approval and lick her orgasmed clit one last time, forcing her to jump back as I stand from the bed and look toward her with need as she continues to convulse.

This pretty, little body is laid out for me like an angel I don't deserve. Her hard nipples. Her bubbled breasts. I kiss each one and lean up to her lips. "Kiss me," I groan. "Taste your pleasure."

Pre-come drips off my cock as I lean into her lips and let her taste the sweet nectar of her flower.

"Fuck me, Declan," she moans. "Please."

"I want to see all of you first. Stand for me... without your clothes. I want to see only you."

"I'm... I'm not good at that."

"You're good at everything, princess. You're beautiful. Let me see all of you."

Reluctantly, she stands from the bed and positions herself in front of me. I'm in fucking heaven. Every inch of this woman is on display for me to enjoy. Shadows from the street bounce between the shades and throw light on her pale skin with no regard for what I need to see... but it's perfect. She's perfect.

My hands run over her hips, up her stomach, then over her breasts, and onto her shoulders.

Her eyes close as she takes in the touch and my heart thumps hard against my chest.

I'm behind her, holding her against me as my cock pokes into her ass. That big, round ass.

Fuck.

My hands wander over her breasts, and I sway with her in my arms, feeling every moment with more emotion than I've ever felt in my life. This woman is perfection. This woman is mine. With her, I'm home.

"I could hold you like this forever," I groan, tipping down into her ear.

She sighs. "You don't know how bad I want that."

"My cock is so hard for you, princess, but I don't have a condom."

She turns toward me, a yearning in her eyes. "You don't need one."

"I won't be able to pull out. I know it already. That pussy was tight on my fingers. It's going to swallow me up and I'm going to lose control."

"So do it, Declan. Lose control. Fuck me. Come inside of me. Make me yours. I want all of you. I want a life with you."

I lean toward her, kissing her pink lips softly. "I love you, Addie."

She sighs. "I love you, Declan."

Hearing those words from her lips are like heaven and earth colliding. Emotions I've never felt before unlock and drip down over my skin, lighting nerve centers that I didn't know existed. She's too good for me. I know that, and I'll spend a lifetime trying to prove my worth to her.

"Please, Declan," she begs. "I need you."

I stare toward her, kissing her forehead before ordering her to bend onto the bed. "Look back at me. Don't take your eyes off me."

She lowers onto the edge of the bed, ass up as she twists her shoulders back. Her hair falls beside her like a soft waterfall on the sheets and my cock hardens to the point where I'm sure it's purple.

I wrap my hand around the girth and position myself at her core.

"Wait," she gasps, "is it going to hurt? You're so big. I—"

"I'll go slow," I groan, as my tip enters her soft mound. "I'll go slow, and you can tell me to stop if you need me to."

She nods, but I feel her body tighten with anxiety as I deepen my length inside of her. My hand lands on her lower back and I rub, hoping to relax her as I thrust deeper.

"Fuck. Are you okay, princess?"

"Yeah," she squeaks. "This is the first time I've done this. Don't stop, though. Go harder."

The first time? "Princess, you should've told me. I would've—"

"Don't stop," she moans. "Please... go harder."

Knowing that I'm the first to press into her tight little core sends a thrill through me. She's all mine.

I lift my hips and push into her, thumping against the round cheeks of her ass as I slide in and out of her wetness.

"Can you do me a favor?" I groan, rocking into her.

She sighs. "Yeah, what's that?"

"Can you touch yourself? Can you rub circles on that silky, little clit? I want you to come on my cock."

Her body jerks and her hand moves into place between her legs as her face is pushed back and forth against the sheets.

Every touch makes her body relax and my cock more easily dips inside of her. I'm not sure how much longer I can hold out.

With my hands on her hips, I thrust harder and harder, deeper and faster. She grips the edge of the bed with her free hand, trying to hold herself in place as I thump into her frame.

Her pussy is hot, and the walls feel thicker. I know she's about to come.

"Don't stop, Declan." She's begging, desperately. I like her this way.

I thrust in harder, and the sound of our bodies meeting sends a chill through my spine until suddenly the orgasm I've been trying to hold explodes and I'm filling her bare cunt.

As the sounds of my pleasure roar out, I feel her tense in my hands. She shakes a little, and I can feel my ear-to-ear grin.

I thump inside of her a little more until we're both exhausted and too sensitive to continue, then collapse next to her, pulling her into my arms to feel her heartbeat against mine. We lay like that for a long moment, sticky and warm against each other's skin.

"Do you remember that pie-eating contest you wanted me to judge?"

She looks up at me and smiles. "Yeah."

"Do they still have room?"

She nods. "It's tomorrow and we're still down a judge."

"I think you're right. It would be good for me to get out in the community. I want to tell everyone myself what happened. I don't want them hearing it from anyone else. So, let's do it."

"Are you sure? People are going to tear you apart."

"My life is here now, with you. And if I'm going to make you happy, I know I need to make the people of Rugged Mountain happy."

She smiles and leans her head against my chest as we both drift off to sleep.

Whatever happens tomorrow, Addie Baxter is mine, and I'm never letting her go again.

Chapter Eleven

Addie

Waking up in Declan's arms is almost as satisfying as the look on everyone's face at the diner when we walk in together. I can't tell if they're jealous or silently judging me. Yesterday, I'd have thought they were jealous. I've heard the way women talk about him in town. They're all enamored by his size, his presence. Today, though, they might be staring because my father already told them Declan's a criminal.

"I'm going to say something first," Declan says, kissing my forehead. "If people are upset, I'll step outside until the contest is over, but I'm not leaving you."

I wouldn't let him leave alone; I'd follow behind. If the people in town can't accept him now, then we'll go to the other side of the mountain until they can.

Declan clears his throat. "I'm sorry to bother you all during your breakfast, but I have a few things to say that I think will be important for you all to know."

It's Sunday morning at the diner, and there's a pie-eating contest on the horizon. Everyone in town is packed into the space, even my father who doesn't look happy that I'm here with Declan.

"When I came to Rugged Mountain and petitioned you all for land and a building permit, I failed to mention some things."

The scent of fruit pie fills the space, despite the tension building in the room.

A tear rolls down my face and I tuck my hand in Declan's as I stare toward my father, desperate for him to do something, anything to stop what he's started.

Declan continues, "I—"

"We all have our issues, Declan," my father says, stepping forward from the back of the crowd. "Every one of us. We're a mountain of imperfect people, and you don't owe us any explanations. You're here, and that means your family."

My father holds his hand out toward Declan, and they shake on something I'm not sure I understand before my dad turns toward me. "You really care about him, don't you?"

I nod. "He's a good man, Daddy."

"I saw that as well," my dad says, "in his background check. Declan has had a tough life. He did the right thing turning that guy in. I'm sorry I only saw the bad at first. Declan deserves a break. Just promise me, Addie, you'll come to me if you need anything."

"I promise, Daddy." I ring my arms around my father's neck and hold him close. "I love you."

"I love you too, Adelaide."

"I can tell them what I did," Declan says to my father. "I came here to wipe the slate clean."

My dad nods. "I know you can, but it was wrong of me to go rooting through your past. You came here for a family, and up here, family is what we do best."

Growing up, my dad has always been my hero. He rescued me from that snake out back of the barn that I was sure would eat me. He listened to me cry when Michael Hoover stood me up at Mullet's bar in town. He showed me what it means to be a hardworking rancher, and he's led me toward a life of simple beauty, all thanks to his love and guidance. He was worried, and he did what he thought was best. Then when he realized he was wrong, he fixed it.

My father's not perfect, but he's a man who loves his family, and he'll do anything to make sure they know that.

The waitress sets pies out on the counter and invites Declan into the chair in front of an apple crumble, strawberry rhubarb, banana cream, and peach pie.

Declan looks back at me, then kisses my forehead, before wrapping his arms around me tight. "I'm going to be honest, and it's going to piss people off."

I laugh. "I think people will learn to like your honesty," I say. "Just don't forget to invite everyone to the hoedown tonight. You can tell them their favorite waitress will be there."

He smiles and kisses my lips softly before making his way back to the counter to judge the pies.

Sometimes, the people you least expect to change your life, are the ones that change it the most. And with Declan Myers, I know my life will never be the same again.

Epilogue

Declan

S ix Months Later

My heart stills as I watch Addie step from the back of the bar. I hope she appreciates my fancy new cowboy attire. We've been doing these hoedowns for a while since they've become so successful, but this is the first time I went all out with my wardrobe. Shit, I've even got the hat on.

"Damn... country suits you."

I grin and settle my thumb on my chin. "Does it suit me enough for you to meet me in my office?"

She can't help but smile. "Yeah, I think we could make that happen. It's customary after all."

I narrow my brows. "What is?"

"Oh, for a waitress to *welcome* a cowboy properly into the hoedown."

"You better not be welcoming any cowboys in here, but me." I take her hand and lead her to the back steps. Slowly I kiss her neck as I lift her, then we make our way upstairs.

When we reach my office, I set her down gently, and rub her belly. "How are my girls doing?"

"We're good. More tired than usual, but nothing we can't manage."

I sigh. "After tonight, you should take some time off or at least sit up here with me. I want to know you're rested, and not on your feet all day."

"I guess I could use a few extra days a week at home with the horses. Do you think maybe I could do half days here, boss?"

I growl and press her further into the couch. "Call me boss again and you'll be too tired to come in here at all."

She smiles. "And why is that, *boss?*"

I groan, running my hand between her legs. "I see you're in the mood to play. Okay... sit on the chair."

She does as she's told, sinking her pregnant body into the chair. I'm not sure what is about the round belly, swollen breasts, and the glow of her skin, but I like seeing my wife like this. Full and happy, with our baby girl... Olivia Jane.

I kneel before her and tug her panties down over her legs, encouraging her to lean back in the chair.

She does, presenting her sweet little pussy for my taking.

My thumb rubs her clit in circles as I lean into her core, desperate to taste her. She's hot and wet, demanding with her hands as she rakes them through my hair, pulling me closer.

"Someone's excited," I groan. "Do you want me to eat this pussy? Do you want to come on my face?"

She moans out in approval, and I slide my fingers through her entrance and lap at her clit. With each inch I travel into her, she gasps louder and louder in the quiet office space. The sounds of the hoedown's banjos are nearly nonexistent up here.

Obscenely wet noises sound between her thighs as I lick her up, frantically moving my fingers in and out of her. "Addie," I groan, "I'm so fucking happy you're my wife."

Her thighs tighten around my face. "I love you, Declan. I need you. I need to feel you."

Since she's been pregnant, there's been no holding off. When she wants my cock, she gets my cock.

I unbuckle my jeans and tug them to the floor. She stands, and leans against the wall, her hands spreading herself wide for me, ready and waiting.

Gripping my cock, I slide into her, softly at first, then hammering. I see we haven't locked the door from this angle, but I don't want to stop. She feels too good, too hot, too wet.

I thrust faster and harder, gripping her swollen breasts beneath her shirt, as I move. My only regret is not being more naked, not stripping her down further.

"Squeeze my cock, Addie. Squeeze it hard." I'm groaning, lightheaded, about to come. She's clamping down, gripping me tight with that soft pussy.

Heavy breaths heave as we hold on to each other. She's small in front of me, rolling her hips, tilting her body to meet each thrust.

The door knocks and a second later, Violet walks in.

My eyes go wide, and Addie and I snap toward her.

She's shocked, standing in the doorway with a look of frozen confusion.

I stop moving, but Addie screams, "Don't stop! Violet, leave!"

Violet backs out of the room, and I grip Addie's waist thumping into her like a greedy animal desperate for release.

Addie moans and grinds against me. "I'm going to come. Don't stop!" The interruption hasn't phased her at all. She's just here, in this office, fucking her boss like a naughty girl. She likes it. She likes the danger. She likes the idea of getting caught. Wet, hot, heat coats my cock as she comes and moans.

It's more than I can take. I hold on to her tight and like a fucking beast, I drive myself home, emptying ribbons of come inside of her.

This is what I live for.

"Oh god," she says, turning toward me to pull her shirt down. "Violet. I should check to make sure she's okay. That was weird."

I can't help but grin. "Really weird. These pregnancy hormones are doing all kinds of things to you."

She smacks my arms playfully and makes her way to the hallway. Violet is still outside the door. Though, in her defense it's much louder in the hallway.

"I'm sorry," Addie says. "That was awkward."

Violet laughs. "No, I'm sorry. I forgot you two were sex crazed animals." She shakes her head. "I just came up to say goodbye. I'm heading out on my hike with the sexy stranger."

Addie has been worried about Violet taking this client for months. He's cancelled twice and everything about him just seems wrong.

"Are you sure you want to go? You could stay here and—"

"And watch you two have sex?" She smiles. "No thanks. I might go out and see if I can get some of that myself, though. You make it look fun."

Addie's face turns red as I grip her waist from behind. "You have that gun," I say to Violet, "and that radio. Don't be afraid to use them."

Violet grins. "I love you guys. I should be back in a couple of weeks. Remember to lock your doors, okay?"

Addie and I nod, before shutting the door as she walks away, locking it tight.

"You know," Addie says, "I used to think the best memories I ever had came from dirt roads at twilight. Now, I'm not so sure they don't come from some office space above a hoedown."

I smile and lean into her forehead, kissing her gently. "I promise you we'll make memories all over this mountain. So many, you won't know which ones are your favorite."

She grins and rubs her hand over the top of her expanding belly, kissing my lips the gentle way she does.

I'm not sure what I did to deserve this woman, but I know without a shadow of a doubt that this country love was just what I was looking for.

Temptress

Chapter One

Violet

Growing up, I was taught to question everything. My mother calls it necessary hypervigilance. My father calls it common sense. Either way, it's become a way of life, a mantra that I live by, a part of my DNA that's so ingrained that I'd say it's a detriment.

For instance, yesterday was a bright, sunny day. The temperature was perfect. I had a great song stuck in my head... you know that new one by Jason Aldean. Well, I'm singing the chorus over and over, and then there's this woman. She looks to be pregnant; I'd say five months. Long brown hair, light eyes, a pierced nose, and a tattoo on her left arm of a dragon. Anyway, I watched a man follower her through every aisle of the grocery store. He was watching... waiting. She didn't notice a thing. I figured I had two choices. I could follow the woman out and tell her about the guy, or I could assume I was a neurotic lunatic and let the woman be on her way.

I chose to follow. Turns out, the man was her husband. They were arguing, and she didn't appreciate the intrusion.

That's not where it ends, though. In a crowd of people, I've been trained to notice every noise, every movement, every person coming in and out of a space. I don't have a filter either. I can't choose to stop just one source of this vigilance. It's all or nothing, and despite the fact that my parents meant well with raising me like a veteran CIA agent, I'm exhausted.

I park my truck at the corner of the hiking lot and hop out, grabbing my backpack from the cab before making my way toward the truck parked on the other end of the lot. It's a black pickup truck which looks typical for the area, but I'm guessing it's a rental. I'm expecting a man I've been talking to for the last couple of months.

Yes, we met online.

Yes, I know it's not safe to meet him alone.

Yes, I realize I probably shouldn't have agreed to take him on a guided hike without telling anyone.

These are the answers I give my brain as it questions my decisions in a slow circle of mind-numbing interrogation. Before I can talk myself out of it, the man cracks his car door and steps out.

My breath hitches. He's going to look different. I know he's going to look different. Every photo I've seen of him has been flawless. I'm talking God-like flawlessness. I'm talking *'why would he talk to me'* kind of flawlessness. I guess it's fine if he looks different. Looks aren't what matters, but he would have lied about it, and I guess that counts.

Okay, head, stop spinning!

"Violet." The man's voice is deep and brooding as he steps from his truck. His voice is the same soul crushing deepness it was on the phone. My heart patters with excitement as he steps out from behind the door and leans in toward me for a hug.

He smells like the woods after a campfire. Like fresh cut cedar or pine with a musk I can't define but want all over me. That, and he's tall. Taller than I expected. I'd guess six foot four inches, and the muscles look as defined and strong as they did in the photos. His eyes are a dark brown that are both warm and inviting and his hair is strung with salt and pepper. He's hot, maybe even hotter than the pictures.

"Thank you for rescheduling so many times. I was afraid you'd think I was a weirdo or something after the third time."

I shake my head, disobeying the internal voice that's sending alarms to run. Nothing about this is right. First off, he could do better than me. Second, he did reschedule multiple times, which is weird. Third, he obviously doesn't need a guide for this trail. He's dressed like an avid hiker in worn boots, camo pants, a black tee, and a camel pack for hydration. Most people that hire my services come dressed in jeans and a t-shirt. Heck, sometimes they come in sandals. Those people I *believe* need a guide. This guy... no way. Truthfully, though, I can't let my stomach get to me. I need this to be a good trip, a break from the norm, a chance at whatever this business was building to be.

"He's given you no reason not to trust him," I say to myself, as I tighten my backpack in place. *"In fact, you've had nothing but good conversation since you started talking three months ago. Hell, at one point, you thought he was going to ask you on a date."* I let out a heavy sigh and look toward him, happy when the pep talk I've been giving myself is over.

"It's no problem," I finally say, unsure if I'm lying or not.

He smiles, resting his hand on the butt of a handgun that's tucked into a holster on his waist.

It's not uncommon for folks up here to carry guns. In fact, most mountain folk would think you were crazy for not carrying, but something about the whole thing makes my stomach turn again. Maybe I should listen.

"Shut up, Violet!" I chastise myself under my breath. I wonder what I must look like to him, having a conversation with myself as he stares back at me politely. Maybe he's more scared of me than I am of him.

"I hope this doesn't make you uncomfortable." He slides his hand over the silver magnum in his holster. "It's for protection. I hear there are a lot of bears up on the mountain this time of year. People say they aren't afraid of anything up here."

It's true, they aren't. Most bears in the area are so used to hikers, miners, and fisherman that they'll walk right up to you out of curiosity, but I'm not sure that's reason enough to bring a gun. Maybe that's just my mountain upbringing, but I've always known to stay away and avoid the trails they use.

"Not at all," I lie again. "I have one too, just in case of emergencies." I pat my backpack as though I have my gun in tow, but I don't. I was taught to shoot when I was three, but I don't like carrying it. Instead, I bring bear spray, which I'm not sure will have the same effect in any situation against a gun.

Hawk laughs. "Got it. Sorry if I scared you. I was hoping our meeting would be smooth."

"You have nothing to be sorry about," I say, doing the people pleasing thing I do in order to hide the million things I'm truly thinking about. "My parents own a private investigator firm in town, so I've seen it all."

He nods and trudges up the hill beside me, our boots suctioning mud side by side. "What? You never told me that. That must have been a fun way to grow up."

I laugh. "*Fun?* More like paranoid. I spend more time worrying about a situation than I do enjoying it, and as a last-ditch effort, I started this business. Fingers crossed that coming back to nature will undo the years of training I've been taught."

Leaves rustle against the wind and a few branches snap as we walk. "I could see that working." He smiles, flipping his ballcap backward. Why did he do that? He's trying to turn me on. He wants me excited. "I could also see how tiring an upbringing like that could be. I grew up with a marine as a dad and he didn't know how to compartmentalize anything. We'd be having family dinner, and he'd tell us all about some raid he did or firefight he got into."

Maybe he does understand. "Is that why you went into photography?"

He looks toward me long and hard before answering, as though something is on the tip of his tongue, but he can't find it. "Yeah, I suppose." He stops there, and I'm a little surprised. On the phone, he'd been chattier.

Maybe he doesn't like me. Maybe he's planning my murder. Maybe, he's committed some kind of awful crime and he's going to ask me to help him hide it.

Ignoring the ridiculous ramblings in my head, I turn my attention to the cedar and pine that stretch high overhead. Birds sing in the distance and a brook is babbling to the west of us. It's a beautiful scene, and one that brings me back to center.

"We're right on the edge of snowfall," I say. "I think some parts of the mountain have already seen it."

He grins softly and looks toward me. "That's what I heard in town. I got here last night and stayed at the Mountain View Lodge. It's a great place with a nice hot tub overlooking the mountains. I almost gave you a call, but I was already nervous enough for our meeting today, and it was around midnight before I was settled."

"You should've called." I brush my fingers back through my hair, wondering how last night could've gone if he'd called me sooner. "I could've brought over some maps and we could've gone through them for today's hike." As soon as the words leave my mouth, I know what a nerd I am.

Can I take them back? No? Okay, thanks for nothing.

Thankfully, Hawk laughs off my comment. "That would've been nice. I collect maps, mostly vintage ones. I frame them or use the pieces for wrapping these guitars that I build. A nice clear coat over them and they're in place forever."

"Do you sell them?"

"Nah. I just make them here and there for friends and family. What about you? What do you like when you're not showing strangers around the woods? You said on the phone that you worked at the country bar for a while. Do you still hang out there?"

I shake my head. "Haven't been back since I quit. It's not my scene. I like hiking, reading, and quiet." I laugh. "My favorite thing is to come up here all alone and sit by the river making up stories or reading someone else's."

"What kinds of stories do you like making up?"

I'm not sure he realizes how invasive a question that is. I shrug. "I don't know, just stories."

He grins. "About..."

"About..." I sigh, and my face turns red. I'm not telling him what kinds of stories I make up! "Stuff."

He stays silent for a moment, then laughs. "Okay, okay... I think I get the picture."

I fold my arms in front of my chest and look toward him with downturned eyes. "Yeah? What picture is that?"

His voice drops an octave, and he looks toward me as he says, "You're a naughty girl! You come out here, you sit by the river, and you make up... *stories*. Have I gotten a role in any of these fantasies?" He's grinning, and he's probably joking, but I'm suddenly shy and not sure what to say. Either that, or my weirdo meter is going off and I'm shutting down to conserve energy for when the inevitable kidnapping begins.

As I'm thinking over that scenario, and possibly making it way dirtier in my mind that in needs to be, I study the cries and screeches that birds make in the distance and the crunching and snapping of leaves and branches under our boots. I try to ignore the wild scent of his cologne that wafts toward me in the breeze, but it's impossible. He's intoxicating. I knew it the moment we started talking, but the more I see of him, the more drunk I get.

Why is a man this handsome out here all alone? There has to be more to it than the freedom. And why Rugged Mountain? There are hundreds of great mountains in Washington and Oregon that would've been much easier for him to get to for a little rest and relaxation.

I swallow hard, then tip up onto my toes and back down again. I should ask him why, but my stomach is turning for some reason. If I were listening to my mom's endless advice, that would be my subconscious telling me something, but I ignore it and push past.

"So, why Rugged Mountain? You have so many beautiful places to hike out west."

His response is quick... too quick. "I've seen all those mountains. I wanted something different. Besides, once we started talking online, I had to see you. You seem a little worried, though. I hope I didn't make it awkward with that weird fantasy joke. I—"

"No. Sorry. My dad is a retired detective out of San Francisco, and my mom is this crazy sleuth who spends every free second solving random crimes." I sigh. "So, you can imagine the types of mental illness that's given me," I laugh, saying the words with a light heart.

"Oh, I get it. As I said, my dad is a retired marine, and my mom is a writer. She loved hearing his stories, and he loved telling them. It was a match made in heaven... for them. For me, it was... interesting."

"And you became a photographer? How do you mix a military father and a writer mother to get a photographer?" I realize how rude the question is after I say it, but that detective part of my brain is always on.

Thankfully, he laughs it off. I'm put at ease until we hear a snap neither of us are expecting from deep in the woods.

I glance toward him, studying the trajectory of the sound. It's too large to be a squirrel and not big enough to be a bear, but it also stops like a human would.

A human. There's only one human I know who lives on this side of the mountain, and he's not a wanderer. Not only that, but hunters aren't allowed in this area, and I didn't see any permits for other hikers. Which means whoever is up here, is up here illegally.

"Must be a woodchuck or a raccoon," Hawk says, holding his position.

In the moments that we're paused, there is no more noise. In fact, there's no sign of life at all. The mountain is still, which I would normally be grateful for. But there's an eerie feeling crawling through my stomach that I can't ignore this time.

"I think we should go." I turn back and face the opposite direction, expecting that he'll follow down, but he doesn't.

He looks toward me, his gaze more discerning than before, more definite. "Nah, let's keep going."

I shake my head and the heavy weight that had been on my shoulders sinks into my stomach as I look into his eyes. "No. I think we should go."

He stares at me, his dark eyes wide as he settles the heel of his hand on the gun at his hip.

Hairs on the back of my neck stand as I slowly begin to regret every decision I've ever made in life.

This handsome man isn't who I wanted him to be, and this certainly isn't playing out like one of the fantasies in my head.

"I'm not going to hurt you," he says, "but I need you to guide me up this mountain. Do you understand?"

I swallow hard and stare back at him, my throat tight with fear. Something tells me, he's not here for pleasure, and I'm about to become one of those cautionary tales moms tell their little girls.

Chapter Two

Hawk

She's clever. I'll give her that. And beautiful... *too beautiful*. It's a distraction. Her big brown eyes, that thick waist, and round ass are all too much. That, or I'm simpler than I thought. But this woman is perfection. She's short, delicate, and steeped in an innocence that makes me excited to explore her further.

What the hell is wrong with me?

"Who are you?" Her voice is firm and confident, though I can sense her fear as though it's a primal instinct. A wild heathen part of me wants to pin her beneath my frame until she's thrashing and whining. It's a dark excitement that steals me away to a place I shouldn't be going. A place where I make her mine, and every other decision is out of the question, despite how wrong it is. Hell, she's got to be close to twenty years younger than me. Not to mention, a thousand times better person. I don't deserve her.

"It doesn't matter who I am," I grunt, reaching back for her hand as I hop over a boulder on the path. "I just need your help getting to the first cabin. When I'm there, and everything is good, you're free to go."

She narrows her brows. "What does that mean? *If everything is good?*"

I debate how much to tell her. If she were to break free and run, she could jeopardize everything. Then again, if she knows what's going on, she might stay closer... if she believes me.

"Are you going to kill me? I'm just curious because I've watched about eight million crime dramas and I thought you seemed sketchy, but I—"

"If I were going to kill you, would I be listening to you ramble on about crime dramas, or would I have done it already?"

She looks away and shakes her head. "Well, it depends what kind of killer you are. Some of them like to play with their victims. Others like to do it fast."

"I'm not going to kill you," I growl, studying her pretty face. "In fact, if it's up to me, not a hair on your head is harmed, but I need you to listen."

She narrows her brows and looks toward me with rigid shoulders and a heaving breast line.

I hold her arm gently. "Can you promise that you'll stay with me until I give you permission to leave?"

She sucks in a sharp breath and stops dead in her tracks, staring blankly ahead as though she's seen a ghost.

I follow her eye line into the darkening woods, but there's nothing there.

"Did you see something?"

She narrows her brows and turns back toward me. "I thought so. I thought I saw a man... but he was wearing a black hood. I think I read about this. It's psychosis. People who've been through a traumatic event experience it. If you let me go, I promise not to tell anyone you're up here. The rangers are going to be looking for me in two days, anyway. Probably sooner if my parents don't get a call tonight." She's rambling. "My mom is relentlessly overprotective. You don't have a chance. Either you let me go, or you're going to end up in jail... or worse. People up here take vigilante justice seriously."

She's not wrong about that one. I did read about a bunch of locals going crazy on a drifter for skipping out on his diner check. But if I tell her all the details of what's going on, she's going to run right back down this mountain and into the house of a retired detective and a mother who has an affinity for crime. Nothing good will come of that.

"I told you," I run my hand over her arm in comfort, "I'm not going to hurt you. So long as you stay by my side, you're safe."

"And when the man in the woods comes after us both, am I safe, then?" She's shaking and that's not what I want.

Why am I letting myself get so attached, so involved?

"How much further until we get to the cabin?"

She squeezes her eyes shut, then opens them slowly and tears make a salty path down her cheeks. "A mile. Maybe two. There's been a lot of rain lately." Tears bubble up until her shoulders are hunched forward and she's shaking.

Fuck, this isn't how I wanted this to go. I was hoping we'd be able to ignore the reason I'm here and enjoy each other's company, and maybe get closer than we'd been on the phone, but I realize now how unrealistic that is.

"He's not with me," I say, cradling her against my chest as I try to calm her tears. "Let's get to this cabin, and I'll tell you everything."

She wipes her face and stares up at me. "And I'm just supposed to believe you? I told you I study crime, right? The first mistake people make is following their captor to a second location."

"Technically," I smile, "this is our first location."

She shakes her head. "Our first location was the trail head. If I follow you to the cabin, that's our *second location*, and then *I'm* a dumbass." Her eyes dart and move, searching for an out, desperate for a place to run, but I can't let her go. Her thick curves bend into a plant on the right side of the path with dark purple berries that cluster together with tiny green leaves. She pulls a bundle off and slides the fruit between her full lips, then passes me a few. "They're goji berries. They're usually a summer plant. This one made it under the radar, I guess." She hands me a few. "They make you feel calm." I've spent enough time in the woods to know that she's right. "You hired me to help you to the cabin, but I'm not going any further. So don't ask."

I nod and stare back at her as the bittersweet goji berry explodes against my taste buds. Maybe I was lying when I said I could let her go at the cabin. Hell, I know I was lying. She knows too much about the mountain, and I need her expertise. Then again, maybe I just need more time to prove that I'm not the man I'm acting like.

Chapter Three

Violet

I've seen the cabin by the river's edge a thousand times, maybe more. It used to be my favorite place to retreat. The building itself is nothing fancy, but the surrounding babbling brook, cedar, and pine lend a sense of magic to the space that can't be reproduced. At least it was all of that, until some psycho dragged me here against my will.

The worst part of all this—I knew better. I had a bad feeling about him at the base of the mountain. Heck, if I'm being honest, I had a bad feeling about him when he changed his appointment multiple times, but I didn't listen.

Why didn't I listen?

"This is nice," Hawk says, striking a match against the logs and kindling already waiting in the fire. It's custom for the previous tenant to leave a bundle of wood for the next. I doubt Hawk will be as kind. Aside from his looks, he's a giant disappointment. A handsome face and a bunch of muscles... nothing else.

I shouldn't have stepped inside, but apparently, I'm an idiot all around today. My mom is going to be so disappointed when she finds me in a shallow grave below this place.

"You're at your cabin. You said I could go." I turn toward the cabin door, but he steps in front of it, blocking the passageway with his oversized frame.

Of course, nothing is that easy. Though, it's expected.

"About that..."

"About nothing. I'm leaving!" I protest, trying to shove him out of the way, but he doesn't budge. "I did my part. You're here. Now let me go!" I hold back from crumbling into a ball of wretched tears, but it's not working. I feel them working up my throat.

Don't cry. Don't cry. Don't cry.

"The man in the woods," he says, leaning against the door frame. "The one you saw earlier, he's Alaskan."

"Okay..." I clear my throat, trying to dismiss the knot sitting at the base. "So you Alaskans are all breaking the rules. Sounds cool. What does any of this have to do with me?"

"You know the mountain. I thought you just knew direction, but you know the foliage as well. I need help finding a plant."

"Too bad!" I bark, lifting my arm to push him away again. I can't help but notice he's not restraining me. He's not even shoving me back. He's just letting me go off while he stands like a statue in front of the door, unphased.

"You're okay, honey." His voice is almost soothing. He's sick. "You're safe here. I can explain everything. I just need you to calm down first."

"*Calm down? Honey?*" I push him harder, but he isn't budging. "You've lied to me since the second we met. I bet you don't even like hiking. Do you? All that talk was just a ploy to get me out here, so you could..." I roll my eyes and lean against the back wall of the cabin, exhausted with shoving.

"Good girl," he says, his voice deep as he grips my arm. He's dragging me somewhere, I think toward the fireplace, but I don't care. My body goes on a rampage again, flailing and kicking, more violently than I had before.

The motion still doesn't phase him, and sickly enough, even in his firmness, he's careful, oddly gentle, holding me against his chest as he moves me. He's hot, his throat beating wildly as he lowers me into place. "Fucking hell," he sighs. "You're a feisty one. If you'd calm down for thirty seconds, I could tell you what's going on."

"It's all lies anyway," I spit, feeling my eyelids begin to swell. "You're a criminal. I should've seen it. I've prepared my whole life for this, and I didn't trust myself."

"My name is Special Agent Hawk Crowley." He pulls out a gold badge and hands it to me to study.

For a second, I believe him. He's said it so honestly. Not only that, but he's kind of bad at the whole captor thing. I've seen it done quite a few times in movies and documentaries. I'm supposed to be tied up, and he's supposed to be a whole lot rougher.

"Twenty-two years in service," he says, sitting on the floor next to me. His large body lowers with a thud. I want to believe him. If I believe him, that means my instincts aren't wrong, which would've been a total blow to my self esteem as I died a slow death in a shallow grave.

"Why are you here?"

His gaze rakes over my body, almost as though he's hungry.

My body responds, though it sickens me a bit to think I'm turned on by this asshole. Then again, maybe this is my opportunity. My chance to use my feminine wilds for the betterment of my situation. Maybe this man is simple. Maybe he'd be turned on by me. Maybe I could lure him in like some indecent proposal situation. We just skip the money part, and I make him think I'm going to have sex with him until I'm close enough to take his gun. Then, I run like hell. Too bad running like hell isn't my strong suit.

I stare back at him, wondering how far I could get with my temptress ways, but the longer I stare, the longer I realize I'm insane. This man is a god, and I'm... not. He's probably looking at me like a hungry wolf because he's literally going to eat me... and not in the sexy way. My father is a retired detective. He would do anything to solve a case. I'm sure back in the day, flattery wouldn't have been off the table. I'm sure that's all Hawk is doing. The few kind things he's said to me have all been a ruse to get me to help him solve whatever crime he's trying to solve.

When my seduction plan fizzles out in my head, I look around the cabin, searching for something that would come in good use, but it's bare, intentionally so. The shack is only meant to be a small reprieve from a storm for hikers who need a break. There aren't any amenities except for whatever food the last person has left behind and the logs in the fire. Even the log poker is too worn to use as a weapon.

When my eyes finally drag back to his, he's dialed on me, watching me, studying my every move.

"What?" I run my hands back through my hair. My skin is hotter than it was before. *Why?*

"You're thinking about leaving," he says. "You're planning it. I saw you doing it on the path as well."

"No. I'm waiting for you to tell me why you're here, Special Agent Something or Other."

He lets out a heavy sigh and straightens his back, setting his broad shoulders wide before pulling his phone from his pocket and swiping a few times. He hands the screen toward me. "Have you seen this man?"

I study the photo of the black-haired man. His beard is grungy, and he has a tattoo on his left temple of a snake that wraps around his neck. "No. Who is he, and why would I know him?"

"He's the guy I'm looking for." He takes his phone back and tucks it into his pocket. "What about a plant called morning glories? It's a late season blue flower that grows on vines with heart petals."

My brows narrow. "Yeah. Historically, people here used their seeds as a hallucinogenic. Fortunately, modern people stay away from them because they taste terrible, and they aren't really cost efficient since it takes a fair amount of seeds to get most people where they want to go." I give him a snide smile. "Is all of this because you're trying to get high?"

He pokes at the fire with the long stick and sparks fly up the flume. "I need you to take me to where it grows in the morning."

"You didn't answer my question. Why do you want to go there? It's not worth anything, trust me."

His shoulders rise and fall slowly. "There's a guy up here from Juneau. His name is Jeramiah Wilcox. He's been traveling to this area for years, collecting the seeds and bringing them back to Alaska to replant."

"Okay," I say as my voice rises and falls sarcastically. "Is that a crime? If it is, it seems it would be Rugged Mountain's axe to grind."

Hawk shakes his head. "It's not that simple. This guy has built a cult around the worship of this flower. He believes that it's a conduit sent by a higher power and that the hallucinations bring him closer to that force, which gives him and his people the answers to whatever is ailing them. Except the answers aren't coming from the flower, they're coming from him. He's mass producing the seeds and gaining followers, mostly young women who believe every sick thing he's telling them." He lets out a sigh. "That's who you saw in the woods. He's here for more seeds. Despite his attempts to grow the same strain in Alaska, they don't do as well as the ones grown natively here. It could be the soil or the climate, but it keeps him coming back as he tries to gather more followers. I've been tracking him around Alaska for months, but he moves. The only way I knew for sure I could get him was here, in the one spot this particular strain of morning glories grows... on Rugged Mountain."

I stare blankly toward the handsome man in front of me. I study his firm, square jaw, and the slight dimple that dots the center of his chin. I can't deny my attraction to him. Even in this stressful scenario, I notice him in a way that's unbecoming. That said, he's full of shit. This is a small town. People would know if some psycho cult leader were hiking into our mountains to harvest hallucinogenic seeds... right?

We would know. Hawk is lying. Even if he's not, I don't want to be mixed up in some chase for a man who's smuggling hallucinogens and brain washing people. I need to run. Hawk hasn't been honest with me. He could be lying again. I can't trust him. In one quick motion, I stand from the chair where I've been sitting and make a mad dash toward the door, pulling it open only to be pulled back into the cabin by Hawk's strong arms.

"This isn't pleasant for me either," he growls. "I don't want to kidnap you."

"Oh really? Then why don't you let me go!"

"Trust me," he spits, "I want to. But apparently, I enjoy the torment."

"You're being tormented?" He's leaned me back against the cabin wall and pins my wrist above my head. "I'm the one being held against my will."

"For good cause. Jeramiah Wilcox saw you. You said so yourself. Do you know what a man like that is capable of?" He looks away, then back again. "One of the women tricked by Jeramiah was my teenage niece. She wanted to believe that there was a fast track to happiness after some rough years in high school, and he was going to be able to take her there. The night that it came across the radio that she overdosed... was the most difficult day of my life."

I stand still for a moment, letting my lungs catch up with my racing heart. That can't be true. Fuck him and his stupid lies. "So what if he saw me? He's long gone by now, I'm sure."

Hawk shakes his head, and his voice is strained as he says, "He's not that humble. The man believes he's the messiah. He won't back down. He's convinced himself that he is the vessel for which others gain help. I can't let you go back down that mountain alone."

"You were never going to let me go once we got up here, were you?" I cross my arms in front of my chest, relishing in another of the lies he's told me. I should've known better.

"None of that matters now." His eyes are on mine, heavy and hot. His hand rests on my shoulder with strength. I'm not sure why it's sexual. It shouldn't be. I hate him! He lied to me, over and over. He dragged me out here. He physically stopped me from leaving. But still, when he touches me, I light on fire and my entire body screams for more. "What matters is... I need your help," he continues, brushing his thumb under my chin, "and I promise I won't let anything happen to you."

Part of me wants to believe him. The other part knows I'm full of shit and probably needs some major therapy. Either way, the detective in me has a feeling, I'm staying put. Meanwhile, the aching between my legs says, I just might like it.

Chapter Four

Hawk

I can't blame her for being afraid. I didn't go about this the best way possible. I could've been upfront from the beginning, but if it had gotten out that I were coming after Jeramiah, the people of Rugged Mountain would have gone on their own witch hunt. I've scoped out the area enough times to know how the people are here. They're steadfast and take charge. They're a community above all else. They protect their own, and their land, at all costs.

"Thanks for the food." Violet leans against the back wall of the cabin near the fireplace. Her legs are stretched out and I can see a new exhaustion on her that hadn't been there earlier. I'm probably evil for loving it. But there's something sweet about the way her head keeps dipping onto her shoulder with a half-eaten granola bar still in her hand.

"I brought you a sleeping bag. I can roll it out for you. We'll sleep for a few hours, but I'd like to move in the dark if at all possible. We have the advantage then."

Her breath hitches and she pulls out her sleeping bag. "You know this terrain isn't easy to navigate. And in case you didn't notice, I'm in shape for novice hikes, not full-blown scaling the side of the mountain type jobs."

Her blue and gray sleeping bag splays out on the hard floor, and she looks up at me, with slightly parted lips, that wake-up parts of me I didn't know existed. "Are you really a cop?"

"True and blue," I say. "Are you really a hiking guide?"

She sighs. "I think today might be my last day."

I laugh, and lay back on my own sleeping bag, staring toward Violet in the flickering light of the fireplace. She's beautiful and strong. She's gathered her sleeping bag up to her neck, and she's staring at me, her eyes drooping with exhaustion as she glares, as though she's afraid to take them off of me.

"You really are safe with me," I say, reaching my arm out for her.

She flinches back at first, then calms, but the violence in her eyes is still there and I know it's a promise, not a threat. The truth of it is, I don't blame her.

I pull my hand away, not wanting to make her uncomfortable, but my palms ache to touch her again. Fuck. What the hell is wrong with me. She's young, and I've kidnapped her. None of this is romantic, but it doesn't change how I'm feeling, what my body is saying, what I need.

"Wait," her voice is small and muffled, so much so that I'm not sure what she's said. "Wait," she says again. "It doesn't make sense, but that felt comforting." She rolls her eyes. "In a *Beauty and the Beast*... fall in love with your captor type of way."

I can't help but laugh. "We're falling in love now? *Wow!* That escalated quickly."

She sighs and turns away from me. "I didn't mean it like that. I'm just... I'm scared. And for some reason, it felt good to have you next to me. Even if you are a liar."

The liar part stings. "I didn't mean to lie to you." I wrap my arm around her and pull her close. "Most of the things we talked about weren't a lie."

"Please tell me that thing about your niece was the truth."

"Every word. She's okay now, but it's been a hard road back for her. She trusted someone, and he let her down." The irony of the statement hits me like a ton of bricks. Am I just as bad?

"So you really do love mountain berry pie?" She hides a grin. "And your mom sang you *Twinkle Twinkle Little Star* backwards when you were growing up?"

I can't help but grin at the details she's remembered. Maybe I'm not the piece of shit I'm thinking I am. Maybe she does have room in her heart for me.

"All true. Just like... whatever is happening here. I... it's real. For me, anyway. I want to hold you." My voice cracks when I speak because I'm not used to talking so emotionally. I'm afraid of how she'll respond, and I'm afraid of how my body will react. This wasn't part of the plan. I never intended to want her so desperately. And I should've known when we were talking online that seeing her in person would only make those feelings grow stronger. The way she's sitting under that sleeping bag now, with her head all tucked low, and her tits heaving beneath, it's inevitable. I have to have her.

"Do you want to fall in love, Violet?"

She balks at my question. "Not with you!" Her words say one thing, but her body says another. There's a pulse in her eyes and they widen gently.

"I think you're lying," I say, slowly inching closer.

She clears her throat, and her breaths are quick and shallow. "You're the liar, not me."

I smile at her comment and brush a silky strand of hair from her face. "I've spent a lot of years analyzing people. And you... you're holding back with me."

She rolls toward me, resting her head on her palm. "Imagine that. Holding back with a guy who lied to me for months."

"Yet here we are, lying next to each other, our bodies proving what we can't admit."

She stays still for a second, then leans in slightly, her voice a soft whisper. "So, what are you going to do about it?" Her breath hitches, and her scent is warm and excited. She's making a monster of me. Those curves, and those lips. She unzips her sleeping bag and rolls on top of me, her gaze dilated, ready, nearly black.

She wets her lips and squirms, looking down at me from above, her legs straddle my waist, and my cock jumps with excitement.

I should stop her. I know I should, but I can't. She's testing the bond, and I'm relishing in every sensation.

A soft moan escapes her lips as she rocks her hips back and forth. "You're the one who's needy, aren't you, Special Agent? Do you want me? Do you want this tight little pussy, and my thick hips pressed against you? Do you want my soft lips on your cock, and my silky hair spread over your stomach?" The way she says the words is almost rhythmic, like a snake charmer, luring me in. I go blank and my dick goes hard. It's working.

She could do anything from this point forward, and I'd be at her mercy. Happily. Willingly. Fully.

Chapter Five

Violet

M en are simple, I learned that when I worked at The Barnyard. It's a country night club that caters to locals and out of towners alike. It seems all it takes is a little sexual interest and suddenly men are at your feet, ready and willing to please you however possible. At least that's what the women did at the bar. I'm not sure what kind of deals they were making, but I saw them using their sexuality to get it.

Then again, I might be as simple as Hawk. Despite the fact that he's holding me against my will, I'm attracted to this big, inked, burly cop laying beneath me and with every word that slips from our lips, I genuinely want him more.

I suck in a deep breath. *God, he smells good*. It's like a walk on a late fall day after a campfire. My plan was to tempt him with something naughty, lull him into a sense of safety, then dart. But now, staring down at his big brown eyes, as his cock presses against me, all I can think is how bad I want to touch him. I wonder what he'd feel like inside of me, what I'd feel like on top of him, what his hands would feel like on my throat, on my stomach, on my skin.

"I need to touch you, Violet. I don't think you understand what you're doing to me." His voice is deep and brooding, almost pained and I want to relieve him.

"What then? I'm a virgin," I choke, nearly whispering. "We fuck, and then what?"

"I don't want to fuck you," he growls, his eyes flaring with some kind of spark I've never seen. "It's deeper than that. I want to know when I have you, you're mine... for good. And it's been a long damn time, Violet. I'm just as scared of all this as you are."

"Please. I'm really supposed to believe that a guy that looks like you, isn't giving it to every woman that asks."

He laughs and turns his head to the side. "And I'm supposed to believe you're a virgin? You're talking like you got an education on seduction. Valedictorian, I'm sure."

My clit throbs as I change positions ever so slightly. His hard cock lays lengthwise in his jeans, hard enough to press against my mound as I move. "Good thing I don't care what you think," I say, lowering toward him. I'm not sure what I'm doing, or why I'm doing it, but my body takes over like it knows best and though a part of my rational brain knows I should be stopping, I don't. I keep moving down until his lips are on mine and my thighs are begging for friction.

I rise and fall to chase the touch of his hand on my back, as an aching whisper escapes my lips.

"You need to stop, if you're playing with me," he growls into my ear, sending a low rumble of tingles down through my spine and into my groin.

I don't know what I'm doing. I don't know why I'm doing it. Well, I did... but that's long gone out the window. Now, this isn't to run. *I want him.* I want the torment to be over. I want him to spread me wide and hold me close to his chest.

"I'm not playing with you, Hawk." I manage the words breathlessly as I cling to his shirt.

He draws his hand up and lands it on my cheek. "Then lay back. I need to taste you first. I need to hear beg me for relief."

"Now who's talking like a valedictorian seducer?"

He grins and rolls me back, taking control of the moment. I can't help but wonder if this is my first mistake. That letting him have control even for a moment will put me at risk for whatever he may have planned. But right now, I don't care. The thought is brief and buried beneath hormones the second I catch sight of his glassy eyes as he dips and pulls at my leggings. I can't help but ache for more. I've lost the battle against myself.

I'm not sure what I expect from the big, burly man, but he takes his time with me, gently drawing out the torture of his touch. His fingertips graze across my needy skin and his eyes rake over me like he's holding a prize, like he needs me, just as badly as I need him... maybe more.

My body isn't as patient, and I feel my hips rising, searching for his face. When he finally buries his beard against my mound, my insides scream, and I let out a sigh so deeply held that it makes him groan. For a few moments, he devours me, like it's been his life's mission to come here to this place and touch me. And in this moment, it's hard to believe I ever thought he could hurt me. He's so gentle.

How is it that a man I've known for less than twenty-four hours makes me feel ways I've been desperate to feel for as long as I've longed for love?

I'm soaking wet, embarrassingly so, but he seems to like it. He laps me up and slides two fingers deep inside, stretching me further than I've ever been stretched.

I cry out, aching as a pinching burns with his touch.

"Fuck, you weren't kidding," he groans. "You're so tight."

I lick my lips and stare down at him. "Yeah, virgin... remember?"

He nods and stares back at me. "I should stop. I don't want you to remember this as your first."

"If you stop, I'll run," I snap, staring back at him with heat.

He grins coyly and dips back between my legs, pumping his fingers in and out gently, as he works my clit between his lips and tongue.

Nothing about this is right, but it feels too good to stop.

I rock my hips against his face as he works my body. Tiny little sighs and moans drip from my lips as energy builds in my groin. I should be repulsed. This man lied to me. He dragged me up here. He refused to let me leave. But for some reason, that only makes my pussy grow wetter.

"Are you going to come for me, honey?" His voice is so deep. It's velvet. "Or should I tie you up first? That's why you like this, right? You're my captor?"

I don't know what to say. I don't know what to feel. He licks up my slit, and stands from the sleeping bag, grabbing a strip of fabric that's tied to the end. He tears it off with one fast motion then turns toward me with a darkness in his eyes that's both soft and possessive.

My pussy clenches. I'm letting him have control. I'm not sure I'm ready. I'm not sure what that means. He could be playing me. *I was going to play him.* If he's going to tie me up and keep me here, this was his best way of doing it.

I want to call him out, but when he lifts my sweater off, and exposes my hard nipples to the room, I lose interest in hating him again.

"I don't hear any objections," he says, wrapping my arms behind my back with the smooth fabric. He's gentle in touch, carefully tying a knot as he kisses the nape of my neck.

My heart races as I stare back at him. Heat stirs between us and his eyes flicker with desperation, an urge, an animal instinct so obvious that my body can't help but react.

"You like the power being taken from you, don't you?" His voice is deep and resonating throughout my body.

"No," I gasp, tugging against his restraint. "I liked being in control." The words leave my lips, but even I know they're a lie. My pussy is dripping wet. So wet, that when he pulls my thighs apart again, there's an audible suction.

He groans and scowls as though my excitement as somehow offended him. "I think your body is telling a different story. Your body says you like the idea of me being in control." He circles his large fingers along my inner thigh as he talks, then moves his hand over my stomach and onto my bare breasts, flicking each nipple before moving between my legs once more.

He rubs his thumb over the top of my clit, tracing circles. He's teasing me and I'm trembling, desperate, aching to come.

"I need to taste your cock," I whine. "I need you to spread me open."

He growls low and smiles, clenching his teeth tight as he looks back at me. "So needy. I'm not sure there's room for me in that tight little body."

My clit throbs again and my nipples harden. I stare toward him as he goes back to work between my legs. I struggle against the restraint, desperate to touch him.

"You're going to come for me first, honey. I need to taste your excitement and relax that little pussy so you're good and ready."

He leans into my thighs and licks at my clit, thrashing wildly between my legs with no finesse. He's hungry, starved, desperate for me.

My thighs lock and squeeze around his head as he works.

"Look at me," he growls, only pulling up slightly. His eyes lift and he stares toward me, as though he's as desperate for the look on my face, as he is for my come itself.

His free hand wraps to the knot he's tied behind my back as his other holds my outer thigh and rubs me gently. The dichotomy of touch sends a chill down my spine and within seconds my body convulses and stiffens all at once as he continues to lap up my juices.

I don't want it to be over, but as I look down at him, my excitement shining on his beard, there's a look in his eye that's turned soft and caring, rather than hungry.

He kisses the inside of my thighs and then my stomach, working his way up to my lips. "Get some rest my sweet little captor"

"What? No. I need you!" I pull free from the knot he's made behind my back without much effort, and lay on his chest, stroking his hard cock.

"Not tonight," he says, moving my hand onto his chest. "This needs to be special. You feel relieved, right?"

"Kind of," I nod, "but also still pretty desperate for that dick. And what about you?"

"Aching," he groans, "but something tells me you're worth the wait."

My heart swells as I lay back in his arms, staring up at the knotty pine boards. This wasn't about capturing me. He genuinely wants me to feel special, and it's working.

Chapter Six

Hawk

My eyes close and all I can smell is her sweet juice on my beard.

Fuck. She's everything. I know it without a shadow of a doubt. I need this woman in my life, and I could lay like this forever.

I'm not sure how long we've been laying here, but I'd guess it's been about four hours, which puts it at roughly around four a.m. It's time to get moving, except she's breathing gently against my chest, her hair is draped down over my shoulder, and I've never felt so content in my life.

I need to get my shit together.

I move my arm from beneath her head and stand from the ground, arching my back as I try to readjust my spine.

"What's wrong?" Her voice is soft and sweet. "Are we leaving?"

I clear my throat. "I am. You're staying here."

I expect relief but instead she offers defiance. "No! Why would I stay here? You needed my help to get around the mountain, remember?"

My jaw clenches. It's true. I did need her help around the mountain, but now, I'm feeling things would be better if I went alone. Not just for her sake, but mine too. She's a distraction. A sweet, pretty diversion that I know is going to throw me off rather than keep me focused, and right now, I need to get back on the trail. "I'd feel much better knowing you're safe, and I think I'd get more done if I weren't looking at your ass the whole time." I smile and pull her close. "Besides, I thought you were happy to be let go. You wanted freedom. I'm giving it to you."

She quiets and rolls up her sleeping bag, tucking it into her pack without saying a word. I'm guessing she's frustrated, though I can't figure why. If I'd asked her to stay back yesterday at this time, she'd have told me yes without question, and probably taken the opportunity to tell the town what an asshole I am.

Maybe last night meant something to her too. I want to ask, but I'm too nervous I'll hear something I don't want to hear, like her vehement distrust in me again. I'm not sure my ego can take it.

"We can stop by my friend Walker's place. He's the only one that lives up here. Maybe he's seen something."

"You have a friend up here?" My brows narrow. "Where?"

"Less than a mile up stream. He lives completely off grid, so I'm sure he has seen something. Though, he's a bit of a hermit so... maybe not. Either way, I'm sure he can help us."

I don't tell her, I plan to leave her there, where I know for sure she's protected. Instead, "Hustle up. We're wasting darkness," escapes my mouth.

She darts me a look of disapproval for my strange use of expressions then tosses her bag up onto her back as I hold open the cabin door.

It's a crisp morning, and the sun hasn't even started to rise. Violet makes her way westward out of the cabin and into the forest of cedar and pine that we hadn't explored yet. She's carrying a flashlight and waving it back and forth as she steps, crunching over fallen leaves and sticks.

"I know you're leaving me with him," she says, turning back, "but I'm not going to let you. He's going to help us. Walker is a veteran. He's seen some of the craziest stuff. You should hear his stories. One time, he told me about this land mine that almost took out his entire battalion."

"How'd you two meet?"

"I was up here hiking one day and he was fishing. He caught a rainbow trout and subsequently had it stolen by a grizzly. I had to stop and laugh. We've been friends ever since. Well, friends in the way that we've had a few conversations, but mostly just wave from a distance. He's not a social guy."

I nod and stare out at the dark forest in front of us, watching as her silhouette moves through the trees. She's careful and steady, even in the black woods. I should ask her now what she thought of last night, and if she regrets what we did, but she turns back first.

"You know, if you want to go solve your case, you should go. I can find my way to Walker's cabin. I'm sure he's up and getting ready for a hunt, anyway."

"No, I'm not letting you take off in the dark alone!" I reach out for her arm, hoping to talk some sense into her, but she flinches away. "*Just go!* Please. Walker's cabin is right around the corner."

"And then what?"

She shrugs. "Then I guess you got what you came for, right?"

"What is this about? I came here for Jeramiah, but I was excited to see you. Hell, last night meant everything to me. I could've laid there with you for the rest of my life. But I have to get this guy so I can move on. And I have to make sure you're safe while I do it. That's all."

Her gaze relaxes, and she moves toward me, her voice soft. "I know. I'm sorry. I'm worried about you now. You're going to be all alone in the dark and who knows what this guy is capable of. My mom has had me watching true crime for twenty years. The cultists are the weirdest of all."

I land my hand on her cheek. "I'm going to come back to you, and we're going to pick up right where we left off last night. Okay?"

She sighs and leans back against a pine tree, staring up at me with tears welling in her eyes. "You better, or I'll have the mountain up here looking for you."

"Fair enough." I kiss her forehead and linger in the moment, breathing in the soft scent of flowers in her hair. *How does she still smell so good?* "Just promise me you'll stay put at Walker's. I need to know you're safe. How far are we from his cabin?"

She nods to the left, and through the trees I see the edge of a small log cabin that looks sturdier than the one we've been staying in, at least from what I can see through the pale light of the moon. "That's his place."

"Okay," I say, kissing her once more. "Let's go get you settled."

She nods, but she turns away before I can kiss her again, and a pit grows in the bottom of my stomach. I know she isn't going to follow directions. That's not who she is. And I'm not sure, I'm in any position to blame her for it.

Chapter Seven

Violet

Walker answers the door straight away, which I'm grateful for. I've heard enough haunting urban legends about Rugged Mountain after dark to keep my heart racing walking around here at night.

The ghost of miners that didn't make it through their expeditions. The wolf shifters that hunt and prowl for a mate out in Saddle Creek. And then there's the unforgiving tale of the night Mrs. Richardson was abducted and ravaged by some kind of purple aliens up on Whiskey Pass. She went into pretty intense detail as she retold the story at Mullet's bar downtown. I didn't hear a lot of it, but from what I gather, there was something about seven-foot-tall aliens and giant dicks that did all kinds of crazy things. Truthfully, it was a more intriguing story than most of the books I've read lately.

Walker rubs his eyes and stares at me blankly. I'm sure he's not used to having company at all, let alone this late. "*Violet?* What are you doing out here?" He holds out his arms, as though he's afraid for me. I lean into his massive chest and hug him hello. We don't talk much, but he seems like a long-lost brother to me.

"It's a long story," I say, rolling my eyes. "I need your help."

"What kind of help?"

"Long story, remember?"

Walker's jaw tightens. "Are you hurt?"

I shake my head. "No, nothing like that. I was helping this detective guy. He dropped me off here a second ago, and now he's out and looking for some cult leader and I'm... I've got to help him, but I don't know how."

"A cop?" His voice cracks. "Looking for a cult leader?" There's a nervousness in Walker's tone that sets me on alert, like maybe he's been up here all these years for a reason, but I don't question him. Instead, I just keep talking. I know my radar has been off, for a while apparently.

"Yeah, I don't know all the details. He's trying to catch this guy off guard."

"And you're going to help? How?" Walker sits on the edge of his rocking chair and looks back at me like I've lost my mind. "Sounds like he wants you to stay here, while he does his work."

"Yeah, but I can't do that. I need to help him. He doesn't know these mountains. He doesn't know the terrain."

Walker runs his big hand over his long beard before making his way toward the stove to start a pot of water. I assume it's for tea when he pulls down two mugs. I've never noticed how well he keeps the place. He's put a lot of effort into making the space his own. There's a set of handmade bookshelves framing the hallway with a hand carved deer in each corner. And the countertops in the kitchen have been sanded and stained to match. The space even smells good, like fresh baked bread and cinnamon.

"I know you love this kind of shit," he says, settling two tea bags into the mugs, "but I think you need to rest here tonight and wait for your detective to come find you. It sounds like that's what he wanted."

Every ounce of me wants to scream for him to stop and take me seriously, but I know better. He'll only laugh me off with that kind of reaction. I need to move slow if I'm going to get his help.

"You're probably right," I say, "and that would make total sense if this were just some random case I was chasing. But this isn't the grocery store thing, or the time I followed that old man down to the riverbank because I thought he'd stolen from the diner. I care about Hawk. I don't want anything to happen to him."

Walker narrows his gaze. "What do you mean you care about him? Didn't you guys just meet?"

"We've been talking for a few months online and I don't know... when I saw him in person... everything just clicked. Then last night we—"

"Spare me." Walker smiles, and hands me a steaming cup of tea. "If I were to help you, what did you have in mind?"

My heart races with excitement at the thought of maybe getting his help. "I was hoping we could use your ATV. I think we can catch up with Hawk and you have guns. We could use them for backup."

"I can't get mixed up with the law, Violet."

"You don't have to," I say, relieving him of the stress of telling me whatever he's been through. "You can remain anonymous. I just need a ride and a gun."

Walker shakes his head. "I'll help you... under one condition."

"Whatever you want."

He pauses for a long moment, then stares back at me. "I'm lonely up here."

"You want me to visit you more? I'll visit you more."

He laughs. "No. Not like that. I want to meet someone. Someone I can talk to and—"

"Oh." I grin. "You want a girlfriend. You want me to set you up with someone?"

"Maybe not a traditional setup, but help me meet someone who has the same interests."

"I'm not sure a woman who won't leave her house and has no interest in people is going to want to leave her house to meet someone," I say with a laugh. "But I'd like to try."

"Similar interests then," he says, grabbing the keys to the ATV from beside the door. "Just someone I can talk to is fine. Hell, I can talk to her online. That way we can chat without a lot of pressure."

I open his gun cabinet and swing a rifle over my shoulder, then grab a case of bullets from the drawer beneath. "Do you get internet up here?"

"Nothing. I'd have to come into town, but it might be worth it."

"Yeah," I say, opening the front door. "I'll help you."

"And I'll help you," he says, locking the cabin up behind him. "Truthfully, I'd have helped you anyway."

I know he would've, but I don't mind helping Walker find someone to spend time with. I can't imagine how lonely he is up here. I consider myself introverted, but he takes it to the next level.

Walker starts the ATV and a loud rumble shakes my stomach as I hold on to the bars on each side of the machine. It won't take us long to catch up with Hawk, but he will hear us coming, and I'm not sure how happy that's going to make him.

Speeding along on the four-wheeler is fast and efficient, and for a second, I close my eyes just to feel the wind in my hair. It's rare that I get to ride trails quickly like this. I didn't think I'd care for it. I rode the back roads with my dad when I was a kid, but I haven't been on a four-wheeler in years. I figured you missed out on too much of the good stuff. The pine needles, the spongy grass, the soft crunching of leaves, and the bright colors. It's all part of the beauty. But moving quickly has its advantages too. Like right now, when I need to know that Hawk is safe.

"I think I see him," Walker shouts back, pointing toward a shadowy figure in the night.

I bend around Walker's large frame and see Hawk in the headlights staring back at us, gun drawn. I should've thought this part over.

"It's me," I shout, waving my arms in the air as we slow the vehicle at his side.

I'm not sure what I should do now that I'm here. *Should I run to him? Should I play it cool? Should I show him my gun and tell him I'm here to help?*

Walker kills the engine and leans forward off the ATV, climbing off. I follow his lead and step toward Hawk, a smile on my face like I'm proud of what I've done. It's unintentional but seeing him has me feeling warm and fuzzy. I reach out for Hawk, desperate to feel the warmth of his arms again. But when I step forward, the ground beneath me disappears and suddenly, I'm falling and screaming, trying to figure out what the hell is happening. Soon, the falling stops, and I'm met with the heavy reality of the ground as the world goes black.

Chapter Eight

Hawk

Looking at Walker, I know he's hiding something. Call it professional intuition, but something about the guy isn't on the up and up. Thankfully, it's not my responsibility to give a shit. I'm here for one guy and one guy only... Jeramiah Wilcox.

That said, the only person in the universe that really matters right now, is a girl. A girl who's laying at the bottom of a trench, motionless.

"Violet!" I yell down, calling out for her. She doesn't answer. I yell again, my stomach in knots as my brain runs a thousand miles an hour trying to figure what to do. "Violet, please!"

"I have ropes," Walker says. "I can run back and grab them."

"I have to go down there," I say. "She could be hurt."

Walker readjusts his stance and stares at me as though I've lost my mind. "How are you going to do that? You could fall and hurt yourself or land on her and do more damage. Just sit here until I get back." He talks like he's had a high position in the military. Having listened to my father bark commands all my life, there's an unmistakable cadence to their speech.

As much as I want to argue, I know he's right. I'd guess the hole is about six feet wide and eight feet deep. It was covered by branches and leaves. It's a trap, usually built by hunters, but this isn't for animals. This was built to stop people. It's a wonder I didn't fall in myself.

Fucking hell. It should be me down there, not her. I should've never brought her out here to begin with.

I study the vines sticking out from the edges of the hole. They aren't perfectly spaced, but they look strong. I doubt they'd hold my weight for long, but I think they might get me down there. Besides, Walker has at least a mile back to his cabin and a mile back. That could take twenty minutes or more. I can't leave her down there that long. What if she's bleeding, or hit her head?

Without more thought, I hop down the shaft and into the hole, skipping the roots as best I can until I reach the bottom. With the light from my flashlight, I look Violet over. For the fall she took, she looks to be in okay shape, aside from the fact that she's knocked out. Then again, I can't see inside of her. I splash water on her face. I know better than to move her immediately in case of a break.

"Come on, sweetheart. You're okay."

Nothing.

I splash water again, hoping and praying that this time she wakes.

"Come on, honey. Just open your eyes for me. Please."

"*Hawk? Where are we?*" Her voice is shallow and crackling as she sits up in a hurry, frantically pulling herself to my chest. "Where are we? Did they get us? Did Jeramiah get us? Where's Walker? It's my fault he's out here." She twists around in a circle, easing my heart that there isn't any major damage, though I'm sure once the adrenaline wears off, she'll start to feel the pain.

"He went back to get some ropes, but I think we can climb out of here if you're up for it. What hurts?"

She looks toward me. "Nothing. I'm okay. Well," she rubs the back of her skull, "I think my head is going to be sore for a while. Am I bleeding?"

Carefully, I move her smooth hair to the side and shine the light toward her head, gently feeling for any injury. "No. The leaves and sticks must have acted like a spring when you fell. You may have passed out from the shock. Can you move everything okay?"

She bends her knees and elbows, then lands her hand on my chest, and stares toward me the same way she did last night. "I'm sorry. I think I just made this worse."

I wrinkle my brows. "That's not possible. Anytime you're in my arms, looking up at me, I have a feeling everything will be okay. I do wish you weren't hurting, though."

She leans into my lips slowly, pressing into me with gentle pressure and my world starts and stops all at once. This woman is everything, and if we weren't sunk in the bottom of this hole with God knows what lurking, I'd take her here and now.

"You need some help?" a voice calls from above. The man staring down at us, is the man I've been looking for. The man with the long dark hair and a beard that looks like it may be hiding birds.

Violet clutches my arm, and a streak of anger rushes through me that I've put us in this mess.

"We're good," I holler, playing dumb. "Got a guy on his way back now. He's bringing a rescue team." I'm lying, hoping Jeramiah doesn't know I've come for him.

"It was for wild pigs, not people," he shouts, throwing down a rope. I saw you fell in on one of my cameras.

Cameras. How the hell does the dude have cameras up here? I don't bother asking. I only stare at the rope he's dangled in front of us, knowing that I've still got fifteen minutes before Walker gets back and I'm not sure I can hold Jeramiah off the scent that long. If I don't grab the rope, he's going to know I'm up to something. Then, who knows what he'll do.

I turn toward Violet. "You stay here until I'm at the top. Once I'm up there, I'll see what he has for weapons, and I'll pull you out once I've stabilized the situation. Okay?"

She looks toward me, a tear in her eye as she leans into me and lands her soft lips on mine once more. The motion is soft and slow and there's so much emotion behind it that I feel torn away from her.

"The second we get off this mountain, you're tying me up again, and finishing what you started."

"Yes, ma'am." I kiss her forehead gently. "I'd love nothing more."

I grip hold of the rope, using the same vines I'd come down on to climb back up. The closer I get to the top, I see Jeramiah is leveraging the weight around a tree, no gun in sight.

Truthfully, I'm shocked. Shocked that he has no gun and shocked that he doesn't recognize me. Though, it's dark.

"See... saved." He laughs. "Now let's get your girl." He turns toward the hole.

"Jeremiah Wilcox, you're under arrest for drug distribution and trafficking." I reach for my gun, but it's gone.

Fuck. I knew I'd get distracted. It must have fallen when I jumped into the hole. I should've checked.

The man laughs. "You followed me all the way here? And now what? I saved your life. You—"

The click of a gun sounds into the night and then Jeremiah flies forward into the pit.

My eyes snap down searching for Violet, but she's gone.

"Right here," she says, her hand on my shoulder, her soft lips pouted in the pale of the night.

"What the hell?" I turn back toward the hole, and see Jeramiah lying flat, and Violet holding a pair of guns in her hands. "How the hell did you do that?"

She grins. "I pulled your gun off you when we kissed, and I pulled his from his holster while you two were talking. I figured I'd come up from the hole the same way you got down here. And I figured if neither of you had guns, no one would get killed. You can thank my mom someday for teaching me the ninja skills that kicked him into the hole."

I've never been more turned on. She hands me my gun back and I tuck it into the back of my slacks as Walker pulls up on the ATV, a smile on his face as he sees Violet standing next to me.

"You're above sea level," he jokes, pulling her in for a hug. "I radioed down to the sheriff and rescue, just in case. I thought you'd be broken to pieces."

"Not even close," she laughs, "and I got the guy we were looking for. He's in the hole."

Walker looks down. "Oh, fuck. Good for you."

"Who knew ending a cult would be so easy?"

I twist back toward Violet and pull her against my chest. "I'll wait here for the local police department. I want to see this guy get dragged away and there's a lot of jurisdictional paperwork to figure out. Why don't you head back to Walker's cabin and warm up. I'll be back there in a bit and then we'll get you home where you belong."

She looks up at me teasingly. "You seriously don't believe I'm leaving you here, do you?"

I nod. "I expect you to. You should get warm, take a nap, have a snack, and I'll meet you back when I'm done."

"No way! I have to be here to protect you!" she teases, nudging my shoulder playfully. "Plus, you're not my daddy."

I growl low and dip into her ear. "Is that so? Because I could be your daddy... and I could make you mind."

She grins. "Good luck."

"Well then, get back to that cabin and—"

"Okay," Walker shouts, covering his ears as he walks back to his ATV. "I know I can't take any more of this. Either I've been lonely too damn long or I'm just repulsed by romance but it's time for me to leave."

Violet grins and kisses my lips. "I'm not leaving you, so I guess you'll have to punish me later."

"Last chance," Walker says, starting up the ATV. I have a feeling he doesn't want to be here when the cops arrive.

"I'm staying," Violet says, hooking her arm into mine. "I'll set you up with my laptop next week. We'll find someone for you to chat with, no doubt. Then again, I think Nicole at the bakery is single. Maybe I could have her drop you some muffins?"

Walker shakes his head and smiles. "I'm glad you're okay. Hit me up when you can." The machine rumbles as he drives back down the path he came.

I look toward Violet, holding her in my arms against the base of a cedar tree. Soon, this will all be a memory, and we'll have a story to tell. Until then, I'm going to hold my girl, just like this, and never let her go.

Chapter Nine

Violet

It's late in the day when we're finally back in town, and I know when I wake up, Hawk will have to go back to Alaska to properly book Jeramiah and figure out the details of the case. Truthfully, I don't know when he'll return, or if he's even coming back. The whole night feels like a dream. I'd say a nightmare, but Hawk is still next to me, and whatever brought us to this moment can't be so terrible.

I stare toward him, a figure on the opposite side of the room, freshly showered and naked, his hard cock pointed out in front of me.

My entire body shivers at the thought of finally having him, and despite how draining the day is, I can't end it any other way.

"How hard should I go?" His voice is deep in the darkness.

I swallow hard. "What do you mean?"

"Should I tie you up again? Should I take control of you?"

His words alone send a shiver straight through to my groin and every nerve center in my body lights with excitement at the thought of my wrists tied with his knots.

When I don't answer, he steps toward me. It's now that I see how large he truly is. And while I've never seen a dick in real life, I'd guess Hawk would win the blue ribbon at some county fair with this behemoth. It's at least seven inches long and wider than what seems to be humanly possible.

He reads the arousal and excitement on my face and lifts the oversized t-shirt I've been wearing up and over my shoulders, exposing my bare body to his.

"You have one minute to tell me you don't want to be tied, then I'm going to assume you want it."

I stare up at him, lost in the urges I see swimming in his gaze. "I want to be tied," I whisper.

He stills before staring down at my feet, dragging his eyes up slowly, then reaches for a necktie that's been tucked in his suitcase.

My blood heats as he bends into my mouth and kisses me gently.

"Arms behind your back," he growls.

I do as I'm told, and relish in every second his large body leans into mine as he ties a simple knot around my wrists.

I struggle against him a bit, but it's for play. I like that he's in control.

With his hands on the knot he's just tied, he guides me off the bed until I'm standing in front of it, facing away from him.

"Bend over," he groans. "Let me see what that tight little pussy can handle."

Excitement rushes through me as he drags his free hand down my spine and onto my ass. Once there, he pauses as I lean my face against the soft sheets. I've been to the Mountain View Lodge a million times, but never like this.

My pulse drums loud in my ears. I'm not sure what comes next, and I like it that way.

"Look at this nice ass. This nice... distracting ass," he groans, rubbing over the top of the smooth flesh that's out in front of him.

I've never been spanked. Hell, I've never done much of anything, but my entire body is aching for him to punish me. For what... I don't care. Just punish me.

"I told you to stay put today, didn't I?" he growls, running his hand over my ass. "Did you?"

"No, but you should be glad I didn't. I got your guy."

He laughs playfully. "You did get my guy... didn't you?"

I nod.

"But you still didn't follow directions. And in law enforcement, when someone doesn't follow directions... there's a punishment."

"Do it!" I beg. "Punish me!" My throat is tight as his cock pokes up against my thigh from behind and suddenly his palm spanks me.

"Hmm," he groans, rubbing against the stinging skin he's left behind. "Tell me you'll be a good girl."

"I'll be a good girl," I pout. "Just fuck me. Fuck me hard." My hips rock toward him, my pussy dripping wet as I call out for him, desperate for his invasion. My heart thumps against my chest.

"Tell me you're mine." He tightens his grip on the knot behind my back. "Tell me you're mine forever."

"I want nothing more," I cry. "Please... fuck me."

"I love to hear you beg," he growls.

"Then I'll beg. Fuck me! Please! I'm aching for you!"

"We don't have a condom. Do you want me anyway?"

"I want all of you," I beg. "I want your come all over me. Inside of me. On top of me. Everywhere. Just spread me wide!" I'm panting as I speak, desperate for his touch, desperate for him, but he's slow with me, teasing, like he had been at the cabin.

His hand reaches between my legs and he runs circles around my clit, wetting me before he begins to edge inside. The grip he has on the rope is steady and the pressure is gentle, though when he moves deeper inside of me, it takes a minute to acclimate.

"You're so fucking tight," he grunts, pressing further into my core.

A short pinch follows a longer one. I try not to scream out, but the noise of uncomfortable pressure escapes before I can stop it.

He pauses. "Are you okay?"

"Keep going," I pant, pressing back into him. "Harder!"

I always imagined myself as someone who liked sex softly. Soft and gentle. I guess I thought that was loving. But with Hawk, I'm someone different. I'm someone I never imagined I could be. I'm wild and untamed. I'm a girl who likes a tight grip, and a harsh ragged response. I'm a girl who likes the feral animalistic chase. It's magic.

I breathe hard against his free hand as it covers my mouth, the other still in the make-shift rope. He's thrusting, hard. Pumping in and out, spreading me wider and wider as I whine with an aching pulse that won't relent.

"Tell me you need to come," he growls. "Tell me now."

"I need to come, Hawk. I need your come too. I need it all. All over me." I pant as I speak, barely able to form words as he stretches me wide.

"Good girl." He presses into me deeper.

Harder and harder, his large body moves me and the bed forward until all at once every bit of pent energy I've been holding to, releases. I cry out and my eyes squeeze closed.

"Good fucking girl," he growls, somehow deeper. I can tell by his voice, that my orgasm has pushed him over the edge. "You take this cock like a good fucking girl." Any bit of gentleness he had is gone, and now, his big, bulky frame heaves against me with the purpose of a ravaging storm.

I love it. I need it. I need him. Always. Just like this.

His warm palm smooths over the small of my back as he releases inside of me. "You feel so fucking good, Violet. Like you were made for me."

My heart warms as he slows his thrust and eventually pulls from within me with a sigh.

I turn back toward him, and lick his cock, desperate to taste the love we've made. As I do, he loosens the tie on my wrists and buries his hand in my hair, letting out a soft groan of approval.

"I love you, Violet." His words are sure and steady. "I love you like I've never loved anyone. Tell me we can make this work."

I pull my lips off his cock gently, swallowing down our sticky sweet juices before lifting to his lips. "You love me?"

He nods. "You're mine, remember?"

"I love you too, Hawk. I never want this to end."

"And it won't," he says, holding me against his chest with the grip of a man who means what he says.

For the first time in my life, I don't question his motive. I take him at his word and I have a feeling, I won't regret it.

Epilogue

Hawk

S ix Months Later

I stand at the mountain's edge and look out at the town below. There's more snow on the ground now and there's a breeze picking up from the east. I'm betting more is on the way.

"Are you coming in?" Violet grips me from behind, wrapping her warm arms around my waist.

I turn toward her, fixing my gaze on my wife. My beautiful, smart, sweet, feisty wife. "I was studying the weather. I think we've got a big one blowing in. Did you let Walker know?"

She nods. "He's been busy talking to his new squeeze, so I'm not sure he cares, but yes, I told him."

"Someone he met online or someone in town?"

"Both," she says, coyly. "I'll let him tell you the details. I invited him to dinner tonight. I hope you don't mind."

I squeeze her against my chest. "Of course not, he's practically family." I don't know Walker's story and I haven't asked. For the most part, he's quiet and stays to himself. That, and we're the only two on this side of the mountain. We need to look out for each other.

"Well, thank you." She tips up onto her toes and kisses my lips as a light snow starts to fall. "Do you ever miss Alaska and all those big cases you were working?"

I stare down at her with all the love in the world. "Never. Being up here in this little cabin with you is everything I ever wanted. Plus, I think your dad likes all the fresh cop talk."

She leans against my chest as we walk back toward the little shack that we rebuilt to be our own two-bedroom retreat. It's not perfect, but it has four walls and good insulation. We're still working on the rest.

"Really? You don't miss it at all?"

I shake my head. "Not for a second. The day I arrested Jeramiah, I knew I was done with that life. I love being here, in this little mountain police station, working for the people. It's like I'm really doing something, you know? Besides," I run my hand over her expanding stomach, "I would rather this life with you and our baby girl any day. Did we decide on a name, though, because I think that was still up for debate?"

I open the cabin door and we step into the warmth of the woodstove burning. "I think I'd decided on Gia and you decided on Nora."

"I vote for Poppy," Walker says, stepping in front of the open door before we close it.

Violet looks toward me. "I kind of like it."

She nods, tipping onto her toes to lean her forehead against mine. "Me too."

"As long as we all understand this baby is going to be the most strong-willed woman on this mountain, I think we're good," Walker laughs, stepping into the cabin with a fresh loaf of bread.

"Hey!" Violet says. "You better mean that as a positive!"

Walker laughs, but I wrap Violet into my arms and press a blazing kiss onto her lips. I never imagined that a cult would somehow bring me to the love of my life, but here I am, warm and content, standing in front of the most beautiful woman I've ever met. My wife, the mother of my child.

My hand brushes her cheek as I look toward her. "If I have a hundred children, as warm and brazen as you, then I've hit the lottery. No doubt about it."

As we sit down for our meal, I can feel myself being examined a little too closely. "What have you done?" my intuitive wife asks with her brows furrowed. God, she's good.

I look at her, unable to hold a solid poker face. "I have no idea what you mean."

"You're hiding something," she says with a smile. "You only sit in your chair that way when you're up to something."

I let out a hearty laugh. "You never cease to amaze me." I look over at Walker. "Can you believe this woman?"

Walker only shrugs his shoulders like he has no idea what's going on.

"Last chance, Special Agent," she says with a smile, holding her fork menacingly.

"Alright. I surrender," I say with a chuckle. I step from my chair and head over to the couch. I drop to a knee and pull a secret box from underneath.

"Oh, what is that?" she asks with a squeal.

"Something for Nora," I say with a laugh. "I'm pretty sure when you see this, you'll let me name her."

Slowly, I open the box and reveal our daughter's first gift.

"Hawk, it's beautiful." I hand a homemade guitar built for a toddler to the love of my life. She scans it over slowly. "Is this a map of Rugged Mountain?" Her eyes start to tear.

"It is. I've been working on it for a while but finding a small enough map to fit was the hard part." I reach for my wife's hands. "I just want her to know that wherever she goes, this will always be her home."

Violet wraps her arms around me and wipes her tears on my shoulder. "I'll always love you, Hawk."

"And I'll never leave your side, my everything."

Lone Wolf

Chapter One

Birdie

Y ou never get a second chance at a first impression. It's a phrase my father said to me over and over again growing up. I'm sure he meant well. After all, there's truth in the statement. I will most definitely *not* get a second chance at this first impression. But the pressure in that... is too much. Especially now, when a first impression is about to make or break my life.

Well, that might be dramatic. But still, if Walker Huxley doesn't like what he sees, this whole situation could get very awkward, very fast. I guess that would be the bonus to sharing pictures before a meetup, but *RanchersOnly.com* isn't set up that way. They claim to be the only website on the market that will find your true soulmate. The one person in the world that you connect with on a level that's heart to heart rather than looks.

It sounds good in theory and up until now, I've been all for it. But suddenly, the thought of trekking up this mountain to meet a man I've never seen is a little... terrifying. In my fantasy, he'd be tall, with tattoos, and a nice, full beard. So, if I can get at least two out of three, I'd be ecstatic. Unfortunately, my fantasy is always dashed by the sight of a man covered in so much hair that you can't even feel his skin. He really could be anything and I need to be calm when I see him.

I wonder what nightmares he's had about me.

Another knot twists as I drive up the long, winding mountain road. What if I'm his nightmare? What if he can't stand short blondes with thick thighs and curvy waists? *What if he hates me?* A bead of sweat rolls down my cheek. I wipe it off quickly and turn up the air conditioning in my little white car. It's not made for treks like this. Then again, neither am I. I don't think I've done anything this adventurous... ever. Granted, I'm only twenty-five. I haven't had a ton of years to bank up the adventure points. So far, the wildest thing I've done, aside from this, is going all out with a new ice cream flavor. I mean, really, who knows what pistachio sunrise is going to taste like until you're at home on the couch cracking it open? There are some balls in that choice. On one hand, oranges and pistachios work for cookies. On the other hand, creamy citrus and nuts in a carton turned out to be trash. God, I hope today is more of a cookie day.

"*Hello?*" I answer the phone too harshly after only one ring, and my friend Montana is quick to respond.

"Ahh," she says in a fake screeching manner. I assume it's for dramatic effect. "Where are you?"

"On the mountain, about two miles from his cabin. I don't know, maybe I made a mistake. Is being lonely really that bad? I'm thinking I should just adopt a dog, or maybe another cat. They're a perfect substitute for a man, right?"

"Umm... no. You drove all this way. You can see what this guy is about. Besides, I want you in Rugged Mountain. It will be nice to be so close."

Montana and I met a while back when she came into Colorado Springs to check out my crystal shop. She was looking to balance her chakras, and I found her the right combination of crystals to work with. That, and some sage to cleanse them all. Since then, we've talked daily online. It makes sense, considering internet relationships have always been easiest for me. I pick up the phone when I want, email when I want, and get-togethers are few and far between.

"I know, but still, *a whole weekend* of just the two of us. What if he hates me? Plus, the pressure of a wedding is more real now, you know?"

"He's going to love you." She sighs. "You guys have so much in common."

"*On paper.*" I'm being difficult, and I know it, but I can't help myself. I'm about to meet my husband. A man that I've never seen. A man that's never seen me. A man that doesn't know my most embarrassing moment. Heck, nobody knows that. "I should turn around." I'm half joking and half serious. Still, my foot lifts off the gas enough that I slow.

"That's a negative," she retorts playfully, as though she knows it's not an option. "Do you know how you're going to introduce yourself yet? What did you decide to wear? I need details! I'm living vicariously, remember?"

She's said it half a dozen times since I started this process, so it's hard to forget.

"I wore that short pink dress, the one with the magnolia on the back. Do you think it's too much? Maybe it's too much. It's a really bright pink. I probably should've gone with—"

"I'm sure you look great. Just be yourself. Have you guys even talked on the phone?"

"No. We could only exchange emails through that little box on the website. They claim that's how they keep people from sharing pictures and physical details, but... I should probably go. It's starting to rain, and it looks like there's a—"

I slam my breaks and stare out in front of me as a man at least six and a half feet tall stalks across the road. He's wild and untamed, with a deer slung over his shoulder, his chest hair spilling from his unbuttoned flannel. Rain falls heavier as he looks toward me, staring with a scowl as though I've interrupted his walk with my car on the road.

"Birdie, are you still there?" Montana presses. "I thought I heard a screech."

"Yeah, yeah... still here," I say, staring at the man as he crosses. He holds the deer on his shoulder and stalks across the road, calling back for the black lab that follows him on the first whistle. The man is massive, intimidating, and if that's anything even close to what my mountain man looks like, I may have bitten off more than I can chew.

"Well, what's wrong then?" Montana continues. "Did you hit something?"

I blow out the wild strands of my hair that have come loose, then watch the man disappear into the other side of the woods before gently laying on the gas pedal again.

"Everything's fine," I say. "I think I'm going to let you go, though. I need to focus on the road. I'm not used to these bends."

"Fine." She lets out a sigh. "But call me the second you can. Oh, and send a selfie of you two. I'm on pins and needles."

I agree to her request, and say my goodbyes, even though I doubt I'll be sending any pictures. It's awkward enough meeting someone for the first time without asking for a photo shoot. Not only that, but if this guy is as intimidating as the man that just crossed, I'm not sure I'll be able to ask for a glass of water, let alone a picture.

Air gets heavier in my lungs, and I roll down the window to suck in some cool, fresh, mountain air. There are still droplets clinging to the windowpane and the earth smells damp and rich with iron. It reminds me of childhood. The tall, green pine, the jagged mountain backdrop, the warm feeling that nature is surrounding you, shielding you between its trees. The dichotomy between this and the life I live in the city is astounding. In the Springs, I live in a high-rise apartment just beyond the rail tracks. It's not pretty, but it's all I can afford. Out here, the only sounds I hear are the light chirping of birds and maybe a few frogs. I could see myself living out here. It's what drew me to *RanchersOnly* to begin with.

It's that thought that drives me up the remainder of the mountain road and soon, I'm face to face with a long meandering driveway with a wooden sign that's nailed to a tree: *No Trespassing*. Beneath that, the number I've been looking for: 7839.

My stomach rumbles and my knees begin to shake as I flick on the blinker. At this point, I have nothing to lose. He's invited me to his ranch, and I've accepted. So… I'm here.

Turning the wheel, I pull into the stone driveway and dial into every detail that surrounds me. Pebbles pop beneath my tires. Tall cedar sway gently in the breeze, and rain pools in the divots of the driveway. To the left, a gray shed with sliding barn doors. Straight in front of me, a log cabin with wood piled beneath the decking and a sweet front porch with two rocking chairs moving in the wind. I don't see any animals from here, but online he said he had horses and a few chickens.

There isn't much decoration to his place, unless you count the deer that's strung up next to the shed as fall decor. Otherwise, it's easy to see a man lives here alone. A woodsy man. A manly man. The kind of man who likes meat for dinner and growls out his replies.

I should go. What business do I really have here? I have no idea what to do with a man like this. I've only ever dated city guys. What was I thinking, making plans to marry someone from the mountains? Besides, I've been sitting in the driveway for at least thirty seconds, and he hasn't come running out to greet me yet. I'm sure he's watching from one of these shadowed windows, trying to figure out how to let me down kindly.

I start up the engine and put the car into reverse when a knock on the passenger door startles me.

My heart stalls and my stomach turns. How am I going to explain why I was backing out? I need to look at him.

Look at him! I say to myself. *Birdie, look at him!* I repeat the prompt over and over, but I can't do it.

"Excuse me," a deep voice grumbles. He doesn't sound happy.

Oh, great. We're already off to a terrible start.

I inch my gaze further toward him, slowly, trying to look as unafraid and as beautiful as possible. After all, you never do get a second chance at a first impression.

"Who are you?" the man grumbles.

With his last statement, I inch toward him faster, holding my breath as I move.

My heart stalls when I see the goliath of a man that stopped me in my tracks earlier. The one with the deer on his shoulder. Up close, he's more attractive than he'd been stalking away, but still easily the most frightening person I've ever been this close to. He looks like he could tear that door from its hinges with no effort and pull me into his lair with a flick of his wrist.

I can't be at the right address.

Grabbing my phone, I check the text again. "Is this 7839 Country Route 56?"

"Who are you?" he repeats, his heavy brows turned down even more than they had been before.

I need to answer him now, or who knows what he'll do.

"Hi. I'm Birdie. I'm looking for Walker Huxley."

As he leans to look into the window, he's broad and bearded, with dark eyes and a stance so wide that I swear he's half the width of my tiny car. "Who are you... Birdie?" His voice is monotone, but intense.

I smile, trying to break the tension, but he's not interested in pleasantries. "I'm sorry. I think I've got the wrong address. Can you point me toward Walker, and I'll get out of your way? I must have written the address wrong." He's a bear. A huge, wild, untamed bear, and he looks like he's about to snap.

"I know who you're looking for. *I asked you who you are.*" I was right, he does growl.

"I'm a crystal dealer. Well, *not a crystal dealer*, as in drugs. I sell crystals in Colorado Springs. The kind that you ward off demons with. But you're probably asking why I'm here. I'm here because I'm looking for Walker and—"

"*Why* are you looking for him?" The man isn't amused by my ramblings.

"Oh, we've been talking online. I'm his mail-order bride."

The man stays silent, staring at me with an intensity that I've never felt before. I swear I feel my skin begin to burn.

"I didn't order a mail-order bride."

My brows bend in confusion. "Okay... but Walker did. So, if you could point me in his direction, that would be great."

The man hunches his shoulders slightly and his jaw tightens as a heavier rain begins to fall. "I'm Walker Huxley, and I'm going to need you to come in and explain all this to me."

My chest tightens and my breathing goes ragged.

What did I get myself into?

Chapter Two

Walker

*W*ho would order a mail-order bride? Especially sight unseen. Some may think I'm desperate, but I'm not that bad.

"Where did you get my name? If you're here from the government, I need to call my lawyer."

She deflates and stares down at her wheel, then glances up toward me through the pouring rain, which I'm sure is turning to ice. "I made a mistake. I think I'll just go."

If I were to believe this mail-order bride shit, then I'd say I was pretty god damn stupid. She's from the government. At the very least, she's a cop. I need to get her inside talking so I can find out what she knows and why she's here.

Reaching down, I pull open the car door. "Come inside. We should talk."

She stares up at me as though I'm asking her to throw herself into my stew pot. "No. I don't know who you are!"

"Yet you've said my name multiple times in the last couple of minutes."

"Well, I know your name, but that's all I know. I thought you were someone else."

She's really playing up this mail-order bride thing.

"Right, well, I'd like to know what you know, but the rain is currently soaking me. So, if we could have this conversation on the porch, that'd be great."

She stares up at me with big brown eyes that look defeated and scared. Yet somehow, she's hauntingly beautiful with long blonde hair and a bright pink dress. Come to think of it, this doesn't look like a government worker at all. But I suppose that's what they want me to think.

"Fine," she finally says, "I'll talk to you on the porch, but you have to keep your distance. Six feet back or I'm leaving." She steps out of the car one bare foot at a time. Her toes are painted pale pink to match the dress. She's gone all out for imagination Walker.

I'm flattered.

"You have no shoes."

She steps carefully over the rocks and hops up onto the front porch out of the rain. "I don't wear them. It's called grounding. We talked about it through emails. You thought it was cool."

My brows narrow. "I thought wearing no shoes in thirty-degree weather in the mountains was cool?" I laugh. "Doesn't sound like me. Shoes serve a very important function. Up here, bare feet wouldn't last an hour."

Her arms cross over her chest and she looks toward me with disdain, as though she's been personally offended. "There are eight thousand nerves in the human foot. When we walk barefoot, our bodies absorb free ions from the earth's surface, which act as antioxidants."

"They're also absorbing hookworms and God knows what else."

She rolls her eyes and turns away. "You know what..."

"Wait, no. I'm sorry. Walk barefoot, whatever. Why are you here, for real?"

"Have you done something? You're awfully afraid of why I'm here. I told you, we were set up for marriage. I guess someone has been using your name, and the app gave me your address. I don't know anything else." She hitches her hip up gently and sways her short frame against the back wall of the cabin.

"I'm supposed to believe that *you* needed to be set up with someone?"

Her gaze narrows, and her frame straightens. "Is that supposed to be a compliment?"

"It's an observation."

"Of what?" She pulls back her gaze. "That I don't look like marriage material?"

"No, that you don't look like the kind of..." Why am I arguing with this woman? "You know what? You showed up on my property. I'm asking the questions."

"And I'm the one who's been lied to, so I can gladly leave if you're going to be rude."

I suck in a deep breath as an icy gust whips into the porch. The woman covers her bare shoulders with her hands and rubs them up and down quickly. She obviously hasn't been to Rugged Mountain in October.

"Stay there," I say, swinging the porch door open to reach for my flannel hanging on the coat tree just inside the cabin. I toss it toward her, and she grabs it without question, drowning herself in the oversized fabric.

"Thank you," she squeaks, wiping away a tear.

God. It might be worse that she's not the cops or the government. I don't know how to deal with all this emotional shit. I didn't sign up for this, not today. I have a deer I have to break down and I still have to drag in the last of the harvest before the freeze, which judging by this wind is right about now. But there's something about this woman that's so innocent and sweet that I feel myself being drawn in. It's almost like an urge that's carnal and barbaric. As much as I want her gone, I can't let her drive back down the mountain in this storm.

"Look, I'm sorry I'm not who you were looking for. But I'm sure with a little time and patience, in the real world, not on that dating website, you'll find someone you can spend your time with."

She straightens and unwraps herself from my flannel as though the decision to be done with me has come all at once. "Oh, well, thanks for the advice." There's sarcasm in her tone as she whips away from me and toward her car.

"I'm not done with the questions yet." I follow after her as she makes her way down the porch and back into the tiny vehicle she rode up in.

She ignores me and slides the keys into the ignition, but I grip hold of the door handle and swing the door open again. "You're not safe driving down the mountain in this thing. The roads turn to ice in rainstorms this time of year."

She sighs and looks up at me with a quivering lip, as though she's trying to hold back the tears and disappointment she feels for finding me at the top of this mountain instead of the man of her dreams.

"There's nothing left to ask. You're not the Walker I was looking for." She turns the engine to her car again, but nothing happens.

"No! No! No!" She turns it again. Still nothing. "No!" Again. "*Please, come on. Please!*" She talks to the car as though begging it to start will solve her problems. I guess that's what got her up here in the first place... false hope.

I'm actually starting to feel bad for her. She might be having a worse day than me.

"The roads aren't good, anyway. Come in for a bit. I'll take a look at your car in the morning."

She closes her eyes and presses her head against the wheel, letting her long blonde hair fall forward with her. Without looking up, she tries the engine one more time.

Still nothing but a painful groan that sounds like a starter issue, which would require a part... and time.

"Can I call an Uber?"

I laugh. "There are no Ubers up here. I can take you down the mountain in the morning, but not tonight. It's too dangerous taking those turns with the ice that's building out there. The whole mountain will be a skating rink. Trust me, tried that once, ended up off a cliff, ten feet in a ditch with a broken elbow and a pretty good gash on my forehead."

She leans up, but stares ahead. "Do you have a pair of ice skates, maybe? I could try—"

"You don't wear shoes. What good would skates do you?"

She glares back, and I swear she's putting a spell on me. "Ha. Ha."

I turn away from the car and step back up onto the porch, out of the freezing rain. "Come on, Birdie. It's just for the night."

"Famous last words. This is the part where you season me up and throw me in the feed bin, right?"

"What? No. I don't season the feed."

She doesn't laugh.

"How am I supposed to spend the night with a guy who clearly has a fear of the government or the police? It's only fair you tell me what you're hiding."

I roll my eyes and hold open the cabin door, clearing the path for the woman I'm mildly happy to trap.

She reacts as I expect, with an eye roll as she makes her way past me and into the warmth of my home.

"Are you hungry?" My voice is probably gruffer than it needed to be.

"No." She's quick with her response, but I know that must be a lie. I'm sure her and imagination Walker had plans for a nice dinner tonight.

"You must be hungry. You drove all the way up here from Colorado Springs."

"It's only an hour and a half. I had some crackers on the way to settle my stomach."

"So, you've only eaten crackers today?"

She nods.

"Then I'm going to feed you."

"Not if feeding me includes anything to do with that deer outside. I don't eat animals."

"Of course you don't," I sigh. "Do you want to tell me what you do eat?"

She bites the inside of her cheek. "Do you have pasta? We were going to make spaghetti together tonight."

"*We were?*" I try not to laugh as I say it.

She nods, holding back a grin of her own. "With tomatoes you'd pulled from your garden."

I suppose anyone could know I had tomatoes in my garden. They're a practical plant to grow up here, but still, who the hell set me up like this? Or rather, who stole my identity? If they knew anything about me, I think they'd want to pass on me for just about anyone else.

Maybe it was something nefarious. Did they plan to cut her off at the pass and take her somewhere else? Did they plan to block me out of the picture and take my spot?

The thought of anyone hurting this innocent woman has my hair standing on end, which is probably my cue to get outside and move the deer to the shed overnight.

"Spaghetti can work," I say. "I'll be back in an hour. I have to move the deer so the bears don't get to him and I need to pull a few more vegetables before this freeze sets. Help yourself to anything, and I'll cook when I get back."

I let out a loud whistle and she jumps. Shit. It's been so long since someone was here, I've forgotten they aren't used to my routine. Lilo bounds in, her tail wagging as wildly as ever.

Birdie comes alive at the sight of Lilo and starts to scratch her everywhere. Despite all of her *feel the ground* nonsense, she can't be that bad. Lilo is having the time of her life with her.

"Lilo, watch our guest. Keep her out of trouble." I turn toward Birdie. "I shouldn't be very long."

She nods and smiles sweetly as I swing open the door, ignoring an unfamiliar rumble in my stomach. It's not hunger, and it's not fear. Though it's nothing like I've ever felt before. It's warm and prickly, and I'm a little lightheaded.

I hold my hand over my stomach and stare back at her again. The same feeling hits. It's a coincidence. It must be indigestion.

"Thank you," Birdie says, as I'm about to close the door.

I glance up at her, taking in her short frame from the doorway. She's innocent and sweet, like a porcelain doll that could easily be broken.

"For what?" I can't figure what I've done that's kind. I was sure I was pushing too hard and being too gruff.

"For taking me in. For protecting me tonight. I'd have done something stupid and tried to walk down the mountain. I appreciate you giving me a place to stay. You don't have to."

My chest compresses and my throat tightens as warmth spreads over the top of me and squeezes my heart. I'm not sure I've ever felt indigestion like this, but when I get back inside, I'm going to need something stronger than an antacid.

Chapter Three

Birdie

There's something about Walker that's real. Gruff and untamed, sure. But above all else, he is outwardly as down to earth as it gets. I get the feeling that with him, I'll get exactly what he says I'll get. Which, in some weird way, I find comforting.

"You made dinner? I was only out for an hour. I thought we were going to cook together. I even put Lilo to bed for the night in the shed. She can't be trusted around food like this. She's the kind of girl who would be begging the entire time we were eating." Walker ducks his head to step into the cabin. From a distance, he's unkempt, but up close, he's quite handsome. Okay, *really handsome.* Like, if he'd been the mountain man I was supposed to marry, I'd be over the moon. He's tall and broad, with dark features, a beard, and beneath his rolled flannel sleeves, black ink tattoos run up his forearms and onto the backs of his hands. That, and he has this deep, velvet voice that draws me in.

What am I thinking? He's not *the him* that was supposed to be *him.* He's a whole different *him.* A *him* who is clearly not looking for a wife.

"Yeah, I figured you'd appreciate it. I saw you outside struggling with that deer. I hope you don't mind."

"No. Not at all." He kicks off his boots and moves closer into the kitchen, taking the scent of the tomatoes I've cooked down into a thick sauce.

"It's just a quick recipe my grandma taught me when I was young. She called it her last-minute tomato masher." I spoon up a bit onto the end of a wooden spoon and angle it up toward his lips. "Coincidently, it's the same recipe she used for her full body sauce, but it just sits a lot longer."

He smiles and lets the flavor linger in his mouth. "Pretty good. I feel bad you've been in here cooking, though. You're my guest now. It's not really the way to treat a bride-to-be."

"Ha. Ha." I pile a twirl of pasta onto a plate, douse it in sauce, and hand it to him before making a plate for myself. "Trust me, it was more selfish than anything," I say with a smile. "You were right. I'm starving. I was too nervous to eat all day."

We sit at a small wood dining table that's situated by a window in the kitchen overlooking what I assume is the valley come daylight. Right now, it looks like a whole lot of my reflection.

"So, are you happy with what you got then?" He twists angel hair onto his fork and stuffs a large bite into his mouth, wiping his beard afterward. Okay, he's not used to company.

"What do you mean, *happy with what I got*?"

"Would you be disappointed if this were real? If I was *your* Walker? I dated a few girls I'd met online, and it all went to hell pretty quick. Turns out, I'm rough by even mountain standards."

I narrow my gaze, wondering for a second if he's some psycho who's playing a trick on me by pretending not to have been emailing, so he has no allegiance to me if this doesn't work out. But I figure that's crazy. He couldn't have faked the anger that was on his face when he saw me pull in. I'm not sure how to answer his question, though. If I'm honest, it's going to sound like I'm into him. If I lie, I'm mean. So instead of answering, I turn the question around.

"Would *you* be disappointed?"

He stills, glancing up toward me before sucking down a long pull from his beer. "This is a trick question."

"You asked it!"

"No, I asked you if you'd be disappointed with me. You didn't answer."

"I did. I answered by asking you the same question."

"You can't answer a question with another question. That's a rule." He twists more pasta onto his fork and stares back at me. "So..."

"So... would you be disappointed?"

"No." The room goes quiet and the only noise is the sound of his fork against the ceramic plate and the crackle of the fire I added to earlier. I wanted him to come in to a nice, toasty cabin and a hot meal. "You're beautiful. And as long as you're not talking... I think we would get along just fine."

I grin. "You had me for a second there. Well, I would say the same about you. Your looks far outweigh your personality."

"Well, at least we both know there's no threat of love here tonight," he says as he takes another gulp.

"None at all."

Silence ensues for another long moment before he starts up the questioning again. "So, what else do you know about me?"

"The real you or the you that's someone else?"

"The me that's someone else."

"Well, the Walker I was supposed to meet is a veteran who served for fifteen years. He was discharged honorably because of an injury from a landmine."

"You're fucking with me," he grumbles, running his large hand through his thick beard.

"No, why? Is that true?"

"Every word. I suppose next you're going to tell me that talking to Lilo makes up most of my yearly conversations and I only listen to country music because the rest of that stuff is shit. Thanks for switching on the radio, by the way. It's relaxing."

I stare toward him with a narrowed gaze. "Yes. That's what you told me. How would anyone else know that?"

He bites the inside of his cheek. "I went into town a few months back to try online dating. I used the public computers. I wonder if someone copied my conversations or something. I need to contact Julie and Maverick. They own the library in town. I bet they could look into it."

"I can't imagine you online dating." I pause. "Or dating at all, really."

He runs his large hand over his beard again and stares back at me with a scowl that's deep and wrapped in thick lines. "You need to even the playing field. I know nothing about you. What else did I like about you?"

I can't help but laugh at the way his sentence is worded... but he's not wrong. Giving up a little information on myself only seems fair after all the drama he's been put through because of me. "Well... you liked all my crystal talk. You said you found it super interesting how much I knew about minerals and you were going to take me quartz hunting."

"I was?" He takes another swig of beer, prompting me to take a swig of mine.

I nod. "Yeah, apparently, according to fake you, there are a ton of smokey quartz stones around here... which the real you could use if you ask me."

His thick brows narrow. "Really, and what's that mean?"

"Smokey quartz helps you open yourself up to the world around you."

He nods slowly, holding back a grin. "Yeah, sounds like something I'd need. What else were you planning on doing with me?"

"Well, you told me how much you loved to dance, so you were going to teach me some moves."

"I was going to teach you to dance?"

I nod. "And you were going to play your guitar for me."

"When those roads clear, I'm opening a major investigation on this because... fuck that guy."

"Why, though? Why would someone steal your personality only to give me your address? That makes no sense. Are you sure you didn't forget we were talking or something?"

He grins and looks away. "No, I'm sure. I know I'd remember a barefoot, crystal loving, vegetarian."

"You say it like it's a bad thing."

"I say it like it's an interesting thing. A thing I wouldn't forget." He takes another drink of his beer. "What were you wanting with a move up here, anyway? Don't you have everything you need in the city?"

I push my pasta back and forth on my plate, trying to figure how to tell someone how messed up your life is for the second time. "My mom passed away last year... car accident. She was all I had left in the city. When she was alive, we'd take these beautiful trips every summer up here to Rugged Mountain. Sometimes, we'd rent a cabin, but a lot of the time we'd pitch a tent next to this pretty blue river with big boulders that had moss on the side and pine trees hanging down from above. We'd walk the shore and pick up rocks to paint back at camp and make pancakes over an open flame. This area always seemed like magic to me. I dreamed that one day I'd come out here and make a life of my own, a little ranch tucked away, a small town with small town drama, and a Christmas parade every year." I shrug. "It's probably dumb."

"No way. I love that story. It's similar to my own. I'd tell you but I'm sure you've already heard it."

I smile. "No, I don't think I have."

"I grew up in Eastern Tennessee, but when I was discharged from the military, I needed a fresh start. I came up here for a few tattoos and met a guy named Henry who helped me relocate. I've been here ever since. I like the quiet."

I'm reminded now about his government freak out and I wonder how honest he's being, but I guess it doesn't matter. I only have one night here on this mountain and then we'll most likely never see each other again.

I chew on my bottom lip as I wait for him to say something else.

"You want to dance?" He reaches his hand out toward mine. "This song is one of my favorites."

My heart stops as his body unfolds in front of me. It's shocking how much larger he is than me. My hand settles into his palm, small and shaky. "Yeah, I could dance."

"I mean, I'd hate for you to come all the way to Rugged Mountain, think you're dancing with your soon to be husband, and not even get a few steps in."

My chest presses against his and my neck cranes upward to look toward him. This close, he smells of cedar, pine, and the spice of something I can't identify, but it's lovely. Manly. Wild.

I almost wish it were him I've been talking to. Well, technically it was. It was everything about him. It was him I was falling in love with, but not him.

My head spins and for a second, without thought, I lean against his chest then immediately pull away. "I'm sorry. I was—"

"Don't apologize," he says, raising his palm to the back of my head to gently put me back in place. He's capable of such roughness, but he's soft with me, careful. "I liked you there."

My heart gushes with warmth and my clit throbs unexpectedly as the song ends too quickly.

I don't want him to let me go. And suddenly, a swirl of crazy thoughts start spinning through my head. Things like kissing him, holding him all night, letting him have his way with me, staying in this cabin, lingering for days, months, years.

What's gotten into me?

Please don't let me go. Please don't let me go. The words repeat over and over in my head as the next song begins.

His body stays in place against mine without missing a beat. And suddenly, I have a feeling, leaving tomorrow is going to be harder than I thought.

Chapter Four

Walker

I ce gathers on the windows as I hold Birdie tight. We aren't doing anything fancy; we're just swaying with the music. One hand is respectfully on her hip, while the other holds her hand against my chest, but as I breathe her in, I can't help but get lost in her. She's delicate, smooth, and the scent of flowers in her hair is like spring and summer all mixed into one.

What am I doing, aside from letting my feelings go awry for a woman that's leaving in the morning to undoubtedly find the real person she's really been talking to? Granted, technically, she was falling in love with me. Did she say love or is that my imagination going wild?

Part of me wants to obsess over who the hell could've done this, find them, and kick their ass. Not for me, but for getting Birdie's hopes up. She fully expected to come here to meet her husband. Instead, she was meant with my grumpy ass. I'm so entranced by this moment with the music, I don't care the cause. Whoever brought her to me, I'm thankful. However she got here, I'm lucky.

Her head is against my chest, her hands wrap around my waist, her nails dancing circles on my back as warmth presses between us. I push away thoughts of laying her down, hoping the shameful rigidity in my jeans retreats before she notices. It's been too long since I've been this close to a woman, and even longer since I've felt something. Birdie is different. She's interesting. She challenges me. She makes me want to break down the walls and try. *Try for something real. Try for love.*

Love. What am I thinking?

There's a soft shutter in her voice before she lifts her head from my chest. "Walker?" She says my name so sweetly that it's as though I feel another part of my heart break free from its cast.

"Yeah?" I inhale her scent as she gets ready to speak.

"If I asked you to let me stay a little longer than just the one night, would you?"

A panicked thud hits my chest and I cough to get the rhythm back again. There are so many ways I could answer her question, but only one way is honest. "I want nothing more."

Her face turns a rosy shade of pink and her gaze scatters from my eyes to the ground and back again. She's cute, re-situating her frame to rub her palm against my back. "Really?" she finally says. "I have to be honest with you, I'm looking for something long-term." She laughs under her breath at how her words are coming out. "That's not to say that I would never leave if you let me stay longer." The way her panic-stricken face gives away her thoughts as she fumbles through her words is so cute that I feel my smile stretch the length of my face.

"I know what you meant," I say trying to settle her nerves. "It's only been recently that I knew I needed to start that next stage of my life. I want love and a family. That's why I dragged myself into town in the first place. My friend Addie set me up with a few websites and I tried them, but I couldn't maneuver them easily, and got flustered."

She chuckles, but her head dips when she does. "Yeah, I can't either. Every time I met someone online who sounded nice, I was disappointed in one way or another." She looks me in my eyes, and I hope she's moving me from one side of the column to the other. Her hand drags up to my shoulder and her thumb rubs soft circles on the collar of my flannel. "I just wanted to fall in love, you know? The kind of love I read about and watch in movies. I see now, that was completely insane. I let my friend Montana push me into it. Otherwise, I'd probably be sitting at home, in my tiny apartment listening to the train go by while watching old reruns of *Glee*."

"Well, I guess I'm glad she pushed you into it then."

She waits ten long heartbeats then stares up at me with big doe eyes that tighten my throat as I try to stop the words that are about to bubble out. It's too soon. She's scared. She's been through too much. I know all the logical reasoning, but still, I can't stop myself. I can't let her go another second thinking she's not worthy of something good.

Her eyes round and glisten in the dim light of the room and her cheeks pink. "Why's that?"

I look down at the ground, trying to gather my thoughts, but they're a jumbled mess. How do I tell this woman that somehow an afternoon with her has meant more to me than any other in my life? How do I tell her that I'm feeling things I've never felt before?

Usually, I'm an antisocial hermit. Right now, I don't want her to leave. Hell, I need her to stay, and the ice storm raining down outside has nothing to do with it.

With my throat tight, my words escape me, but my body reacts leaning into her small frame with intention. Our lips graze against one another and within seconds, my aching palms are on her soft skin.

She sighs into my mouth, relaxing in my arms as I pull her closer.

Her hot breath is against my mouth as our lips massage each other's, and I need more. I have a feeling I'll always need more of her. In my arms it's easy to feel that she's going to be addictive.

An easy addiction that I'll never want to kick.

I run my hands down over her chest and palm each breast. They're large and heavy with two hard beads pressing against her dress.

My lips trail down her neck and settle beside the lobe of her ear. She's precious... perfect.

Every beat of my heart slams against my rib cage as I fight with myself for wanting her so desperately.

"I should stop," I whisper, rocking her back against the cabin door. "It's been so long since I've been with someone. I don't think I could stop myself if I go much further." I've never said a truer statement. There's a craving waking inside of me, a desperation to have her, to claim her.

She draws her heavy gaze up slowly and pouts her bottom lip. "But I want you."

Fuck!

"I want you too," I growl, "but you've been through enough tonight. Not only that, but what happens when the storm is over? You're young. Did the other me tell you what an old man I am? You deserve the world. Definitely more than I can give you here."

"Are you forty-four?" She leans into my ear and grips my hard cock in her hand. "Because I was told you were forty-four."

I nod and clear my throat as every bit of blood I had left in my brain surges to my dick. "And that doesn't bother you?"

She shakes her head. "I like that you're older. Is it weird that it turns me on?"

A laugh sticks in my throat. "Kind of. What are you, in your early twenties? You have a lot of options. I shouldn't be one of them."

Her hand runs up my chest and onto my beard before her gaze locks with mine. "I don't know who I was talking to for months, but I know that guy was an awful lot like you... and age only made you better. Better at... everything." She perks an eyebrow and leans into my lips again. "I want to do this, Walker. I want to make love."

"And what happens when you find who you were really talking to? If I claim you right here and now... I'm not letting you go. You'll be mine. My bride. My woman. My heart to hold."

She tugs at my belt and looks up at me. "I've been saving myself for this moment. Make me yours."

I blink down at her in a daze. She's a virgin. A young, untouched virgin. She has no idea what a wild, untamed animal I am, and I'm not sure I could even describe it. My brain is short-circuiting. All I'm thinking about is pressing into her heat.

My arm lifts over her head and my free hand glides to her throat. I'm going to spoil her, treasure her, ruin her for every other man. The fireplace crackles behind us and I lean down into her lips, hovering over the top of them as I speak.

"Are you sure you can take me? I'm not as careful as I wish I could be."

Her eyes lift to mine. "I think that's what I want. I want you to be wild. I want you to touch me like you can't control yourself. I'm not fragile, Walker. I want to be fucked... hard." Her breath hitches as she speaks and the final drip of control I had left spills out onto the cabin floor, leaving me helpless to her touch.

I growl into her neck and bare my teeth against her skin, sucking in her softness before gripping her arm and lifting her onto the small dining table. Dishes fly everywhere, cracking and breaking against the pine wood floor as her thighs spread before me.

My hands slide up her dress and pull at her panties like a beast, desperate to taste her, desperate to map her reactions, and feel her pleasure ripple throughout her body.

Palming over her mound, I take in her desperate gasp and move with her frame as she lifts and presses into me harder, begging for relief.

"Please fuck me."

"Shh... shh... shh..." I lift a finger to mouth and quiet her pleas. "I'm going to take my time with you. I'm going to make you shake and beg until you're so needy, you come at the slightest touch. Then, I'm going to lick you from top to bottom and slide my cock in so deep you'll feel it in your stomach."

Her cheeks turn pink and she leans back, swallowing hard as I tear the side of her thin, lace panties and strip them off her body, tossing them onto the ground with the broken dinner plates.

I kiss the inside of her thighs and make my way toward the scent that's been drawing me in all night.

Delicate fingers lace into my hair and her legs lift up over my shoulders as her ankles lock behind my neck.

A groan escapes me as I dive into her, lapping up her juices before concentrating on a rhythm at her swollen clit.

She bends and rocks, lifting her hips and grinding. Slick and warm, she spreads her silk over my beard as though she's desperate for relief.

"Your beard feels so good," she pants, rubbing against me.

I grip her hips tighter and press into her core, twisting my tongue around her clit over and over again as I growl, sending vibrations deep into her.

How did this happen? This morning, I was hunting, depressed that I was set to spend another winter alone. Now, I'm between the legs of a woman I just promised to marry. A woman who somehow knows me despite us never meeting.

The wind howls through a crack in the window and a cool breeze penetrates the warm air of the cabin, forcing goosebumps down Birdie's arms.

I palm over her skin as I devour her juices. Then slide a finger into her tight little pussy, rubbing at her walls with a come-hither motion that I'm hoping makes her come. Or at least, gets her close. I don't intend on letting her have that pleasure until I'm deep inside of her.

"Don't stop," she moans, tightening her thighs against my cheeks. "I'm going to come. Please... don't stop!"

As her fingers grip tighter in my hair, I pull back from her core. "You'll come while I'm inside of you. I want all of you on my cock."

With a red face, she sits up from the table and stares at me with pent up energy. "You better make me come hard. I need it!"

What is it about the look in her eye that drives me insane? Am I a monster for making her wait? I don't know, but the desperation in her gaze is driving me insane.

She tugs at my jeans, and they fall to the floor. "Oh god!"

"Oh god, what?" I wonder for a second if I've hurt her, or if she's disappointed by what she sees.

"You're enormous!" she gasps "How am I ever going to fit that in?"

"Enormous is probably a bit much."

"You're being modest. That's not a typical cock. I'm a virgin, not blind. I've watched porn. Even by those standards your big."

"So do you want to stop?"

She looks toward me as though she's considering it, then leans back again. "No. Just go slow."

"And condoms... we don't have any."

She nods toward her bag on the coat tree. "I do. There in the front pocket... but I don't want you to use it."

My brows narrow. "Why? You could get pregnant?"

"I'm assuming you're clean if it's been so long, and if I get pregnant... would that be the worst thing?"

The idea of this beautiful woman carrying my child is a fantasy come to life and somehow turns me on more.

A hiss escapes my lips, as I stroke my girth and lean into her soft core, gently pressing my cock into her. Slowly, I inch into her heat, letting her tight, wet, pussy strangle my cock as her legs move up onto my shoulders.

I'm barely inside of her when a loud popping noise snaps behind us. Then another, and another. At first, I ignore the sound, focused only on diving deeper into the tight, heat in front of me. But as smoke begins to billow, I pull from her core and turn my attention to the burst of fire working its way up the cabin wall.

"Do you have a fire extinguisher?" Birdie jumps from the table and swings open the kitchen cupboards frantically looking for a red tube of foam.

"It's under the sink." I reach for it and pull the pin quickly, spraying the fire from the base up, hoping to stop the spread. I'm wishing now I'd bought a bigger extinguisher. Nothing like this has ever happened. Then again, I usually have nothing going on. Tending to the fire is my one and only purpose.

When the flames have died and the wall is charcoal, I turn toward Birdie who's standing in the corner shivering.

"It's my fault. I put more logs on the fire. I wanted the place to be warm for you when you came inside and—"

"It's not your fault." I pull her against my chest, my nerves calming again despite the drama of a fire raging through the cabin. "It's all good. We can't stay here tonight, though. It's not uncommon for coals to reignite. That and there's a lot of smoke. We'll have to take our chances down the mountain."

She nods and shakes her head. "I guess you could come to the city and stay with me, or we could stay at the hotel on Main Street. But your beautiful cabin, I ruined it!"

I grip her face between my hands and stare into her eyes. "You are the best thing that's ever happened to me, and if you burned this whole cabin to the ground tonight, I'd feel the same damn way."

She bites the inside of her cheek as though she wants to believe me, but I know a part of her doesn't. I'm even more convinced when a heavy thud hits the side of the cabin door. At first, I think it's a branch from the storm, but when it hits again, I'm sure it's a knock and I have a feeling this isn't going to be good.

Chapter Five

Birdie

When Walker pulls on his jeans and swings the door open, my mind goes blank. A second ago, I was leaned against the dining room table with his cock pressed into me. My biggest problem was the orgasm he was teasing me with and the dishes I was feeling bad to have broken. Now, I've burned down half the cabin to char and I'm staring at Montana for some unknown reason.

"Is everything okay?" I figure something awful must have happened for her to come up here so unexpectedly. Besides, how does she know his address?

She pulls at her long, dark ponytail and looks away before glancing toward me again with a look as though someone has died.

"What happened?" I'm impatient now, demanding with my request. "The roads are awful; how did you get up here?"

"What? The roads aren't bad. They're fine. It's just raining."

I glance back at Walker who's standing like a silent pillar behind me with crossed arms. So he lied about the storm. Then again, I guess I'm the dumb one who fell for it.

"It's just rain," she repeats. "Cold, yes. Freezing, no."

"I don't listen to the weather," he says. "I go off my gut. I brought in the last of the harvest because there was a frost moving in. When the frost moves in, the roads tend to freeze over. I was just being cautious."

I appreciate his cautiousness, and truthfully if he hadn't been, tonight wouldn't have happened, but I can't help but wonder what else he's left out about his life. I was so quick to dismiss the secrets he was holding back about the government earlier. That said, right now, I need to figure out why Montana is here.

I cross my arms over my chest and stare toward her. "What's going on, Montana?"

She bites the inside of her cheek and steps inside the cabin, closing the door and the cold behind her. "I made a mistake."

"What kind of mistake?" The way tonight is going, I'm not sure what to expect.

"I'm Walker." She says the words plain and flat then stands in the entryway like a child who's waiting to be scolded.

When no one speaks, she continues.

"I'm sorry. You were lonely, and the other day I was at the library when I saw his profile open on another site. I was going to close it, then I thought, maybe I could intervene and play Cupid. In my head, I thought everything would work out." She takes a long sigh. "My backup plan was that if it didn't, you would call me, and we would go to lunch. We could talk about what happened and then I could talk you into moving here. You would have seen the town and how lovely it was and even if Walker didn't work, you might want to move here, and we could hang out all the time. I hate that you are all alone in the Springs and I thought this would solve everything."

Walker and I look at each other with confusion.

"Then today, when you were coming up here, and I didn't hear from you for so long, I got nervous that maybe he would be a crazy mountain man or something and I panicked. Now I'm here to make sure you're okay." She lets out a sigh with her last word and stares down at the ground. "I'm so sorry. I overstepped huge and—"

"You most certainly overstepped huge," Walker growls, walking toward her. "You used both of us. You invaded our privacy." He sucks in a deep breath and lets it out slowly. "Yet, somehow, you inadvertently helped me find the love of my life. And as angry as I want to be right now... I can't."

"What?" Montana sucks in a deep breath. "You guys actually hit it off? You're like a thing?"

"Almost," I say, turning toward Walker. "There's still the issue with why you're so afraid of the government coming after you."

He looks toward Montana, then toward me, and I wonder if she knows whatever he's been holding back.

Walker sighs and my stomach turns. I'm not sure I want to know. Maybe I want to keep things the way they are. Tonight was perfect. We danced, we held each other, we nearly made love. Hell, I agreed to marry the man. Either I'm insane, or I felt a genuine connection. I'd like to think it was the latter.

"It's okay," I say, stepping to his side. "Are you currently in any trouble?"

He shakes his head. "No, but—"

"Then I don't need to know," I say gripping his hand in mine. I turn toward Montana. "Thanks for coming up here, but I think I'm going to let this go."

Montana stares at me through long lashes as though I've lost my mind. "Okay then... I guess I'll just head back down the mountain."

I should be worried. Maybe he's done something horrible, something I can't even imagine. But when I look at him, I can't see it. When I look at him, the paranoia I usually have is gone, and all that's left is unbridled affection.

"That's okay," Walker says. "We're headed down, anyway. We don't dare sleep in the charred cabin overnight." He grabs his coat off the rack and wraps his flannel around my shoulders before turning out the light behind us. "I'll call the fire chief when we get reception. They'll send someone up here to check out the damage. I guess we'll follow you down."

Montana nods and looks toward me with the same look she had when I first tried to convince her that quartz was going to help her with anxiety. She was skeptical. Truthfully, she probably still is. The girl is one of the most anxious people I've ever met.

But when it comes to this mountain man, I don't have a doubt in my mind. Walker Huxley is the one for me. Not despite his past, whatever that may be, but because of it.

His hand links into mine and he helps me up into his truck. "I appreciate your loyalty, but you don't owe it to me. I can tell you what I did. Why I worry that the government is after me."

"I'm sure I'll find out in time," I say, squeezing his hand, "but I want to remember tonight as the night I met the love of my life and burned down his cabin. Everything else can wait for some other day."

A smile lifts onto his face and he kisses my hand gently before making his way to the driver's side of the truck. Between us, a stark white sheet of paper glints in the dim light of Montana's headlights as she drives down the long stone driveway. I look away at first, but instinct brings me back. On the top of the paper is a notice from the Eastern District Court. Beneath that, an eagle with the state of Tennessee emblem hammered into it.

The State of Tennessee vs. Walker Huxley

It's all I can read before Montana drives out into the road and the light dims again, leaving the space between us dark, and my imagination to run wild.

Chapter Six

Walker

The ride into town is quiet, and the urge to tell Birdie what I did is overwhelming. Also, I don't want to scare her away. What I have against me needs to be explained with finesse.

"Should we stay at the Mountain View Lodge?"

Her demeanor has changed. She's withdrawn. "Actually, I had a great night, but Montana is really upset now and I'm wondering if I should check on her. She pulled over about a mile back and started texting me. I think maybe I should ease her mind. It would probably be best if we slowed down a bit, anyway. We don't want to rush into anything crazy."

I stare toward Birdie and resist the urge to flip the truck around and drive her back up the mountain where everything made sense.

"I shot a man." I twist toward her. "I had just gotten home from my accident, and I went to a local store to grab my mom some sugar for an apple pie she was making. I'd seen the man's face on flyers all over. He was a suspect in the kidnapping of a young girl in town. I couldn't let him walk away."

Birdie's face goes pale. "So that's it? You shot him? Did he have the girl?" She swallows hard. "It doesn't matter, Walker. I jumped too fast with all this. I need some time to breathe." She opens the truck door and hops out, pacing down the street quickly before bumping into Henry as he leaves the tattoo shop for the night. The man owns most of the land up in the area and has run the tattoo shop on Main since way before I got here. He's also the only one who knew my story until tonight. I'm wondering if he told Montana.

I know I should respect her wishes, but I hop from the truck anyway. Birdie keeps walking.

"Birdie, stop... please. Let me explain."

She turns back, her face dark red as she stands beneath a streetlight. "I thought maybe you had a few parking tickets, or you were a conspiracy theorist. I didn't think you'd shot someone. Is the man dead?"

Henry stops in his tracks and runs a hand down through his beard. "Everybody okay?"

I suck in a deep breath and swallow hard. "I'm going to need someone to look at the cabin. I set the place on fire tonight."

He nods and pulls up his phone, texting. "I'll let Trevor over at Fire and Rescue know. They'll send someone straight up." He clears his throat and looks toward Birdie. "Everything else okay?"

She nods. "I just got some interesting news is all."

"I heard." Henry tucks his truck keys back into the pocket of his jeans. "I couldn't help but overhear. Is this about Walker's arrest warrant? You know that was dismissed, right?"

Birdie steps forward. "Dismissed?"

Henry nods. "The man Walker shot was found with the child in question. Walker's lawyers talked the judge into a lesser charge. He's a hero to our country, and to that family."

"So what were you charged with?" Birdie directs her attention back toward me.

"Disturbing the peace. I had to pay a fine and promise to leave the county. I figured it was better to leave the state. That's how I ended up here. I bet your friend found some news articles on me while she was waiting for you to call her tonight. Some of them are pretty bad. People don't take kindly to pulling the trigger before you know for sure, but I couldn't see letting that man get away."

Birdie looks toward Henry as though searching for guidance, and I don't blame her. Tonight has been a whirlwind.

"I don't know what the relationship is between you two," Henry says, "but I don't sell land to just anyone. Walker is a good man. He served our country, and he followed his code. Civilian life may not have called for it, but if my daughter had been taken, I'd be damn grateful for a man like Mr. Huxley. The law has made him feel like he's done something wrong, and I know he's always watching his back, but up here, he's one of us and that means a great deal in these parts."

"I see that," Birdie says, running her hand back through her golden hair. "I'm sorry for the trouble tonight. I guess I should've taken my own advice and slowed down a little."

Henry laughs. "If we were good at taking our own advice, there'd be a lot less therapists around. You two take care and I'll make sure your cabin gets looked at right away, Walker."

We nod and Henry makes his way toward his truck on the opposite end of the street. Thankfully, the rain has stopped except for a light drizzle. The temperature is still cool, though. I'd guess somewhere near freezing.

"I'm not proud of what I did." I look toward Birdie. "I think that's why I don't talk about it."

Without thought, she crashes into me. "You don't need to think about it Walker. I didn't want to judge you and I did. I'm so sorry. I—"

"You needed to know, Birdie. We're about to share a life together. You can't be left in the dark about something so huge."

She looks away, twisting at the ends of her hair.

"What's wrong?"

"There's something you need to know about me. Something embarrassing that I've been holding back too. I wanted to tell you the whole time we were talking online, but I didn't. Well, I guess you wouldn't know that, but either way..."

"Okay... what is it?" I can't imagine anything she says is nearly as bad as the things I've done, but I'm curious, nonetheless.

"Remember when I told you I was a virgin? Well... it's deeper than that."

"How does it go deeper than that? Is there something before virgin?"

She smiles and looks away. "I've never kissed anyone before you, Walker. What we shared tonight was the first of everything for me." She sighs. "It's so embarrassing. I'm twenty-five years old!"

I land my hand on her face and pull her into my orbit. "So, you're telling me that you saved all of yourself for me. Every last drop?"

She nods and her pretty pale skin turns rosy. "All of me. I've never been unwrapped. I wanted to give myself to my husband and I want that man to be you, Walker. Though, I think I might have to text Montana back soon. She's blowing up my phone with random texts. It sounds like someone at Mullet's bar thought he knew something and started spreading some rumors, that's how Montana found out. She's apologizing now for not doing a background check on you. I'm glad she didn't."

I suck in a deep breath and rest my chin on Birdie's head. "I'm glad too. I'm sorry this has been so confusing, but I promise without a shadow of a doubt that I'll look after you, protect you, and keep you safe until the day I take my last breath. You can count on that above all else."

She kisses my lips gently. "I know I can, and I can't wait to be your wife." She grins. "And... to finish what we started earlier."

I wrap my hand into hers. "Don't you want to have the ceremony first?"

She shakes her head. "Something about your intensity says you're not letting me go. Besides, after getting a taste earlier, I'm not sure I could hold out for a ceremony. Don't those take months to plan?"

"We could do something quick tomorrow. I know a few pretty spots by the river."

"Even tomorrow is too far away." She grips the collar of my flannel and meets my gaze. "I need you now, soldier. That's an order."

I can't help but smile. "Well played. I've never ignored an order, and I'm not about to start now." My cock twitches as she kisses my lips, the thought of pressing into her tight little pussy again is enough to rocket me out of the headspace I've been in.

I need this woman, and I need her now.

Chapter Seven

Birdie

I updated Montana on the walk back to the hotel, and while she isn't on board as fully as I am, she respects my decision to stay, and apologized again for pretending to be Walker. If things hadn't worked out, I suppose there would be more to be angry about, but as I stare at the massive man in front of me who's now sitting on the hotel bed, there's little to regret.

He's kindhearted, skilled, and he'll protect me and the family we build at all cost.

"Every inch of you was made for me," he groans, running his hands over my frame. He moves carefully, mapping me with his touch as a bolt of heat shoots into my core.

"You can't tease me this time," I groan. "I need you... bad."

"Tell me again you'll be my wife," Walker says, spreading warm heat over my neck.

"I'll be your wife. Tomorrow morning, by the river." I pant out the words, desperate for his hands to touch me everywhere. "We'll live in your cabin, and we'll have babies. On the weekdays, I'll start a little crystal shop here in town that's all my own. And on the weekends, I'll gather while you hunt, and we'll live off the land. It'll be perfect, Walker."

He grips my waist and holds me tight, slowly pulling each strap of my dress down over my shoulders with a feral look in his eye that tells me he likes my plans for the future.

Inch by inch, my hot pink dress falls to the floor and pools at my feet, leaving behind my bare body for Walker to explore. I expect him to take his time, touch every inch of me, explore my body. Instead, his eyes glaze over and a low growl heaves from his chest.

"Bring that pretty little pussy to me," he demands, squeezing my ass. "I need to take you." His hand slides over my mound and a single finger slides in, then two. He's only there long enough to pull sticky sweet juices from within me. Bringing his hand to his mouth, he licks me off with a groan. "Still sweet and ready."

I tug at his jeans, letting them fall to the ground as he pinches my nipples and licks the lobe of my ear, my throat and my collarbone growing goosebumps when cold air hits the heat he's spread.

"Do you want me deep?" he groans, moving his lips toward my nipples.

"Yes," I sigh, "I want you as deep as I can have you."

"Bend forward onto the bed," he growls. "Reach back and touch yourself. I want you to feel the moment I come inside of you."

My clit throbs and I start to feel lightheaded as he steps between my legs and presses into me. From here, every sensation is focused on his massive dick sliding in and it stings.

He rubs the small of my back as he enters, but nothing prepares me for the pinching pain that commences as he spreads me open. Inch by inch, he slides in further, destroying me for all other men.

"Good girl," he groans. "You're taking me in so good. A few more inches..." I figure I'm bleeding at this point, but I'm finally relaxing enough that the pain is subsiding. I doubt I'm able to take all of him in, but he's dug himself into me so far that I feel full and satisfied.

I suck in a deep breath and grip the sheets with my free hand as the other bounces over my clit. The intent is to stay in sync with his movements, but he pounds into me with such feral desire that it's impossible to hold rhythm. Thankfully, it's best this way. The way he moves is wild and makes me feel desired.

Instinctively, my hips lean back into his and he thrusts harder. He grips my hips with one hand and my shoulder with the other and with each move I become more and more desperate for his seed.

"Tell me again what your plans are for us," he groans. "Tell me you want to have my babies. Tell me you need them." His voice is rushed and fevered, sending a shock of excitement through me.

"I want your babies, Walker. I want your come. I need it. I need *you*." I pant as I speak, unable to catch my breath from rocking into him so hard.

He leans into me, his hot breath on my neck as he continues to thrust. "Say it again. Say you need my come." His lips lean into my neck and he sucks at my flesh.

"I need your babies, Walker. Fuck me. Come inside of me."

As a growl works its way up his throat, my pussy swells and every nerve on my body ignites and vibrates against his. I cling to the sheet as he holds me in his arms, still thrusting against me.

"Good girl," he growls. "I'm going to give you this come and you're going to lick off what's left."

I love his eager demands. They only drive my orgasm harder, sending heat over me like a cresting wave, which sends him over the edge. He holds his breath, and thumps into me again and again, still holding me close as his massive cock beats against me. Then, I feel it. The explosion of heat. The wet, sticky pleasure dripping and spilling from his cock into my pussy. I rub my fingers in what spills and relish in the thought that his seed is inside of me, searching for a place to grow.

He holds himself inside for a long moment before pulling out with a heavy sigh and I spin to suck the last of him dry.

Twitching, he jumps at my touch, but I have no mercy for him. I take as much as I can into my throat and lick the head wildly. I get off on him squirming, begging me to stop.

When I don't, he pulls me from his cock and lays me back, licking my pussy again, tasting us both together, sucking my clit. I jump and thrust into him, still sensitive from coming, but I don't want him to stop. I want him to take me over the edge again. Again and again until I'm drained of all fluids and I need to be rehydrated intravenously.

He slides his fingers inside of me and eats me like his last meal. Sucking, pulling, thrusting, licking. Everything about Walker feels so right. The sex, the conversation, the dance in his cabin earlier today. He's the man I've been looking for—despite how we found each other.

My thighs clench around his face and heat warms my cheeks as another orgasm works its way down from my spine and into my groin.

Walker growls as I come, vibrating warmth throughout me, doubling the pleasure... again.

My legs shake and my heart stops as I grip hold of his hair and cry out in pleasure so loud that the people begin beating on the wall beside us. They don't say anything, but we know what the sound means... *shut up*. Lucky for them, I couldn't take anymore tonight, even if I wanted to.

"That's an interesting first experience for you," Walker says. "You screamed so loud you woke up the neighbors."

I lean into his arms and run my fingers through his chest hair, trying not to drift to sleep. "Thankfully, there are no neighbors up on the mountain to worry about."

He chuckles. "I didn't hurt you, did I?"

"No. I wouldn't change a thing. Not about the sex, or tonight, or this whole thing. And I've never been more thankful for a meddling friend."

"And you still want to marry me? That wasn't just hormonal sex talk?"

I lean up and look toward him, my eyelids heavy with pleasure and exhaustion. "You still want to marry me, right?"

He grins. "More than anything."

I kiss his chest again and again. "Me too. Tomorrow next to the river, near your cabin. I wonder if your friend Henry could do the ceremony. It only takes a few minutes to get ordained online, right?"

"I could ask." Walker rubs my shoulder slowly. "We'll talk about it in the morning. For now, we should rest. It's been a long day. And Birdie..."

"Yeah?"

"Thank you."

"For what?"

"For giving yourself to me. For showing up. For changing my life. For showing me what love is."

I smile against his chest and try to hold my eyes open long enough to formulate a thoughtful response, but before long I'm deep inside my mind, and my will to speak turns into fog and mumbles. That said, the one thing I'm sure I say is, "I love you," because that's something I'll never forget.

Epilogue

Walker

Six Months Later

Montana sits on the front porch of the cabin and stares out at the surrounding view while she scratches Lilo's ears. She's spent a lot of time with us since the wedding. At first it was to apologize for the meddling... profusely. Then, it was because she and Birdie took on the crystal shop together. Now, they spend most afternoons here sketching out where they'll hike for the best gems or figuring what mines they need to order from.

I've learned since opening the crystal shop that one does not say things like *'I thought those things were manufactured in a warehouse.'* That's the wrong thing to say. Instead, I've learned that hiking alongside the girls with my pickaxe is most useful. Turns out, we live near one of the largest smokey quartz mines in the west, which has been great for the shop. Birdie and Montana have people coming from all over the world to mine their own gemstones, and they pay big bucks to do it. Though out of respect for the people of Rugged Mountain, we only allow two miners a year.

"Do you think this guy is weird, or what?" Montana says, showing Birdie a photo of the man, she's chosen to mine come November. "He looks savage. I'm not sure we need a guy like that up here."

Birdie runs her hand over her swollen belly. "What's so *savage* about a guy mining quartz? Does he have some major anxiety he's looking to bust? Does he need clarity in his life?" She laughs. "If the guy is really that interested, I say let him mine."

"I don't know, I might just be imagining scenarios now. Look at this guy." She holds her phone up again. "I don't know if he's house ready, but I bet he can put it down."

Birdie laughs out loud. "I thought your life was less about *putting it down* right now and more looking for a date to your brother's wedding."

"I mean, it is, but a girl can't just settle, right? Someone needs to come along and do more than just take me to a wedding. I need a man who's able to send shivers down every woman at this thing."

Birdie shakes her head and steadies herself on the rail of the front porch as she stands. "On that note, I think I'm going to call it a day. My shivers these days are Baby Boone kicking his mama like crazy. I need to put my feet up and feed him marshmallows... strawberry flavored. It's all he'll eat right now."

"Okay, okay..." Montana relents, twisting her dark hair into a ponytail. She climbs down off the porch and heads toward her car. "I'll see you tomorrow at the shop. Don't forget your laptop! We need it for inventory."

Birdie waves goodbye to her friend, and moves inside, before sitting on the couch and lifting her legs with a sigh. There's nothing more beautiful than seeing this woman pregnant. I don't mean to fetishize it, but it's caught me off guard how much it turns me on. Her breasts are swollen, her nipples are always hard, and she's glowing.

I sit next to her on the couch, my dick already shamefully hard. "You look too good." My hand slides up her thigh and down again, rubbing her smooth skin without intention, though I wouldn't be upset if she were interested.

"Fatherhood looks good on you too, Mr. Huxley." She grins and runs her finger down over my arm.

I think that's a green-light, though. I'll tread lightly.

Gently, I kiss the inside of her thigh and then her stomach, lingering between her legs as I catch the scent of her.

Fuck. That scent. It's changed ever so slightly with the baby and it drives me insane. I don't know what it is, something hormonal I assume. A pheromone that can't be identified by a man like me but must be acted upon. It's carnal and instinctive.

I growl. "I need you."

"Then take me," she whines. "Take me hard, like you mean it."

"I want you on top of me. I want to watch you bounce on my cock. Can you do that?"

She nods, and I lay back on the floor. We could move to the bed, but there's no stability there. On the floor, she moves as she chooses without risk of instability knocking her over.

With her panties on the ground and her dress over her head, my wife lowers her swollen, naked body down on top of me. Inch by inch I penetrate her core. I'd swear my cock has never been so hard, but I nearly swear the same thing every time we touch.

"Right there, good girl." I grip her hips and settle her onto my cock, watching her bounce as her full, heavy tits swing back and forth. Long, blonde hair falls over her shoulders and teases her erect nipples.

"Oh god, Walker." She grinds against me. Pushing back and forth, then bouncing again, over and over as tiny whines escape her.

It's too much and I feel myself nearing orgasm already. My eyes close in an attempt to hold off, but she feels too good, and I know in seconds I'm going to come whether I want to or not.

Then all at once, I feel her pull off and the excitement subsides.

"And where do you think you're going?" I groan, reaching for her hand.

She grins and looks down at me. "Oh, I'm just teasing you a little. I figure you'll come when I'm ready."

That smart little mouth puts me over the edge, and I flash to our wedding day by the river. Henry was about to marry us when Birdie realized I was wearing shoes. We couldn't finish the ceremony until I was grounded with her with my bare feet in the soil. She knows what she wants, and she demands it. I admire that strength, and I hope every child we have carries that beauty.

That said, right now... this woman is getting my seed, and she knows I like a little fight with my steam.

"Bend over, beautiful. I'm going to fuck you hard."

She grins, and grips my cock in her hand, pumping me gently. "Or what?"

"Or... I'll tie you to the bed and set that vibrator on your cute little clit until you're about to come. Then, I'll take it away and leave you begging."

She pretends to hate this, but we both know she loves it. In fact, I'm almost sure that's why she lifted off of me when she did.

"I guess that's a price I'll have to pay then." She leans back on the bed and assumes the position, readying her arms for the silk ropes that I tie around her and the wooden bed frame.

Flicking on the vibrator, I lay the head on her clit and let the soft pulses take her over as I lick and suck at her nipples. She thumps and thrusts her hips forward as her eyes open and close.

"Do you want to come? You know what I need to hear."

She sighs and whines, pulling against the restraints. "I need to come. Please let me come."

"What do I need to hear?" I press the vibrator into her harder, and she jumps in pleasure.

"You need me to tell you to fuck me. Fuck me hard. Fuck me so hard. I need your come. I need your come so bad, Walker." She pants as she speaks, and I can tell that the words alone trigger a response within her.

I pull the vibrator away. "How do you want me?"

She whines and her legs flail wildly as she squeezes her thighs together. She knows how this game is played, and she's playing it well. "I need you to bend me over and take me like a wild animal. Take me like you need me, like you can't get enough. I need your come."

I press the vibrations back into her and she sighs, leaning her head back against the pillow as I lick her throat. "Good girl."

Her hips grind upward into the vibration, but I don't let her have it.

"I'm going to turn you around and you're going to hold this on your clit. I want to feel it vibrating as I push into you, okay?"

She nods and swallows hard as though she can't take anymore, but we both know she wants what's coming next. It's what most of our love making evolves into.

I untie her and she bends forward, arching her back, and holding her ass up. Her long pale hair drapes over the sheets as she holds the vibrator between her legs.

I run my hand up her back, over her shoulders, and onto her breasts before rubbing her stomach and settling on her hips. As my cock presses into her core, she's ready for me. Soaked and hot, swollen and sighing. Inch by inch, I thrust inside. Slow at first, then faster, thumping against her ass as vibrations travel upward and into her tight little pussy. She was made just for me, and I don't take it for granted, not for a single second.

"Oh god, Walker. I can't hold it anymore. I need to come."

"Come for me, beautiful. Come hard for me. Come all over my cock."

As I watch her skin ripple forward with each thrust, I know I won't last a second longer. She grips the sheet with one hand and presses the vibrator harder into her clit, orgasming within seconds.

Silky, wet, sticky come spills out over my dick as she convulses against me.

I lean down and wrap her in my arms, bottling her up to feel the energy of her release, but it's short lived as I myself spill over the edge and come, painting her walls with my pleasure.

She sighs and rolls onto her side as I tuck in behind her, holding her naked body close to mine. Nothing in the world compares to this and nothing ever will.

"I'm starting to think you'll want me pregnant and barefoot forever," she laughs.

"Well, you've got the barefoot thing down." I kiss her forehead. "So, I figure why not keep you pregnant."

"I think that might work for me. Except for one thing." She grins and turns toward me, her expanding belly pressed between us.

I rub my hand over the top of her, feeling for a kick. "And what's that?"

"You have to promise you'll make love to me just like that... forever."

I roll her onto her back and climb on top of her small frame, leaving room for her belly. Even pregnant, she's dainty next to me. "Is there a crystal I can swear that on, or will you take my word for it?"

She smiles and reaches her hand under the pillow to pull out a velvet satchel.

"What's that?"

"Open it." She hands me the bag and I pull the string, dumping six tiny stones into my hand.

"Have you been using crystals on us this whole time, Mrs. Huxley?" I say the words playfully as I push my hair back from my vision.

"Only the smokey quartz. I've been planting that all over the cabin since you rebuilt that wall after the fire."

"Are you that worried about my clarity? I feel like I've been pretty clear about what I want."

"Thanks to the smokey quartz! You're welcome!"

"And how does this tie into you being barefoot and pregnant?"

"Well, another property of the stones I just recently learned has to do with sexual energy. Apparently, it stimulates your sexual organs as well."

I can't help but laugh. "Well, to be honest, my sexual organs have been stimulated, but it has nothing to do with crystals, and everything to do with you."

Her eyes widen. "And the crystals."

"But mostly you."

The smile I've come to love the most, lifts onto her face. It's a cross between thinking I'm funny and fed up with my nonsense. The truth of it is, she could build a house of crystals and I'd gladly give them all the credit if it meant I spend my life loving her. My barefoot, crystal shop, mail-order bride, that I didn't know I needed.

Savage

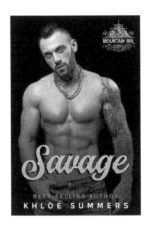

Chapter One

Montana

I lean against the crystal shop window and suck in a deep breath of fresh mountain air. I love Rugged Mountain all year long, but this time of year it's especially beautiful. The leaves are changing to brilliant reds and yellows, and I can wear my favorite hoodie every day. Not to mention the homemade apple cider donuts that every shop keeps close to the register.

"This is the third time this week you're wearing that hoodie," my sister Pearl teases. "If you're going to re-wear clothes, you should pick something less noticeable than a bright purple Denver Rockets hoodie. No one is going to forget that rocket ship. Besides, you don't even like basketball."

"It's comfortable," I shrug, following her toward the truck she's parked out front of the shop. Though we're identical twins, my sister and I are nothing alike. Where I'm a naturalist, she's all about bling. The brighter it shines, the more she wants it.

"Comfortable isn't going to catch you any fish, Montana. You're always whining about wanting a boyfriend, then you leave the house everyday dressed like Cinderella... before the makeover. Let me help you!" Her voice turns to an irritating whine that I brush off because I know she means well. "Seriously! I can take you to my boutique and we'll get you fitted in whatever you want. I have some great fall dresses that just came in."

"Dresses?" My eyes squint. "I don't know if I'm a dress person. How am I supposed to ride a horse in a dress?"

She rolls her eyes. "And how are you supposed to find a man for this wedding, dressed like one?"

I smile, letting her comment roll off my shoulders. Originally, I wanted a date for our brother Owen's wedding, but now, I think I can manage going alone. "I love you, sis. I really do, but if you could give me a ride to the train station in peace, that would be kind of you."

Her lips purse and she twists toward her bright pink truck. Truthfully, it's a mockery to trucks everywhere. "Why are you working on the train, anyway? You know Mom and Dad will pay for anything you need."

"I know they will." I slide into the truck and wait for her to come around to the driver's side. "Just like you could ask Mom and Dad to hire someone to drive you around, but you like the drive." I shrug. "I like to work."

"And you do work... at the crystal shop. You did that girl Birdie a huge favor by opening a shop for her."

I sigh. "I didn't open the shop for her. We did it together. She paid for half, and I paid the other half."

"So then, why are you worried about the train? That thing is way beneath you."

"It's not beneath me, Pearl. That train is part of the community, and it brings people in from all over the world. We get to show people our mountain. I get to meet people I'd never have met. I donate every dime I make right back to the railroad."

She rolls her eyes again as though she's unapproving, then pulls out onto the road with her engine roaring. Most everyone on the mountain drives a truck, so I get the appeal, but she's the only one with a pink one. I blame my father. He spent our childhood trying to get us interested in every kind of truck there was. I know more about C-10's and F-150's than anyone not selling them should. Then again, the knowledge has come in handy on trivia night down at Mullet's bar. I embarrassed every man in that place when I hollered out the answer to *'What was the name of the first truck?'* Most everyone went silent, but I knew right away it was the Daimler. If there had been bonus points, I'm sure I'd have had them there too. I've listened to my father rant for twenty-two years about trucks. I could beat them all. When they were younger, my mom even made my dad a calendar of racy pictures, all posed with different trucks. We were all subjected to it every time we went to the garage. My brother made fake vomiting noises whenever he saw it, but I thought the gesture was romantic. I loved watching my parents together. I still do. They have a dance in the kitchen kind of love. I want that.

Ugh, why does everything divulge to love?

"What are you all in your head about?" Pearl switches on her blinker before turning into the train yard that sits on the edge of town. "You zoned out on me."

"Sorry, I was thinking about Dad."

"Yeah, right. You were thinking about that guy." She looks toward the black steam engine on the opposite side of the road and notes a tall, dark, inked man in a navy-blue jumpsuit hopping from the train with a clipboard. Her eyes peel back toward mine and a wide grin settles onto her face. "So, you're into the hard-working type. The big, muscular mountain men. Get it girl!"

My brows narrow and my arms instinctively cross over my chest as she pulls into the train yard. "What? No. I'm not into him. He's my boss. Well, technically some random face at the American Historic Railroad is my boss but Cord is a close second. He runs the whole train."

The car stops just outside the big, black train engine and my sister glares at me again, the same Cheshire smile still on her face as her pretty brown hair falls onto her shoulders. "Okay... well, you enjoy your pseudo office romance and I'm going to go find you a dress for the party. I figure you'll look good in whatever I pick."

I shake my head and sigh as I lift up out of her car. I could be angry with her for pushing with the dress thing, but I really do need an outfit for the wedding and I hate clothes shopping, so if she wants to pick it up for me, I would actually be thankful. "Nothing too fancy, please. I want to look modest, not—"

"Trust me." She peeks her head out the side window and looks toward me. "He's looking at you..."

"No, he's not."

She nods, and talks with her lips barely moving as though she's sly, but she's not. She's as obvious as a girl in a hot pink truck. "He is!" she continues. "Ask him to the wedding! He's so cute, and he's coming this way."

"Stop, no he's not." My cheeks turn red like a schoolgirl, hoping that Cord is in fact coming this way, but I play it down. "You should focus on your own wedding date."

"I've got it locked down, but—" She nods toward me, and I simultaneously feel a hand on my shoulder. Not a finger, but a whole hand... and it's huge.

I twist back and swallow hard, willing my cheeks to flush to a color other than pink. Then again, maybe I'll blend into the pickup truck, and he won't notice me. "Hey," I finally say, looking toward the man attached to the massive hands.

"I'm Montana's sister," Pearl says, somehow now standing beside me with her hand stretched out toward the man of my dreams.

Okay, the man of my dreams might be too much, but he's pretty close. He's tall, dark, handsome, big, and over the last three weeks, whenever we talk, he treats me like I'm the only woman he's ever seen. I pinch my lips between my teeth and center myself before chastising my sister for getting out of her truck.

"Don't you have a Fall-Fest, wedding, or something to plan for?"

She glances toward me and smiles. "Oh, the wedding! How crazy that you brought that up. You're still looking for a date to that, aren't you?"

I could kill her. I could murder her right here and now, bury her under the train tracks, and no one would find her. I could pretend to be both of us. It's the perfect plan. Thankfully, Cord cuts the tension.

"You're twins!" He looks toward me with the darkest eyes. "Montana! You didn't tell me you had a twin! You two look nearly identical."

I haven't had much practice with dating, but I already knew I wanted to wait at least fifteen years before telling anyone that I have a double running around. I love Pearl, but she does *me* better than *me*... and that's... embarrassing. She stands taller, wears her clothes better, uses bigger words, and she went to college despite all the money being dumped on our lap. Then, she opened a fancy boutique downtown and it has everyone clamoring over her latest fashion trends. She's small-town Madonna.

I nod toward Cord and force a smile. "Yeah, twenty-two years now. It's crazy."

"Oh, that was dumb of me," he groans. "You probably get that all the time. I'm sorry. I've heard twins like being treated like separate people, and I fell right into the trap. It's just so weird to see two people that look exactly the same. Ah, I'm doing it again. Sorry... I'm from a small town." He says it as though it's an excuse, an excuse I know too well.

"Same," I laugh. "Born and raised here in Rugged Mountain."

"No way. I was raised just outside of here in Whiskey Falls."

"I think I'll take this as my nudge to leave," Pearl says, turning back toward her still running truck. "But if you happen to be free Saturday..."

My stomach turns and my eyes bulge out toward my sister, begging her to stop. I know she understands my gesture, and it has nothing to do with twin symbiosis. This is human communication... but she ignores me.

"Montana could really use a date to this wedding. Our grandma won't stop with the spinster jokes."

"That's enough Pearl. I'll see you in the morning." My voice shakes when I say it, not because I'm scared of Pearl, but because I'm humiliated.

"Okay..." She smiles and nods as she climbs in and drives away. There isn't a river cold enough to cool down my face right now.

I twist back toward Cord, whose smile is a little too wide.

"Sounds like you really need a date to a wedding." His voice is deep and graveled.

"No." I shake my head and walk toward the steam engine with him side by side. He's enormous next to me, which isn't something I normally feel. "I don't need a date. I'm sorry. My sister is—"

"A lot like my brother," Cord laughs, his voice deep and rumbling as we stand in front of the train steps. "He's been trying to set me up with someone for way too damn long, but I'm not having it. I'm fine alone. Always have been."

My dreams of the two of us falling in love after this awkward push from my sister sizzle out and I'm left trying to recategorize my feelings for the man in front of me. I mean, they weren't *real* feelings. More so, fantasies of a life with a man I barely know. Well, I mean, I know he likes his coffee black, that he wishes the train ran all year long, and that he lives on a ranch in Whiskey Falls. Other than that, we're strangers.

"Yeah, yeah," I say, running my hands through my long, dark hair. "Me too. She's always trying to set me up with people, but I'm totally not into it. I love Saturday nights alone on the couch much better than spending it with someone trying to hold me and stuff." I've taken my lies too far, which Cord calls me out on with an even bigger grin.

God help me.

"I was going to say I'd be happy to accompany you to the wedding, but maybe you don't want the plus one."

I straighten and try to untangle the confused battery of thoughts rushing through my brain. *He's asking me as a courtesy, right? He's being kind. Would that be so bad, though? Grandma can be terribly annoying with her constant questions about why I'm single, followed by her worldly advice on how to snatch a man. Apparently, if you cook generous meals and offer a man your lady parts on a regular basis, a husband will fall right into the trap. Any woman can clean, but a woman who can cook and offers her man sex, well, that woman has a husband. I can hear her voice as she says it, and I can't help but laugh. It would be nice to show her up for once. Then again, it would all be fake and I'm sure I'd get a more extensive lecture at the next family gathering.*

"Are you okay?" Cord's hand lands on my shoulder again as a crisp breeze blows a pile of colored leaves into a swirl behind us. I've zoned out again. I've been doing that lately.

"Yeah, yeah, I'm good. Thank you for the offer, but I wouldn't want to put you out."

"You'd actually be doing me a favor as well. My brother is on this train. Any chance that we could do a little trade? Two happily single people doing each other a favor?"

Two happily single people doing each other a favor. I stare back at him, studying his large frame, calloused hands, and the dark blank ink that winds down his arm. Maybe a trade wouldn't be so bad.

Chapter Two

Cord

The railway was built by convicts, working under the gun. Not much unlike how I'm sure I've just made Montana feel. If it wasn't bad enough that she was getting shit from her sister, now she gets me with a trade offer that begins immediately.

What the fuck is wrong with me?

"Montana, I'm sorry. I shouldn't have sprung that on you. When your sister asked about the wedding, I thought of my brother, and I understood the concept and I—"

"I'll do it," she says, biting her lower lip as she looks toward me with her big blue eyes. She's gorgeous. I've thought it since the second we first met three weeks ago. Hell, every night I go home and think of Montana, imagining her in ways I probably shouldn't be. Especially since she's so young.

"Are you sure? I don't want you to feel obligated. Besides, there's quite an age gap here. You're—"

"Old enough to know what's good for me," she snaps. "Should we say hi to your brother now."

"Once the train gets moving. I have to run and get the engine ready for the trip. Should we do the usual?" The usual consists of her holding the clipboard to check things off while I verify that the pistons, rods, and flywheels are in working order. Usually, this is my favorite part of the day. She and I moving around the train and my arm brushes against hers or we bend into curious poses to check locations. Today, though, there's more tension in the air than there usually is.

"You're the boss," she chides, twisting toward the train ladder.

"*Boss.* Fuck. I forgot I'm technically your boss. This is probably a terrible idea."

What the hell was I thinking? I'm not trying to get either of us fired. And Lord knows I won't be able to control myself... even if this is just pretend.

"Does anyone need to know? I mean, besides your brother and I? And well, my entire family." She grins. "If I don't make a big deal out of it, I'm not sure anyone else will."

I look down the long track and study the people boarding each train car. Some come with cameras in hand, others with children and bags of snacks. It's a three-hour trip that takes us up the Balsam Mountain to see the changing leaves, around Whiskey Falls, and back and it's become a tourist destination October through December when the train turns from a fall excursion to a Polar Express trip. Sometimes, we'll do summer trips, but that's only on rare occasion and by request from Maddox, the owner of most of the land here in the mountain. I'm hoping someday there is a demand for year-round work, but for now, this is when we operate. Either way, that's a lot of people moving in and out of the depot. I bet no one would notice if we pretended to be a couple for one day, and her brother's wedding wouldn't involve anyone at the train yard. Besides, looking at her now, I'm not sure I could back out of this. She's so sweet, so innocent looking, and every part of me wants to know her better.

"You're probably right," I say, stepping up onto the first step of the train. I place a hand onto the rail, then turn back for Montana, who stretches her short arms toward me with a grin she's trying to hide. My hand slides under her arm and I pull her up a foot and onto the first step. Our bodies are close now. So close that I smell her sweet perfume and her soft hair brushes my face. She blinks up at me and I'm reminded of how archaic I am.

A soft breath escapes her and breaks into a shy smile. "I'm usually right." Her voice is so soft. It's like a whisper and suddenly, my palms ache to pull her close.

Fuck. I need to get a grip. There's nothing happening here.

I look away, trying to gather myself, but like a boomerang, my eyes are on hers again and I can't help but smile back at her.

"I'm not really dressed for a meeting with your brother. I only have this. I thought I'd just be grabbing your coffee, helping you do checks, and chatting with a few travelers today."

"You look great." I push a stray curl that's hanging from the side of her neck and hold the touch too long.

She narrows her gaze, and her cheeks turn pink. "To meet your brother? Don't you want me in a sexy little dress, or something more—"

"No." I don't leave her vision. "I like you just like this."

"In a hoodie, with a messy updo, and no makeup? My sister just about died when she saw me leaving the house in this."

"You look like someone I'd want to spend time with."

"Is that supposed to be a compliment?"

"It's the truth."

Her eyes dart down, and her cheeks turn fire engine red. "You better get the train ready for departure." When her gaze finally meets mine again, it's soft and curious and her lips are twitching. No one has ever reacted to me like this. Hell, I've never reacted to anyone else like this. We're in a makeshift chemistry lab and everyone on this train is in danger of an explosion. She feels it too. I see it swirling in the blue of her eyes before she looks away again, this time for good. "I'll catch up with you in a bit." I guess that means we're not doing rounds together this morning. My heart sinks with disappointment.

Without looking back at me, she stalks into the next train car, and I lose sight of her, only to be interrupted by my second in command.

"You're in trouble," he says with a laugh. "Messing with a Dunn girl."

My brows turn down. "What does that mean?"

"She's rich. Like mega rich. Her dad has old money. He's not going to like her messing with some train guy."

I stand rooted in place between cars as the wind carries the sweet and salty scents from the popcorn factory just next door. "Rich? Why is she working on the rail car if she's rich?"

Robbie shrugs. "Beats me, man. But I've known you for years. You wouldn't mix with a girl like that, and I see it on your face already. You're smitten."

"Smitten? Who the hell says smitten?"

"You're changing the subject. Just trust me. I dated her sister in high school. Twins are the same at their core, right? The girl gave me nightmares for the rest of the school year."

"Forgive me if I don't base my opinion of a girl I like on your experience with her sister in grade school."

"*High school.*" He shrugs, checking the lock between cars. "Don't say I didn't warn you."

Subtle rage tenses my muscles and muddies my brain. I'm not sure what Robbie is talking about. The guy is habitually late and is known for his unsolicited advice.

I suck in a deep breath and start my rounds, wondering if Robbie's right about Montana. Her sister *was* dressed to the nines and drove a custom truck that probably cost more than my house. That said, Montana is down to earth, and nothing like Pearl. I squeeze my eyebrows together and shake my head as I jump from the train and move to the engine block. The sooner we get moving, the sooner I get to see Montana again. Maybe we both have a past to disclose... I know I do. I just hope she doesn't hate me for it.

Chapter Three

Montana

W hen I see Flint, I know right away he's Cord's brother. They have the same jaw line and the same dark eyes. I bet if I talked to him, he'd sound similar too. I wonder what he does, and what secrets he has about Cord. I wonder if he'll even buy that the two of us are dating. Truthfully, it makes zero sense. Cord is built like a hard-working blue-collar man with bulging biceps, strong shoulders, and a chiseled chest that you could grate cheese on. Cheese that I would use for pizza because I'm not shaped as godly. My body looks more like something from a fun-house mirror. I'm not saying I hate my body, because I don't. In fact, I quite love my lumps and bumps, but I've never loved them so close to a man that looks like Cord. And I understand why society would be confused to see us together. Outwardly, we don't value the same things.

"Are you the drink lady?" Flint draws up a single finger as he calls for me. "I'm awful thirsty and I thought the train was supposed to take off ten minutes ago."

I could tell him I knew where his brother was and guide him toward his location, but instead, I point him toward our coffee station and let him know drink service starts in thirty minutes. I don't tell him that I'm not a waitress and that I'm dating his brother. Well, fake dating his brother. If I tell him that, I'm sure he'll meet me with a barrage of questions that I shouldn't answer without Cord. I need to talk to him. I need to see him again. I need to find out whatever I can so we can make this look as real as possible... but I'm stopped by Flint's voice again.

"Do you know Pearl Dunn? You look an awful lot like her."

Of course, my sister knows Flint. I sigh and turn back toward him, unsure of how to answer the question, knowing a lie won't suffice considering the identical twin thing and all. "She's my sister," I manage, twisting back. "How do you know her?"

"Then your dad owns that pizza shop in town on Main?"

Wow. He knows my dad, too. How lucky am I?

"Yeah, that's the one. How do you know them?"

The train starts moving forward and my throat tightens as people talk low to themselves on each side of the car. For the most part, their eyes are glued on the scene passing by as we move out of town and toward Balsam Mountain and Chicory Pass. Townspeople wave at the train and soon we're passing by the field where Fall-Fest is currently being held and where Winter-Fest will be setting up come November. I fantasize about hopping off the train, running into the woods, and pretending this whole day never happened, but right on cue, Flint brings me back again.

"Your dad bought a truck from me a few months back. Your sister came along for the ride. I thought we hit it off, but apparently, she didn't feel the same way."

I hesitate on whether or not to tell him that my sister can be a bit of an elitist who's been seen with multiple men in town, but decide on a simple, "I'm sorry, she can be like that."

I've ragged on my sister all our lives for her shotgun approach to dating. She's a cut-to-the-chase kind of girl. She knows within moments if she's interested and starts trying to seduce them on the spot.

Truthfully, I might need a little more of that in my life. Every time I've been into someone, I've waited for the perfect moment that never came. I'd spent months getting to know my crush, only to have them start dating someone else since we were *just friends*. With a man like Cord, I might need to push myself out of my comfort zone and be more aggressive.

"Anyway," Flint says, clearly noticing my excessive inner monologue, "you think you could let my brother know I'm here?"

"Your brother?" I play dumb.

"Oh." He holds out his massive palm. "I'm Flint Masters. The engineer is my brother, Cord. Have you met him?"

My eyes widen, and my heart constricts. I've met him alright.

"Yeah, we're..."

"What?" Flint gasps. "Don't tell me you're the new girl he's been seeing. He's told me all about you. *Shit*. I'm so stupid not to have seen it. You look just like the girl he described. Sit." Flint gestures for me to join him at the table. "Here I am, ordering drinks and rambling on about your sister. Damn. That's weird. I'm asking for your sister's number and all the while, my brother is dating you." He laughs. "I guess it's true brothers have the same taste in women."

Fun. I glance back toward the engine. "I should go get your brother. He wanted to invite you up front, I believe."

Flint stands without hesitation, towering over me. They grow them big in Whiskey Falls. "If you don't mind, I'll just follow you. I'd like to surprise the guy. It's been a few months since we've seen each other between the railway keeping him busy and the rodeos I've been traveling with."

I'm not sure if Cord wants a surprise visitor, but I can't stop what's happening. The whole situation is so awkward that I don't say much at all and the man is sideways scrolling through the train car with me.

The train is still moving slow, but that doesn't stop the cars from rattling back and forth. My legs wobble as I grip the back of each seat and we make it toward the tender.

As we pass through the final car, I glance toward the engine room and my stomach tightens. I'm not a good liar. I'm, in fact, the worst liar ever. In middle school, the drama teacher moved me to set design because I swayed too heavily to be a tree. It's bad, and I'm afraid this imaginary relationship might end before it's even begun.

Chapter Four

Cord

U p until today, I thought I'd missed my brother. Right now, I want him to leave me alone with Montana. She looks scared, and I want to relieve her of whatever fears she's having. I want to rescue her from this mess I've put her in.

Flint, he doesn't seem to have a clue. He bends forward, twisting around Montana, and hugs with a single pat on my back. "Hey, man, long time no see. If I hadn't met your girl up front there, I'm not sure I'd have gotten back to you. You're not answering your cell. I had to buy a ticket."

My blood boils at the thought of what he's already put Montana through. "You could've asked someone at the ticket booth. They'd have radioed in for me."

He straightens. "Damn, brother. On edge?"

I sigh and my gaze darts toward Montana, whose pretty lips bow up neatly.

"He has a lot on his plate right now, is all. Once the train is out of town, his focus won't be so split." She says the words like she knows me, like she knows the train route, like she's watched me carefully for years, though it's only been a few weeks. I can't help but wonder if maybe she feels the same way as I've felt about her. Though, if she's as elitist as Robbie says, I'm sure I'm making all that up.

"Well then, I'll shut my trap and watch," Flint says, lowering into the seat next to mine. He's a good guy, a little goofier than me. He doesn't take life nearly as seriously, which I suppose I could use from time to time. Then again, he could use a little urgency in his own rite. He stares out the window for three seconds, then turns toward me. "I didn't see you dating a rich girl. That's a twist."

I narrow my brows and glance back toward Montana. "I'm sorry, sweetheart."

She waves it off and I gauge her reaction to see if she truly is as rich as Robbie and apparently Flint thinks she is. "It's okay. Apparently, he knows my sister and my father. Some truck deal..."

I suck in a deep breath and stare toward him for a long moment before looking away again. Great, everyone knew she was rich, but Flint knows her family. I don't even know what her father looks like. I'm jealous. He knows a part of her that I don't.

He glances up at Montana. "You never did tell me what a rich girl like you would want with a train riding roughen like Savage here."

She laughs. "Savage?"

"Yeah, that's what his buddies call him. He's the bad boy of Whiskey Falls. He didn't tell you about all the trouble he causes back in town?"

She shakes her head and smiles wider and though the view is beautiful, my ego is bent. I thought we'd get more time to talk this morning, more time to tell each other our stories. I can't have Flint running off at the mouth.

Flint tosses his feet up onto the control board, crossing them over as dirt kicks from the heels. The man is on my last nerve. "Well, I guess I should let him tell you those stories." Finally, he acts like a brother.

My shoulders relax as we take the corner on a bend around the side of the mountain. I suck in a deep breath, letting the cool air from the cracked window beside me fill my lungs. This was a terrible idea. At least that's what I've convinced myself of until Montana's hand lies on my shoulder, and something shifts deep in my chest.

"You know," she says, "Cord and I haven't known each other that long, but he's been the kindest, gentlest man I've ever met. I can't imagine him ever being *savage*."

I grin at her comment and reach up to cover her hand in mine. Fuck. If Flint weren't here right now, I'd put her on my lap and claim her to be my own. But I'd have to tell her the truth first, the truth about why I have the nickname I do, and that's something I was hoping I could hold secret until we'd been married for twenty years and this whole fake relationship thing is a joke in our past.

Montana holds her hand in place, and we watch out the front window at the fall scene unfolding in front of us. Reds and yellows fall gently from the trees as we pass the glittering turquoise river. I should say something, start a conversation that's about anyone but Montana and I. Sadly, that only leaves conversations about Flint.

"You should tell Montana about that time in Cheyenne when you rode your first bull for almost five seconds," I say, glancing toward him for a moment. "That's a good—"

"That's boring," Flint says. "She wants to hear about you. And I'm sure you've already told her all the good stuff. Let me tell her the stuff that you're leaving out."

I know what he's trying to do, and it's pissing me off. He thinks he's saving her from something. I sit back in my chair and suck in a deep breath, quietly letting it out as I bite the inside of my cheek. I'm on my best behavior right now. If we were alone, I'd have put him in his place by now, and he knows it.

"Anyway," Flint continues, "Savage here has some good stories for you. Don't let him get away with not telling you. I can see he really likes you. That doesn't happen often for him."

My fingers twitch and my eyelids flicker without thought. I do like Montana... a lot. Hell, my skin heats just thinking about her velvet skin, satin hair, and the innocent way she smiles, like she isn't sure if she should be or not. Earlier, I'd have guessed she was feeling the same way. Now, I know that must have been my imagination because I can't imagine what a beautiful, wealthy girl like Montana would want with an asshole like me.

"I'm going to grab us some drinks," Montana says sweetly. She tucks her head in close to mine and the soft scent of her drugs me again.

Fuck.

"Do you guys want anything special?"

I'd sit her in the chair next to me and make Flint get us drinks if I didn't want to tell him to fuck off so badly.

"I'll just take whatever is easiest," I say, staring out the front window again.

"Do y'all have Dr. Pepper? I've been dying for some since I left the ranch."

"Of course we do," Montana says, sliding open the train car door. A breeze blows into the chamber before she shuts the heavy metal door again.

I glance toward my brother with the intensity of an acetylene torch. "Are you having fun?"

He laughs. "What? I didn't say anything. I'm just fucking with you. If you guys date for real, she needs to know though."

My stomach knots. "What makes you think we're not dating?"

"Your shoulders, they flinch every time she touches you like you want her to go further."

"So?"

"So... you haven't looked like that since fourth grade when Mrs. Rolando brushed your shoulder to give your eraser back." He laughs. "You always had a thing for an age gap, didn't you?"

The thought that Montana is some fetishized version of what I want makes my stomach turn. "What? No! It's not like that. She needs a date to a wedding, and I needed to shut you up, so we swapped help. The end. I don't know why you have to make it sick."

A drumbeat thumps in my chest as I stare back at my brother, desperate for him to shut up. I'm not one to talk about my feelings, especially not with him.

"You like this girl. Don't you want her to know all of you? The good, bad, and ugly. It's what got you here, in this engineer chair."

"I'll tell her about my past when I'm ready. Until then, you should get back to your seat in first class. Tell them I sent you. I'd recommend the chicken. It's much better than the fish."

My brother sucks in a deep breath and lets it out slowly. "I'm in Rugged Mountain for a snow rodeo that runs through the new year should you find yourself with some time."

I nod and squeeze my eyes shut as he stands from beside me and heads out the door, letting cold air in when he leaves. As much as I don't want to hear it, I know he's right. Montana needs to know who I am... all of me. Past, present, and future. Pretending is only going to leave us both broken hearted. Or, maybe that's on me as well. She has been gone an awful long time. Maybe she's put everything together by now. I'm an asshole, and she's a rich girl. The two of us shouldn't be drinking from the same fountain.

I sigh and watch tall pine and cedar pass as we make our way up Balsam Mountain. A turquoise lake on the left leads way to a gorgeous cliff and about twenty dozen maple trees, all of them various shades of red, yellow, and orange. There's a family in a rowboat and two people kayaking beside them. Though the water is freezing this time of year, the rapids are low, so it draws people into the river with smaller boats.

The door slides open again and another blast of cool air hits my back, this time though, it's followed by the warmth of Montana's voice.

"I just saw Flint. He said he was going to eat in the first-class car. Is everything okay?"

"Yeah," I lie, my chest tightening. "He's just..."

"Did I do something wrong?" She hands me a mug of black coffee and lowers herself into the chair next to me with a sigh. "I'm so sorry. I knew I was going to say something stupid and I—"

"You didn't do anything wrong," I say, reaching out toward her.

She leans into me willingly and my heart stiffens. "What is it then?"

"I should've told you something earlier, Montana."

"If this is about us, I want to know you better too, but I haven't been completely honest." She pauses and strides toward me with heavily lidded eyes and a sashay in her step that wasn't there before.

I need to say what I need to say, because I'm about to be helpless. Helpless to her and everything she stands for.

She leans into my lips and straddles my lap. "But I have to tell you, you've been on my mind nonstop for weeks. I lied to you, Cord. I'm not *happily single*. I'm fantasizing about you every night and watching you work... has me all revved up again. I want to know all of you." She trails her hand down my overalls and unzips the fabric slowly, her eyes on me. "Every part." Her lips press into mine, and a rush of warmth runs through me and my toes tingle. Everything that had been inside me slides away until all that's left in my brain is the way her curves feel against my hands. I slow the train and set it to autopilot as we straighten around the bend. I know Robbie is close by feeding the train with coal, but my hands don't stop. They slide over the curve of her hips until all that's left are thoughts of her body against mine and I can't stop myself from acting on them.

Fuck, I want to act on them.

My cock prods out shamelessly and presses against her stomach as she continues to kiss my lips. Every nerve in my body buzzes and my brain turns to a muddled mess of hunger and excitement.

"I'm distracting you." She breathes the words out hot and slow on my neck and I can't help but lie.

"No, but I wanted to tell you something."

"What is it?" She pants between kisses, and it's hard to imagine that this is the same shy girl that's been working with me for weeks. Now, she's in control, sexual, needy... and I like it. I like both versions of her. I want it all.

The train pumps forward with the turquoise river disappearing behind us, the wooded mountain face in front. We're okay on auto for a while, but I'll need to take over manual again before we hit the ridge.

God, I sound like a fool. Anyone could see through that window, Robbie most likely.

"Is this pretend?" She sighs. "Is it all part of the ruse? Do you really need me? Because I have feelings for you Cord. I have since the first second I saw you and I don't think doing this is going to help that if you're not in the same place."

My heart slams into my rib cage and I roll my shoulders back as my palms slide upward, over her arms, and onto her neck. "You're the girl I've been describing to Flint for weeks now. I can't stop thinking about you, Montana." Blood roars in my ears and my cock stiffens to the point of no return. I want her. I need her. But not just for tonight, I want her for good. I want to know when I press into her, just like my fantasy, she's mine.

Her body grinds against me slowly as her eyes close and her neck arches back. Her breasts press forward and I'm desperate to pull off her hoodie. I'm eager to feel the curves of her skin. I'm falling, plunging out of control in the best possible way, but we need to slow down. I have to tell her who I am. I have to tell her my secrets.

Chapter Five

Montana

Cord stands and lifts my hoodie up over my head, pressing me against the cool black wall of the steam train. His hands run wild over my skin and my pulse thunders in my throat.

What am I doing? Who am I? Maybe I'm dreaming. Maybe I'm in bed and I'll wake up alone, reaching for my vibrator again. I could blame it on hormones, the gentle vibration of the train, or the way Cord looks taking control, but I know my feelings for him run deeper. He's wild and rugged and when he talks, he sounds like home. A home I've been looking for my entire life. One where materialistic stuff isn't at the forefront and life sounds like a steam engine rolling through the mountainside.

His lips move from my mouth to the lobe of my ear. "You're going to have to tell me to stop, sweetheart. I have so much to say to you still. So much to tell you about my life. Things you should know, but I can't control myself with you."

"I'm not sure I want you to," I pant, opening my eyes just long enough to see the sun as it filters through the balsam trees ahead of us. I hadn't noticed how loud it was in this room until right now. The engine growls and the train cars squeak as they shift back and forth and the thumping in my ears doesn't help either.

Cord's giant, calloused hands lift up and over my frame and press against my throat lightly as he growls into my ear. "You don't know what you're saying. I'm not a kind man, Montana. And when I get ahold of your sweet little body, I'm going to wreck you."

My heart thumps harder. Part of me thinks his words are dirty, wrong, and the least romantic thing I've heard. Another part is desperate to hear more of what this animal has to say as though there's something sexy about a man whose carnal instincts take over. His boots thud closer and his cock presses into my stomach. I'd guess he didn't plan it that way, which makes it more arousing.

Every second is long and agonizing as he touches me slowly, drawing his hand over my breasts, onto my stomach, and onto the buckle of my jeans.

Our gaze meets and my stomach turns and twists, excited for him to do whatever it is he's about to do.

His jaw tenses and his fingers snap, loosening my jeans before his hand slides in, and air knocks from my lungs. Slow and strong, his hand takes over my mound. A low growl escapes him as he leans against my shoulder and presses a finger then two inside of me, thrusting them through wet, hot, excitement.

I cling to his shoulder, but my head arches back, and my lips drop open as heavy panting ensues.

There's a scowl on his face as he works me over. If I didn't know any better, I'd say he were angry, but I know that's a lie. He's hungry. Hungry for me, and I want to give myself to him.

His beard rubs against my neck and the lobe of my ear as he thrusts his fingers inside of me. "That's right, sweetheart. Give into me." His groan is primal as he inhales my scent.

I dig into his shoulder and hold him tighter as my thighs squeeze his fingers. My head collapses on his shoulder as he works my clit with his thumb. He smells like engine oil and pine trees, like the present and forever mixing into one. Heat pools between my legs and the ache to have him inside of me gets worse.

"I need you," I pant, unbuckling his jeans. I have no idea how long we have. There's a porthole behind us and a train that's driving itself about five miles per hour less than usual. Someone will come check on him soon.

His free hand glides to the side of my face and he lifts my gaze until our eyes meet. "You're mine. Do you know that? The second I touched you. No other man is ever going to touch you like this, right?" There's possession and demand in his tone. I like it.

I know some women would be turned off by a man taking what he wants, but I can't get enough. The more he claims me, the more my legs shake against his hands.

"I'm yours, Cord." My voice shakes as I say, "I've never been anyone else's."

He pauses for a second and looks toward me, tipping his thumb beneath my chin as he continues to work my pussy. "*Never?* What do you mean?"

"I've never been with anyone else. This is the first time... I've even gone this far." My face turns crimson as the words slip from my lips. I realize in this moment how inexperienced I must be compared to this man. He's twenty years older than me. He's got a life, a career, everything. I'm just figuring myself out.

I'm not sure how I expect to react, but he growls and leans into my neck, and I swear it sounds like satisfaction. "So, I get this pretty little pussy to myself?" He growls again and again, rumbling power through his chest against my throat.

I sigh in approval, and stare toward him, desperate to give him all of me. "It's yours. Take me. Please."

His hard length prods me again, as he slides his hand from within my core, and licks his fingers clean, groaning as he tugs my jeans to the floor.

My heart races and stalls all at once, as I bury my face back into the crook of his neck. His pulse is rapid against my lips and I'm pretty sure I'll die if he takes his rough hands off me.

I hadn't been able to picture Cord as a savage before, but now, I see it. I see the ancient parts of him that hold no promise to modern civilized men.

A cool breeze filters through the cracks in the engine door and a hard pounding slams against the glass where my head lays.

"Fuck," Cord groans. "Don't move your head." He pulls my jeans back up into place and orders me to lift my arms so he can slide on my hoodie. I wonder how much the person outside can see, but I don't let that monopolize my thoughts. Instead, I focus on my breathing and the hard thump between my legs. "I'm sorry, sweetheart." He kisses my forehead. "Let me get rid of whoever the hell this is."

****

The train rocks me back and forth as I make my way through each car and toward the bathrooms in the back. No one ever uses them so they're the cleanest on board and right outside is a nice open-air balcony. I could use some cool air right now. My core is still straining, desperate for Cord, but Robbie had other plans. *Something about driving a train.*

"Montana." Flint notices me right away. I wasn't sure what car he'd been put in, but I was hoping I'd fly right past him unnoticed. Sure, he was nice to talk to earlier, but I'm not sure I have much more to say. "Where's my brother? He kick you out too?"

"Kick me out? No. You didn't get kicked out either. He said you wanted to eat."

Flint laughs and taps the silver table as though he wants me to sit.

"I shouldn't. I'm still on shift."

"If anyone bothers you, I think you know a few people at the top."

I bite the inside of my cheek and lower into the velvet backed chairs. This car was built in 1927 and the railway has worked hard to maintain its original look. Blue paisley wallpaper lines the ceiling and walls and tiny tea light lamps sit on the end in front of each picture window. I focus on my surroundings when I'm stressed. Outside, all I can see is the shale stone chipping away and the steep drop below the canyon's edge. So, I focus on the wallpaper again.

"You look scared," Flint continues. "I hope I didn't make too bad an impression."

"No. Sorry. It's been a weird day. I was on my way to get some fresh air."

"I'll keep this short then."

My heart pounds against my chest, heavy and hard. All I want is Cord.

"Sure. What is it?"

"I love my brother," Flint starts, setting the tone for a conversation that I know isn't going to go well, "but he's in trouble and I think maybe you can help." He clears his throat and looks out the side window before turning back.

I narrow my brows, thoroughly confused. "Huh?"

"He really hasn't told you any of this?" Flint bites the inside of his lip and runs his rough hands over one another. The sound is like sandpaper. "I don't want to be that guy. I love the man, but he doesn't look out for himself at all."

I'm getting impatient. "You told me to sit. Tell me something!" I bark, clearing my throat afterward as though the outburst were a mistake, but it wasn't. I like direct people. Flint is being everything but. "Is this about the Savage thing? I'm sure he'll tell me when he's ready."

Flint pinches his fingers on the bridge of his nose then looks up at me. "It's important. I don't know if he'll tell you if he hasn't already. How long have you guys known each other?"

I puff my cheeks and blow out a heavy sigh.

He leans in. "I'm sorry. I want to tell you. I thought I could, but I don't want to blow up his spot."

"Is he in trouble?" My brows narrow and I respond with edge as I say, "Tell me what's going on, Flint!"

Flint sighs and runs his hand over his beard, before looking up at me again with round eyes that spell concern. "Cord is an animal. He's always been more in tune with his primal instincts then those around him. He uses that to hunt... for men."

I'm dizzy. "*Hunt for men?* What does that mean? *He kills people?*"

"He bounties out in Whiskey Falls and he has no regret for who he takes or when he takes them." Flint leans in. "He once took a man out at his dining room table, mid bite. The man's wife was sat three feet from him."

"What did he do?"

"He was wanted for murder."

My stomach turns. "Okay... so he was a bounty hunter. He's not anymore, right? He's a train engineer."

"For three months out of the year. The rest of the year, the man hunts."

"So... a lot of guys up here bounty. It's a way of life for some. I don't understand."

"He's made a lot of enemies. The last one he made, stalked him before ultimately shooting him. Cord ended up surviving it, but the shooter promised to come after his family someday. Why don't you ask Cord what happened next."

I narrow my brows and lean in close to Flint. "Tell me right now what happened. I'm not waiting."

Flint looks toward me, and takes off his trucker hat, snapping it in his hands over and over. "Savage found the man and killed him."

My heart thumps hard against my chest and the train spins around me as steam billows out into the mountainside. "In cold blood?"

Flint sighs heavily. "Not exactly. The police were after the shooter, but he didn't have a bounty on him." He looks me intently in the eyes. As he does, I can feel my blood pressure rise and my hair stand on end. "Luckily for Cord, he had a friend at the local police station who saw it the same way he did. So, the police ruled it was a drug deal gone bad and there was no evidence to find the killer."

I bite my tongue and stare out the window, trying to calm my chaotic mind. A man sought revenge for a bounty that Cord collected, shot him, and threatened Cord's family. Does that make murdering him okay? I scratch my nails into my palm over and over again as my mind comes to terms with this. Can I love a man who is so violent and could justify that violence as he sees fit?

"Montana?" Flint's interruption shakes my soul. As I come back to reality, I feel my breathing return to a normal pace, and I can see my palm looks like I tried to pull a cat from under a couch. "That life isn't good for him. He needs to get out of the business. Maybe you can be the one to convince him of that. He's going to end up dead someday and I can't keep worrying that every time he goes hunting, he isn't coming back."

"No pressure," I scowl, standing from the table, my stomach turning as I try to make sense of all Flint's just said, but my head won't stop spinning.

"I'm not trying to pressure you, Montana," he sighs. "I guess I'm asking for your help. No one else can get through to him."

"And what makes you think I can?"

Flint smiles and looks away. "I see the way he looks at you, Montana. It's special. He cares about you. Maybe you can convince him to stop hunting. We've all tried, everyone in the family. He doesn't see it like we do. He thinks he's invincible."

I stare toward Flint with the weight of the world on my shoulders. Of course, I want Cord to be safe but suddenly I'm thinking I moved this whole relationship way too fast. I need to slow down. I don't even know him. If he's done this, what else has he done?

I blow a stray hair up out of my vision and slide up from the table. "I'll think about it." I walk toward the caboose, holding onto chairs as I move through the crowded first-class cabin, feeling like an idiot for throwing myself at a man I didn't bother asking what he did the other nine months of the year.

Chapter Six

Cord

"I'm sorry. I don't know where she went." Flint's jaw locks as he stands in front of me. People file off the train and rejoin society with smiles on their faces, pictures to show their family of the idyllic fall getaway in hand. I search for Montana in the crowd, but I don't see her anywhere.

"She disappeared after she left the cabin. I know you had something to do with that. What did you tell her?"

He sucks in a heavy breath and leans against the train, staring at me with a glare that says it all.

"What the fuck, bro? I was planning to tell her everything."

"It's not about her knowing, Cord. It's about getting you to stop. I thought maybe she could talk you out of—"

"What the hell is wrong with you? She's twenty-two years old. She's... we barely know each other, Flint." A growl works its way up my chest and I fear that whatever shot I had with Montana is wasted and no one is to blame but myself. I should've told her what I was hiding. I should've told her what I've done, who I am.

"Do you have her number? You could call."

My mouth dries. "I don't. I could start working through her friends to see if anyone would give it to me, but I expect that she'll be prepping them on how to avoid me going forward." I slowly walk around and kick the rocks beside the rails. "I should really take this as a sign. She got off the train and didn't look back. She doesn't want to see me. I shouldn't hunt her down and make her. She's a grown woman who knows what she wants, and I don't blame her for not wanting me."

A breeze stirs between train cars and the holler of children releasing pent up energy echoes in the narrow path between the train and the row of shops on the opposite side of the tracks. I could blame Flint, but like the rest of my family, he's only doing what he thinks is best for me.

"I know you're sorry, man. It's all good." I slap his back gently. "When does that rodeo start? I can pop over for a show while I'm in town."

"Tonight," he says, looking down at his boots. Something stews within him that's bigger than this moment, but I don't ask. I'm sure his wheels are turning about how he can get Montana back, but I don't want to press the issue. She's too good for me. I knew it the second I touched her velvet soft skin. Now, I just have to learn to live with myself knowing that it's my fault I'll never hold her again.

****

The day is long and dragging, so by the time the rodeo starts I'm glad when Flint takes the ring to ride. He's great as usual and the crowd goes wild. The full eight seconds, as always. I expect he's got another buckle in his future.

I squeeze my eyes and look out at the crowd hoping to see Montana. Hell, I'd even take a Pearl sighting at this point. She seems like the kind of wild card that would give me Montana's number.

No such luck. Instead, I see a few folks from Whiskey Falls who've made their way out here for Fall-Fest and Maddox Baxter. He's a big, robust looking guy who looks busy with his own, though. Like most folks, he's enjoying a cheesesteak sandwich while his wife works over a funnel cake. It's this kind of atmosphere that makes me love small town living. Simple pleasures, community, and the woman you fell in love with still by your side twenty-plus years later. It's too bad things like that don't happen for guys like me. Guys like me never learn. We play on the wrong side of the tracks. We get burned and we go right back for another shot because life has taught us to be rough.

"Cord!" Maddox says, reaching out for my hand. He's looking older than he was the first time we met, nearly five years ago. His normally black hair has been blended with gray and white and his beard is nearly all the same. "Are you staying in town for Flint's tour?"

I shake my head. "I'll be in and out of town until the end of December. I'm sure I'll catch a few more shows. What about you?"

"Ah, just here for the night with the family. I think the wife wants to stop at the crystal shop on Main before we head home. Have you been in there yet?"

I shake my head. "No. Can't say I've had a big interest in crystals lately."

He nods and crosses his arms over his chest. "I thought maybe you'd have stopped by since you work with Montana. I guess I thought she'd talked about it."

My blood runs cold. "*Montana?* Rich Montana?"

Maddox laughs. "That's the one. She's not there tonight. She's got a big wedding for her brother Owen at her family ranch up on Route 56, but you should stop by sometime. It's a weird, hippy type of place, but interesting none the less. Emma loves it." Emma is his wife. A short, brown haired woman with gemstone earrings who's still in place on the bleachers eating her funnel cake.

Thoughts scatter as Maddox shakes my hand and excuses himself toward the bathroom on the opposite side of the field. He's just told me more about Montana than I've learned in three weeks. She has a crystal shop. Of course, she does. That, and her family's ranch is on Route 56, which is where the wedding is being held.

Warmth radiates throughout my body and my heart races. I'm rejuvenated, alive at the thought of what we'd shared earlier coming back again. She was so soft and sweet... so perfect held against my chest. And despite what we hadn't learned about each other, our bodies reacted instinctively. I can't deny that. I can't give up on her shy smile and the way she says my name. Maddox has given me a sign, a map to find Montana, and I won't stop until she's in my arms.

Chapter Seven

Montana

"Come on, Montana. You've got to get dressed. Owen's counting on us today."

I stare up at my sister in a pale pink dress, her hair perfectly coiled, her nails perfectly painted. She's beautiful and put together as always while I sit in my robe on the edge of the bed and stare out at the mountains.

"I know. I just wish you hadn't told Grandma I was bringing someone. I mean, you didn't even know that Cord would say yes."

"I spoke to Flint the other day. He said Cord really misses you and he wants to talk. Maybe you should give him five minutes. I mean it's only five minutes. He's only asking for enough time to drink a cup of coffee or eat a cupcake." She tips her head to the side. "Well, actually, the cupcake thing might take two minutes. So maybe coffee."

I smile and stand from the edge of the bed. "He's a bounty hunter, Pearl. If he wanted to find me, he could. And besides, I don't know what to say to him. He killed someone!"

"Someone who was going to kill his family. That sounds like self-defense to me. It's not the same as murder. The police saw it that way too. Besides, he's hot and I've never seen you get so torn up over a guy before. You need to call him."

"Need to call who?" Dad says, knocking on the door softly before stepping into the room. Mom is behind him wearing a vintage pink dress that pools on the ground, crystals adorning the belt that goes around her waist. She's beautiful and when she looks at my father, their love radiates.

"Cord," my sister says as though she's been talking to them about me.

I suck in a deep breath and let it out slowly. I love being from a close-knit family, but sometimes I wouldn't mind keeping some things to myself.

My mother grips my hand in hers and sits at the edge of the bed. "You remember how your father and I met, right?"

I nod, but I know it won't stop her from telling the story.

She looks at my dad and smiles, then squeezes my hand again. "I already had Owen when we met. Your dad took care of both of us. He didn't have to do that, but he saw something in me that no one else did, and now look at all we have. You two girls, a wonderful home, a life we've built together."

My father leans down onto his knees like he has a thousand times over and I feel like a kid again being coached after getting a poor grade on a test. He's gentle and kind with his words and his hand is warm and comforting. "You should never put yourself in harm's way, Montana, but if you have feelings for Cord, talking to him is the only healthy way out of this." My dad kisses me on the top of my head then stands again, a creak in his knees as he does.

"I appreciate you guys," I say, looking up at my family, "but this is Owen's day. We should get back out to him. I'm being selfish in here whining over myself."

My mother twists my hair lightly as it rests on my back and holds me against her chest. "You're a good girl, Montana. You're going to find love." She grips my sister's arm in hers as well. "You both are."

I smile and kiss my mother's cheek, grabbing the dress off the back of the door as I walk toward the bathroom. I know my family means well, and I'm sure they're right. Talking to Cord could make things a lot easier. Or at the very least, it would help clear a lot of things up, but I wouldn't know what to say or how to act or how to hold myself back from jumping all over him and letting my body react the way it naturally does when I'm around him. And that's.... confusing.

Pearl straightens and pulls her hair to the side of her shoulder as she smiles and looks at our mother. "I think Flint, that rodeo guy, Cord's brother, is interested in me. He called me after he broke some state record at Fall-Fest last night. He wants to go to dinner or something, but I don't know. It's weird, right?" She twists toward me and gasps. "Unless... you and Cord get together and then we're dating brothers! That would be so fun. Our kids would grow up together, and we'd always be at the same family functions. Call him! If not for yourself, do it for me."

"That's enough," my mother says, in tune with me enough to know when I need my space. She links into Pearl's arm. "Let's give Montana a few minutes to herself." When they leave the room, I hear her rattling off to my mother about how Robbie called her last night too. Leave it to my sister to be caught in the middle of some love triangle. How is it that our cells are identical and were raised the same, but have completely different life experiences?

Maybe *my* life would become infinitely more interesting if I got a pink pickup truck and wore the newest dresses. No, it's not worth it.

I grab my dress off the back of the bedroom door and step into the bathroom, staring at myself too long in the mirror as I curl every last strand of my hair and feather on too much mascara. I've done weddings alone before; I can do it again. I can wear this pink dress and walk down the aisle smiling for everyone like I mean it. I don't need Cord's big arms around me, or his graveled voice in my ear, and I surely don't need his hot breath on my neck, whispering my name.

I'm sure of all of this until I step back into the bedroom and see him standing in the doorway, tall and wide wearing a crisp black suit. It's then, that I know for sure, I'm a liar.

Chapter Eight

Cord

"I can go if you don't want to talk. I just—"

"No," she pants, still breathless with the shock of seeing me. Maybe it was a mistake that I came. Today is a big day for her family, and she could see me as a distraction. "Stay. How did you find me?"

"Flint has been talking to your sister. They're planning Winter-Fest together." I laugh and try to displace the awkward energy in the room, but my throat still tightens at the sight of her in that gown.

"You look incredible." I shrug. "I'm not sure as incredible as you did in your hoodie the other day, but I'll take it."

She smooths her hands down over her hips and looks toward me. "You too. You wore a suit. Does that mean you're coming to the wedding with me?"

"A deal is a deal," I say, stepping toward her, my hand outstretched for hers. "I made a mistake, Montana. I should've told you what I'd done way before. I wanted to, but your body felt so good that I... I don't know... I wasn't thinking straight."

She looks down at her bare toes, then back up at me, biting the inside of her lip. "I don't know what to say."

"You don't have to say anything. I'm done with all that. No more bounties."

"Flint told me about how you were shot, and... what happened next."

"He told me." I sigh deeply. "The man who shot me was a criminal, and I was afraid for my family's life. I wish I had the time to wait for a bounty to be issued on him and done it properly, but who knows where he would have been by then. I knew right where he was and... I had to act. I'm not proud of what I did, but it was necessary." I move my hand to her face. "I needed to make sure no one I ever cared for was ever hurt because of my job. I loved being of service to my community, but you have to know your limits."

She holds my hand in hers. "But I worry what this means for us. Are you always going to need to be Savage? Is the need to be violent just part of who you are?"

I smile a soft smile. "My goal was to do exciting things and serve a purpose. That's all bounty hunting was for me." I brush her hair from her face. "But now, I think I've found something that can be exciting and meaningful... with a lot less risk of bodily harm."

She smiles back and my heart flutters. "So, what about work? If the train isn't going, will you have to leave to find something?"

"Funny you should ask. I ran into Maddox last night at the rodeo and he called me this morning with news. He said they think there's enough interest to keep the steam train in service all year long. I could stay here in Rugged Mountain. We could build a little cabin up by the lake, and you'd still be close enough for your crystal shop." I look down and swallow hard, trying to loosen my throat. "I know I don't deserve you. I know you're better than me a million times over, but if you'll let me, I could try every single day to be the man you need."

That shy smile creeps up onto her face again. The one that knocks the air out of my lungs and makes me question every choice I've ever made that kept me from this moment.

"And what do I need, Cord?"

I pull her into my orbit and look down at her sweet face. "I reckon you need a hard-working man who'll do anything to see that smile... and maybe a horse or two." I grin and kiss her forehead, holding her against me until she pushes back.

"I can't believe you're actually here, Cord."

"I couldn't have you once, and not try to get you back, Montana. You're one of a kind."

"Actually," she smiles, "there's another one of me running around downstairs, probably patting herself on the back for getting you here."

I lean into her lips and brush them against mine, soft and slow. "No. There's only one Montana Grace. I know that without a shadow of a doubt."

She stares at me through long lashes and presses her curved frame against me all at once, crashing against me like a wave and deepens the kiss. "You know my middle name now and that I'm part owner of a crystal shop? You must have asked everyone in town about me."

"Something like that. Also, Google. Apparently, I'm a creepy internet stalker now." I hold her against me and stare down at her sweet blue eyes. "I want to know everything about you, Montana. Every detail, and I think a family wedding might be the perfect place for that." I smile and she pokes my ribs playfully.

"My grandma is going to have a field day with you," she laughs.

I grip her waist tighter. "Is that right?" Every part of me wants to take her harder and longer right here, but now isn't the time. I hold her back, willing my cock not to embarrass me, but he has other plans. "We should get downstairs. The wedding should be starting any second."

That shy smile returns as she reaches for the door, turning the lock, before bending onto her knees before me, looking up with light blue eyes that stop me in my tracks. Slowly, she unbuckles my belt and the slacks I bought this morning fall to the ground.

Fuck. I wanted to be a gentleman. The kind of guy who takes his time and claims his virgin the right way. But she's too sexy, and though I want to stop her, I can't.

She pulls my cock from my boxers and strokes it in her hand over and over, licking just the tip as she moans.

"You're huge. I knew you were. I could feel you through your pants."

"And your family is right downstairs," I say. "They've been so nice to me, helping me up here to surprise you. I want to start this out right."

"We will." She smiles coyly, then slides my cock into her mouth as deep as she can, gagging when the tip hits her uvula.

Fuck. Fuck. Fuck.

I run my fingers through her hair and wet my bottom lip as my eyes go hazy.

"Get up off the floor, baby. Let me taste you." My voice is low, but I doubt it's low enough that someone standing outside the room couldn't hear, especially with how labored my breath is.

She ignores my request for reprieve and continues to suck, pumping her fist up and down as she works.

My head tips back with a groan as she licks my shaft and bobs on my head. I try to be careful with her hair, but my fingers curl into her pretty updo before I can catch myself and pins that were holding something in place fall.

She isn't fazed. She keeps her lips suctioned onto my cock with ragged groans that send a soft prickle to my scalp and down my spine. She moans harder, the vibrations licking at my dick like another tongue, desperate to make me come. But I won't, because when I come, it's going to be inside that sweet, tight pussy. And like the savage I am... I won't take no for an answer.

Chapter Nine

Montana

M aking sense of my actions would only slow me down. Right now, I'm riding on emotion alone. Cord showed up, on his own. He wants me as badly as I want him and that's all that matters. Maybe that's all that *should* ever matter. Maybe we let reason have too much space in matters of the heart. Maybe we should let our bodies decide what's right and what's wrong.

My jaw aches as I take Cord's girth in deeper. I've never done this before, but as I suck his warm cock, I know without a shadow of a doubt that I want his come. I want it all over me. On my lips, in my throat, on my breasts, on my stomach, in my pussy... everywhere. And it's because of who he is that I want it. The parts that have been broken, the pieces that I hope to put back together, and the protector in him that wouldn't let me go through this wedding alone.

He grips my shoulders and lifts me up from the ground, his gaze dialed on me with intensity. "Are you sure you want me to fuck that tight, little pussy? It's probably going to hurt."

His eyes have glazed over as though he's in a world of his own. A world driven by animalistic urges and desperation to release. I know, because I'm experiencing the same thing.

"Make me come," I whine, blood pumping in my ears as I lean up onto the bed and lift my pretty silk dress behind me. I'm not sure what I'm doing, but I've seen this position enough times in movies that I figure this is the way men like it.

He runs his hand over my ass and down my thighs, moaning as he pulls my lace panties off with his teeth.

I could come right now. My thighs squeeze together instinctively as his giant body works behind me. At first, his palm runs over my mound, then his lips press against my thighs, before he slides his tongue over my pussy. I'm not sure what to think at first, but with a few more wet, hot licks, I melt for him.

"I'm going to cover you in my come. Do you hear me?" His voice is low but graveled. "You're going to go downstairs and sit through that wedding with my hot come dripping out of you and everyone who comes within a foot will know you're mine."

"Fuck me," I say as my voice shakes, and he licks my mound again. I never imagined it would feel so good. So good that I'm delirious with pleasure. Someone could burst into the room right now and I don't think I could stop.

"Condoms," he says. "Fuck. I don't have any."

"I don't care. I want you inside of me, then I want you sprayed all over my body. I want your come on my skin. I want to taste you, Cord." I'm breathless and panting with urgency.

"Your dress..." His voice comes out fevered like he needs to fuck me now. He lifts the dress off my frame and tosses it to the floor, then presses into me gently, spreading me wide, filling me up, scraping against my walls.

I'm not sure what I expected sex to feel like, but for a solid minute, there's just pain. I bite my lip and bear through it as he presses in further, stretching me wider than I thought possible

He leans down and rubs my clit gently, kissing the small of my back. "You're okay, baby. Just breathe."

Breathe. I almost forgot to breathe.

I let out a slow, steady breath as he thrusts deeper, moving his hips against me with a rhythm that catches and bursts every aching whimper I've ever fantasized about.

Harder and faster, he thrusts into me, and I feel my pussy clamp down on his girth as he rounds my clit.

My mouth drops open and I grip the sheets tighter, holding on for life as he slams against me like an out-of-control animal desperate for release.

Where there had been pain before, there's only pleasure now. No, it's more than pleasure. It's euphoric. His needy hands take my body, claiming me from all other men.

"Don't stop, Cord! I'm going to..." He covers my mouth with his free hand as he thrusts.

With his voice low, he growls, "Come for me, baby. Come hard. I'm going to bathe you in my pleasure."

The thought of his come on my skin sends me over the edge and in seconds I'm convulsing against him, pushing into his cock as he holds my screams in the palm of his enormous hand.

When the convulsing subsides, he returns his grip to my hips with both hands and slams up against me. Skin on skin sounds unmistakable, and while I'm not trying to make a scene, I can't help but wonder if it's unavoidable.

"Here's what's going to happen," Cord growls. "I'm going to come in that pretty little pussy, then I'm going to come on your stomach, your tits, and wherever else you want me... and you're going to beg me for it."

He doesn't have to ask me to beg. I'm all in for begging. "Do it, Cord. Come. I want you. Claim me. Make me yours, forever."

He grips my hips tighter and his battle subsides as ribbons of come empty into my core. He stays there for a second, pumping.

"Come on me," I beg. "Come on my tits. Rub it in."

"Turn over," he growls, pulling from me with a sigh.

I do as he's asked and flip onto my back, staring up at his enormous body as he jerks his cock to eject the last of his seed all over my stomach and breasts.

"Put it in my mouth," I whine. "I want to taste us."

A low groan rumbles up from his throat as he kneels beside me and lets me take him in my mouth. He's salty and musky, and I lick him clean. Every remaining drop of him ends in my throat, hot and warm.

This is what I've been missing.

When I've been properly coated in his cream, I stand from the bed, an utter mess and extremely late for my brother's wedding.

"I don't want to wash you off," I whine, desperate to lay in the bed with him for all eternity.

"So don't. It's soaked in, and it will be under your dress. I want to know you're covered in me when you walk down that aisle."

His dirty words have me sopping wet again with urges that I know for sure I can't indulge in. I know this because I have two missed calls and eight texts from my sister.

Pearl: Where are you?

Pearl: You're lucky the ceremony is outside.

Pearl: I'm pretty sure Grandma knows what's going on.

Pearl: She does. She's telling everyone.

Pearl: I'm happy for you... but hurry.

Pearl: The ceremony is about to start.

Pearl: I can't make any more excuses.

Pearl: Seriously!

The last one was sent a minute ago. I turn toward Cord and grin.

"What?" His face goes blank as he pulls his pants back in place in a hurry. "Could they hear us?"

"It sounds like Pearl heard. I don't know about anyone else, but we should get down there."

He nods and zips up the back of my dress as I attempt to fix my hair in the mirror behind the door.

"You look hot as hell," he groans, kissing the back of my neck. "And I'm so glad you're mine."

"Forever." I smile. "But before then, I'm going to need you to tell my grandma I didn't cook you one meal yet."

He grins. "Well, you did feed me."

I link into his arm, poking him playfully as we make our way downstairs to the waiting crowd. He's right, I did feed him. Maybe Grandma was onto something all along.

Epilogue

Cord

O ne Month Later

Montana and I stand at the caboose of the iron horse where our story began. She wears a short, simple, lacy white gown while I stand before her in jeans and a white button down with the sleeves rolled up to my elbows. I hold her small hands in mine and look into her bright blue eyes in the crisp late autumn morning.

Our friends and family stand behind us, the clergyman in front as the train chugs along the track. Today, it's engineered by Roy, my former mentor. He taught me everything about locomotion and it only seemed right he was here for my big day. He's a big, burly man, and about the same age. Where I needed to find my way to the train yard, Roy was seemingly born here.

As I stand in this moment, my intention was to absorb every second of the ceremony and memorize every word she said. Instead, I find myself memorizing every breath she takes, every smile she blesses me with, and every soft whisper she places on my ear.

When it's my turn to say my vows, I'm awe struck. My head is light, my chest is expanding, and my mouth is dry as worries and the past drift away. Right now, in this moment... it's only us.

"Montana Grace. If someone told me I'd be married to the sweetest woman in the world, I'd have called them a liar. Not only because I know I don't deserve you, but because at this point in my life I wasn't sure I'd ever find a woman like you. You've blessed every one of my days with love and beauty and I'm beyond grateful for what we share. I promise to love you, protect you, and honor you all the days of my life and beyond. I promise to work hard to solve disagreements and always be your best friend, because you're the first person that has ever felt like home... and I'm never letting you get away."

Tears well in her eyes as the clergyman announces our union. "You may kiss your bride."

I lean into my sweet, young bride and pull her to my chest, holding her like the prize she is.

The small crowd behind us cheers and bubbles blow in the wind up and over our heads as the steam whistle blows.

We link hands, Montana's bright smile bigger than it's ever been as we walk through the train car toward the first-class suite. Our reception will be on the train, as we climb Balsam Mountain. But before then, we get a few moments alone together as cocktails are served.

The stateroom is 1920s glamorous with an art déco design and wingback velvet chairs that stay bolted to the ground.

Montana takes my hand in hers and guides me to the chair, unbuttoning my shirt as we move. "I'm thinking we need to consummate this marriage or I'm not going to be able to focus on anything else tonight." She unbuckles my belt, and I don't stop her.

Instead, I rub my hand over her round ass and lift her pretty little dress up just far enough that she can sit back and ride me while she looks out the window at the mountains passing by. I expect her to like this view but once she's angled down on top of me, she leans back against my chest and circles her hips slowly as her face buries into the crook of my neck.

Hot, wet, heat spills onto my cock as she bounces.

My hands clamp onto her swaying breasts, as my heartbeat booms in my ears.

"You're so hard," she pants. "Are you going to come for me?"

I growl into her ear, taking in the floral scent of her hair as I thrust upward into her tight pussy. We fit together, like two pieces of a puzzle, and though I've had her dozens of times over the past month, I still want more.

Leaning forward she bounces harder, slapping her ass down on my lap as she works my cock. The small of her back bends and arches as she finds the right spot to ride. And when she does, it's all out war.

Her hands grip my thighs as she rocks and grinds. Moan after moan slip from her lips and I grab a fistful of her hair and suck her neck.

"I'm going to come, baby. You better get yours."

She works faster, slamming into me, tightening her muscles, and twisting with need. Thunderclap after thunderclap of hard waves ripple through her ass and onto her back. It's too much. I'm going to come.

My cock stiffens and sweat blooms on my chest. The room smells like sex and there's no denying it. We're animals desperate for touch, desperate for each other.

"Come, Cord. I'm going to…" A heavy breath and a loud sigh expel from her lips as her muscles seize and twist erratically. That's all it takes. I spill my seed inside of her, thrusting upward over and over as she squirms.

Our breath is ragged, and I can't move.

She collapses backward into me and sighs. "Ugh, I have a feeling I'm never going to get anything done with you."

"Is that a bad thing?" I groan, holding her tight against my frame as my dick softens inside of her.

"No." She turns her head toward me and kisses my cheek. "I'm just going to need more time in the day."

"Well, that I can do, Mrs. Masters. You see, I drive a train, and up here in the mountains, there's no such thing as time."

She smiles and leans up off me, reaching her hand out for mine. "So, I guess if we never leave this room, everyone out there waiting for us will never be the wiser?"

I stand from the chair, my legs like jelly as I pull her close to me. "I think that's what I'm saying. Good thing we bought a cabin in the mountains as well."

She laughs. "Technically, the crystal shop is in the mountains too, so I guess time doesn't count there either." She nods. "I think we're good."

I kiss her forehead and step outside the room letting my shoulders relax as I hold her in my arms. The sounds of our family and friends in the next car spread throughout the train, a scent of vanilla and bourbon in the air.

Some people call a wedding that happens fast a shotgun. They say it won't last. They say it's lust or infatuation. But when you meet a girl like Montana Grace, you don't stand still and let her run away. You find the track you're looking for and you ride that baby home.

Delivery Man

Chapter One

Pearl

I stare at the pile of journals next to my bedside table. A bullet journal, vision journal, line a day journal, dream journal, travel journal, focus journal, and in my lap, a gratitude journal. I know there's something to be grateful for. They're all I brought with me from home and technically, I suppose I do have *something* I could put in here, but right now, I'm caught in an appreciation white-out. Oh... maybe I should write that in my quotes journal.

As I'm reaching for a pen, the phone rings. It's my friend Roxie. I haven't told her any of my news and I'm not sure I want to. Sometimes I think my friends are only my friends because I have money. I take them on trips, buy them nice things, and let them have whatever they want from my boutique for free. I guess my dad saw the flaw in my plans because he stepped in last week and stopped my dysfunctional choreography.

"Hey, Roxie." I sound more depressed than I'd planned. Hopefully, she doesn't notice.

"What's wrong? You sound like your dog just died or something."

"No. I'm just tired. What's up with you?" I should ask more poignant questions, but I don't have the energy.

"Umm... *everything!*" Her tone rises and falls as though I've forgotten something important. My stomach twists as I scan through my memory for her birthday... *June 28, July 28, May something?* Okay, it's summer sometime. I'm sure of that. "You forgot, didn't you?"

"No! How could I forget today? It's like the biggest day ever!"

Her voice drops. "You forgot."

I sigh. "Okay. I forgot, but in my defense, I've been under a crazy amount of stress lately."

"You're dripping in money. What kind of stress could you possibly have?"

"Rich people have stress too, ya know." I could tell her that I'm not exactly rich right now, but I haven't said it out loud yet, and I'm not sure my ego could stand the reality check.

"Okay, my bad. What kind of stress are you under?"

I shake my head. "That's not important. What's important is today. What did I forget?"

She sighs. "Winter-Fest. The rodeo. Everyone in town is going to be there... even Flint."

Flint. His name conjures up a series of pictures that I've been flipping through for nearly a month. Most of them involve zero clothes and a lot of touching, but I digress.

"I don't want to see him. It's weird now. It's better if I just stay home."

"What in the world is going on with you, Pearl? You've been reclusive for weeks, you're not answering your phone, and I thought you liked Flint."

"I do. I just..."

"Just what?" Her voice is short and punchy, as though she's a little annoyed.

"Like I said, I have a lot of stress right now and then with Flint... things got weird."

"Weird how?"

"Weird like... I don't want to talk about it, weird."

She sighs. "You could at least come and be a wingman for me. I'm desperate to get out of the house and I really need to meet someone."

Roxie is *always* there for me. She listens to me rant about whatever new dress I'm designing, she gives me honest feedback, and she's probably the sweetest, most genuine person I know. That said, I still don't want to say yes. Sure, I want to go to be supportive of Roxie, but seeing Flint after the mess I got into last month will be ten out of ten embarrassing. Besides that, there are people I'd rather not run into. Then again, I can't *actually* say no to my friend. That might make me feel worse.

"Fine," I sigh. "I'll go, but we're leaving before the dance."

"No way. I'm going *for* the dance. Did I mention the rodeo is in town? All those hot cowboys... looking for love. I'm not missing out on that. You shouldn't either. Flint is down for you. I saw him in town two nights ago and you're all he would talk about."

I bite the inside of my cheek and run my fingers through my hair. Sure, whatever we started is over, but I still need the details. "What did he say?"

"The normal stuff. He wanted to know how you were, what you've been doing, and why you wouldn't return his calls." She chuckles. "I told him you weren't returning mine either, so..."

"He's too old for me." I snap the words out with little regard for how they sound in the air. It's a fact she can't argue with. Flint's forty. I'm twenty-two. He's too old for me.

"Yeah," she pauses. "Probably. But what's wrong with that? I mean, every guy I date my age is so terrible. They don't appreciate what they have. Maybe older men do? Plus, he's like six foot five and mega hot."

Okay, maybe she *can* argue with facts.

"Maybe, but it doesn't matter. I messed things up. Now, I have to preserve the last bits of pride I have and move on gracefully."

"Move on from what? You guys didn't start anything. You just did this weird little dance around each other until you freaked out and dropped off the face of the earth."

"If you only knew..."

"Knew what?" she balks. "Just tell me you're coming tonight. I need a friend.... at the dance too!"

I suck in a deep breath and let it out slowly, knowing full well what a train wreck this whole thing is about to be. "At the dance too."

"Okay then..." I can almost hear the smile in her tone. "We're doing a thing! I'll be over in a bit to get dressed. Or maybe we should stop by your shop and grab new dresses. I haven't been by lately. You must have all this new stuff in by now."

The sign is still up on my storefront on Main. She must not have noticed the lights have been off. I should tell her I want to. Letting this pressure go would be nice right now, but I don't. Instead, I make up a lie. The dumbest lie of all time.

"The shop is being cleaned. Remember those raccoons that are notorious for getting into the bakeshop? Well, they got into my shop last week and tore up a bunch of stuff. I may even need to borrow a dress from you."

"That sucks," she sighs. "How much damage did they do?"

"A lot," I say, desperate to change the subject away from my idiocrasy and back toward the night ahead. "Do you still have that cute skirt with the tulle... the black one? I have a shirt if I can borrow that."

"Of course." She sounds confused. "But why wouldn't you want to wear one of your dresses at home? They're so much nicer than mine."

She has way too many questions.

"Not true. You have lots of stuff from my shop, the tulle skirt included."

"I guess," she says, her voice rising and falling again. "I'll be over in a few minutes. Do you need anything else?"

"No! I'll come to you. I'll be there in an hour."

"*You're coming to me?* Why would you come to me? I always go to you. I live in a shoebox. Plus, my parents are here, and my brother is... being annoying. We'll be better at your place, trust me."

I remember as she's talking that my ride is a beat-up farm truck that my parents so kindly gifted me before they cut me off and took away my hot pink pickup truck. I can't show up in that thing. Roxie will know I'm broke. It has over two hundred thousand miles on it, rust around the wheels, and it sounds like it's going to rattle apart every time it starts.

"Okay, maybe you're right, but my parents rented me a cabin for the week up on Cedar Pass. You can't miss the place. It's the first house by the river, and it's super cute. You'll have to meet me here." I'm talking the place up. It's most definitely not super cute. It's something along the lines of basic and bare bones, with a major hint of minimalism.

"Okay..." I can almost see her eyebrows squish together. "I'll be there in twenty."

When she finally hangs up the phone, every siren in my head alarms and my stomach turns.

What am I doing? Why am I lying? I'm not a liar. In fact, I suck at lying. One time, when I was seventeen, I tried telling my family that I was going to a friend's house for a sleepover when really I was going to the bonfire with a bunch of local kids on the ridge. It took less than three minutes for my father to figure out every detail of my story and only asked me two questions. I learned that day that my tell is my entire body. Apparently, I move differently when I lie. The tone of my voice gets weird, and I stutter a lot. Yay for good decision making.

The room spins until I sit on the nearby rocking chair that's been carved from old Balsam taken from the surrounding area. This cabin is nothing like what I'm used to. My family owns one of the largest ranches in Rugged Mountain, but none of that applies to me since I've been exiled to Cedar Pass to *'learn a lesson'* on the meaning of a dollar. Roxie is going to demand answers when she sees this place, let alone the truck parked outside.

The truck. I can move the truck.

I pull on my boots and head outside into the freshly fallen snow. There's less than an inch on the ground, but it's already looking like Christmas with heavy white branches and tiny footprints in the powdered snow. Usually, I'd be excited for this time of year. A time when shopping and gluttony are imposed. This year, I'm not so sure. I guess I'll be making pinecone ornaments for everyone or picking berries for jam.

Are these berries even edible?

Ugh. I'm sure this lesson could've been taught in January instead... or maybe not ever. I know the value of a dollar and if my parents would've listened to me, they'd know what was going on, but they refused. Apparently, seeing five hundred thousand leave the bank account overnight put them in shock.

I climb up into the old truck, avoiding the springs poking through the seat and try to turn over the engine, but it stalls. This is nothing new. Usually, it stalls a few dozen times before it actually starts. I'm not sure what lesson this is teaching me, but I don't much have a choice left in the matter.

Rolling my eyes, I turn the ignition again, but this time the truck makes a different sound. It's a sputtering that sounds like a start until it spits back out somewhere in the snow behind me.

Great! Another problem. Just what I needed.

Maybe my dad will have mercy on me and let me have my truck back for the night. Sometimes, he's weaker without my mom. I should get him alone. I dial his number and he answers right away.

"Hey, sweet girl. What's up?"

My stomach tightens. "Dad! This truck you bought for me won't start and I have to get to town for the rodeo tonight."

"We didn't buy it for you. We loaned it to you. Are the lights turning on?"

I roll my eyes. Maybe he isn't going to be as easy to push over as I'd hoped. "Yes, Dad, the lights are on."

"Put the phone on the seat and let me hear the sound."

I do as he's asked and turn the engine again, listening to it sputter out the way it had before.

"Check the gas gauge, Pearl. Is it empty?"

I groan and draw my gaze down to the dashboard. Sure, I usually have someone fill my truck up for me, but I'm not dumb enough to drive this thing to empty and not fill it up.

"Jeez, Dad. Have some faith in me. I..." When my eyes hit the gauge, it is indeed on 'E.' *Shit.*

"Well, do you have gas? You can't leave it this low in these temperatures. It freezes. I told you that."

I sigh and blow my hair up and out of my face, staring out the window into the woods before answering. "I know."

"Okay, so what do you do when your car is on empty?"

"I get it, Dad, but how am I supposed to get gas up here? Can you bring me some?"

He sighs long and hard into the phone. "Pearl, you know we love you. This isn't a punishment. It's a learning experience. You need to figure out how to get the gas on your own."

If I weren't so frustrated with myself for making terrible decisions this week, I'd be more patient, but I don't have much stamina left and I lash out. "You didn't do this to Montana! We're twins, aren't you supposed to like... treat us the same or something?" When my sentence has finished, I realize I sound like a child. A spoiled child that probably deserves to live in this cabin with a run down truck and a hundred dollar allowance.

"I did. We treated both you girls the same for twenty-two years. Montana isn't perfect either, but she saw the hard work that goes into earning money." He sighs. "Your mother and I won't be here forever. That's why we bought Montana the crystal shop and you the boutique. We thought you'd make your own money and have pride in what you do. Instead, you turned it into a personal shopping spree for all your friends and that withdrawal you made last week was too much. Five hundred grand? Where did it go, Pearl?"

I grip my hands tight on the steering wheel and stare back into the woods, unsure of how to tell my father what I did. Ever since that bonfire when I was seventeen, I've avoided lying. But this last month, I could use my Pinocchio nose as a bridge to cross the gorge up on Hideaway Rock.

"Well," my father presses, "I'll ask you again. Are you in trouble?"

"No. I'm sorry I took the money."

"What did you take it *for*, Pearl? You say we're not listening to you, but I'm right here... asking."

He's right. I know he's right. That's the worst part of all this. I betrayed my family to help a guy who didn't deserve it. A guy who's gotten me pregnant and threatened my life. A guy who would most definitely hurt anyone who knew where that money went.

"I better go. Roxie just pulled up."

My dad sighs and I hear the trouble in his voice louder than ever. I've been a brat in the past, for sure. But this time, I really got myself into it and I'm not sure how I'm ever going to get out.

Chapter Two

Flint

How is it that I can ride a real-life bull for eight full seconds almost every time, but a mechanical hunk of metal knocks me off in three seconds flat? It's embarrassing and I blame the operator. I think he sees me coming and needs to get his money's worth.

I climb up off the ground and settle my Stetson back in place, making my way to the bar for another beer. Maybe this is why I'm not staying on as long.

Alcohol, the excuse for all of life's problems.

Then again, I always have a few beers before I ride. It's kind of my thing. A mentor of mine used to say it helps loosen your joints for the ride. It's the one piece of advice I've followed all these years. Hard to argue with advice when you've come out of nearly every rodeo with only a few bruised ribs.

"Flint," Mullet says, sliding a beer across the bar. It's a local IPA made up on Balsam Mountain and it goes down real smooth, "getting kind of old for that thing, aren't ya?"

"You're one to talk. What are you... pushing sixty now?"

He laughs without a smile. "Hey, only fifty-nine, you young whippersnapper, but loads of wisdom to go with it. To start, I know well enough that I can't handle old Tessa anymore." He runs his hand down over his gray beard and finally grins.

"I guess I'm still waiting on that lesson," I chuckle, knocking back another sip of beer.

The bar is fairly slow tonight considering Winter-Fest is the happening event in town. Most folks are already in the rodeo stands, drinking hot chocolate near the vendor stations, or strolling through the village shops that have marked everything at half price.

"I guess that lesson translates to your taste in women, too. I saw you hanging out with the Dunn girl a few weeks ago. What are you doing messing around with a young, rich girl, anyway?" He pours vodka into a short glass and grins. "Not that I can judge. I married a girl way too young for me, but man, times were different back then. Women weren't so..." He leans his palms against the wood counter. "Doesn't matter. Your problem is that you have no follow through."

My brows raise. I can't remember the last time I was schooled by an old man with a mullet, but here we are. "Not sure the follow through was the problem. We were hitting it off great, something happened, and she flaked."

Mullet laughs. "You think she liked you, right?" He slides the shot he's poured toward a man who sits down beside me in a black business suit.

I nod. "Yeah, I mean, we were set to meet for a horse ride out by the gulch and she cancelled last minute. Haven't heard from her since."

"Maybe she wanted you to go after her." Mullet leans into the counter. "Women like to be pursued, man. They like to know you'll go the extra mile or two for them."

"She seemed pretty adamant that I leave her alone. I'm not sure she'd have appreciated a surprise visit."

"It's not a surprise visit. It's effort. I hate to be that guy, but you should know that by now." He chuckles. "It's a pretty standard trait to all women that if you try, they'll be more inclined to be interested in you."

"No, they don't," the man beside me chimes. He's a shorter guy with gym muscles and a tattoo across his left forearm. "I was dating a girl up here and she most definitely wouldn't like me showing up out of the blue."

"Is that right? I know a lot of folks up here. Who were you seeing?"

He laughs and pulls back a sip of the vodka he's drinking. "I was just poking holes in your universal theory. There are some bitches who are never happy and no matter what you do, nothing changes that."

Mullet laughs a sage laugh. "Spoken like a true romantic." He grabs a rag for the bar and begins to wipe it down. "But back to your girl in question. You said she was from here. It's probably someone I know or one of their kids. Any chance you still remember this harpy's name?" he says with a condescending smile.

"Pearl. Pearl Dunn. Do you know her?" he says as he looks at both of us.

My chest tightens and my mouth goes dry. Is he the reason she dropped off the face of the earth? He ain't shit. I know that much. The dude isn't even Pearl's type. He's wearing a business suit, for fuck's sake.

Mullet starts to speak, but I jump in, blocking off anything he might say that would make this idiot stop talking with, "Never heard of her. How long have you two dated?"

As I tip back my beer, I'm not thrilled that I'm lying about knowing her. Truly, it's none of my business, but if she isn't going to answer my calls, I may as well get the closure I need to get her off my mind. Maybe I was forcing myself on a girl who's already spoken for... even if he's a fucking loser.

"On and off since we were eighteen. She's a real pain in the ass, though. You wouldn't believe what that whore bitch did to me a few weeks ago."

Whore bitch? My palms itch with an urge to knock the fucker out, but I play along with the conversation.

"What did she do?"

"She ran off on me and owes me an ass ton of money. I figure she'll show up at this rodeo shit." He leans in. "I think she was seeing someone else, too."

I struggle to stay composed. *Was she with this asshole when the two of us were talking? Is that why she dropped off the planet?* Besides, her family is rich. How does she owe anyone money?

My brows raise and my throat grows tight. He can't be talking about Pearl, not like that. "How much money does she owe you?"

He laughs with darkness and runs his hand back through his thick black hair. "Too much. And I'm going to make sure she pays... tonight."

Is this fucker threatening her? I glance toward Mullet, then toward the mechanical bull where a woman in her seventies has been riding for at least three minutes. I swear that thing is rigged. "How are you going to *make her pay?*" My voice is gruffer than it needs to be, but I'm teetering on the edge of making this guy blind.

He chugs the rest of his vodka and sighs. Beneath it is a chuckle. A dark, menacing chuckle. "I don't talk about things like that, partner. But know... that bitch will pay."

I've never been much of a fighter. Sure, in grade school I had an occasional scuffle with the boys in the playground over king of the hill or games of kickball, but I've never felt enough rage to hit a man and cave in his face like I do right now. The truth is, I don't care what Pearl did. She doesn't deserve to be talked about the way he's talking, and she surely doesn't deserve the fucking threats.

My hand balls into a fist and my jaw clenches as an overwhelming urge rolls over me. I know I'm not perfect, far from it, but fuck this guy. Without thought, I stand from the stool and release my eager fist, landing my energy straight on the man's jaw. This is nothing like a playground brawl when you're eight years old. Aside from the obvious fact that I'm much larger than this man, there's an odd amount of blood and the paunchy sound of a fish trying to escape his destiny as he's reeled in from the river.

The asshole falls backwards and for a second, I'm reeling with gratification, sure that I've solved the problem until Mullet starts talking.

"What the hell, man? Take a breath. Outside... now!" When he's done barking orders, his hand goes to the man on the floor as he helps him up from the ground. I decide not to hold this against him. He's got a business to run and I've reacted like a barbarian.

It's now that I notice how quiet the bar has gone. The few people tipping back drinks are wide eyed and staring toward me as though I'm an out-of-control zoo animal.

Maybe I am. I'm not sure what came over me, but I know I'm not going to apologize.

I suck back another sip of beer and settle the glass bottle onto the bar top before heading out into the crisp mountain air. My eyes squint as I take in the bright sun reflecting off the snow. Out here, the normally quiet town is buzzing with people that are here for holiday shopping, Winter-Fest, the snow rodeo, and probably a tattoo at the most popular ink shop in the west.

What was I thinking? I'd be kicked from the rodeo if Waylon knew I was causing trouble like that in his hometown, especially during one of the biggest times of the year.

I suck in a deep breath and let it out slowly, gathering myself before heading toward the coffee shop at the end of the row. I'll grab a cup and use the bathroom to wash this blood off my hands. Then I'll call Pearl and let her know this asshole is in town.

"*Flint?*" It's my buddy Dustin. He's a ranch hand working for Waylon's family, but he travels with the rodeo as needed. He's a great guy, though a little stiff in his viewpoint on most everything from sugar consumption to political affiliations.

I tuck my hand into my pocket and hope he doesn't notice my bloody fist as I turn around. "Hey, Dustin. What's up?"

He laughs. "Well, I just saw you deck that Johnny guy, so I thought I'd see if everything was alright. I've seen you do a lot of things, but never throw yourself into a punch like that." He laughs loudly as he says, "Your form is terrible. You're a little old to be out here throwing punches like you're throwing around bales of hay."

Of course, he says that. Everyone's a critic. "Everything's fine, man. Thanks for check-ing." I don't make small talk, as I'm desperate to get as far away from the bar as possible before the logical side of my mind collapses under the weight of my lizard brain, demand-ing we go back in and finish the job. Unfortunately for me, Dustin isn't quite done yet.

"I've seen that guy around. He's an asshole, and probably deserved what he got."

"How do you know him?"

Dustin shrugs. "I don't. I've just heard people in the bar over the years. Everyone has a story. You know, people come in from the Springs, and they think they can get one over on us small towners. He's a swindler."

I can't help but wonder if that's what he did to Pearl, but I don't ask more questions. I'll ask Pearl herself. No more of this, *he said-she said* bullshit.

"I'd love to hear all about it, but I gotta grab a cup and get washed up before I hit the chute. I don't need issues with Waylon."

Dustin holds up his hands and grins. "Got it, buddy. Just making sure you're okay." He turns away and I'm immediately relieved until I hear his voice again. "One thing, though. Was this about that Pearl girl? The one I saw you with a few weeks back? I heard the guy say his name and—"

"So, what if it is?" I'm on the defense and I'm not sure why.

"Just wondering if maybe you hit your head too hard on that mechanical bull earlier."

I manage a fake laugh. "And why's that?"

"Well, she's a rich girl, for one. And you're... *a you*."

My patience is thinning. "What does that mean?"

"I don't want to see you get hurt, is all. I know how lonely it gets on the road. I see it happen all the time. Guys get homesick and they think they're in love with some girl they've known for five minutes."

"It was longer than five minutes, and *love* is probably a little strong." I turn away from him and start walking toward the coffee shop. "That said, I get your point. I'll catch up with you later."

He follows after me. "Woah, woah, woah, dude. You do have feelings for her, don't you?"

"Feelings are a strong way to put it." I'm lying. Feelings are exactly how I'd put it, but I don't answer to Dustin.

He laughs, still beside me as I dodge oncoming people and walk toward the end of Main.

"I got to you just in time, then. I'll take you to a bar on the other side of the mountain. It's a country music club... The Barn Yard. I bet there will be tons of local women there ready to help you with all your *needs*."

I stop amidst the people and turn toward him. My jaw is tight, and my voice is unapologetically gruff. "I *was* that guy. I was that guy for so damn long, Dustin. It's empty. It's a novelty. And once you meet that one person who's more real than anyone you've ever met before... you can't see anyone else. All you want is them."

He studies my face for a second, then grins and I'm sure some smart-ass remark is coming. Instead, he surprises me with, "Why aren't you two together, then?"

I shake my head, thinking back to a few weeks ago when everything made sense. We connected on a level I've never had with anyone. She understood the words coming from my mouth when I barely knew what I was trying to say. And in turn, I felt all of her passions with every word that left her beautiful lips. Truthfully, it was... more than I was expecting. We were in sync, and then, just like that, she was gone. She stopped answering my calls, wouldn't respond to texts, and I assumed she'd realized she didn't want to be with a working class cowboy. So, I let it go. I don't say any of this to Dustin. I only shrug my shoulders. "It's complicated."

"If you want her, you should probably go get her."

"That seems to be the popular advice around here," I say. "Unfortunately, I'm into boundaries and all that shit."

"It's popular because it's true."

"Maybe, but something tells me it's not that easy," I chide. "I've got to figure this out at my own pace."

Dustin nods and glances behind me as a wide Cheshire grin grows on his face.

"What's wrong?"

"Oh nothing, man. It's just... you may not have to overstep boundaries after all."

My stomach tightens as I guess what he's about to say. "And why's that?"

He nods forward, that excitedly, pleased smile never leaving his face. "Because your girl is coming this way."

Chapter Three

Pearl

"You're really not going to tell me what's going on?" Roxie's voice is like fingernails on a chalkboard, and I wish I was saying that figuratively. If she asks me one more question, I know my ear drums are going to rupture and I'll lose all hearing for eternity. Which, at this point, might be a good thing.

The longer I try and keep up with my lies, the more stress brews in my chest and the more awkward I feel. *I have to tell her what's going on.*

I twist back, sigh, and push the stray strands of hair from my face as my volcano of lies bubbles over. "I'm broke, okay? I'm broke. Like broke, broke, broke, broke, broke."

Her eyebrows twist inward, and she pulls her cotton dress into place. "What do you mean, you're broke? I saw your dad yesterday at the market. He looked fine. Your mom was carrying the biggest bouquet of roses I've ever seen. She was treating *herself*. Broke people don't do that."

"*They're* not broke. *I'm* broke."

"What happened?" Her hand goes to my shoulder in comfort, and I suck in a deep breath of relief. It feels good to finally tell someone what's going on. "It's my fault. I gave a bunch of money to Johnny. My parents think I took the money for something else. It's a mess."

"Yeah, you left out a lot of details there. Care to back up?"

"Not really." I stare up at the bright blue sky, then back toward my friend who's obviously got too much time on her hands. I need to make sure she gets set up tonight.

"Well, you've got to give me more than that! How much did you give Johnny? I thought you guys broke up a while ago. Why are you still giving him money?"

I sigh, hard and heavy, hoping for relief, but it doesn't come. "Can *I'm broke* be enough for now? I really don't feel like talking about it."

She stares back at me long and hard before leaning into my ear whispering, "I know you're pregnant."

My chest tightens and my head pounds, the world around me spinning like a top that I'm riding. I open my mouth but nothing comes out.

Roxie leans back and crosses her arms in front of her chest. "How long were you going to lie to me for? I'm your best friend!"

I swallow hard and stare toward her, unsure of what to say. "I only found out a couple months ago."

She narrows her brows and looks down at my stomach. "You're clearly pregnant, Pearl. Have you looked in the mirror?"

A bead of sweat breaks onto my forehead despite the frigid temperatures. "I thought I was gaining weight. I'm under a lot of stress."

The crease between her eyes only deepens. "I'm worried about you. Whose baby is it?"

"Johnny," I say in a near whisper, embarrassed for myself that I let him get that close to me.

Roxie's face goes pale, blank. Her eyes drift upward, and an eerie feeling settles into my stomach.

Someone is behind me. Someone else has heard my news.

My palms go sweaty and my heart races. I'm afraid to turn. The look on her face says it's my dad or God forbid, Johnny. I haven't talked to him in weeks. I owe him money and I don't have any to give him. Not only that, but I'd be fine with him never knowing about the baby. I slap my hand to my face, covering my eyes as I spin toward whoever has left Roxie speechless.

"*Are you pregnant?*" Flint's voice is deep and shaking. "Pearl, is it that Johnny guy's?"

How does Flint even know about Johnny?

Okay this is worse than I thought. Any chance I thought I had with Flint is in the trash now. I already brushed him off once, and now I'm eight months pregnant with another man's baby. I'm sure that's not going to get him all hot and bothered for me.

"You weren't supposed to hear that." I press past him and walk down the street, desperate for escape.

"Pearl," Flint calls, chasing after me. "Do your parents know? Who else knows?"

My heart pounds as I make my way through the crowded downtown area. Christmas music plays in the background and the lights are lit and glowing back at me, taunting me with everyone else's happiness. I move faster through the streets, trying to ignore the trail of concerned people I've left behind, but Flint moves faster than I can and soon his big hand is linked onto my arm and he's stopping me in my tracks.

"Pearl. Stop. You're in trouble. Tell me what's going on." His eyes drag down toward my stomach in disbelief. "Are you really pregnant?"

"Keep your voice down!" I shake my head and pull him into an alley between the tattoo shop and the bar. "Yes. I'm really pregnant. Eight months. I haven't told anyone. Well, except Roxie and now you." My finger goes to his chest and my eyes stare up at his. "And that's the way it's going to stay!"

His eyes graze over my body again and his voice tightens. "What did he do to you? How do you hide a pregnancy for eight months?"

"I wear my coat and I don't leave the cabin!" I snap in frustration. "None of this matters, Flint!" I want out of this conversation.

"I met the piece of shit earlier today, at Mullet's bar. He said you owed him money. He said some pretty shit things about you. Does he know about the baby?"

My cheeks heat as I finger the heart shaped necklace my mother gave me when I was twelve. I would give anything to tell her my secrets. She's the only one who's ever been able to comfort me. But this could kill her... quite literally. "I'm fine. He doesn't know about the pregnancy. Please don't tell him. In fact, you'll be best off not letting him know you and I ever met."

Flint stands taller and runs his hand over his beard. He's as handsome as ever. Tall, built, tight jeans, a flannel shirt, ink rolling down both arms, and a cowboy hat in place. The man could have any woman he wants. Why is he talking to me?

"What is that supposed to mean?" he grumbles. "I need to know what he did to you so I can help."

I let out a heavy sigh and look down the sidewalk before dragging my gaze up toward Flint again. He's so much bigger than me in every aspect. His neck alone is as thick as my thigh. Not only that, but he's handsome and I can't help but drown myself in what-ifs.

What if I'd taken him up on his offer to help plan Winter-Fest?

What if I'd let him take me to dinner the night of my sister's wedding?

What if I'd fallen for him like I wanted to instead of running back to Johnny out of obligation?

What if I'd met Flint sooner?

Maybe I'd be pregnant with his baby. Maybe I wouldn't be sleeping in a hunter's cabin alone. And maybe, *just maybe,* I'd be wrapped up in Flint's big strong arms with a promise of forever on the horizon.

"Hello..." Flint waves his hand in front of my face. "You're zoning out on me."

"I did?" God, I'm turning into my twin sister, Montana. She's constantly zoning out into la-la land. "Sorry, it's probably all the hormones jumping around inside of me. What did you ask?"

He rolls his eyes to the side and his jaw tightens. "What did this guy do to you?"

I scan the alley. To the left is the field that leads to Winter-Fest and the rodeo. To the right, the streets of Rugged Mountain and Roxie who's making her way toward us with her head shaking as though she's been searching.

"It's nothing." I look away. "You have a rodeo to get ready for."

He looks down at me with narrowed eyes and his giant hand runs up and over my shoulder. "I'm not letting you off the hook that easy. You need someone beside you right now."

My heart warms and my breath picks up as he stares back at me with dark brown eyes. I'm not sure what to say or how to react. I've wanted Flint since I first saw him. He bought a truck from my dad a while back and I couldn't help but be infatuated with him since the beginning. And even with our limited interactions since then, I know he's funny, courageous, and somehow, he makes everything feel okay even when it's not. I should've realized that sooner. Now, if I tell him I'm interested, I'm only dragging him into a mess I created.

"I'm fine, Flint. I'm a grown woman. I can take care of myself, the baby, and everything else. The last thing I need is some man rushing in to rescue me."

"I'm not trying to rescue you, Pearl. I'm—"

A bell rings and an announcer speaks over the loudspeaker in the grandstand. "We're riding tonight for the golden mustang folks. Who's ready?"

"That's your cue," I say, linking my arm into Roxie's who's standing like a fly on the wall beside me. "I'll catch up with you later. You've got another buckle to win."

He groans out and looks toward the ring before turning back to me. "I'm not going unless you promise to meet me tonight at the dance."

My heart swells when he asks and every part of me wants to say yes, but if Johnny's here, that's only going to complicate everything.

I shrug. "Maybe you'll see me there."

"Maybe isn't good enough," he continues, his voice deep.

I stand in silence for a long moment, wondering what a night with him would mean. Most likely he's moved past the being interested in me thing and feels an obligation to help the pregnant woman with a weirdo chasing her. I can talk him off that ledge later. Right now, he can't miss his ride.

"Fine. I'll meet you after the show."

He nods and grins, though I see behind his eyes that part of him doesn't believe me. I can't blame him after I stopped communication with him a few weeks back.

I'm such an ass.

Sucking in a deep breath, I turn toward Roxie who's twisting her brown hair onto one shoulder with a grin.

"Well, that wasn't obvious or anything. I hope you don't plan on blowing him off again. Did you see the way that man looked in those jeans? I bet he could give you three more babies tonight." She grins. "We're talking science miracles here."

I stare down the alley as he jogs toward the rodeo stand. "I know. But... it's not that easy. I have to figure out what I'm doing with everything else first. Besides, do you not see Flint? He's like the nicest, hottest guy in the world. I'd only be dragging him down."

"Why don't you think you deserve him, Pearl? He likes you. You could use people on your side right now. If the man wants to give you love, let him." She shrugs and grips my hand in hers. "Give him a chance."

"He's just being nice, Roxie. It was a miracle the first time he talked to me. What would a guy like him want with a big, round, puffer fish about to give birth to someone else's baby? The man could have anyone in those stands. And God knows they're throwing themselves at him."

She rolls her eyes, and we walk forward down the alleyway toward the rodeo where people are cheering, and whistles are being blown. "Can we at least watch him ride that bull then? The man's biceps are a download straight from heaven."

I laugh and we make our way up into the bleachers, stopping for a hot cocoa at the stand just outside the arena. It's then that I see him. The man I've been avoiding since he shoved me down to the ground a month ago. My stomach twists and my cheeks flare red as he grins and turns toward me. I should've known better than to come here.

Chapter Four

Flint

I grew up on the rodeo. My dad was a bull rider, his dad was a bull rider, and his father was too. There's something about the roar of a crowd, and the feel of dirt under your boots that helps make sense of everything else in this fucked up world. My dad used to tell me that if something makes you happy, it's worth doing, even if it isn't always easy. And he's right. Here I sit at forty, the oldest in the family to sit up on a bull. I'm not sure if that's a good thing or not. It's wreaked havoc on my back and I'm sure it's damaged other parts of me I'll find out about when I'm sixty-five trying to bed over to put a fence post in. Right now, though, the aches and pains don't matter. I'm here, in front of the crowd, putting on a show, and that makes me happy.

The best part is, I know Pearl is watching. I give my cowboy nod to the judge and the chute opens. My beast begins to buck, immediately testing the freehanded style that I've mastered over the years. Tonight is the night I break the state record I set with Little Bubba a few months back. I can feel some history making numbers with the amount of energy I'm feeling tonight. Black Tornado here rides different, but I've got just as good a shot. I hold tight as he bucks counting the seconds the way I've been taught.

One Mississippi. Two Mississippi.

The crowd roars as dust and mud flies. The good thing about a snow rodeo is that the bull isn't at an advantage. The ground is slippery, and his footing is slightly compromised.

Three Mississippi.

From the corner of my eye, I catch a sight of Johnny's face. His grin is wide, and his hand is on Pearl's back. What's happening over there? Is Pearl okay?

My record-breaking energy for the nearly one-ton beast I'm battling shifts priorities and I light on fire. I kick my leg over the bull's head, like my grandfather taught me, and keep myself small as I run for the gate. Now here, most riders would take their bow, having reached safety, but I have something much more pressing that needs my attention.

I clear the arena and never stop running through the stands. Johnny's eyes are wide as I crash into him and climb on his chest, my hands on his neck. So much for my battle with my lizard brain, but... I'm okay with it.

The crowd quiets, and the announcer says something about 'getting that guy some help' but I've lost all control. This man will never touch Pearl again!

Pearl gasps. "Flint! Stop. You're killing him. He's—"

"A piece of shit?" I punch him again, this time striking the opposite side of his jaw. Snow flies into the air and the crowd gasps in chorus around me. I stare down at the man I'm attacking. "What did you do to her?"

As I gear up to hit him again, I start to feel the crowd pull me off of Johnny. I struggle against the mob, but there are too many of them. Don't they see what a monster this guy is?

"Seriously, Flint," Pearl says again. "You don't know what he's capable of."

"Yeah, Flint," Johnny chides, with a grin as he lifts to a knee. "You don't know what I'm capable of."

"Whoa, cowboy." I can hear Waylon's voice and feel his hand on my back, as my sanity starts to return to me. "You're going to get yourself disqualified. Who the hell is this guy?"

Johnny stands from the ground and swipes his hand over his wrinkled suit. "None of your fucking business."

I crack my knuckles and stare toward him with flaring nostrils and bared teeth. I'm an animal. This man has turned me into an animal. Or maybe it's Pearl. The thought of her being hurt is what's turned me. She won't be disrespected in my presence... period.

Johnny turns back, straightening the cuffs on his suit. "I'll be back for you, Flint Masters. I promise."

I lunge toward him, but Waylon holds me back. Jonny just continues to smile with his perfectly white teeth. Little does he know, I can see a few of them aren't as complete as they were when he came in here tonight.

"Who's taking him home?" Waylon looks toward Pearl and Roxie. "I've got a rodeo to finish, and Flint can't be trusted tonight. He's lost his mind."

"Pearl can take him back," Roxie chimes, as though it's the best idea she's ever come up with. She turns toward Pearl. "I'll be okay here. I see Montana and Cord. I can hang off them until I get to the dance. You go... *help* Flint." She winks her left eye, and her voice rises and falls as though she's speaking a secret language that's not all that secret. I wonder if they've been talking about me, or maybe about Pearl and I together.

"Are you sure?" Pearl reaches out for Roxie's hand. "I can come back to the dance once I get Rocky here home."

"*Rocky?*" I lift my hat off my head and run my fingers back through my hair. "I think he'd have knocked that asshole out with one punch."

Waylon rolls his eyes and scuffs his boots against the snow and dirt that's built up in the shaded corners of the venue. "Are we good here? I've got to get back to it."

Pearl nods. "I'll take him."

"Good," Waylon says before turning toward me. He's a big man with tattoos covering nearly every inch of skin, except for his face. To be honest, the looks of him are intimidating as hell. Half the time, his attitude is too. The man doesn't have a joking bone in him. He's all business, all the time. I guess you have to be if you're going to run one of the biggest ranches in the west. Usually, he has no mercy, and I don't expect him to. Right now, though, the wrinkle between his eyes tells a different story. "Figure this out, cowboy. People pay good money to see you ride, not fuck off."

The crowd roars loud beside us as another rider takes to a bull.

I nod. "Understood."

He doesn't say another word. He stalks back toward the chutes, and I turn toward Pearl who's standing in the sunlight just right with bright golden beams painting her hair with shine. She's beautiful.

She bites her bottom lip and looks up at me with the sweetest gaze. "You're getting in trouble."

I smile, placing my hand on the small of her back as we make our way up toward my truck parked at the opposite end of the lot. "It was worth it. Maybe now you can tell me what's going on."

She sighs and pauses for what seems like forever before she speaks again. "I'm having a girl. Do you know what little girls need more than anything else?"

I shake my head as I study the worry on her face. Worry that I'm desperate to take away.

"They need their father," she says. "My dad is still so important to me. He taught me how I should be treated. He showed me what a man could be. Granted, I've done a shit job at finding it, but still, I know what good is out there." A tear rolls down her cheek. "Faith isn't going to have that."

I open the truck door and take her small hand in mine, helping her up into the seat. My question this whole time has been focused on what Johnny did to Pearl, but I never stopped to ask how Pearl was doing. She's holding a child all on her own. A time that should be filled with joy, laughter, parties, and celebrations has been spent running and hiding.

I climb up into the truck and start the engine, pulling out onto Main before turning right toward the mountain. I'm not sure what to say to her, and everything I'm mulling through sounds like some over the top romance novel.

"You're not alone, Pearl. I'm right here. I'm not leaving."

She laughs, short and quick. "Thank you, but we both know that you can find way better than me and this mess."

"Why don't you let me decide what I want. Okay? You decide what's best for Pearl and I'll decide what's best for me."

She twists toward me. "So, after our two-week friendship where I left you on read and didn't return your calls, you're ready to take on a crazy pregnant woman with an ex who has quite literally threatened your life?"

I pull the truck to the side of the road, nestling between a row of pine and cedar. "You're so much more than any of that. Let me show you. Let me treat you the way you deserve to be treated."

Her eyes flicker. "I want to believe you."

"Then believe me." My voice is nearly a whisper. "I'm not the one who ran, Pearl. I wanted you the first second I saw you. You had your hair in a braid on your shoulder and your eyes were lit up with such beauty that I never stopped thinking about you." I pause and stroke my hand over my beard. "Tell me what happened with this asshole and why he's still coming around."

Her breath goes jagged as she sucks in air. Tears fall from her cheeks. "I met Johnny on my eighteenth birthday. I was doing a fashion show in Colorado Springs and he was an investor. I thought he was *so cool* and I was completely smitten. We were dating for," she shrugs, "seven months maybe, and he came to me with a proposal. He said my designs would be on models all over the world. He said I'd be famous. He said celebrities would be wearing my dresses to the Oscars. All I needed was a small investment. At first, it was fifty thousand." She wipes away a tear. "I was so dumb to believe him. The more money I gave him, the more lies he told. At one point he made me believe that the dress I'd made was being considered by Beyonce, but that she'd changed her mind at the last minute." She sighs. "He's done this for three years. Every year it's more money, more promises."

My hand goes to her leg in comfort.

She draws in a deep breath. "When I told him I couldn't get more money, he told me he was in love with me. I don't know why I believed him. I didn't love him. I knew I didn't, but I was in so deep. I thought if I went along with it all, maybe I'd find the success I was looking for, but I didn't, and before I knew it he was forcing himself on me and I didn't stop him." She holds her head in her hands. "He demanded five hundred thousand shortly after that. When I couldn't get it for him, he threatened my family. So... I stole the money from my parents and my dad cut me off, closed my shop, and told me I needed to learn my lesson. And he's right, I do."

"It's not your fault. If you tell your parents what's going on, they'll help you."

"They wouldn't know how to help me. They're good, humble people. Their fortune was inherited." She shakes her head. "They would get hurt. Johnny would hurt them."

I nod and pull Pearl close to my chest, running my hand down over her hair as she cries. "I'm not going to let that happen."

"I found out I was pregnant a couple months ago. I can't tell him, Flint. I don't know what he'll do."

I look toward her, my hands on either side of her face as I lean into her lips. The motion is natural, unforced, and pure, though it's laced with desperation, longing, and the wild urge to take all of her pain away.

My heart races as our lips meet and my fingers tangle in her golden hair. I can take all her problems. I can make her life good. I can be the man she's been looking for. I can make that asshole, Johnny pay.

Chapter Five

Pearl

It's so much harder being alone with Flint than I thought it would be, especially with all this emotional honesty floating around. Normally, I'd be superficial, tell everyone I was fine, and go about my business. Now that the flood gates are open, I'm not sure I can stop the leak. And with his lips pressed against mine, and these pregnancy hormones rushing through me, the odds are even lower.

His large, calloused hand moves up the side of my face and his eyes stay on mine as a growl leaves his throat. "I shouldn't have kissed you."

"What? Why?"

"I knew what this would start for me, and I did it anyway."

"What does it start for you?"

He sighs and runs his hand over his beard. "I've been thinking about you non-stop Pearl. I've tried to forget. Hell, I thought the best thing was to forget. But still, every morning you're there. Your face, your voice, the way you talk with all your heart." His eyes dial in on mine. "How can I forget something that could've been so perfect?"

I stare back at him, silent, unsure of what to say, how to act. There's no denying that he means what he says. I feel it when he talks. I see it in his eyes. And though I'm terrified to take a leap, his words set me on fire.

I lean into his chest and brush my lips against his, wrapping my arms around his shoulders. His beard tickles my face, and his big hands grip my waist, holding me close and for the first time since I left my parent's house, maybe longer, I feel like I'm home.

I pull away and pluck at the hem of my dress, suddenly terrified for the hurt that inevitably comes from giving myself to someone. This time, I'm not choosing for me alone. I'm choosing for Faith, and I have to be careful. I can't get involved with someone haphazardly. I need to think of who I want around my baby girl.

He brushes my hair back and runs his hand over my expanding stomach, his gaze back on me. "You're scared, aren't you?"

"What? No. I'm not scared. I—"

"You know that you're falling for me. You know given time alone, you and I would find more love than you've ever felt. That terrifies you."

I pause for a long moment, then drag my eyes up to his again. They're dark and warm and his biceps flex against my skin. My heart constricts and my throat tightens. I think I've having a stroke. I want to dive in without abandon. Everything about Flint is right. The way he listens, the way he responds, the way his gaze stays intent with mine through every beat.

"It's okay to be scared." His whispers vibrate against my throat.

My clit throbs and my nipples go tight.

"Is it? You deserve better than someone who doesn't know what she wants or who she is."

He kisses my skin. "I bet if you let yourself go, you could tell me what you want."

His breath is so warm on my neck that every nerve in my body awakens and the thumping between my legs grows stronger.

"I know I want you." My voice is a squeak, afraid to trust the emotion I have for him... but it's real. I knew he was a good guy the first second we spoke, and all I've done is think of him since I pushed him away. "I want you so bad, Flint." The words slip from my lips with abandon.

He groans low and cups the side of my face. "Say it again."

"I want you..." My words are still a whisper as a flood of emotion drowns my heart. He wants to hear me say I want him... and I do. *I want him so bad.*

His eyes close as his hand grips the back of my neck. A slight growl leaves his throat. It's a natural, primal sound that drives desire straight through me. I'm soaked, and my desire quickly turns to an urge. A need. A desperate, uncontrollable, yearning.

I kiss his bottom lip, lingering on his touch. "Take me back to your place, Flint. I need you."

"Are you sure?"

I nod in confusion. "Of course, I'm sure."

"I need you to know that when I take you, Pearl, I'm keeping you. You and that little girl. You're both mine. I'll love you and take care of you both, but there can't be any question about it ever again. Once I'm inside of you, you're mine." His words come out in a series of rumbles that sound archaic and possessive. Usually, I'd be repulsed by such control but with Flint, I want it. I want him to own me, claim me, possess me in every fraction of the word. And I want it... now!

Chapter Six

Flint

I've wanted to hold Pearl like this since I first laid eyes on her. I've thought about what her soft hips would feel like in my hands, what she'd taste like, how she'd sound, what my fingers would feel as they ran through her silky hair.

I've imagined scenario after scenario. In the stables, in the hayloft, in the bed after a long day, in the cabin against the wall, in my truck as we try not to hit the shifter. In none of these fantasies was she pregnant, but as she stands nude in my warm cabin, the sight of her round belly, full breasts, and tight nipples sends me to a place I hadn't realized I needed to be. She's perfect, at the peak of her beauty as she grows a life.

Hot, rushed fever washes over me as I try to decide where to put my attention. I'm like a kid in front of a cookie plate. I want every flavor, every crumb, every sprinkle, and I want it all at once.

"You're making me nervous," she says, her voice shaking. "I'm not usually this... naked."

I groan and step toward her, tracing my thumbs over the curve of her lips, then her collarbone, and finally those full breasts that are begging for attention. "You're hot as hell. I want to map you, study you, remember every inch." My cock presses against her stomach and my free hand cups her throat.

Her breath snags as she pushes my jeans to the floor and grips my cock in her hands. "You're huge. I can't..."

My cock pulses in her hand, desperate for whatever warmth it can get. "We'll go slow, princess. I promise."

"*Princess?*"

I suck her neck and bite the inside of her shoulder gently. "Do you not want to be my princess?"

She tips her head back and gasps, holding onto my shoulders as she makes room for my teeth against her skin. "I want to be your princess, Flint. I want to be your everything."

Her words are the permission I need to let my greedy hands explore her body further. Slowly, I back her against the wall of the cabin and press my palm into her mound. She's soft and warm, already soaked.

Fuck.

I slide a finger inside and watch her face as her lips spill open letting a soft sigh into the universe. It's a sound I'll never forget. I thrust into her further, scraping upward in a come-hither motion that makes her body shake and moan.

I want more.

Sliding another finger inside, I push deeper, pumping in and out of her tight pussy as she sighs over and over in my ear.

I hiss and grip her closer. The light of the Christmas tree in the corner illuminates her curves and soon there's a need raging within me that I've never felt before. It's carnal and heated with urges from some cave in some country I've never been. It's barbaric, uncontrollable, desperate, and needy.

"Fuck me, Flint," she begs. "Fuck me hard. Please. Please, just fuck me hard."

I pull my fingers from within her and lick them clean, tasting the sweet juices of her core before turning her around.

She places both hands on the wall as I stroke my cock behind her and kiss her neck with desperation, scraping my teeth along the bone like a savage.

I grip her hip with one hand and her opposite thigh with the other, holding her steady as I anchor into her core. It's now that I'm remembering the gap in our age. She's tight, strangling my cock with need.

What am I doing? She's too young. She has her whole life ahead of her. I'd be holding her back. The thought only lasts a beat as my body takes over again.

Holding onto her close, I slide in further.

"Oh, god," she moans. "Just go slow."

I wrap my hand from her hip to her clit and rub the swollen knob until she relaxes and I'm able to push further inside. Her round ass bounces and strained moans leave her throat as I root myself inside of her. My hands struggle to stay in place. I want them everywhere. In her hair, on her throat, on her hips, slapping against her ass.

She rolls her body back against mine as we move. "I need to come, Flint. Now!" She's panting, hungry, desperate for release and it only gets me harder.

I notch myself against her tighter and thrust with purpose, trying to keep rhythm as I circle her clit.

Her ass squirms against me and draws my cock in deeper.

My eyes squeeze closed as she rocks her hips. There's a scent of sex and pine in the air. Moan after whining moan escapes her lips and soon there's no going back. This is a sound I want to hear for the rest of my days. This is a feeling I want forever: Pearl Dunn and her wet, warm, tight pussy gripping my cock as she whines for release.

"Fuck," I growl, breathing against the back of her neck. "Come for me, princess. I need you."

She whimpers and squirms in my arms as I thrust harder. "I'm going to, Flint. I have to come."

Every nerve in my body is awake and alive. I didn't think sex could be like this, but I'm high. I'm high on her and I never want to come down. My teeth clench as our bodies seal tightly against each other.

"I'm going to—"

A hard bang hits the cabin door, and then another. It's followed by some muffled yelling. I should stop and see who it is. There are windows surrounding us. Whoever is there could come around the corner and see us together. They could see my forty-year-old ass pressed up against a twenty-two-year-old Pearl. They'd judge us and they'd tell everyone in town. They could see her breasts sweeping against the logs of the cabin wall. They could hear her begging for more.

"Who'd be here so late?" She's breathless. "Don't stop... please. Just let me finish."

Neither of us are thinking straight, but I don't stop to question it. I grip her tight and thump harder and harder, spreading her wide as the pounding on the door only gets louder.

She reaches back for my forearm, as though securing me in place, letting me know I'm not to stop under any circumstance. Her pussy clamps down on my cock and I feel her pulse against me.

I breathe into her neck, letting go all the worry I've been building. This woman is about to be mine, and I wouldn't have it any other way. "I'm going to come, princess. Are you ready for me?"

She whines and nods her head, then screams out in pleasure warming my cock with her come.

The door creaks and for a second I fear who's on the other side, but that doesn't last long. The sounds of her pleasure still echo and my cock can't take it. I grip her hips and make her mine, painting her walls with my come as I growl out with relief.

In my fantasies I hold her, protect her, let her know how safe I'll keep her. Sadly, reality has other plans and as the cabin door comes crashing open, I see we're back to square one.

Chapter Seven

Pearl

I stare blankly toward the open doorway while Flint is all action. He tosses me his flannel while he pulls his jeans on and grabs his shotgun from the wall. It all happens in a matter of seconds, but it may as well be hours. I'm like a statue. A big, bloated, pregnant statue staring at the one man that shouldn't know about my baby.

"What the fuck?" Johnny rasps. "Are you fucking pregnant?" He's looking at me nearly as shocked as I'm looking at him. I think it may be the only thing keeping him from using that gun he's pointing. Not the fact that I'm pregnant, but the shock that I am.

I don't answer. I just stand there naked and shaking wondering how I get myself out of this lie.

Flint doesn't act as slowly. While Johnny's attention is on my stomach, Flint is able to get to his side, grab Johnny's gun hand, and press the nuzzle of the shotgun into Johnny's ribs. "Drop the gun now!"

Johnny does as he's instructed while his eyes never leave my stomach. It isn't until now that I'm startled into feeling the cold freeze from the open door.

I slide Flint's flannel into place, drowning in the fabric as I reach down for Johnny's gun.

"Back up, Pearl," Flint commands. "Go to the back room and lock the door."

I know he's trying to protect me, but right now, I don't want to be protected. I want Johnny out of my life for good, and I want to be the one to make that happen. I want it to be my lips Johnny hears telling him to leave. I don't want him lingering, thinking he can be part of Faith's life, because he can't.

I look toward Flint, and I know he can see the wild in my eyes.

"Please," he begs. "Think of the baby."

I aim the gun toward Johnny as Flint holds him.

"What?" Johnny laughs. "You're going to shoot me now? Over what? Helping you get your dreams?"

"You stole my money, Johnny. My family's money. I—"

"You gave that money to me, Pearl. You took it out of the account, and you handed it to me, because you're a selfish bitch who wanted fame over everyth—"

Flint leans into Johnny's throat choking out his words. "I think you forgot she's holding a gun."

Johnny's words are strained, but he doesn't stop himself from talking. "She won't shoot me. She doesn't have the guts."

My hand shakes and my stomach turns as I aim the gun toward him. He's probably right. I don't have the guts. I don't even like swatting at mosquitos when they're sucking the blood straight out of me.

"She might not shoot you," a deep voice says from the door, "but I will."

My gaze draws up slowly. "Dad?" My father stands six and a half feet tall in the doorway with the shotgun he keeps hung over the front door of his own cabin. In twenty-two years on this planet, I don't think I've ever seen him take it down. I didn't even think the thing worked. He nods toward Flint and grips Johnny by the collar. Slowly he starts to walk Johnny out the door, his gun never leaving Johnny's back.

"What are you doing here? How did you know where I was?"

"Roxie called. She said you might be in trouble. I guess this asshole threatened her before leaving Winter-Fest for Flint's rental. Are you two okay?" My father looks toward Flint and I both, and for the first time he sees my pregnant belly rounding out in front of him. "Pearl... why didn't you tell me this was going on? I'd have helped you."

I let out a heavy sigh and stare up at the ceiling, holding back tears as I shrug. "You don't even know the half of it, Dad."

Flint rounds to my side and holds me against his chest in silence and warmth radiates throughout my body. I close my eyes to gather myself, but the tears keep falling.

"I'm not trying to raise some fucking baby," Johnny spouts. "I was trying to help Pearl. She said she wanted her designs to be on everyone in Hollywood. I was trying to make that happen."

"Does the baby belong to Johnny?" My father straightens as he asks, still holding the man I was dumb to trust in his grip.

I want to lie. I want to be as far away from Johnny as I can get, but what good will that do me? He'll probably sue for custody anyway then get some lawyer to say I'm insane to get full custody.

I wet my lips and open my mouth slowly. "He's—"

"I'm the father," Flint's voice rasps. "We've been hooking up for a while now." He looks toward my father. "I'm sorry we didn't come to you sooner, sir."

My heart stalls, warms, races, and drops all at once.

Did he really say that he's the father?

I know my dad can see straight through Flint, just like he saw through me, but Johnny can't.

Johnny's face turns beat red as he laughs. "You really are a whore. I was just saying it, but—"

My father grips him tighter. "That's enough out of you." He looks toward Flint and I as he says, "I'm going to take care of this guy. You two take care of each other. I'll catch up with you at Winter-Fest."

"*Winter-Fest?* You're still going? What about all of this?"

He looks toward Johnny and scoffs, shrugging his shoulders like he'll be no big deal to get rid of. "I'll be done with this in twenty minutes. I left your mother at the rodeo. Besides, everyone in town is asking where you are. They miss you and your shop."

I look down at the ground, switching my feet back and forth over one another. "I don't know what to tell them."

My dad sighs, holding tight to Johnny who's cursing and pulling from his hands with little effort. Turns out he's only tough when he's messing with women.

"Tell them you'll be open by the end of the week. You have a baby to provide for. You're going to need the income." My dad smiles and ducks as he leaves the cabin, dragging Johnny behind him.

I turn toward Flint and lean into his arms. "Why did you do that? You—"

His lips meet mine in a soft kiss. "I know we didn't talk about it much, but I meant what I said before we made love, Pearl. You're mine now. You, baby Faith, all of it. I'm not letting you go."

"What about the rodeo? You travel all over, and your ranch is in Whiskey Falls. I can't take you away from all that, Flint. You'll resent me and then what? You're stuck here, raising another man's baby while you dream of a life that you wish you had?"

"Don't say that ever again." His voice is deep and gritty.

"Say what?"

"That I'm raising another man's baby. That man didn't deserve you, and he doesn't deserve Faith. You're both mine. End of story." He kisses my forehead and sways me back and forth in his arms. "And for the record, I'm not going to miss long, lonely trips. And my animals, they can eat their dinner just as well here. Long as I have you, everything's going to be okay."

I suck in a deep breath and let it out slowly as Flint's words sink in.

"Should we head back down to Winter-Fest? I think I have a dance or two I'd like with you."

I stare up into his eyes, letting them warm me from the inside out. Flint is the kind of man who will defend me, protect me, love me, then fuck me like an animal. And afterward, he'll dance with me in the middle of a snow-covered field with our friends and family all around while he raises a baby he didn't have to raise. It's now that I see that money isn't everything. Hell, in reality, it's nothing. Because right now, in my arms, I have everything I've ever dreamed of and no amount of cash could ever replace him.

Epilogue

Flint

Two Weeks Later

Sweat beads from my hairline as Pearl digs her nails into my shoulders and sighs.

"I'm so full. Fuck me harder, Flint." She's panting as she speaks, digging her knees into the mattress further.

I grip her hips and let one hand search for the soft bounce of her tits as the other holds her expanded stomach.

"Fuck. Hold it there, princess."

"I can't," she whines, fisting into the sheets. "I'm going to come."

I should pull out, toy with her, drag the orgasm out, but her tight little pussy feels too good clamped down over my cock. I'm not sure how anyone plays like that, really. Once I'm inside of her, there's no stopping me.

"Come for me. Come all over my cock."

She whimpers as I thrust into her harder. Her breaths are ragged and her hair sweeps over her left shoulder and onto the mattress.

I grind harder, listening to her sounds as I lean forward, and suck a loving kiss onto her neck.

She reaches back and touches her clit, rubbing circles around the swollen knob as my own orgasm works its way down my spine. This is what I live for. These intimate moments alone with Pearl. Whether we're snuggled on the couch, doing dishes side by side, or fucking like animals, I need her next to me.

"Fuck, princess. You're going to have to come or I'm going to—"

A thunderclap of screams leaves her throat as she grinds backward into me. The motion sets me over the edge and within seconds, I'm coming hard, filling her up with my pleasure. I thrust for a second longer, but she twists around and latches her lips onto my cock, drinking out the last of me as she moans.

She sucks and groans, twisting her tongue around the head, then takes me as deeply into her throat as she can before twisting off and laying back on the bed.

I'm motionless as I watch her frame collapse. She's relaxed and still, her eyes shut as her smooth, silky legs run over one another in comfort.

"Come lay next to me," she groans. "You're too far away."

I lay beside her, admiring my wife. "That was... a perfect way to start this marriage," I say, noticing her breasts are leaking milk.

She leans up when the white juice drips down her swollen chest, but I don't let it linger. I bend in and lick up the liquid, circling her sensitive nipples with my tongue.

Her eyes close and a sigh releases as I growl into her neck.

"You taste good, princess."

She grins. "So do you. It's so nice to relax together. The past couple weeks have been insane."

"It should slow down now... until the baby comes. Then, there's Christmas and I still have the rodeo to tend to. Waylon was good enough giving me a few weeks off for the wedding and the move. I'm not sure he's going to be as cool with time around Christmas. There are so many tourists around that week. He sold out the grandstand."

Pearl rolls into me as her fingertips wander through the hair of my chest. "You don't need to worry about Faith and I. You've given up enough for us already. We can come visit you at the grandstand, and you'll only be gone for a few hours at a time."

I look toward Pearl and cup her face in my hand. "I didn't give anything up. You're what I want. Every time I leave this bed, I regret it." I rub my hand over her expanding stomach. "You're my everything."

Her face contorts, and she leans forward and moans. This time, it's not in pleasure. She's in pain. Slowly, her eyes drag up to mine. "I think my water broke."

"You're not due for another three weeks. How'd your water break?" I feel the bed beneath her as I speak. It's soaked. Adrenaline shoots through my system and a tingling starts in my chest. "We won't make it down the mountain right now. The plows haven't been through since the storm. I'm going to call Dr. Atlas and Alex Baxter to drive her up here. Maybe they can make it in time."

Pearl groans louder and rolls onto her side, practicing the breathing techniques we've been reading about in a book she borrowed from the library. "Faith is coming, Flint. Call my parents. I'll text Roxie and my sister." Another loud groan leaves her throat. This time, it's more labored, and she's bearing down. "Never mind. We need hot water and clean blankets. I'll text everyone if you can toss me your phone."

My chest tightens as I rush around the small cabin, heating water on the stove, and grabbing a few clean blankets from the linen closet. I'll tackle a guy to the ground with no problem, but delivering a baby, I don't even know where to start.

"They're on their way," she pants, spreading her legs apart as she groans out in pain, "but I don't think I'm going to last that long. My contractions are so close. You're going to need to deliver the baby, Flint."

"I'm not a delivery man. I'm just a guy who rides horses. I don't know what I'm doing."

"*Delivery man?*" She smiles between groans. "I hate to tell you, but you're gonna have to be, cause Faith is here."

Pearl grips the sheets beside her and bears down, pushing as naturally as she breathes. It's as though she's done this a thousand times. She hasn't, and I know that, but none of that shows. Nature takes over and I slide between her legs, watching as my daughter's head crowns. Time slows and though I'd been terrified a second before, that's all drifted away. All that's left is this moment that I'm desperate to savor.

"You're doing good, princess. Keep pushing."

Without thought, Pearl does what needs to be done. She pushes hard and steady, and soon Faith's head is out. Within seconds her shoulders follow and before I can take another breath, her small body is in my arms. She shakes, cries, and she's covered in a white film I wasn't expecting.

Pearl grabs one of the blankets from beside her. "Wrap her in this."

I do as I'm asked and hand the tiny bundle back to her mother, where she's immediately soothed, and I'm left staring in awe at the miracle that's just happened.

"Are you okay?" I run my hand over Pearl's forehead and wick away the sweat that's gathered.

She closes her eyes and sucks in a deep breath. "Yeah... I'm perfect."

"Yes, you are, princess." I kiss her head, then move to our baby girl, kissing her as well. "And so are you, angel."

The baby is still attached to the placenta and I'm sure there are a million things that I'm doing wrong, but for just a second, I memorize this moment. The way Pearl's smile curves up gently, her eyes softening as she looks at her daughter, Faith's stares back at Pearl, those tiny hands clenched closed, and her cries as they turn to soft coos.

"Knock, knock..." The door cracks open. "Can we come in?"

"It's my mom and dad," Pearl says. "Do you mind if they—"

"Of course not." I stand from the bed and peek down the hall toward the front room, waving her family to where we are. They aren't alone. Dr. Atlas is with them. So is Roxie and Pearl's sister Montana.

"We were hosting a charity event at Winter-Fest when we got your call. Your dad has that big truck so we figured we could grab Dr. Atlas and haul up here faster than she could. Roxie and Montana were nearby, and they wanted to come see the baby. I hope it's okay." Pearl's mother talks as she washes her hands in the bathroom sink. "My girl, are you okay?"

Pearl looks up at her mother as Dr. Atlas goes to work where I left off. I should pay attention in case this happens again, but I can't take my eyes off Faith and Pearl.

"I'm good, Mom. Flint's a top-notch delivery man," she laughs.

Her mom smiles but doesn't get our inside joke. "And he's brought you the most precious Christmas gift, sweetheart." She leans in and brushes her hand over the baby's head, as her father stands behind holding her mother close.

"Okay, I'm officially jealous," Roxie says, squeezing Pearl's hand. "This is storybook shit. I need it... now." She laughs. "I'm happy for you, girl. You deserve it. Every second of it."

"No luck down at the rodeo? We've got to find you a man before all those cowboys leave town!" Pearl moves the blanket down that's covering her and offers the baby to latch as she's talking.

She's a natural mother. Faith takes to her right away.

Roxie sighs. "I met a couple of guys that I like, but that Waylon guy was talking at tonight's show, and he said the rodeo is here to stay. He's done traveling. They signed a deal with the landowners to keep the show in town."

"What?"

"Yeah," Roxie continues. "That's good for you, right? That means you can keep doing what you love without all the traveling."

"That's great for me." My brows lift in surprise. "Fantastic, actually. Though, I don't know how many years I have left in me, anyway. Especially now that I have this little girl to wrangle." I tuck back in beside Pearl as she feeds the baby.

"We're all set here," Dr. Atlas says, taking off her gloves. "You're going to need to get to the office for an official check up of you and the baby on Monday, but everything looks good. You're lucky cowboy here was quick to act."

I don't need the praise. I'm only happy that everyone is healthy, but there's a part of me that wants her pregnant again already. I want my seed inside of her, expanding and growing us a houseful of children to love.

"Your father and I are going to run Dr. Atlas home. We'll be back in a bit. You three need time on your own, anyway." Her mom glances toward Montana and Roxie who are standing over Pearl, admiring the baby.

"Oh yeah," Roxie says. "You guys probably need time to yourselves. Which is fine. I have to internet stalk some Dustin guy I met at the rodeo. I can tell he's too old for me, but it looks like it's working out for you guys so maybe I'll give him a shot. He's a bit of a hard ass though." She shrugs. "I don't know. We'll see."

"He's a buddy of mine," I say. "You're right, he is a hard ass. I'm not sure you mess with him. He's got this anti-love, anti-Christmas, anti-happy thing going on."

Roxie grins and rolls her eyes. "Sounds like my type. I'll catch you guys later."

Montana kisses Pearl's head and squeezes her sister's hand. "I'll stop at the store and bring you back a few things. Text me a list."

"Thank you," Pearl says, squeezing my hand, "but we have everything we need right here."

Montana smiles and makes her way out the front door with her mother, but Pearl's dad hangs back pulling a set of keys from his pocket.

"I guess it's about time I give you these back."

"My hot pink pickup! People will finally see me coming again. Are you sure? I don't mind riding with Flint. His truck is big enough for the three of us."

Her father shakes his head. "I want you to have your truck, Pearl. I'm proud of the way you turned the shop around the last week. Your business plan was a nice touch. Besides, I'm not sure who else would want a hot pink Silverado."

She grins wide. It's obvious she appreciates her father's approval. "Thanks, Dad. Whatever happened with Johnny? He's not coming back, right?"

"Oh, he's not coming back, sweetheart. You three focus on your family and trust that your father took care of things."

"How do you know he's not coming back?"

Her father kisses her head and runs his hand over Faith's hair before looking toward Pearl. "I know."

Pearl glances toward me as her father leaves the cabin. "What the hell was that? How does he *know*?"

I suck in a deep breath and hold her in my arms. "I gotta tell you, whatever he did, I don't blame him. Seeing that little girl come into the world... I know I'd do anything to keep her safe."

Her breath is soft as she relaxes her shoulders. I'm sure she'll have a thousand more questions in months to come, but right now she's exhausted. "I love you, Flint."

"I love you too, princess." I kiss her head gently. "I love both of you... now and always."

"Now and always," she repeats, closing her eyes as she leans against my chest, baby Faith still in her arms, suckling on her breast.

This is what life is about. These small moments and quiet hours. It's not the bulls, roaring crowds, or dressing celebrities. It's holding your wife and newborn daughter in your arms and knowing that you hold the world. Don't get me wrong, I was raised on bulls, dirt, and stop watches. I know how to hold tight with one hand and let go with the other. I know when to break free and when to tighten my grip. But most of all, I know that if there's even a slight chance at finding something that makes you happy, it's worth the ride. Every. Single. Time.

Scrooge

Chapter One

Roxie

M usic thumps from the speakers in front of the field stage as a bluegrass band plays *Foggy Mountain*. The composition is a slower version of the normally fast rhythm song with banjos and fiddles. Usually, I love this song and I love the way the local band plays it, but right now, it's so loud that my blood vibrates in my veins. I seem to be the only one bothered by it, though. Everyone else in town is dancing and laughing. I should be more like them, fun and free of complicated emotions that only lead to headaches and drama. At least that's what I imagine as I stare at my sanity role model, Mrs. Robinson.

She's an older woman with long silver hair and pretty blue eyes. Her outfits range from 1960s skirt suits to 1970s hippy with flowy tops and big, chucky jewelry. Tonight, she's wearing a thin floral dress that peeks beneath her mod coat. Her life has been spent in Rugged Mountain and everyone knows everything about her like the local legend she is. Her home stands out as the last original house on the east side of Main, her sons always back to help keep it standing, and her loving husband who can't seem to keep his hands off her after forty years, always by her side.

Her head leans back and her eyes close as he dips her on the dance floor, then leans down to whisper something in her ear.

My heart tightens. *Ugh*. That's what I want. A love where stolen whispers are still a thing after forty years.

I bite the inside of my cheek and make my way toward Ian, who's bent over the outdoor bar chatting up some girl I've never seen before. His blonde hair is twisted and messy and his t-shirt is stained from the mustard dip that didn't make his mouth. In his hand, the sixth or seventh bottle of IPA I've seen him with tonight. I'm getting the vibe that he will never be the Mr. Robinson I'm looking for, but he might be for the girl he's whispering to.

In my fantasy, the whispering with Mr. and Mrs. Robinson was romantic. Here, with Ian and the whore, I mean the flirty blonde at the bar, the whole thing looks tragic. *Are some women really this simple?* You whisper one thing in their ears and they're all giddy?

"Roxie," he says as his voice rises and falls while he looks toward me with bleary, bloodshot eyes. "You're here. I was just talking to my new friend, Angela." He looks toward the blonde with big tits spilling from her dress. "Angela, this is Roxie. Roxie, Angela."

I give the woman my most polite nod, but she seems oblivious to the situation at hand, and smiles wide back at me, showing off perfectly white teeth.

God, why am I even standing here?

I turn away from the bar and head back toward Main Street. This is the smallest town in the universe, so I'm not sure how I'm going to get home, but walking up the mountain would be a better option at this point.

"Roxie, wait!" Ian's voice slurs behind me. "We still haven't done the mistletoe dance thing. That's why we came."

I freeze and turn back slowly, trying not to let the evil bitch brewing inside of me out around all these people. News travels way too fast in a small town like this. One blow up and the whole town will be talking about me. Last year, my friend Lilly had a breakdown over some guy who screwed her over and somehow, she ended up being the crazy one that everyone talked about. It was years before people stopped *'blessing her heart'* wherever she went. And trust me, while in most places *'bless your heart'* is a term of endearment, here it's just a nice way to say how crazy and dumb you are.

"I think we're good here, Ian."

"What? No. My mom says you're perfect for me. If you're worried about Angela, that wasn't anything. If you can't tell, I'm drunk."

His mom says he's perfect for me? Who the hell did my brother set me up with?

"Oh, you're not hiding it. Trust me." I shake my head and turn back toward the dirt path that leads from the field toward the street. "I'll catch my own ride home. Have a good night." Fog leaves my lips as I let out a sigh of relief, hoping I can move on from this nightmare, but he grabs my shoulder and turns me back toward him.

Great, he's an aggressive drunk. If I'd seen this side of him two dates ago, I'd have never come tonight. But up until now, he's been oddly decent with his stories of teaching kids in Hong Kong how to speak English and earning a lacrosse scholarship to a prestigious school. I wonder which was a lie and which was the truth. I can find out later when I'm grilling my brother over this set up that's clearly going to end in severe regret.

I stare down at Ian's hand clenched tight around my forearm. His eyes glass over like he has some kind of cowardly, alcohol infused power. My stomach turns.

"Come back to the dance." His voice is low and steady, as though he's using all his focus for this moment.

I flinch away, but his grip only grows tighter. "Ian! You're hurting me. Let go!"

The fiddles play on in the background and from where we stand in the shadows of the buildings behind us, it's dark. I've really only been out with him a few times. The first time was dinner at a diner just around the corner. It was nothing spectacular, but I've been lonely, and he knew my brother, so I figured why not give him a second chance? The second time we went hiking with a guide named Violet. She took us up the side of the mountain toward the river and we had a great afternoon floating leaves over the rocks and talking. That's when he told me about his scholarship and work abroad. He also mentioned that he wanted to be a teacher, and I thought that was an admirable profession. Staring at him now through the darkness, I'm not sure he'd be an admirable anything.

"Let go!" I shout the words again, hoping this time he loosens his grip, but it only makes him tighten.

I know I could scream for help, but I doubt anyone would hear me over all this noise. I guess there's a possibility that the guys working the popcorn stand would hear. They're only fifty feet away, but who knows what drunken Ian will do when I draw attention this way? My mom has sent me too many articles about out-of-control college guys that my imagination goes wild and soon I'm picturing my own body floating down the river like the leaves we'd been racing last weekend.

Without thinking, I move closer toward him and lift my knee with force.

Ian doubles over in pain, wincing as he falls to the ground like the spineless ass he is. I don't stay to find out how his story ends.

I turn the corner onto Main and jog down the street, losing myself in the small crowd gathered by the display windows of the bakery and market. The owners have set up vintage lights and Christmas trees that everyone from town comes down to see this time of year. Usually, I'd be right there with them, but right now, I want my bed, a cup of hot chocolate, and some sappy book that's going to release so much dopamine that I pass out in a puddle of my own tears.

First, though, I'll take the long two-mile uphill hike home... in the dark. At least it's not too cold tonight. I'd say it's around fifty, which for December in the mountains is like summer anywhere else.

I gaze upward, noticing how clear the night is tonight. It's so clear that every little star shines and sparkles brightly, giving me a little light to work with as I cross Main Street and head up onto the mountain. I guess that won't last long as I head through the pines, but it's nice while it lasts. I could call someone, but I'm embarrassed that another date didn't work out. This is the third guy I've tried dating this year. They're all douchebags... every single one. Tommy was too quiet, and he had this collection of puppets that he was really obsessed with. Eric, on the other hand, didn't shut up. He was easily the loudest guy in the room wherever we went, but I'm not sure he ever said anything real. In the month that we were together, I don't even know if he told me what he was majoring in. Then there's Ian, and well, that's not going to work either... *for obvious reasons.*

Maybe this is the part where I should try out for one of those dating shows. I could use a professional approach to relationships. I'm surprised more people don't. I mean, you're making a lifelong commitment to someone and instead of running numbers and calculating negatives and positives, we gauge the whole decision on feelings.

I think it's all a broken system.

My arm throbs as I walk up the mountain. At the time, I didn't think he'd grabbed me so hard, but this might leave a bruise. I pull my jacket off and tie it around my waist, letting the cool air soothe the sting as I suck a shaky breath of fried food and pine. The corn dogs and funnel cake travel for miles up here, which isn't a bad thing. It reminds me of every Christmas I've ever had on this mountain. Things were so much easier when the only thing I had to worry about was getting to Winter-Fest for the ice-skating contest instead of babysitting asshole college dates while they drunkenly hit on some out-of-towner.

Maybe I don't need a dating show as much as I need a sabbatical from men.

The rumbling of a truck sneaks up behind me and my blood stills. I roll my stiff neck in circles and duck into the woods, stepping into a mossy patch that sinks my cute black flats into the earth.

Damn it! Whoever this is owes me a new pair of shoes. These are never going to dry right. My eyes squint through the dark, trying to see who's pulled over, but everything looks like shadows from between the trees.

What the hell? The truck door slams and a man hops out. A man too big to be Ian.

Did someone follow me up here? What was I thinking walking around alone at night? My mother warned me of things like this. I'm such an idiot!

I squeeze my eyes shut and duck behind a massive pine, holding my breath as the large man crunches over leaves in the forest toward me.

All I wanted was to be dipped on the dance floor. Now, I have a feeling my float down the river is inevitable.

Chapter Two

Dustin

This weekend has been the worst. *Something* has gone wrong every night. A bull jumped the fence and went running through the crowd Friday. Thankfully, he didn't injure anyone, but he scared the hell out of about three hundred people. Saturday night, we had a fight break out at the pie stand over who stole whose recipe, and tonight I see some asshole grabbing a girl outside the fairgrounds.

I'm ready for a break. A long trail ride on my horse, just me, the trees, and the crunch of the earth beneath Comet's feet. Tomorrow morning, I should have time if this girl comes out of the woods without any drama. Though, if I know women, I doubt it will be that easy.

"Miss?" I holler into the forest, hoping she'll answer without a scene. But nothing comes back. Not a sound. Not even a squirrel running through the leaves, or a raccoon chattering.

"Miss?" I holler again, making my way down the ravine and into the woods.

I can't figure why anyone in their right mind would think walking up a mountain road at ten p.m. was a good idea, but she's probably been drinking. Most of these young kids are. They come down from The Springs for winter break and they cause all kinds of trouble in town. The locals let it roll right off their back, but I've been hired to watch the Winter-Fest grounds in the evenings after the rodeo and I don't have the same blasé attitude.

Truthfully, all of this kind of boils down to babysitting adults. *Look at me, I'm some irresponsible toddler who will do something potentially life threatening, but I'm afraid to talk to a stranger who's trying to help me.*

"Miss?" I holler again, this time with more frustration. "I'm here to keep you from getting hurt. You can't be wandering around in the dark back here. You'll freeze to death or get eaten by a bear."

Still nothing. Not a peep.

I shine my flashlight through the trees and crunch over fallen leaves, twisting back and forth as quietly as possible. She can't have gone far. She only had a two-minute lead on me.

"I have no idea what you think is going to happen to you if you answer. I'm not going to slap you and take your Christmas away like some Scrooge. I'm just a guy who's being paid to keep people from dying at Winter-Fest."

I pause to listen for movement again. Nothing. Maybe I need to rethink my strategy. Being direct isn't working, so let's try soft and cute. "I'm just so worried that if something happened to you, I'd never be okay again. Please come out so I don't have to live with your death on my conscience for the rest of my life."

A tree branch snaps behind me. Thankfully, *something* worked.

I spin back and the light follows, illuminating a thick waisted woman with long dark hair that tumbles down her shoulders. She's wearing a black dress with a red jacket, and her shoes look like they're for dancing, not hikes. That said, she's gorgeous. So much so that even the faintest glance at her has my brain wavy like an old tube TV that needs a smack to go straight again.

"I don't need help getting home." She turns further into the woods and walks away from me.

"Nope..." I follow behind her. "You're going home... on the road. Get in the truck. You're not going to wander through the woods all night long. You'll get lost or—"

"Get eaten?" She turns back, and scowls as dark locks frame her sweet, freckled face. "I heard."

"I'm glad you're listening because I've had a long weekend and I'm ready to get to some down time."

She turns back toward me, her arms crossed in front of her chest. "Then go. I don't need help just because I'm a woman."

I get it. I wouldn't take a random ride from some guy showing up in the woods with a body like that either. I really should have workshopped this a little more instead of simply taking off after her.

"I saw what happened back there at the festival. I was hired as security. I'm supposed to watch everything that happens. I saw you run off, and I worried you might be drinking."

"Do I look like I've been drinking?" Her arms wave up into the air and I see a dark bruise on her pale arm.

"Did that asshole do that to you?"

She rolls her dark brown eyes and brushes her hand back through her hair. "I'm over boys."

"You should be over that one, that's for sure. What's his name? Next time I see him, I'll make sure and kick his ass." Smooth one, Casanova. Convince a young lady in the woods who's afraid you're violent to come with you... with promises of future violence.

"It doesn't matter. It's over," she says, buttoning her coat up tighter. "You might be right about that ride, though. I thought it was going to be warm tonight."

"The overnight low is always colder. I'm glad you're coming to your senses. You should text someone and let them know I'm giving you a ride up the mountain."

She beams a coy smile toward me. "You've done this before... given rides to broken women on the side of the road?"

"Not unless you count my memaw who likes to take long walks to nowhere. We've spent a lot of nights out looking for her. That's up in Whiskey Falls, though. But I guess now that this rodeo is going to be a permanent draw here, I'm going to be moving up this way. The timing is all up to my boss, Waylon, but I'm thinking it'll be just after the new year."

She purses her pretty pink lips. "Is that a good thing? I'm not sure I like all this ruckus. I liked it when the town was quiet and peaceful, and the Christmas windows were just for me."

"Hell, I remember a time when this place was literally a two-shop town. Rugged Mountain Ink and the bar. You had to go into The Springs if you wanted groceries. The crowds will calm down after the holidays. Tourism is always good for the area, but I agree with you. I like the quiet too."

She grips hold of a sturdy branch and digs the toe of one shoe into the hillside, pulling herself up the ravine as she holds the back of her dress down. It's a smooth, steady move that tells me she's a born and true country girl.

"Are you sure you don't mind taking me? I'm kind of out of the way."

I nod my head, opening the truck door as her cool skin brushes against mine. "Not at all. Wherever it is, we can manage. I've got my buddy Carlos covering for me, anyway. Come on."

Her shoulders relax as she pulls her seatbelt into place and a sense of contentment washes over me, knowing that at least she'll be home safe. Though something tells me she'd have found her way home in the woods tonight regardless.

"So, by your talk of the Christmas windows, I'm assuming you've lived up here your whole life?"

"I was born in the same cabin I was raised in, so I like to think I'm pure mountain woman." She laughs. "Well, minus the coon-skin cap. What about you? Were you always from Whiskey Falls?"

I nod and glance toward her, noting her flushed cheeks. I think she got colder than she'd thought. "Same deal for me. Born and raised in Whiskey Falls." I pull a blanket from the back seat of the truck while I keep my eyes steady on the road, then hand it toward her and crank up the heat. "I've spent the last few years traveling with the rodeo, though. It's nice to have traveled the country, but I'll be happy when we have a residence here in Rugged Mountain. The good thing about it is that it's only a thirty-minute drive up home. I can still see family often."

"I saw you at the rodeo a few times. I'm surprised they have you doing security. Seems like a waste of talent."

I laugh. "I appreciate the break, to be honest. Riding was easy when I was young. These days, it gets harder and harder."

She glances toward me with the blanket tucked up to her neck. "It didn't look like you were having trouble."

"I'll take the compliment." I clear my throat and wonder when she'd have seen me ride. I must have been on my game that night... *thankfully*. Lately, I've been getting thrown in less than two seconds, which is a disgrace for as long as I've ridden. But that's what age does... it changes a man. Some for the better, some for the worst. I stare out the front window, watching as the dark night splays out in front of us. The sky is clouding, and I wonder if a storm is rolling in.

"You should." She glances at me. "You must ride all the time to be that good."

"When we were kids, we'd lay behind the mountain ridge and sneak up on the wild horses. Took me years to mount one. I was fourteen when I finally did, held on for dear life."

"So that's where you learned? Wild horses?"

"I broke my collarbone and my shin that summer, but the second I was healed, I was back out there again." I laugh. "At my mother's disdain. She'd have chained my brother and I to the bed if she could've, but we didn't let her. We just smartened up and wore our dad's motorcycle helmets while we were trying to ride. What about you? What do you do aside from wandering through the woods at night?"

I glance toward her as she tucks a strand of hair behind her ear, the faint scent of flowers in the air. She's so pretty.

"Nothing as exciting as riding wild horses. I work at the bakery on Main during the week and I spend weekends helping out at the library." She smirks. "When I'm not going on horrible dates."

"Yeah, I saw that bruise on your arm. Is that what that asshole did to you?"

Her mouth twists. "Something like that."

My teeth grind against one another, my chest tightens, and my blood heats. Who the hell would ever hurt this woman? "I was hoping I was seeing things wrong."

She shakes her head. "It's over and I think it's safe to say there will be no more dates."

As she talks, I run the numbers on finding this guy and giving him a taste of his own medicine, but then she says something that stops me in my tracks.

"Tonight sucked, but now I'm in a truck with a wild horse-riding cowboy. So... I think I'll call it a win."

I want to hold it back, but a grin spreads across my face like some shit-eating animal that doesn't know what's good for him. She's being polite, not hitting on you, cowboy. I tell myself the truth as I know it, but there's a part of me that hopes it's more. *A sick part.* The sick part that's okay with a woman in her early twenties hitting on me.

"This is me," she says, pointing toward a small cabin tucked under the pine trees. With the snowman earrings she's wearing, I was expecting to pull up to a gingerbread house, but the place is rather plain. The house itself is a shoebox size log cabin with dark moss growing between the logs. On the front porch sits a single rocking chair and what looks to be a wreath that hasn't made it to the door yet.

"Pathetic, isn't it?" She stares ahead at her place.

"No. It's just not what I was expecting for you. You seem so... cheery."

"Oh. Well... I am, but this is my first year in my own place and I haven't had the money to fix it up much."

I nod slowly, resisting the urge to spend the night tacking Christmas lights to her roof. I can't imagine the smile she'd have from seeing colored lights strung just right.

Fuck me. I shake my head and hop from the parked truck to open her door. This is just a ride home. I can't be thinking about her Christmas lights or her fucking smile.

Her cheeks turn pink as her tiny hand is swallowed in mine. "Thank you. I'm not sure anyone's ever opened a door for me before. I'd invite you in but—"

"Oh, I've got to get back to the grandstand anyway. I just wanted to make sure you had everything you needed for the night." It's a lie. I'd go in if she asked me. I'd go in and overstay my welcome. I'd go in and fix that crooked front step, hang her lights, and chop some wood... among other things.

Her cheeks are pink again when she looks up at me. "Well, thank you... for the ride and the conversation. I really appreciate it. I think you're right, I'd have probably frozen out there." She tips up onto her toes and wraps her arms around my chest, pressing her small, curved body against my frame. Her breasts sit against me as her gaze draws to mine. I shouldn't notice such a small detail, but I do.

She's beautiful.

My hands cup her cheeks, and I lose my fingertips in her silky hair. I pull her in tighter, like I own her, like she's mine. Except she's not... and I'm only supposed to be dropping her off.

What the hell is happening?

My gaze meets hers and my hand moves over her back slowly, as I will my cock to stay tucked away. I tell myself this is only a hug. A thankful gesture from a kind woman who was in need, but I'm not sure my brain listens and suddenly, I don't want to let go.

Chapter Three

Roxie

I t's been four days and one hour since I've seen Dustin, but he's been the only thing on my mind. Yesterday at the bakery, I wrote *Happy Birthday Dustin* on a birthday cake meant for an eight-year-old named Nicole. Who knows what I'll write today? Maybe I'll wish him happy retirement or congratulate him on graduating high school.

I'm just glad I fixed it before anyone saw. I'm sure the shop owner, Josie, would've laughed it off, but still, it would've been embarrassing.

If I could help it, I would. Mostly because it makes zero sense to fawn over a man I can't have. He's grown for one. Like, grown, grown. Grown man grown. Forty-year-old plus kind of grown. Second, he hasn't contacted me since I last saw him. Obviously, he's not having the same feelings for me. It was a ride home and a hug that I clearly read too much into.

I pull on a pair of jeans and a Christmas sweater with a 3-D snowman from the back of my closet. I have half a dozen to choose from, but the snowman is calling to me today. Maybe it's the giant carrot standing at attention.

God, I need to get my mind out of the gutter and back on track but everything I look at reminds me of Dustin's big shoulders, his wide, barrel chest, his gritty deep voice, or the way he held me close against him and for a few minutes, I felt safe. Safe from everything around me. Safe from the world.

I close my eyes for a second and try to remember the way he smells. Cedar, pine, and a natural musk that I can't identify. Trust me, I've been trying every night when I lay in bed and fantasize about him taking me over.

Ugh. My clit throbs and my heart swells at the thought of his hands all over me. It's probably a good thing that I promised the girls at the library I'd help out all day. I need a distraction until this feeling dissipates, and spending all day Saturday watching sappy Christmas movies isn't going to do me much good. I have enough fantasies stored up to last me a lifetime already. Another Hallmark movie and I'll be certifiable.

My phone rings as I walk toward the back door. It's Ian. He's called every day since that incident at Winter-Fest. The first call was an apology, and though I hate him and think he's a poor excuse for a human, I appreciated the thought. The second, third, and fourth call, though, I'm not sure what to think of that. He hasn't left a message and I have no idea what he could possibly need. He has to know there's nothing between us now, right?

"Hello?" I immediately regret answering the second he speaks.

"You picked up. I was starting to think you hated me."

Oh, I do hate you.

"Is something wrong? You've called every day this week."

"No. I was hoping we could work things out. I know the other night was weird, but that's who I am. I had too much to drink, and I did things I regret. I'm sorry, Roxie. You didn't deserve that."

Four days ago, I'd have probably taken his red flags like a dozen roses. Happy to be handed anything, and appreciative that he was putting in the effort to apologize, like that was meaningful. But now, having spent time with Dustin, I can't help but see the flaws in not only Ian's actions, but also his apology. Now, I know what it's like to have a good man touch me and I can't forget it.

My eyes clench shut with the thought. I'm such an idiot. It doesn't matter what it felt like with Dustin. He's not interested, and he's way too old for me.

"I appreciate your call, but I've got to get to work."

"Library or bakery today?" He's talking to me like I've forgiven him and we're moving on.

"I better go." I hang up the phone and grab my keys off the hook beside the door, locking up behind me before climbing into my jeep.

Ian is crazy if he thinks I would settle for someone like him after meeting Dustin. Sure, the chances of Dustin and I having a life together are slim to none, but meeting him was like finding a long-lost friend. It's like I've known him forever. Like we've spent a lifetime before now together and we've just found each other again.

I turn over the engine to the jeep and lean my head against the wheel, trying to summon the reality I know I'm missing.

The truth is, Dustin hasn't tried contacting me in four days. That's not what someone does when they're into you, and I need to face it.

****

The library is busy with its normal Saturday in December activities. Lilly is reading *The Christmas Mouse* to a group of kids in the back, while Janie is stacking books into a Christmas tree in the lobby. We work together every Saturday and they've become my closest friends.

"You need help?" I grab a book off the rack she's working with and stack it on top of the circle she's started.

"Sure, if you're going to spill all the tea you've been holding in."

My forehead crinkles. "What?"

Janie is a natural blonde with a curvy waist and bright blue eyes. She's beautiful without trying. I've always been envious of that. Also, she's like the sweetest person in the universe. This year, she took every tag off the tree to buy gifts for children in need. She didn't even tell anyone she was doing it. When the tags disappeared, Lilly and I checked the security cameras, and saw she'd brought gifts in herself.

"What do you mean, *what?*" She laughs. "You've been sulking around, and you've been getting lost in your head. So... who is he?"

"What? No. How do you want these stacked... left to right?"

She laughs and grabs another hardcover book off the rolling rack beside her. "Oh god, you've got it bad. I'm jealous! I need details!"

I haven't talked about Dustin to anyone, and I think I like it better that way. Right now, he's a fantasy in my head. Anything goes. The second he's free floating in the universe, I'll be subject to the opinions of others, which I'm sure will crash and burn every dream that I'm having.

"Come on!" she presses. "I told you all about that terrible date I went on with Tyler Michaels, so don't hold out on me."

"I hardly think calling his mother by the wrong name is equal to what I'm about to tell you."

Her lips curl upward in a sinister grin, as though she's greedy for more. "You're teasing me now. I need to know. And for the record," she swings her hip, "calling a woman Hairy, when her name is Mary, is incredibly embarrassing."

I can't help but laugh. "Okay, that does sound kind of funny, but Tyler was dumb for breaking up with you over it. See... that's why older men are better."

She pauses and her jaw drops. "*Older* men?"

My face crinkles. "Did I say that out loud?"

"Yeah, really loud. So loud I'm sure all those kids in the back room just heard what a daddy's girl you are."

"Gross, stop! It's not like that. We only met once. Besides, none of this talk matters. He doesn't like me back."

"What happened in that *one* time you met?"

"Nothing. We just talked, and that was it."

Her voice drops. "That was it?"

"That was it." I grab another book for the pile. "Well, I mean... I think we kind of connected, but I don't know."

"Connected how?"

"He looked at me really intently and there was this exchange. I don't know... it was nothing."

She bites her bottom lip and nods slowly. "Looked at you, *how*?"

I can't help but grin. "You're a toddler, stop!"

She shrugs and grins again. "I don't think I can! Your story is so much better than *The Christmas Mouse!* Tell me all about what a daddy's girl you are! I need a little jolt this morning."

I shake my head and laugh. "Nothing happened. He doesn't like me. I'm a dreamer, and I need to forget him."

"Yeah," she laughs. "Looks like you're doing a great job at that."

Kids flood from the back room quietly, all of them tip toeing with the imaginary marshmallow shoes that Lilly puts on them before they leave the room. They smell like sugar cookies with vanilla icing, and their eyes are wild with pent up energy. I'm thankful for the interruption. I've barely said three words to Janie, but I'm already regretting the conversation.

"You're not getting off that easy." She sets the final book in the center of the stack and grabs the Christmas lights off the shelf beside her, wrapping them around carefully. "You owe me so many details."

"I'm not sure I owe you any—"

"Roxie?" The deep, graveled voice catches me off guard as my gaze draws upward, my heart stalling. I know who it is. I've been memorizing his voice since Saturday night.

"Dustin? What are you doing here?" He's even bigger in the light of day, with broad shoulders, thick forearms, and tattoos inked down his arms and onto his hands. His beard is dark, and he's wearing a black t-shirt with a red and black flannel thrown over top, his sleeves rolled to his elbows.

"I thought I'd come by and see if you had any books on..." He's paused as though he didn't think his story through before he walked in.

Did he come here to see me?

"I've got some. See, I've been trying to..." He looks down at his dusty boots, then up at me again. "Hell, I don't well remember what I came in for now."

My heart swells and for a second, I feel dizzy.

I think he did come in to see me.

His big hand lifts to his head, and he brushes his hair back with a sigh. "I'm starting to forget things now. That's not a good sign. This gray hair is starting to prove me right."

I can't help but smile. "I think the gray is nice."

God, did I really just say that?

I haven't taken my eyes off the giant in front of me, but I can feel Janie's stare like lasers on my skin.

"This is my friend, Janie," I say, nodding toward her.

She reaches out her hand then looks toward me with wide eyes and a slight grin before mouthing, *oh my god.*

I'm not sure if Dustin has seen her obvious gesture, but I turn him away from her and toward the library before she gets another chance at embarrassing herself.

"How's your arm?" Dustin asks. "I've been worried about you, but I thought it'd be creepy to show up at your house, and I didn't know your number."

"Yeah, you're right. Showing up at my place of work is much less creepy." I laugh, hoping he gets my joke, which judging by the smile, he does.

"My arm is good. A little sore, but the bruising has gone down."

"Good," he says. "I haven't seen that asshole around, but if I do, I'll make sure he doesn't get away with what he did to you."

"That's really not necessary. It's over. This will heal."

His thick brows crinkle together. "You're letting him off too easy. He has to learn his lesson."

I laugh. "Well, the way I figure it, the universe will straighten him out." I clear my throat. "You never did say why you came in today. Is there a book you're looking for, or..."

He runs his large palm over his beard and looks toward me with light blue eyes. "Yeah, I... I came to ask you a favor?"

A favor? My mind races with thoughts as it tries to piece together what kind of favor he could be looking for. Maybe it's a date. Maybe he wants me on my knees for him. *Spoiler alert, that's the kind of favor I can get behind.*

Get it together, girl. It's probably something simple like he needs help at the grand-stand.

"Sure." I swallow hard, a little nervous for what he's going to say next. "What kind of favor?"

He looks down at the ground, then draws his gaze up slowly, before crossing his giant arms over his chest.

My heart flops and my pulse quickens. Something tells me his favor isn't going to be the fantasy I'm looking for.

Chapter Four

Dustin

I've spent four days thinking about Roxie. The way her hair falls on her shoulder, the way she smiles with her eyes, the way she felt pressed up against my chest—it's all perfect. But there's more, more to her than that. It's the easy conversation, her sweet responses, and the tenacity she had to get away from that asshole at the rodeo. I'd be a fool to ignore what we have. Then again, I'd be a fool to indulge. She's young. Much younger than me and according to my brother, *'if I had a brain in my head, I'd best use it to stay away from her.'*

My relationship history isn't a very extensive one, but according to my brother, the choices I've made are all wrong. I have to say, he might be right about that thus far.

That didn't stop the endless cycle of thoughts this week, though. God, I fantasized about her so many times. I imagined my hands on her hips again, my lips on hers, her body naked against me as I thrust inside her and claim her for myself.

"Is everything okay?" Roxie's face has gone pale, and she's crossed her arms over her chest, giving prominence to the carrot nose on her sweater.

I nod. "Everything's fine. I just..."

A nervous smile tries making its way on Roxie's face, but it's dampened out by the resting worry on mine. Truthfully, I'm not sure why I'm here. I didn't get to the excuse part of the visit. I convinced myself that showing up to the library on Saturday was a perfectly normal thing to do. Considering this is the first time I've set foot in this place, I see now, it's probably not.

She rolls up her sleeves and stares toward me with big doe eyes that need answers. The fucking bruise is still there and in the light of day I can see every finger mark that asshole left on her.

I swallow down the lump growing in my throat as I try to find a reasonable response to her question. "I was hoping to get a pie."

She nods with wrinkled brows. "A pie?"

"Yeah, something with apples with a tangy after taste."

"What about apple-cranberry? We sell a lot of those this time of year." She's answering my question, but I can see she's confused as to why I'd come to the library to ask her about a pie.

"Yeah. I can bake you up a fresh one tomorrow morning. What time do you need it by?"

"That's great." My words are quick and shallow. I'm such a fucking ass for coming all the way here and not telling her how I feel.

"What time works for you?"

Her brows crinkle together. "Well, I go in at four in the morning and it'll take a little time to put together, but anything after seven should work."

"I'll stop by around seven then." I swallow down another lump in my throat. What the hell is happening to me? I've gone from a rough and tumble man to chicken shit in less than five days.

She waves her hand back through her silky hair and that bruise makes an appearance again. "Let me see that thing."

I reach out for her arm with the intent of inspecting the bruising, but as she lowers her arm into my hand, I realize it's more than that. I wanted to touch her. Her soft skin in my rough hand is a place she doesn't belong, but I can't stop myself.

"I think it's getting better," she says, looking up at me with the sweetest gaze.

I hold her small arm in my hand and study the marks the asshole has left behind. Her skin is cool to the touch, and she's peppered in tiny goosebumps, but the swelling has gone down and aside from the discoloration, she's healing well.

I hold on to her longer, not wanting to let go. "You're never seeing him again, right?"

Her face crinkles. "Seriously? No. I'm done with boys." Her gaze lifts to mine and my stomach sinks.

Is she saying what I think she is? I should act on it. I should tell her why I really came here. I should be the fucking man she wants. Instead, my throat closes, my chest tightens, and words fail to form.

Thankfully, Janie interrupts. "Sorry to bother you, Roxie, but I have to take another group of kids to the back and Lilly has craft duty. I need you to check some people out." Her face is crinkled like she really doesn't want to interfere.

Roxie looks toward her and nods. "No problem. I'm on my way." She glances back toward me and smiles, bright and happy like the morning fucking sun. "I'll see you tomorrow morning then. Do you need anything else?"

Seeing her face again should be enough. It's all I've been thinking about for days, but there's a greedy part of me that wants more of her. An archaic gene that's itching at my palms to pull her close and make her mine... now!

Another second can't go by. I need her right here in this library on top of these books.

"Nothing else," I say, lying straight through my teeth.

She bites her bottom lip, and that smile happens again. The sweet one that's cute and eager to please. "I'll see you tomorrow."

I nod and head out the front door, my head spinning with a high I've never felt before. Maybe age is just a number after all.

Chapter Five

Roxie

I've never spent more time on an apple pie than I have this morning. I carefully measured each scoop of sugar, candied the cranberries twice, sliced the apples as finely and evenly as I could, and made sure the crust was baked to perfect crispness. I even made little pie crust cookies for the top in the shape of snowflakes. This year, I think there was a tie for best apple pie at the Winter-Fest bake-off. Not to be narcissistic, but I'd have broken that tie with this pastry.

I'm not sure why I've gone to the trouble. Our meeting yesterday confirmed that he is absolutely not interested in anything about me... and that's okay. He's too old for me, anyway. I can't even imagine what everyone in town would say if they saw me with him. I mean, I told Janie, and she about lost her mind with the drama of it all. Then again, I'm not sure anything could stop all the fantasies I've been having about him.

Is it wrong to imagine his giant body pressed against me with his hand on my throat while he whispers in my ear in that graveled voice?

The bell on the bake shop rings and I'm startled from my drooling. It's only six a.m. and technically we're not even open yet, but I left the front door unlocked knowing Dustin would be stopping by before I flip the open sign. Maybe he's here early to profess his undying love to me.

A girl can dream.

But the second I step into the front room, my stomach turns, and all those dreams fizzle and burn. "What are you doing here?"

"I had to see you. I feel so bad for what happened the other night. I just—"

"You just what? How many times do I have to tell you no?"

He steps closer toward me, and I already smell the alcohol on his breath. He looks like he's been out all night, probably partying on some back road with a bunch of friends. "Come on, forgive me..." His voice is slurred. "I know you want to."

"I'm going to ask you nicely, one last time. Then—"

"Then what? You're here alone." He moves closer. "No one else is around."

I know we only dated a few times, and I know the other night went south really fast, but I still wouldn't have pegged Ian for the kind of guy that would show up at the shop and threaten me, but here we are and truthfully, I'm not sure what I can do about it. He's not muscular, but he's not small either. If he wanted to overpower me, I think he could.

I back into the kitchen and head toward the rear door, but he's on top of me before I get to the sink and soon I'm backed up against the wall with both hands holding firm to each of my arms.

"I told you not to run. I just have a question for you..."

"No more questions!" I pull my knee up and get ready to nail him again, but he's onto me this time. He pushes me with all his strength, sending me flying into the counter behind, spilling my award-winning Christmas pie all over me.

For a long minute, I sit in the crumbled apple mess, and wonder what's next. I seem to have shocked Ian with my fall. Though, not enough for him to actually care. He's just standing over me with bloodshot eyes contemplating what he should do next.

I sigh and dig my phone out of my back pocket as I stand from the scattered pie pieces. "Just leave."

He stares toward me blankly as though nothing is computing the way it should.

"Now!" I shout. "I'm calling the police!"

Without more thought, he scurries out the back door like a rat caught in water.

Note to self: Never listen to your brother for dating advice, ever again.

Phone in hand, I text Josie before calling the police. She's owned the bakery for years and though she's not set to come in for another two hours, I think she'd like a call before I reach out for the cops. Besides, I'm not in any immediate danger. Ian is gone and I don't think he'll be dumb enough to circle back today.

As I'm sending the text, the bell on the front door rings again and my stomach tightens. *Okay, I was wrong. He would come back again. Who knows what he's planning this time.*

Scanning the kitchen for a weapon, I grab a knife from the back counter, and stalk to the front of the store with shaking hands. "Get the fuck out!"

"Woah." Dustin holds up both his hands. "What's going on?"

I set the knife down and relax my shoulders, letting out a heavy breath like finally I'm safe. "I'm so sorry. I'm all shook up. What are you doing here?"

Dustin rounds the corner and pulls me against his chest with purpose ignoring the pie smattered all over me. He holds me there until I feel the beat of his heart slow my own.

His massive hand runs over the back of my hair. "You're okay. What happened?"

I swallow hard, then stare up at him with teary eyes. "Your pie is ruined. I'm so sorry."

"It's okay." His voice is deep and gentle despite his massive exterior. "I just need to know you're okay."

"It was such a good pie. I used this nutmeg that came from Indonesia, and I candied the cranberries twice. Now, it's all over me... and you."

He backs away from me slightly and swipes a dollop of the filling from my chest before licking his finger, groaning when the sugar touches his lips. "You're not kidding. That's the best pie I've ever had." His massive finger goes back for another scoop, followed by a long groan.

I bite my lip hard and stare up at the massive giant in front of me. I'm not a small girl, but with him, I could be a doll. A soft, delicate, breakable doll that has to be touched carefully.

My clit throbs and my brain goes crazy with fantasies of him bending me over the bake-rack and taking me... *hard.* "I'm glad you like it." My gaze goes to his softly as my skin melts and every bit of fortitude I had left dies right there on the bakery floor. I don't care how old he is. I don't care that I have apple pie smeared all over my body. I don't care where we are, or what time it is, or how we got to this spot. I need him and I can't wait any longer.

"I don't like that you're here alone in the morning. You should keep these doors locked, baby girl."

A lump catches the air in my throat. "*Baby girl?*"

"Does that bother you?" His gaze is so intense with mine that my breath catches.

"No," escapes my mouth in a near whisper.

He makes a soft winded noise that's filled with both pleasure and pain as he stares toward me. "I'm about to lose control, Roxie."

"Lose it," I pant, desperate for his touch.

He backs me up against the brick interior wall of the bakery next to the vintage Santa clock that ticks back and forth with eight tiny reindeer. A hum from the clock buzzes against my ear as Dustin presses into me. His hand moves up my waist, over my chest and onto my shoulders, lighting me on fire as though he's Zeus with a bolt of lightning and I'm his willing adversary.

I've never been touched like this, not by anyone, and I don't want it to end. My eyes close and I lean my head against the wall, breathing heavy as he wanders my body. Our lips haven't touched yet, but I'm waiting for it like a beat about to drop. Any minute now, his lips will touch mine, and he'll groan into my throat and taste me with wild abandon. *Like he needs me. Like his whole life has led up to this moment.*

I run my hands over his firm body and through the back of his hair, taking in the heavy scent of cedar on his skin. He's not wearing a t-shirt today, only the flannel button down. Chest hair weaves its way through the peak at the top. I lean my face against him, sucking in the scent as his hands wander me. We're like animals, groaning and sighing, smelling and moaning until all at once our eyes meet and the world stops spinning.

What I'd thought was need before, is nothing compared to the aching urges currently thumping between my legs.

His shoulders rise and fall, as his eyes dial in like a wolf, and our lips move closer together. It's happening. His lips are going to touch mine.

The front bell rings. "Roxie?" Josie gasps. "What's going on?"

Embarrassment flushes my cheeks dark red as Dustin backs off me, running his hand down over his beard.

"Yeah, oh. Nothing. I..."

She glances toward Dustin, then toward me. Her own cheeks pink as though she can see what she's walked into. "I got your text, and I thought I should get over here. Are you..."

I slap my hand to my head. "I'm fine. Ian left a bit ago. This is Dustin. He's my... friend."

Dustin looks toward me with narrowed eyes. His voice rasps as he says, "Ian was here? Why didn't you tell me he was here?"

"We just sort of..."

"Did he hurt you?" Dustin glances down at the pie still stuck between us. "Did he do this to you?" His jaw is tight, and his fists are clenched.

"He didn't hurt me. He backed me into the table, and I fell trying to get away from him."

"But he threatened you? He tried to make himself a big man again?" Dustin pulls in a deep breath. "I'm going to find him."

"No." I grab his shirt. "You're going to get in trouble over something that doesn't matter."

He leans into my lips and finally the moment I've waited for happens. Slowly, softly, his rough kiss lands on my lips. He lingers for a moment but pulls away too soon. "You matter, and he's not going to do this again."

Josie rounds to my side in comfort as Dustin takes off out the front door. I know they're both trying to help, and Ian *could* use an ass kicking after what he just did. But truthfully, I don't care about any of that as much as I care about getting back into Dustin's arms.

"You should get washed up," Josie says, running her hand through her crimson red hair. "I'll clean up here, but what's with the big guy, and all the touching? Are you two dating? Does your mom know? He's quite a bit older than you, Roxie." Her tone is kind, but a little judgmental considering I think she and her husband share an age gap of their own.

"We're doing *something*," I rebut. "I'm not really talking about it until I figure out what."

She grins and reaches out for my hand, squeezing it quickly. "I'm here if you need anything. Okay?"

I appreciate her kindness and I'd love to stay and fill her in on all the details, but right now I need to go find Dustin before he does something stupid. If his boss, Waylon, finds out he's getting into fights in town, who knows what that could mean for his job.

As I head out of the bakery, I notice I have three missed calls, all from Janie with follow up texts.

Janie: What's going on? Lilly was driving by the tattoo shop and saw your man out front taking Ian down.

Janie: Hello?

Janie: Call me!

Janie: Okay, why does nothing good ever happen when I'm around?

Janie: You're literally on your phone all the time. Why are you ignoring me?

In a panic, I poke my head into the street, and look down the road toward the tattoo shop. It's a few hundred feet, but surely, I'd notice a massive bear and a mountain goat fighting in the street. So would the few people speed walking down Main with cups of coffee in their hands.

My shoulders relax as a deep breath releases. Maybe Lilly needs to get her eyes checked. I dial her number just in case. She picks up on the first ring with more enthusiasm than I'm expecting.

"Are you dating the rodeo guy? The hot one? With the tight jeans, and the hat, and the husky voice? I saw him. He was beating the shit out of Ian."

"Slow down. What's going on? Janie said you saw him outside the tattoo shop. Was he with anyone?"

"Girl, yes! I tried calling you!"

Her call must have been buried in all the messages from Janie.

"Sorry, it's been a weird morning. What did you see? I'm looking down the street now and I don't see anything."

She sighs. "Your guy threw a punch and sent that little creeper straight into the Christmas window at Rugged Mountain Ink. There was glass everywhere. I called Henry right away."

Henry is the owner of the tattoo shop, and most of the land in the area. He's a big, burly type who found romance here long before I was born. He's also the nicest guy you could ever run into, and I hope he doesn't press charges. Maybe if he hears how absolutely horrible Ian has been, he'll be forgiving of Dustin, and let this whole thing go.

"Thanks for the update. I'll call you later."

"You better! I need every juicy detail. Single mom life may as well be forced celibacy. Do you know how horrible that is?"

Considering I'm a twenty-two-year-old virgin, I might have a clue, but I don't bother with details. Right now, I need to find Dustin.

"I'll call you later. I promise!"

Half a second passes from when I hang up the line with Lilly to when Dustin is yelling my name from down the street. His deep voice carries.

"Baby girl!" He's leaning against the brick exterior of the tattoo shop with his boots kicked up as he takes a drink from a bottle of cream soda.

I meet him with a tangled expression, and wait for his response. "I'm confused."

He grins. "About what?"

"What happened?" I lean to the side to see the glass on the display window is broken. Tiny shards lay scattered across the sidewalk. The pretty Christmas display has been ruined by his barbaric act of protection. Inside, Ian is sitting in one of the chairs barely conscious.

"I took care of a problem," Dustin says. "Now, I'm waiting here for Henry so I can repay him for the window. Also, gotta make sure no one gets cut on this shit. I made a mess."

My jaw drops. "Yeah, you fixed a problem alright, but you can't... you just..."

His voice tenses. "This asshole tried to hurt you, *twice*. I stopped him."

I have to admit, somewhere inside of me there's a princess hiding in her tower, just waiting to be rescued by a man in some way, but not like this.

"I didn't ask you to defend me. I don't want you fighting my battles! I can take care of myself."

Dustin leans up from the wall and looks down at me. In this light his normally blue eyes are a steely gray. His shoulders widen and his chest expands. "I didn't ask permission... and I won't. I'll always do what I need to keep you safe."

My heart gallops slowly, coming to a full and complete stop as I stare toward him. He's not messing around, and for the first time in my life, I want to be rescued from my tower.

Chapter Six

Dustin

I f I were less a barbarian, I'd grab hold of Roxie's hand, drive her home, and make love to her by the fire with soft music playing in the background. We'd talk about the past, the future, the present, and everything in between. I'd stroke her hair, I'd kiss her neck, I'd savor every last drop of her touch. But it's been too long since I've felt a connection like this with someone and I can't wait another second. I need her now.

"Where are you taking me?" Roxie's voice is peppered with excitement and apprehension. It's a sound that wakes a fire inside of me. "I'm too heavy. Put me down."

"You're not heavy, and no." I'm grunting out words like an animal but it's all I can manage. Blood pumps so hard in my ears that it's like I'm underwater.

"If you're not going to let me down, you can at least tell me where we're going. People are staring, Dustin," she whispers.

"Let them stare. We'll give people something to talk about."

Her ass balances on my shoulder, vibrating with each step I take. It's unbearable. Then again, the last five days have been torture. Every waking minute, thinking about her, dreaming about her, wondering what she tastes like, what she'd feel like on my skin, on my cock, in my mouth. Wondering how she likes to be touched, and what sounds she makes when she's coming. Wondering how her thick thighs would feel squeezing my face. Wondering if she'd like hearing me whisper all the dirty things I've been thinking.

I'm not a good man. I'm evil. Dark. Fucked up. I shouldn't want her like this. She's young, sweet, innocent, but I can't help myself.

I don't want to help myself.

We've nearly made it to the grandstand where I know of a little place to hide, when Mrs. Robinson stops us in the street. Every part of me wants to keep walking and pretend like I don't see her, but Roxie has other plans.

"Mrs. Robinson!" Her voice is sweet and patient, despite her current situation.

Reluctantly, I set her down, and she looks up toward me with a crooked grin as though she's gotten away with something.

I lean down, and whisper in her ear. "You're going to pay for this."

She keeps her cool, but I see the way her thighs press together, as though she's managing her excitement. "How are you? I meant to stop and talk at Winter-Fest, but things got crazy that night."

Mrs. Robinson waves Roxie's distress away. The silver bracelets on her wrist clank together as she moves. "We're all busy, honey. Don't worry. I did see a lot of drama going on at the tattoo shop this morning. Anyone want to fill me in?"

From what I know about Mrs. Robinson, she's been married for the better part of her life to one man. A man that all the guys in town affectionately call Moose because of his size. The man is nearly seven feet tall. Mrs. Robinson is lucky to be five feet in heels, and she's known as the town gossip. Not the nasty kind that people can't stand, but the sweet, cookie baking kind that people find endearing.

Roxie glances back at me as though she's asking if I want to tell the story.

"You go ahead," I say, wrapping my arm around her waist. "I'd rather the town gossip hear the story from us then someone else."

She looks back toward Mrs. Robinson. "Ian, that college kid I was seeing... he was messing with me, so Dustin took care of it. The window at the tattoo shop got broken. Henry came down and covered for Dustin with the police and Ian agreed to go back to The Springs when he sobers up. It could've been crazy, but thankfully... hometown heroes."

Mrs. Robinson nods and looks toward Dustin. "Good thing you had this scrooge around who didn't care about breaking the nicest bit of Christmas we have in town."

I look down at Roxie unsure of how to take what she's saying. Roxie looks up at me with a smile. "She's messing with you."

Mrs. Robinson laughs. "Not everyone would want confrontation, but the locals do try their best to take care of their own here. I'm just glad you're okay, dear. It's nice you have a man that will protect you. I know how special that is. Will you two be at the Snowman Swing this evening?"

I want to blurt out no before Roxie can answer. I want nothing more than to dance with her forever, but right now I have other plans.

Roxie smiles softly and tilts her head to the side. "I'm not sure, but I saw you and your husband at the dance last weekend and maybe it's weird to tell you this, but the way you looked at each other during that dance was beautiful. I hope someday I'll have that too."

Mrs. Robinson's cheeks turn rosy. "That's sweet of you to say, honey. Of course you'll have that someday. By the looks, you have a good start right here."

Roxie glances up toward me with wide eyes and the kindest grin. She leans into me, tipping up onto her toes to crush her lips against my neck. "I think so too."

"Well, I'll leave you two love birds to it then. I'm going to grab a few pictures of that broken window for the gazette."

Mrs. Robinson leaves, but Roxie stays glued to me, breathing me in.

"I was going to take you to a secret spot and have my way with you," I groan, staring down into her pretty brown eyes. "But now... I think I need to make your dirty dancing fantasies come true first."

"Dirty dancing fantasy?" She grins. "What are you talking about?"

"You spoke so sweetly of Mr. and Mrs. Robinson and that dance they had last weekend. You deserve to feel that way too. I want you to know you're special, Roxie. You're not like anyone else."

Her eyes brighten, then glass over as her hand lifts to my chest. "I think maybe we have other things we could do first. Besides, I've always been a fan of *secret spots*. I'd love to see yours." She looks up at me with slightly pouted lips and my brain slides right back to the archaic place it had been a few minutes before. I'm not sure if you could even call what we shared at the bake shop earlier a kiss. It was more a brushing of lips than anything. And though any fraction of her against me is a win, I'm aching for more.

Her hand wanders up my chest and her fingers scratch at my beard. "I want to hear all the dirty things you want to do... but I need to tell you something first."

She had me at whispering dirty things, and though her features have turned down as though she's about to say something serious, my cock is going hard in the middle of Main Street.

That's a first for this forty-year-old man.

"What's that, baby girl?" I brush a strand of her hair back as I impatiently wait for her to talk.

She sucks in a deep breath of cool, winter air then looks down the street both ways before tipping up onto her toes and leaning into my ear.

I bend down toward her slightly, unsure what she could possibly have to share.

Hot breath releases against my earlobe as she sighs, "I'm a virgin, Dustin. I've never done this before."

My brain isn't sure how to respond, so my cock makes decisions on its own. Apparently, the thought of her saving herself for me is a turn on. Though, as everything above my waist catches up to the news, I'm not sure how I feel about myself knowing my truth. *I'm a sick, fucking ass.*

"Are you okay?" Roxie's voice is sweet and gentle. "I know it's weird. I contemplated even telling you because what difference does it make, ya know? But I've read it can hurt a little and," she sighs again, "I thought I should tell you."

An involuntary growl bubbles up my throat and the beast inside of me speaks. "Do you want me to fuck you, baby girl? Do you want me to stretch that tight little pussy wide?"

She sighs gently. "Yes," she says in a near whisper.

"Then you have to do as I say."

She nods and smiles coyly, tucking her small hand into mine as I guide her down the street past the Christmas windows dazzled with lights, past the shoppers shopping, past the green and red lampposts dressed for the season, and past the bakery spilling scents of peppermint and chocolate cookie dough. Roxie is about to be mine, and this time, nothing's going to stop me.

Chapter Seven

Roxie

I didn't think I'd like taking direction as much as I do. First, I thought it would be a huge affront to my independence as a woman. A setback for feminine energy everywhere.

Why would I listen to a man? Why would I let a man protect me? Why would I let him order me on my knees the way Dustin just has? I am a young, capable woman who sets her own line of rules and doesn't listen to anyone... especially a man.

"Good girl," Dustin groans, rubbing his large palm over my bare ass. "Such a good girl."

Why would I like someone to call me a *good girl*? I should be repulsed by it. I should stand up right now and bend *him* over. I should call him a *good boy* and see how he likes it.

The sheer fact that I know that's *not* going to happen is enough to wet my pussy further. He's too big for that, too strong. I couldn't overpower him, even if I wanted to... and I'm okay with that. I'm at Dustin's mercy. I want him to control me. I want him to take me over his knee. I want him to keep telling me what a good girl I am.

I want to be *his* good girl.

My heart thumps loud and fast, slamming against my ribcage as his cock prods against me. I haven't gotten a good look at it yet, but judging by the pressure against my ass, I'd bet he's huge.

He runs his big, rough hands over my body as he groans in appreciation, then sits back on the couch of his RV. He keeps it parked at the grandstand. This must have been what he used when he was traveling. Though, I don't take the time to ask. Since we stepped inside, it's been all heat.

"Come up here, baby girl."

We've barely kissed yet, but I'm staring at his naked body relaxed back on the couch. I was right about his dick. It's huge. I'm terrible with measurements. All I know is that it's big enough that I'm not sure it's going to fit.

I climb onto his lap and run my fingers through the hair on his chest, breathing him again. Pine, cedar, and an undefined musk.

His fingers tickle my bare back as I close in further. Between us sits his big cock, hard and ready. I'm desperate to touch it, but I'm waiting for permission like a schoolgirl needing a pass for a trip to the library.

"You're going to have to stop squirming, or this is all going to be over really fast."

His request only antagonizes me and I wiggle back and forth more liberally.

"Fuck," he groans, gripping my hips closer toward him. "You're asking for it now."

I grin playfully. "What am I asking for?"

He leans into my shoulder and bites down lightly, then sucks on my neck with a growl. "You want this cock on your cute little tits. You want my come dripping off your lips. You want me lapping up your juices while you moan and cry for me to let you finish."

"I do. I want all of that, Dustin."

He presses a kiss to my forehead, then grabs a handful of my hair, and leans into my lips.

My throat goes tight as he drinks me in, holding my bare body against his with ferocity and intent. I shudder in his lap, my breath held as his hands work over my skin.

He's groaning and growling like a caged lion fighting for relief.

I need to give it to him.

He leans me back against a soft velvet pillow and dives between my legs, scratching his beard over my mound before diving in deeper. His tongue wanders into my crease and he crosses a line he can't go back from.

His touch is warm and gentle, yet firm and concise. "You keep this mound so soft, baby girl." His lips brush against me and I shudder as he slides a single finger inside. One is enough. I can't imagine two, and I definitely can't imagine his dick. It's so thick and there's no way he's going to fit inside of me.

Slowly, his thumb works my clit. "That's it, baby girl. Try to relax. I need you nice and supple for my cock."

Is it too soon to say I'm in love? Everything he's doing is better than I've ever imagined it. Juices swell at my entrance and threaten to spill from within me as he works. My back arches, moan after moan escapes me, and I'm pretty sure I'm about to hear angels sing.

He's romantic but unapologetically firm and even-keeled. He's my soulmate. He centers me. "Don't stop, Dustin. I have to come."

His tongue bumps over my clit as he paws at me from the inside. "I'm not sure I can let you come yet, baby girl."

"What?" I gasp irrationally loud. "No. You have to let me come. I'm so close."

"I know," he growls. "I can taste you, but I want that virgin come on my cock."

Heat washes over me like I've just stepped my toe into hell itself. I'm not sure anything hotter has ever been said... to me, anyway.

"You're all red, baby. Are you okay?"

I shake my head and pout my lip playfully. "I don't think so. I'm aching for you like I've never ached for anything."

"Mmm," he growls. "I guess that means you're ready to ride."

"Ready to ride?"

He lays flat on the floor between the sofa and the kitchen. There isn't much room in here, but none of that matters right now. I follow orders as he lists them, and I do it with butterflies and excitement in my stomach. I'm finally going to pop my cherry, and I'm doing it with the hottest cowboy in Rugged Mountain. How did I manage this? How is he here? How is he real?

When he's situated himself on the floor, he calls out for me. "You're going to lower yourself on top of me really slow. I want you to feel me stretching you. I want to feel that soft pussy taking me in." He takes a deep breath, and his eyes change their tone. "Shit. I don't have a condom, though. When I came into town, I wasn't expecting any of this."

I want to scream out how badly I want his babies, but that might put me in some sort of weirdo category that I'm not ready for yet. Thankfully, he doesn't have a problem speaking his mind.

"Unless you *want* my come." His gaze locks mine in the dim light of the room. "Do you want my come, Roxie?"

Ugh, I've never wanted anything more. I nod.

He groans as he says, "Good girl. Where do you want it?"

Truthfully, I want it all over me. I want it on my skin, on my breasts, and in my mouth. But most of all, I want him painting me from the inside. I want bits of him dripping from me for days. I want to smell like him when I get up in the morning.

"I want you inside of me," I pant. "I want it now."

"Are you sure, baby girl? What if you get pregnant?"

My eyes light as I lower onto his thick cock. "I don't care, Dustin. I want your babies. I want you. I never want this feeling to end." I close my eyes as the words fall from my lips. I've only just brushed his cock with my pussy, but I'm afraid I've crossed a line with my thoughts, and I wait for a response.

He growls, "What are you waiting for? Be a good girl and lower down slowly. I'll fuck you hard. I'll give you babies, and I'll hold you close. But you have to know once I'm inside... you're mine. There's no going back. Are you sure you're ready for that?"

I hold his gaze as I lower slowly, swallowing hard as a pinch of pain resonates through me. There's no stopping me now. I want to belong to Dustin. I want to be his good girl.

"Yes," I whimper, taking more of him in. "I'm ready."

Chapter Eight

Dustin

Roxie's breasts sway and bounce as she moves, and I can't look away. Her long locks tangle over her shoulders and spill onto her chest, bobbing with her movements, as if I wasn't hard enough already. There's something about knowing she's saved herself, knowing that I'm the only man that will have her, knowing that as I stretch her open that she's molding to fit me and only me.

Reaching up, I rub her clit as I watch her move. There's inexperience in her body, but I like it. It's erratic and surprising. It keeps me guessing, which I like.

"Does it hurt?"

She whines as she twists in circles, bouncing up and down as she sees fit. "A little, but I like it." I watch as she swallows down her pain. A single lump travels down her throat and into her chest. I don't want to hurt her. I want her to feel good.

"Are you sure? We can stop."

"I'm sure." She's breathless as she grinds over me. "I need you, Dustin." Her nipples are hard and beading as though aching for touch.

With my freehand, I work on each side, squeezing and pinching the hard buds, but it's not enough. I want to feel her against my tongue. I want to push into her deep and let go of the tension I've built. I've let her have control. I let her gauge how deep she could take me. I let her move at her own pace. But now... I need to take the power back.

"On your knees again, against the couch, baby girl. I have to have you."

She grins and rocks her hips a few more times before standing to bend over the couch. Her gaze draws to me so pure and innocent as though she wants me to praise her for doing as I've asked.

Fuck. She *likes* the praise. Her eyes are begging for it.

A low growl settles into my throat. "Mmm... you're such a good girl, bending over for me like that. Do you want my cock, baby?"

A soft sigh of approval enters the space as her hips wiggle back and forth enticing me to stretch her wide.

"It's going to be rougher and harder than you were going. Are you okay with that?"

"Please hurry," she pants, circling her own clit while she waits. "I need you so bad."

Standing behind her round ass, I stroke my cock, and settle the tip at her entrance, moving in slowly. I slide in easier this time, but she's still strangling my width.

Her small hands grip the couch cushions as I thrust in harder. I'm slow at first, then move quicker, rolling into her hips like rough surf against the shore.

Every thrust is bound with sparks of pleasure and desire for more. More of this moment, more of her heart, more of a life with her. Children, grocery lists, chores, and evenings by the fire. I need it all.

"I'm going to come, Dustin." There's a whine of desperation in her tone that excites me beyond belief. "Lean into me. Hold me."

I do as she asks, and lean forward, holding her tight against my body as I thrust into her harder and faster.

Her fingers are on her clit circling, as my hands hold her hip and breast. She's hot and flushed, and I lick the salt from her shoulder, biting down playfully with a growl.

"Good girl. Come on my cock."

Her body tenses and she clenches down on my dick, tightening the already tight space.

Whine after delicious whine leaves her mouth as she convulses against me, losing control of her body.

The erratic behavior sends me over the edge and all I see is red, hot, need. I grip her tight and thrust in harder and harder, a rumble of vibrations echoing through my chest as I shove deep, then come.

Roxie reaches back and grips my hand in hers, holding me close to her as I ripple against her thick ass, sending ribbons of pleasure into her cavern.

"Fuck." I thrust a few more times until the tip of my cock is so sensitive, I have to pull out.

She turns toward me with bright eyes. "You felt so good. I want to do that every day forever."

I invite her naked body against me and hold her close. "Oh, we will. Multiple times a day if you'll let me."

She runs her fingers through my chest hair and smiles. "I'll let you."

"And you'll also let me take you to the Snowman Swing tonight. I want to spin you around that dance floor until you feel like you have everything you've ever wanted, Roxie." My hand cups her small face and my heart warms as her eyes glisten in the sparkling light of the Christmas tree in the corner.

"I don't need a dance with you to know how I feel, Dustin. I have everything I need right here, and I never want to leave."

I kiss her head and hold her close, memorizing the way her chest rises and falls against me. "I love you, baby girl."

Her lips brush my chest and a soft whisper releases. "I love you more, Dustin, and I always will."

I kiss her forehead and hold her tight, saving the *I love you more* fight for another day. Because right now, the words are stuck in my throat behind a wealth of emotion.

Roxie is everything I've ever wanted, and I can't wait to spend forever showing her that.

Epilogue

Roxie

T wo Weeks Later

"Please be careful!" I shout up at Dustin as he balances on a ladder stapling colored Christmas lights to the eves of the cabin. He's been begging me to do it for weeks now, but I've managed to convince him that staying in bed with me is more important than lights on the house. Granted, the lights do look great, and they'll be super festive when we have our party tonight.

"I'm always careful," he says stapling the last bulb in place. "What do you think? Does everything look even?"

I nod and brush my arms up and down over one another, trying to generate some heat. It's been bitterly cold this week and I don't think a heat wave is in the forecast. I should've thrown a jacket on.

Dustin climbs down the ladder and settles it beside the cabin before turning to me. "Are you out here without a coat on? Get your ass inside. You're going to get sick!" His hand meets my ass with a playful smack as he chases me onto the front porch. "Let's go. I'm ordering it."

"Is that right?" I grin, leaning against the cabin door. "What if I refuse to go in?"

His hand lifts above my head and he stares down at me, with narrowed eyes like an animal who's about to assert his dominance. I don't like being a brat, but I do like the way he tries to put me in my place. Sometimes I listen, sometimes I don't. I suppose that's what keeps it interesting.

"Get inside," he growls into my ear, sending heat radiating through my body.

My eyes light and my clit throbs. "I think we only have thirty minutes before people show up. I—"

"Gross! Stop! Not on the front porch." Janie covers her eyes as she makes her way up the steps. "I know I'm early, but not early enough to be subjected to this cruel and unusual punishment."

Dustin looks toward Janie then back toward me. "You need to set her up with some-one."

"What? No way! I don't need some whirlwind romance and a shotgun wedding like you guys had. Next, you'll be telling me there're babies on the way."

I look toward Dustin and bite my bottom lip, trying to hold in the news we've just found out.

"What?" Her jaw drops. "You guys aren't pregnant. You can't be. You only met a few weeks ago. You just had your wedding."

Dustin grips my waist and pulls me close to him before glancing down to nod in approval.

I glance back toward Janie. "Don't say anything to anyone, but I had some routine bloodwork scheduled, and my HCG was elevated."

"Speak English," she says. "What does that mean?"

"It means we're pregnant, but it's still really soon, so we're not telling anyone yet. You have to keep it a secret... okay?"

Janie's eyes widen. "You two win the record for the relationship speedrun. Is that a thing?"

"Let's get inside," Dustin groans. "You two are not dressed for this weather."

He's not wrong. Our cookie party is pajama themed. I'm dressed in a gingerbread onesie and Janie is dressed as a snowman. The outfits are not ideal for the snow that's just started falling, though we are going to look really cute for pictures later.

"So wait," Janie says, following us into the cabin, "when are you telling people?"

"Christmas Eve. We'll be about six weeks along then. Henry is going to let us use the tattoo shop's repaired Christmas window to make an announcement. Dustin has been working on a wooden cradle for the Dickens' based family we're building. I thought it would be a fun way to announce it since everyone on the mountain goes to town to do the window walk every Christmas Eve." I tuck my hand into Dustin's. "What do you think? Too much?"

She slides down into a chair at the dining room table and pulls a baked sugar cookie to decorate. "Can I be honest with you, Roxie?" Her face has turned down and her normally bright smile is replaced by something more somber.

"Yeah, of course you can." I sit beside her at the table and pull out a cookie of my own.

Dustin takes this as a cue to leave the area and I hear the front door of the cabin shut behind him. I'm sure he has more Christmas lights he's dying to string, anyway. Something tells me that though this place is small, he's happy to have a place of his own too. For years he's been living out of that fifth wheel traveling the country. Now, he has a few acres all to himself.

"What is it, Janie? Is everything okay?"

She nods and smooths frosting over the top of her cookie slowly, darting her vision from the cookie to me. "Yeah. I'm fine. It's just..." she sighs. "I'm a virgin, Roxie. And while I'm happy for you and excited for how well your life is going, I'm starting to feel a little... behind."

For the most part, Janie and I spend our time working together at the library. Sure, we have conversations about girl stuff like guys and romance novels, but we've never talked about sexual experiences.

"I was a virgin too, Janie, up until like two weeks ago."

Her brows crinkle inward. "Seriously? You're so... pretty. I figured you'd have been with a lot of guys by now."

I shake my head and reach for her hand, squeezing it in mine. "No, and I'm glad I waited. Giving myself to Dustin has been the biggest gift. He's so appreciative of it. He loves that I saved myself for him."

Janie sighs. "See, that's the thing... I don't think I'm going to save myself. I was thinking of auctioning it off online," she shrugs, "for the money."

My eyes widen. It's a comment I'd never have expected to hear from her. "What? You can't. You're... you'll regret that, Janie. I didn't even know that was a thing!"

"Me either, but a friend of mine up at Waylon's ranch has been talking about doing it. She said these guys online will pay huge bucks to take it and I don't know... what's the big deal? I won't be behind anymore, the whole virgin thing is out of the way, and I can pay off my last semester of college before I get kicked to the curb."

I'm not sure I fully comprehend what she's saying. Janie's always seemed very responsible to me. She's in college to be an official librarian. Right now, it's like she's a different person.

"How about we talk about this again in a couple of weeks? I'm sure you'll change your mind after we get you down to Winter-Fest to meet someone. Who knows? You could find the love of your life like I did."

Dustin knocks his boots on the threshold of the cabin before stepping back in, carrying with him the freezing cold wind that's blustering outside. "It looks like my brother is here. So is Lilly and a few other folks. I think we're going to need more seating. Can you help me in the shed for a minute, baby?"

I reach out to Janie for a hug. "I love you. We're going to figure this out. Just promise me you don't go listing yourself *Pretty Woman* style tonight."

She grins. "Of course not. I'm too busy with cookies for that. Can we keep this between us, though?"

I nod and squeeze her hand one last time before her attention goes back to the frosting. I meet Dustin at the door, hugging our friends as they make their way into our cozy little cabin.

"We'll be right back. We forgot the extra chairs in the shed."

Dustin hands me my coat, then grips my hand in his, and we run across the freshly fallen snow toward the back field, avoiding the shed all together.

"Where are we going?"

He grins. "I already grabbed the chairs. I just wanted a second alone with you before the crazy starts." He pulls me into his arms and holds me close to his chest as we stare up at the dark night sky where ice crystals fall onto our noses.

"You know this is dangerous, right?"

"How so?"

"Well, now that I'm outside, I really don't want to go back in. I'm thinking we snuggle out here and watch through the window while everyone decorates cookies."

He grins. "Ah, kind of like our own live action Christmas window?"

I tip up onto my toes and nod as our lips brush together in the cool night air. It's moments like these that I didn't know I was missing out on. The unexpected second, he pulls me aside when we're hosting a party. The way he stares at me from across the store while we're getting groceries. The way he reminds me what a good girl I am when we're making love. Or the way he pins me against a wall and spanks my bratty ass when I'm being naughty.

Janie's right. Two weeks isn't very long. Dustin and I really did figure this out quickly. But that's the thing with love. It hits you when you least expect, then challenges you to surrender to it, and finally... you can't see your life any other way.

Innocent

Chapter One

Janie

My mom always says, *'Why fit in, when you can stand out?'* It's a nice sentiment for someone like her. She's tall, thin, elegant, and somehow managed to be exceptionally smart as well. To this day, at nearly sixty, everyone she knows is still envious. For her, standing out was a good thing. For me, not so much.

I spent most of my childhood being bullied for wearing my hair too short and playing video games with the boys. I won't apologize for enjoying the escape act of diving deep into a world that doesn't exist and pretending to be someone else for a while, but it hasn't exactly led me to popular waters.

"Are you off to work, sweetheart?" My mom kisses my head as she walks by me in the kitchen. It's seven p.m. and she's still dressed like she's expecting an important visitor. I'd ask her if she was, but this isn't new for her. She stays perfectly primped until she crawls into bed at night. She knows I'm not that girl, though. Usually, the second I get off my shift at the library, I sling off my bra and toss on the longest, biggest oversized tee I can find. Tonight, I uncomfortably sit in a short black dress and a pair of Spanx so tight that I'm sure I'll have heartburn later. She knows something's up.

"Yeah, we'll see how it goes. I'm a little nervous. Mark was telling me that this place is swarming with people this time of night and I'm not sure I'm ready for that much socialization."

"I gotta say, Janie, I was surprised when you took the job. You have all those hours at the library and you're still finishing up your online classes at the university." Her eyebrows crinkle as she pours herself a cup of tea. "And the tattoo shop doesn't seem like your thing."

I bite the inside of my cheek and stare at her blankly. I knew this question was coming, and I've been mulling over a good response in my head for days, but I haven't found one yet.

I shrug. "Pushing myself outside my comfort zone, I guess."

My mother glances up at me, then back down at her tea, squeezing a smidge of honey into her cup. "I love you with all my heart, dear, and I'm all for you getting out of your comfort zone, but the tattoo shop? Your ears aren't even pierced. You did a final paper in eighth grade English about how tattoo ink causes allergic reactions and should be avoided at all costs." She grins after she says it. I know she's razzing me, but I'm not in the mood. My nerves are too frayed.

"It's only for a couple of days while Mark is visiting his girlfriend in the city. I'm just setting appointments and answering phones. It's no big deal." I hop down off the stool, unrolling the top of my Spanx that have rolled down my stomach. These stupid things are a pain in the ass. I have no idea why I wear them. Well, technically, I do. My dress won't zip if they're not on. So, there's that. "I'll see you in the morning. I won't be home until after eleven."

She smiles. "Okay, hon. Be careful, and have fun. You look great, by the way."

If she weren't my mother, the compliment would mean a lot more, but I think she might be obligated to say nice things. I'm not sure. Besides that, any minute now, she'll be able to see straight through me. I'm not a tattoo shop kind of girl. I'm a library, pet store, fruit stand woman. And I'm definitely not into a busy Friday night with loads of people. I prefer to spend the little free time I have locked in my quiet room with my video games and romance novels. That said, Mark really needed the help and I need a few extra bucks to pay for my last semester of college. Besides, I wouldn't mind saying hi to Mark's dad, Huck. It's been too long, and I've always had the tiniest crush on him. He's tall, rugged, inked everywhere, and he has this presence about him that's always driven me wild. Of course, none of that matters. He's about two times my age and my best friend's dad. Besides that, he's *way* out of my league.

"Thanks, Mom." I give her a quick squeeze and head out the back door and hop into the pickup truck I was gifted on my sixteenth birthday. That was six years ago now. Back then, my family was living in The Springs. We weren't rich, but my dad had a successful law firm, and things like trucks for your birthday were a thing. Now, things are very different... for everyone. We live in a small shoebox of a cabin just outside the main street of a small mountain town and money is harder to come by.

I crank up the radio to the local country station and head out into the snow toward the tattoo shop that sits on the corner a few miles up the road. From the outside, the place doesn't look like much. The highlight is the Christmas window that's decorated with a snowman family and twinkling white lights hanging above. It's simple and gives small town vibes like every other brick building on this street.

I pull up outside the shop and head inside, readjusting my dress again before stepping into the warmth of the large tattoo shop where *Outlaw Country* is blaring. It's a bluegrass sound that's amped up with a few guitars. I'm used to the vibe. Most people around here play it, but it sounds different through the deep bass speakers of the shop.

The bell above the door jingles and everyone looks up from their stations to greet me. There's Maddox, a big, burly guy with mostly gray hair, who owns the shop. Henry, a similar looking guy who's his brother and co-owner. And Huck, Mark's dad.

I immediately regret coming. It's been a while since I've seen him. *How is Huck hotter?* I try not to stare, but I can't help but glare up as I situate myself at the small office space in the front of the shop.

"Hey, Janie! Thanks for filling in this weekend. The last time Mark went away, Maddox was answering phones, and he messed up quite a few appointments."

Maddox laughs and shuffles his fingers back through his hair. "And apparently, I'm not friendly enough for phones." He grins. "I'm friendly, right?"

"No one said you're not friendly, Maddox," Henry calls out as he returns to his work.

My heart stops as Huck makes his way to the front counter, drawing his inked hand down over his heavy salt and pepper beard. His arms stretch out toward me for a hug. "Janie... good to see you. It's been too long. What have you been up to?"

Where have I been? A hug? I figured I'd be staring at him and watching him work. I sure as hell didn't expect to be touching him. The shop is packed, and he has a guy on his table. There's no time for chatting. He's busy. Go... be busy. I shoo him away with my eyes, but I think they've betrayed me, because he's leaning in.

"Here and there, I guess." I lean into his wide barreled chest for a hug and suck in the scent of cedar and pine, flooding back a thousand memories of Mark and I getting lost in the mountains while listening to Bon Jovi. We'd write our own songs over their lyrics and make up goofy sounds to every track. Then, we'd have lunch by the river and get drunk on wine coolers. For a while, I think Mark thought he and I would be more, but there's no way I could've focused on a relationship with him, knowing how I felt every time I saw his dad.

I can still hear the rumble of Huck's truck as it roared up the mountainside to pick us up, stones popping and the bright summer sun filtering through the pines. Looking back, I'm sure he knew we'd been drinking, but he never said anything. We'd go back to the cabin, make lunch together, and eat outside by the granite rock overhangs above the river's edge. He didn't say much in those hours we spent together, but he was steady, strong, capable. His presence alone was enough to incite a reaction from my body that I didn't understand.

His chest reverberates as he pulls away from the hug.

God, how long did that last?

Was I awkwardly holding on as I fantasized about having lunch with him by the river when I was seventeen?

My clit throbs, but my cheeks turn dark red. This is what happens to anti-social girls who play video games and read romance novels. They end up drooling all over their best friend's dad at a tattoo shop they don't work at.

I can't imagine what Mark would say if he knew. He'd probably vomit. Then, he'd take me to The Springs for a CT scan... *if he could ever look at me again.*

"Well, I better get back to my client," Huck says, backing away. "Good to see ya, kid. I'll catch up with you again before the night's over."

Kid.

I contemplate stomping my foot on the ground, crossing my arms, and pouting out a lip while screaming, *I'm not a kid*, but that might not prove the point I'm going for. So instead, I roll my stiff neck in a circle and plop down at the reception desk, staring at the blue buzzing screen while I catch my breath and try to rationalize the very simple, meaningless exchange we've just had.

It was nothing. Just a hello. He thinks I'm a kid... because I am to him. That's normal. I tell myself these truths, then stare back at the computer screen, trying to look busy.

The air in the shop is cool, and the music drowns out any conversations going on around me. I can't believe I have to come back here tomorrow. I'm an embarrassment to myself! Of course, I'm a child to him. What did I expect? Did I really think he was going to sweep me up and tell me he'd been in love with me for years?

That's insane.

I'm insane.

The worst part is, I'm still the same kid I was at seventeen. In the same town, still working at the library, still playing video games, still reading raunchy romance, still wishing on some broken star that I'll fall in love and get my happily ever after.

I bury my head in my hands and suck in a hard, heavy breath. There's no way I'm coming back here tomorrow.

Chapter Two

Huck

Floorboards creak as I roll my stool to the side and work the opposite corner of the eagle I've been trying to finish. It's a black ink piece that has an elaborate wing design and hundreds of detailed strokes. I used to loathe the details, but now I look forward to them. The nuances in art have made me notice the subtitles in life. Small things I may have never noticed before. Like the lines in someone's face, or the way a blade of grass leans, or the way a raindrop slides off a windowsill, leaving a streak of moisture behind it.

I ink another dark line down the feather contour of the bird and glance up at Janie sitting behind the counter on her phone. With her, I'd need to stare for years to soak in every detail. The way her hair falls in soft curls. The way her lip wrinkles just above the bow. The way her nose crinkles when she's happy or nervous. The beauty mark that sits on her right breast at the top of her cleavage line. I could stare forever and never soak her all in. Nor should I. The fact that I'm attracted to her at all is fucking sick. It was when she was eighteen, and it still is now that she's twenty-four.

I'm such a fucking asshole. What kind of a guy lusts after his son's best friend? A best friend, I'm pretty sure he had feelings for at one point. What kind of man wants a woman twenty years younger than him? What kind of man thinks about that woman for years and years and years, despite the obvious reality that they could never be?

I clear my throat and stare back down at the wing I'm supposed to be working, desperately trying to push away every gross old man feeling I'm having, but the more I push it away, the more it wants in. Like the scent of mold on the soil after a heavy rain... it's both intoxicating and revolting. I'm desperate to escape it, yet eager to take one more breath.

I suck in a tight gasp and focus down on the fine detail of the underwing, dotting in texture as I try again to scrape Janie from my mind, but it's useless. It always has been, and seeing her face only makes it that much worse. That pretty mouth, and those blue eyes. *Fuck.* It's been too long since I've seen her in the flesh and every old emotion I had has come flooding right back.

I've consistently wondered what it would be like to head to the library and sit in her presence for only an hour, hoping to give myself a chance at peace from my screaming desires. But I fear it would end with me carrying her back to my place over my shoulder and that wouldn't do much good for anyone… but me.

"Hey, man." My client twists toward me. "I think I'm going to call it for tonight. Can we set up to finish in a couple of weeks?"

"Yeah, of course. Everything okay?"

He grins and sits up from the stretched-out table. "That's a rough spot. I wasn't expecting the pain. If my wife asks, though, you had to cut the session short due to some emergency. Okay?"

I nod. "You got it. We'll settle up when you come back in." Usually I don't do things like this, but paying would mean going to the front desk where Janie is and I'm not sure I could take the heart attack right now. I need to stay to myself, clean my station, draw out the tattoo I have tomorrow night, and ignore every feeling creeping under my fucking skin.

"Huck…" I'm turned toward my station when the haunting sound of her voice slinks through me, threatening my evolution as a man.

I twist toward her, taking in the soft scent of citrus on her skin, keeping my eyes firmly planted on hers, trying not to notice the way her body has filled out. She's gorgeous. "Yeah, what's up?"

"Oh," she twists her mouth to the side, "sorry to bother you, but that guy didn't pay, and I didn't know if it was my responsibility to stop him. So…"

The way she hangs off the word has me suddenly awake and buzzing with energy. I need to be closer. I need to find a way to touch her again. I need to sweep my hand across her back or touch her face. I need to hold her hand in mine or feel the weight of her hips against my body.

Fuck, I need help.

"No. Don't worry about that guy. He's an old friend. He's good for it. How's your first night going? A lot of calls?" What am I even asking?

She smiles coyly and turns her head up from the floor, drawing her stare around the room. "Nope, nothing. I've been keeping myself busy with this profile online." She pauses, as though she's caught herself saying too much. "I guess I should be doing something productive, though. Do you guys need anything cleaned, or… what does Mark usually do between calls and clients?"

"You're doing it," I say, flinging my glance between her and the ink bottles lined at the back of my counter. I don't dare stare too long for fear of fucking up everyone's lives right here and now. "What kind of profile are you making? Not dating, I hope. Those websites are awful. I joined one a few years back and lasted less than twenty-four hours."

She grins. "Yeah, I don't see you as the online dating type. I see you as a, *found the love of my life while fishing type.*" Giggles bubble up from her throat and she covers her lips with her index finger to keep from laughing uncontrollably. "Anyway, mine isn't a dating profile. I'm selling something."

My brows crinkle. "What are you selling that you need a profile? You know those online sales sites are just as bad. Who the hell knows who'll show up at your door? You should list whatever it is up on the local board at the diner. Everyone in town is up there, anyway."

Her eyes roll sideways, and she bites her bottom lip softly. "I don't know if this is the kind of thing you'd list on the wall at the diner."

I can feel my eyes wondering the room while I think. I can't imagine anything that can't be sold on the wall at the diner. "You selling something illegal?"

She laughs awkwardly and twists onto her heels before stepping back toward the desk. "It's nothing. But really, I only have like ten minutes left here anyway tonight. If you don't need anything else, I'll catch you tomorrow?"

Oh, I need things.

"Yeah, you're good to go. Thanks for covering tonight."

She nods and twists away, leaving me with a view of her round ass that stirs me alive again. It's apparent I haven't been as coy as I thought I was being when the second the front door has closed behind her, Maddox starts with his bullshitting.

"Fucking hell, dude. Could you be more obvious?"

My brows turn down and I wave him away as I stalk toward the front computer, desperate to see what profile she was making and what the hell she could be selling. Maybe it's wrong to snoop, but if she was willing to do it on a public computer, I guess I have the right to make sure she's safe doing it.

Maddox, though, who's been cleaning, isn't done with his questioning. He runs his hand down over his beard and sweeps the last bit of dust from the shop into the pan that sits beneath the counter. "So, you've taken up lying to yourself?" He laughs, but it's a fading noise as I dial into the profile buzzing in front of me on the screen.

I ignore him as a black and pink website populates from a subcategory of Reddit. At first, I think *LoseitNow* is a weight loss page and I'm frantic with opposition. She doesn't need to lose weight. She's perfect, just as she is. But that's not what this webpage is.

"Dude," Maddox barks, making his way behind me. "What the hell are you doing?"

The hairs on my arm stand on end and a burning rage boils through me. How could sweet, innocent little Janie be selling her most precious gift? And why was she in such a hurry to do it here at the shop? I stare at her sweet, beautiful smile, and count the freckles along the ridge of her nose to calm myself, but another bidder joins the party as I'm counting, and I lose focus.

Thirty-six hits on her profile already, all of them trying to buy her virginity, and I'm about to kill every one of them.

Chapter Three

Janie

D id I erase the history on that computer? I think I did. I must have. I wouldn't have looked at something like that on a public computer and not erased it, *right?*

I did get distracted by that conversation with Huck, though, and I don't remember going back to the desktop.

Oh fuck. Did I not erase the history?

My heart slams against my chest as I stare up at the dark ceiling of my childhood bedroom. If anyone ever finds out what I'm doing, I'd have to dig myself a hole and bury myself deep. I can't imagine how humiliating that would be. It might be almost as humiliating as going to the tattoo shop to begin with.

I'm genuinely the most scatterbrained person on the planet.

My phone buzzes against the bedsheet next to me and a streak of panic turns my blood to acid.

It's someone from the tattoo shop. They went through the history, they found me pathetic, and they're going to tell the whole town what a disgusting whore I am. I know it! Someone kill me now. Take me out of my misery.

With closed eyes and a hammering heart, I flip the screen around and stare down at the caller. It's my friend Kate. She's Waylon's daughter. Their family owns the rodeo in town and lives up on a huge ranch up stream. We've been friends for a few years now, and she's the one that told me about the virgin website. I text her to let her know I'd posted. I'm sure she's curious about how it went.

Thank God. I'll live another day.

"Hey... you're up late."

"Well," she bubbles, "I knew you were setting up your profile. You already have almost thirty takers. The bidding is up to eight grand. I think it's that Christmas hat you're wearing. Nice touch, by the way."

My stomach turns. *"Eight grand?"* Okay, the pathetic sinking feeling in my stomach subsides, but it's replaced by a whorish feeling I can't describe. "That's enough to pay off my last semester of school." I sigh. "I could really use the money. I know my mom doesn't have it, especially this close to the holidays. Plus, I'll be glad to finally get rid of this cherry I've been carrying around like a lead weight."

I can hear the shrug in Kate's voice. "You only live once. People sell their sperm and their eggs. What's wrong with selling your virginity on the dark web? Seems legit to me. This website is supposed to vet everyone who applies."

Somehow, her reassurance isn't as reassuring as I was hoping. "But do you think it makes me a prostitute?"

"No!" she gasps. "It's a one-time thing. An act that gets you some much needed cash, and gives you the power of choosing how you lose your virginity. I might be on the site next." We both know that isn't true. If her father found out she was doing something this crazy, he'd go on a killing spree, then lock Kate in their root cellar. But I don't have anyone looking out for me like she does. Hell, I think even my mom might think this is empowering somehow. She's that kind of woman. Though, I'm sure she'd be worried about whether or not the guy is an axe murderer.

"Think of it like selling your hair, or an organ. No one puts limitations on which organs you can sell."

"Actually, they do. You can't sell your organs. I think it's against the law."

"Well," she huffs, "I'm sure you can in some places. My point is, you're not doing anything bad. You're being proactive. You're doing what you need to do. You're going to the gym and you're having someone else stretch it out a little, so it's ready for Prince Charming."

I pause and purse my lips, staring up at the ceiling again without words. Why is her way of convincing me only making me more skeptical?

"What's up with you?" she continues. "You were so convinced earlier. Now you're being all wishy-washy again. I thought you didn't want to be a kid anymore."

I'm not sure my virginity makes me a *kid,* but it does make me feel like one. Either way, after seeing Huck, I'm confused.

"I probably need sleep." I manage a fake yawn. "It's been a long day."

"Okay! I'll keep an eye on your numbers until I fall asleep. We'll talk in the morning."

"I have library hours tomorrow. I'll catch up with you when I get home." I slap my head. "Nope, not then either. I have the tattoo shop. Maybe I'll have a second to text."

"I'll be around," she says. "I've got your back. Don't worry so much."

Mark introduced me to Kate a couple of years back and we hit it off straight away. She's wild and free like Mark, but there's something about that personality that draws me in. Maybe it's because I can live vicariously through it. I can pretend I'm a crazy person who puts their information on the dark web for men to bid on, when in reality I doubt I could ever show up to cash the check—even if it were huge. What I really want is for Huck to see me. Like really see me. Not as a kid, but as an adult, completely unrelated to the girl he's known for years. I want to meet him again as an alternate, adult version of myself. Maybe losing my virginity will give me that power. The power to look and feel like the woman I'm desperate to be.

The clock ticks on the wall and I close my eyes, letting reality chew at the inside of my stomach. I can think Huck is the most handsome man on Earth. I can love the way his big rough hands feel on my skin. I let him slither through my thoughts with wild abandon, but I know nothing will ever come of it. He's off limits. He's the tall, strong, bearded, inked, dark eyed man that I can never have. And that's a reality I should come to sooner than later.

My eyes close and I try to imagine a different man, different arms, another body against me... but I can't. All I smell is cedar and pine and all I feel are Huck's giant hands against my waist. Softly, my clit throbs, and within seconds, I'm sucked back into the fantasy of the two of us together. This time, it's more intimate and the pictures are like they were when I was younger. I'd come back from a weekend at Mark's with sexual energy pent up like a wild animal. Then, I'd spend the week reading romance novels and putting his face into every hero I read. At night, I'd touch myself under the sheets to the thought of his low grumble in my ear.

I let my hand slide into my panties and run my middle finger through the silky wet mess I've made thinking of Huck.

My eyes close and a shutter of warmth rattles through me as I spin circles on the swollen nub.

No!

I pull my hand from below and tuck the sheet around my body tight, as though I'm a psychiatric patient tied to a gurney.

I'm twenty-four years old. I'm not some dumb kid. I have to make better decisions and the first is going to be not jerking off to thoughts of my best friend's dad.

Chapter Four

Huck

I spend the night up bidding every fucker on this fucking website. I'm currently the highest bidder at fifteen thousand, but LocknessCock isn't far behind and pushes me out of the running every few hours.

Who the fuck are these assholes?

"You didn't kill anyone," Maddox laughs, as I swing open the shop door. "That's positive."

"Not yet," I groan. "I don't know how to get to these guys. Addresses are all blacked out. You don't think they could be people in town, do you?"

"I wouldn't think folks would be into something like that here, but you never know. I mean, look at you... Mr. Claus. I'm not sure I'd have expected you to be bidding."

I keep my head down and grumble as I head back toward the printer. He must have seen the bullshit name I gave myself on that website last night. We're still close enough to Christmas to make Mr. Claus work. "You know why I'm bidding," I finish, pulling the printed photo from the printer. I have an early afternoon job that's going to take most of the day. It's a mural of The Little Mermaid with King Triton, Ursula, and Ariel. The client wants the image finished to Disney standards, which should be interesting. "You know why I'm bidding."

"And what are you going to do when she finds out?"

"I hadn't gotten that far. Right now, I'm just trying to keep sicko assholes away."

"Why don't you talk to her about it, as a figure of authority? She respects you. You've known her since she was a kid. Besides, aren't you going to run out of money soon? Fifteen grand is a lot to cough up for something you could just talk to her about."

What is he getting at?

"I've got it handled," I grunt, holding my hand out as the printer feeds me a crooked image. *Fuck.* Now I've got to reprint this damn thing again. I slide another sheet into the front and press the large blinking button as I stare out the side window of the shop. Thankfully, Maddox gets the point and leaves the room.

There isn't much to see outside except the brick wall from Mullet's bar, but the natural light centers me as I focus on the detail of the bricks. Each one of them is distinct to itself and holds the history of Rugged Mountain. Every line, every crack, every widening pore has seen the growing pains of a small mountain town. They've heard secrets and memorized stolen kisses. They hold tears and heartache. They remember love and growth. These bricks and all their details are the backbone of our town. They're the reason we've been here for three generations.

"So where are you going to get the fifteen grand?" Maddox flips the shop sign to open and turns up the radio, peeking his head into the print room before heading behind the counter to organize a box of nose rings that just came in. "Last weekend you were bitching about the six grand you had to spend on a new water heater."

I stare down at my phone and see LochNessCock has bid me up again. "Looks like eighteen grand now."

Maddox's eyes bulge. "Eighteen grand to sleep with some stranger? What the hell? Talk some sense into her, get her to take down the listing. What if you can't outbid this guy? Who the hell knows what she's messing with? And if you do win, where are you going to come up with eighteen grand?"

"Twenty," I say, hitting the button to bid. I can't let this fucker win.

Maddox laughs. "So, does that black market shop have a section for body parts? Maybe you could sell a few limbs."

"Probably wouldn't go for a fraction of what I need," I refute, turning toward the front door as the bell chimes. Janie steps inside with a tight grin and a quick nod of the head. She's nervous about something. Maybe she can see that Mr. Claus is me.

God. I should've been more creative. Mr. Claus wouldn't be buying the virginity of a twenty-four-year-old online. Maybe she's upset because that asshole LocknessCock is contacting her privately. I see there's a place for direct messages.

Fuck. I need to ask her.

She tucks the hem of her little pink dress beneath her round ass and sits in front of the desktop, dialing in on the screen. Something has happened.

I lock eyes with Maddox and nod back toward Janie, hoping he'll take the reins, but he only holds up his hands and grins before making his way to the storage room in the back of the shop.

Fuck me.

With my hand on my beard, I stride toward her and start talking, hoping the words come to me as I go. "Everything okay this morning, Janie? You're looking a little tired."

Her cheeks turn pink, and her hand runs down the back of her hair. "*Do I?* I guess I was up late last night. Then I had the library this morning and," she sighs, "it's been a weird day." She's talking, but she's focused on the computer, clicking and scrolling with wide eyes before finally looking toward me. "How was your night?"

I contemplate telling her that I spent the night bidding on her virginity, and that I'd do anything to make sure she was safe and smiling, but I'm not sure she'd appreciate the sentiment.

"Worked on my truck last night."

She cocks her head to the side and smiles. "The Ford? You still have that?"

"It was my dad's. Can't figure a time when I'll ever get rid of it. Hell, I just got the thing running again."

Janie hums. "I remember you used to work on that thing all the time. Do you still have the same seats as you did back then? I remember helping you pull out the old ones."

I remember that day too. It's one that sticks in my head. Mark was inside taking a call from his girlfriend, and Janie stayed outside to give them some space. The seat I was pulling got stuck on the rails, and I needed another set of hands. Janie grabbed the opposite side of the seat and helped me lift it off the bar, but I couldn't focus on anything but her. The way her hair fell down over her shoulder, the way her breasts crept up from the low scoop neck of her sundress, the way the sun fell on her pale skin like a halo of an angel standing in front of me. She lost her bracelet on that day too. An important one that had been handed down on her dad's side of the family with pink gold roses. I've always felt bad about that and looked for it for what felt like an eternity. I've thought of that moment we shared, hundreds of times over the past few years.

"Same seats," I finally say. "You'll have to come take a ride now that I've finally got the thing running again."

Fuck. Did I really just say that? I turn away and busy myself with the box of nose rings Maddox left on the counter. "Someday, I mean, maybe with some of your friends. Or a boyfriend. I could let you two borrow it for a date." The thought makes me sick, but the words sound better out loud than the alternative of her and I alone for a long ride together in a truck I've imagined laying my filthy hands on her in too many times to count.

"Yeah." She pauses. "Of course. Thanks for the offer." There's disappointment in her tone, but I can't figure why.

"Or maybe you don't want a ride in the old truck at all. I'm sure it's pretty lame for someone your age, anyway. It's just a—"

"That's not it." She gnaws at the side of her cheek like she's holding something back. "The way you rebuilt that truck always," she pauses, then shrugs, "it always amazed me. I've thought of it a lot over the years, actually."

Shit. I try not to let her words go to my head, but before I can stop them, they're there, poisoning the last bits of reasoning I have left.

"Really? What about it had you amazed?" I ask sarcastically as though rebuilding the truck isn't that big a deal, but I'm anxious to hear her response.

She shuffles her feet beneath the counter and stares up at me with big blue eyes that take me right back to that day, four years ago when the sun gifted her a halo. "You looked so strong and capable. So smart to know where to oil and place each bolt." Her teeth sink into her bottom lip. "I'd love to go for a ride with you. What about tonight, after we get out of here? It'll be late, but we could go look for aliens up on the ridge like we used to." She laughs. "Remember all the stories we used to tell up there?"

Warmth pools below my rib cage and my heart slams against my chest. She can't mean it the way it sounds. She's being polite, and as perfect as all this seems, I'm not sure I can trust myself alone with her. "I think Mark might be home tomorrow. He would probably like to see you, too. We could go then."

Janie flashes her gaze to the side before centering on me again. "I have to work at the library all day tomorrow. Then, I have a thing to take care of." She diverts her gaze again, and I'm reminded of why I started the conversation. I was going to tell her I knew about the virginity website. The one where she makes good on her promise Christmas Eve. "Anyway," she exhales hard, "I'm up for tonight if you are."

The doorbell rings and my Disney obsessed client walks in. It's an older woman with silver hair and an arm full of tattoos already. At least she knows what she's getting into. I nod toward her and smile. "Go ahead and grab a seat at my chair. I'll be over in a second."

The woman smiles back and steps up into the parlor, looking for my name on the wall.

My glance returns toward Janie. She's gone back to the computer as though the conversation was a passing thought to her. Maybe I'm reading into what tonight could mean. Maybe it would be good for me internally to prove I have self-control. I don't need to make this difficult. Janie is nostalgic, that's all. "Tonight sounds great. After I finish, you can follow me up to the cabin. I'll even grab a couple slices of pie on my break for the ride."

She grins so wide that I fear my heart will stop and burst right here and now, but I can't read into it. I can't let my head go to a place where I have a shot with Janie. What good does that do me? What good does that do anyone? Whatever I feel is inconsequential to the bigger picture. Janie is my son's best friend and everything about her is off limits.

Chapter Five

Janie

I t's official. I've lost my mind.

Huck's old truck is rumbling beneath me, sending a shiver into my stomach. It's either that, or his mere presence that's turned me alive. Either way, it's stranger than I'd imagined. He's in the driver's seat in a flannel with rolled-up sleeves, showing off dark ink that runs up his arms. Between us sits a picnic basket of hand pies from the diner on Main and a bottle of wine I brought along because I figure that's what grownups do. Though, now I don't think I need alcohol to loosen me up. I need an antipsychotic to rein me in again.

How did I get here? How did we have a conversation that led to this moment? How are we in the same truck, on a dirt road, heading toward the lookout? The same place Huck used to drag Mark and I home from when we were younger.

It's all so wrong, and though I haven't technically done anything to betray Mark, I can't help but feel like I'm hurting him somehow. What would he do if he knew I was riding up to the ridge alone with his dad? How would he feel? *God, what am I doing here?*

"So," Huck sucks in a deep breath, letting it out slowly as he breaks the silent air around us, "what do you think? Is the old truck what you remember?"

I stare at him through the dark, the only light on his face a reflection of headlights off the snow. God, he's gorgeous. His biceps flex unintentionally as he shifts the truck. My nipples poke at my bra.

This is the part I remember from all those years ago. Huck's giant body moving, flexing, working. Just watching him dig up a patch of dirt out back for his garden or lift a heavy piece of the truck and put it in place gets my body pulsing like a second hand on a clock. He's effortless in everything he does. Whether it's the manual labor of his small ranch, or the way he uses his hands at the tattoo shop. He's so careful and methodical, etching in every detail with precision.

My clit throbs again and again. Tick, tick, tick. I lose myself a little more with each pulsating ache.

"Yeah. It looks brand new. Are you going to sell it or..."

"My dad would roll over in his grave," he chuckles. "This truck is the only thing that's been passed down in the family. Not sure who it'll go to next. Mark doesn't want it."

"Do you ever think about having more kids?"

He laughs. "At my age? No. I did the kid thing. I love Mark to death, but I don't see myself being in a relationship again and well... I raised Mark without his mother, but I'm not sure that was the best thing for him."

"You're selling yourself short. You're only forty-five, right? You have like half your life left. You can't really think you'll spend the rest of it alone."

He pulls onto the top of the ridge beneath a few snow covered pines. It's the best spot I know to see every star in Rugged Mountain. Huck looks toward me, his arm still on the wheel as the other lies on his lap. "I guess if I found the right person, I'd settle down again, but that's a shot in the dark. Most women don't like guys like me."

"*Guys like you?* How so?" Part of me knows what that means already, but I'm curious about what he thinks of himself.

He nods and looks out the curved front window. "I don't know... assholes." He laughs. "Women want everything sugar coated. I'm not that guy. If I think something, I'm going to say it, and it's probably going to come out rough as hell."

At least he's self-aware.

"I kind of like that about you." I twist my thumb and forefinger together, trying to compartmentalize the nervous energy working its way up my throat. "I mean, I always thought it was cool the way you just spoke your mind." I look toward him, watching as the stress of what he's said settles onto his shoulders. The way he stiffens his back has me thinking he's keeping something from me. It's unnatural for him, and his body tells that story.

I wonder if it was the mention of Mark's mom. I've known Mark since I was eighteen and he's never talked about her much. From what I know, she and Huck were never married. They had Mark together young and went their separate ways when her mom got involved in drugs. Huck has spent his life devoted to raising Mark ever since.

"Well," he clears his throat, "you'd be the first woman to ever think that." He cracks his door open. "You want to check for these aliens?"

I've made him feel awkward. This big strong man who speaks his mind is holding back with me. Because to him, I'm a child. A kid he used to know. A girl who's spent way too much time pondering a fantasy that will never be. I bite the inside of my cheek and lean against the hood of the truck next to him, twisting off the cap on the bottle of wine I brought along. "We don't have glasses." I hand him the bottle and he takes a swig, then hands it back to me, fogging up the air with sweet raspberry on his breath.

"You're cold." He looks toward me, then turns back to grab a blanket from the truck. He wraps the fleece around my shoulders and rubs his hands together, mist escaping from the warmth from his breath. "When was the last time you were up here?"

"Oh, god, probably with you and Mark right before he left for college. I remember he was telling us that story about the seven foot aliens with the spiral di..." My face turns red as I realize I'm about to talk dicks with a man whose dick I've been thinking about nonstop since I was seventeen. "Anyway, he'd heard some crazy stories of the abductions up here. It's always some lonely woman who's been kidnapped and never returns."

Huck laughs. "Yeah, I used to hear some shifter stories when we first moved out here. Bears going wild with need and turning to men. Men going wild and turning to wolves. I think it's all just mountain stories. Something to keep people busy on cold nights like tonight." He looks toward me, casually running his giant hand down over my arm. "You warming up? We can get back in the truck."

"No. I'm fine." My gaze goes to his and for a long moment we're stuck there, our eyes locked in the waxy glow of the crescent moon with half a foot of snow crunched beneath the car and our boots. "Are you?"

He groans beneath his breath and a shot of excitement goes through to my core, thumping my clit, and tightening my nipples harder than they'd been. Is he feeling this too? Does he want to touch me as badly as I want to touch him, or is this all in my imagination?

It has to be my mind playing tricks. He's tucking his hands into his pocket. That's for sure the international sign for please let this end.

"We should head back down," I say, turning quickly back toward the passenger's side of the car. "I have an early morning and I'm sure you're exhausted from your day." As I turn, my bare knee catches the edge of the license plate and I let out a howl that scares an owl from his perch in the tree above us.

"Shit!" I drop the bottle of wine and stain the clean white snow, dark purple and red as my bleeding leg begins to drip. "God, leave it to me! I'm sorry. I don't want to get your truck a mess."

"I'm not worried about the truck. Let me see." Huck bends down in front of me. His knees hit the cold snow, and he grips my thigh with his big hand. He rubs his palms together and breathes warmth into them before he touches me. "Fuck, honey. Come sit down." With his hand on my back, he helps me to the truck, lifting me up onto the bench seat sideways before handing me his cell phone. "Here. Hold this light for me while I bandage you up."

If I'd known cutting myself would get him this close to me, I'd have sliced my leg open years ago.

Opening the glove box, he pulls out a decently sized first aid kit and props it up on the dash. I move the light to the box while he fumbles through for some antibacterial wipes. "This is going to sting," he says, lowering back down to my cut, "but we need to get it cleaned out good."

I close my eyes and brace myself for the inevitable sting, breathing slowly as I wring my fingers into my jacket.

"Hold on to my shoulders," he says, looking up toward me. "Give me a tap if you want me to stop."

My mind goes to places other than the cut on my leg. Dirty places. Places I shouldn't be.

I do as he's suggested, leaning forward onto his shoulders as he swipes the wipe over my cut, but there's no sting. Instead, I only feel the heavy touch of his warm hand.

He reaches up into the box for a large bandage and wraps white cotton around my leg once before taping it down. He's squatting between my legs, working my cut, and I can't take my eyes off him. Huck is quiet too, working slower now, swiping his thumb over the edge of the tape multiple times before standing. "You should be set until you get home. But make sure and take that off and wash it good with some antibacterial soap before bed. I'm sorry that happened. I need to get something around that, so it doesn't happen again." He stands slowly, rising up like a giant, the scent of his woodsy cologne in the cold air as he moves. *God, why does he have to smell so good?*

A litany of small confusions fills my head. Do I want to stop him from getting in the truck or not? Do I want him to stand or stay kneeling? What is the right answer to keep him with his hand on my leg until a world exists where he can do more to me.

He grips my legs and helps me in sideways, babying me as though I'm the most precious being on Earth. He's careful and methodical in the way his hands graze my body. The broad center of his shoulder brushes mine and he's close enough that I feel the warmth of his frame against my face.

I want to reach out for him, grip him close, pull him in, tell him I've had this feeling for years, that I wonder every second of every day what a life would be like with him.

But I'm not crazy, so I keep my lips sealed shut. Which right now, I should get an award for because feeling every ragged breath as it drags in and out of his body is near torture.

"You don't need to do all this," I say, my voice almost a whisper. "It's just a little cut. I can still move my leg."

His hand drags up to the side of my face and his gaze dials in on mine. "You're precious. You should be treated as such."

My heart pounds hard as my hand lands on his back. Our eyes lock. I'm not sure who is leaning in. Maybe it's me. Maybe it's him. Maybe it's the world pushing us together. I'm not sure, but I swear our lips are getting closer.

"This is wrong," he groans out as his lips brush against mine.

"It is," I whisper. He's so close now that I can't see him clearly. I can only feel him against me... and I want more.

His lips brush past mine and he nuzzles into my neck, sucking in my scent. "You've no idea how long I've wanted to hold you."

My nerves sing beneath his touch and my neck arches back, letting him in further. He nuzzles against me, growling under his breath as he holds me close. "You're so fucking beautiful. Do you know that?"

My eyes close and for one holy second the entire world makes sense. Huck's big arms are around me, and mine on him. His breath's on my neck, his hands in my hair. Everything is right, even though it's all wrong.

He grips me tighter. His hand wraps around my wrist as his jaw clenches against my face, a low growl emanating as though he's struggling with stopping himself.

"Do you know how long I've wanted you, Janie?" His forehead presses against mine.

"I reckon just as long as I've wanted you."

His lips sink into the space between my collarbone and my neck. The soft scratch of his beard against my skin tickles and wakes me up from the inside. My eyes close and every touch of his big, rough hands against me is like magic. Real, true, aching, dark magic. Magic that stirs parts of me that had been starving for a kind of love, affection, and touch that I didn't even know existed until now.

I need him.

Huck's hand wanders down my frame, his gaze never leaving mine. "You know we—"

"*Dad?*"

Somewhere in my mind, I know the voice belongs to Mark, but I'm frozen against Huck. I can't move. Even if I could, I'm not sure where I would go. There's only this small truck, and the frozen tundra. I suppose I could run for a tree, but I'm not sure Mark wouldn't put everything together sooner or later.

Huck stands, his hand still on my chin, his gaze on me. "I'll handle this. It's okay." He pulls away from my body, his absence leaving cold behind as he takes a step toward Mark.

I can only see him in the rear-view mirror, but I already know he sees me. There's no denying that from the look on his face. It's shock, horror, disgust, and something I can't identify.

"Mark, just hear me out." Huck tries to talk, but Mark's backing away slowly, disappearing toward his truck parked behind the trees.

I can't let Huck do this alone. I suck in a deep breath and stand from the truck with him, staring toward my best friend with more guilt than I've ever felt in my life.

"I'm sorry, Mark. I—"

"*You what?* How long has this been going on?"

"No. Nothing is going on. We were just—"

"Don't lie to me! You're up here, after midnight with my father leaned over you humping you like a feral dog."

I have nothing to say. He's right. He's right and something is wrong with me, because I wouldn't change what just happened between Huck and I for a second. I've never felt so good, so warm, so alive. That said, I can't ruin his relationship with his son. And this is my fault. I'm the one that mentioned coming up here in the first place.

What the hell is wrong with me?

I glance back toward Huck, whose eyes have gone dark with an emotion I don't want to identify. Mostly because I'm sure it's embarrassment, or maybe even regret.

God. Someone kill me. I'll be so empty if he regrets what happened.

"I'm going to walk back down the mountain," I say.

"No. You're going to ride with me. It's after midnight, freezing cold, and there's God knows what out here. Get in the truck."

If he were wrong about even one of those things, I'd start walking. But he's not. It's about ten degrees and pitch black out. Not only that, but I've heard at least three wolves howl and after all those shifter stories, I'm not sure I'd make it the few miles back.

"Nice!" Mark hollers. "Just get in the truck and pretend I didn't show up. Makes complete sense."

"Ignore him," Huck grumbles, hopping into his side, before hollering back to Mark. "We'll talk at home. It's not what you think."

Huck starts the engine of the truck and I look toward him.

"I'm so sorry. I didn't mean to cause all this."

He narrows his brows and looks toward me with an angled gaze that's more serious than he'd looked at me before. "He's confused. We've shocked him. That'll wear off. He'll understand everything with time."

"Understand what?"

"Whatever's going on here." He brushes his thumb against the back of my hand. "He'll understand after I talk to him."

I sigh and look out the passenger's window. I appreciate Huck's willingness to talk this out with Mark, but I know who Mark is. He's stubborn, like his father. Except he doesn't have the wisdom of forty-plus years behind him. He's not going to understand. I turn back toward Huck, my voice shaking as I say, "I thought I could do this. God, you have no idea how bad I want you. How bad I've always wanted you. But now, seeing Mark's face, I can't hurt him like this. I can't get between you two."

He lets out a heavy, gruff sigh and leans his head against the steering wheel, groaning out with a pain I'm not sure I've ever heard from a grown man. "Don't make any decisions yet. Just let me talk to him."

I pause for a long moment wondering if there's a world where Huck and I work... but I know there's not. He's my best friend's dad. He's twenty years older than me. Whatever this is, it's not destiny. And the sooner I come to terms with that, the better off we're all going to be.

Chapter Six

Huck

I've never wanted someone like this. I've never had an urge so deep that I couldn't satisfy. An ache so relentless that I can't relax. A thirst that won't let me think anything else.

Body wound, I sit in front of the computer screen staring at Janie's profile. Now that I've had her sweet body curved against mine, it makes me even more sick to see her being bid on like a piece of fucking meat. Besides that, LockNessCock has bid me up again. I swear I'm going to fucking kill this man. Twenty-four grand. I click the button to raise it another two. I'll be glad when this is over tomorrow.

A truck door slams outside and heavy boots thud against the porch before the front door opens and shuts with fire.

Mark has every right to be upset. I've crossed about six thousand boundaries even having thoughts about one of his friends, but he's always been a rational person, and everyone is of age. Maybe he'll understand. And if he does, maybe I can convince Janie to take a real shot at this.

"Can we talk?" I stand from the office chair and move into the kitchen. "Just for a few minutes?"

Mark rolls his eyes. "Which part would you like to talk about, Dad? The part where you're sleeping with a woman my age, or the part where you—"

"I'm not sleeping with her, Mark. It's... it's complicated."

Mark's head bobs back and forth and his shoulders roll back like they did when he was young and angry with me for not letting him take the snowmobile out to Whiskey Falls with his friends. "So, you're not sleeping together, but you're necking her at shifter lookout? What the fuck is wrong with you?"

I sigh, unsure myself what's going on with Janie. I've gone from being rational and methodical to being at complete mercy to my heart. It's uncomfortable. "I don't know what we're doing is what I'm saying. I only know how I feel."

Mark laughs. "How you feel?" His tone is sarcastic. "Tell me, Dad, how do you feel, messing around with my friend? I always thought you were looking at her weird, but I ignored it because I thought I was crazy. Turns out, you're the crazy one."

Fuck me. I'm a prick. I can barely stand Mark looking at me like this. I've raised him on my own, and what he thinks of me is all I have in the world. But a life without Janie, especially after having her in my arms, is too much pain to comprehend right now.

"I know it's awkward, Mark. I wouldn't have chosen to fall for one of your friends, but she's—"

"What, Dad?" Mark laughs psychotically and spins in a circle. "She's what? She's beautiful? She's smart? She's strong and funny and what? I know things! She's *my* best friend. And last I checked it was off limits for a dad to be messing around with his son's best friend. You know we almost dated, right?"

I suck in a deep, ragged breath. Maybe I underestimated how understanding Mark would be about this. "But you didn't. You're seeing Carrie and you two are happy, right?"

He rolls his eyes to the side. "That's not the point." His back straightens. "You know Janie's on one of those websites, right? The ones from the Reddit forums that take you to some black-market shit? The one where you sell your *virginity* to some stranger online?"

"Fucking hell, Mark. She told you about that?"

He laughs. "You know already? And you're still pursuing her?" His voice drops an octave. "Dad, you're twenty years older than Janie. *She's a virgin.* Have you lost your mind?" Mark shakes his head, crosses his arms over his chest, and heads up the stairs, disappearing behind the wall and into his room before slamming the door shut.

What the hell is wrong with me? It's like years of urges all focused-on Janie have built up to create a monster. I need to get ahold of myself. I need to stop thinking about her. I need more discipline, more self-control. I need to erase her sweet scent from my mind and ignore the way she sighed when I nuzzled against her. I need to forget the way her skin felt against my rough hands and the way she looked me straight in the eye and told me she felt this too.

Fuck. I swing open the front door and step out onto the porch, sucking in a deep icy breath as snow falls around the cabin. It's heavier than it was when I came in and I can't help but wonder if Janie got home okay. The roads bend and wind up this way and it's easy to hit a patch of ice and go flying. I hate that she drove herself home this late. I should call and at least make sure she got back okay. If nothing else, it's an excuse to hear her voice again.

Man, I'm going to need to check myself into rehab for this one, or I'm going to be finding excuses to run into her for the rest of my life.

The phone rings twice when her soft voice answers, "Hello?"

"Hey."

"You shouldn't be calling me, Huck. We made a mistake tonight."

"It didn't feel like a mistake." I hadn't planned to start the conversation this way, nor did I plan to fight for her again, but here I am, doing more things I never thought I'd do. "Can you honestly say it felt like a mistake to you?"

She sighs softly into the receiver. "It feels like we should've known better, Huck. Mark is your son. He's my best friend. I betrayed him. I can't get in the middle of you guys anymore. Which is fine because I don't think Mark is talking to me ever again, anyway. And you'll forget all about me in a few weeks."

This is the part where I should agree with her. I should let her go. I should let wounds heal and prove to myself that I'm not the monster I'm acting like, but I can't let her think things that aren't true.

"Janie, I'm not going to forget about you in a couple of weeks." I scoff. "No one has ever made me feel the way you do. I can't forget something like that."

Her voice shakes and increases in volume. "And maybe, if we're lucky, there's a universe out there where this works. Maybe, there're versions of ourselves on some alien planet where we're standing in falling snow and your arms are around me so tight that I can feel your heartbeat. And maybe, that version of us goes inside to sit by the fire, drink wine, and listen to music while we whisper sweet things in each other's ears." She sighs. "I hope it's true, Huck. I hope somewhere, somehow, a version of us gets to be in love. But it's not here, and it's not now." She sucks in a heavy breath and lets it out slowly. "I'm going to bed. I'm sorry for all the trouble." The phone goes dead, and I'm left standing in the falling snow staring through the trees and into the dark forest, wondering how I'm ever going to find this universe where we get to be, because this life without her... wouldn't be worth the trouble.

Chapter Seven

Janie

"It's the Virgin Mary," Kate jokes as she sits across from me at the library counter. She and Ann are both staring at me with wild eyes like I have a story to tell, but I don't.

"Ha. Ha. Not funny." I scan another book into the library from the return bin and slide it up onto the shelf.

"Well, you did set your Lose-It-Date to December 24."

"I think the Virgin Mary had some kind of miracle immaculate conception. She didn't sign up for a website to lose her virginity on Christmas Eve." I laugh, though it's caught in my throat, so it sounds sarcastic. "You guys are sick. Besides, I think that's sac-religious or something. Get help. It's Christmas."

Ann laughs. "Don't judge. The truth is, I'm just as desperate for a cherry pop. Besides, I wouldn't mind all that cash you're getting from it. What's it up to now?"

I roll my eyes. "It's ridiculous. There are two guys bidding each other up. It was at twenty-seven thousand last I looked."

Kate gasps and takes a sip of her iced peppermint coffee. "That's more than I've ever seen anyone go for."

"Well, I'm feeling kind of dumb about the whole thing. I might even pull the listing."

"What?" Kate gasps. "You can't! That'll pay for your last semester of college and give you enough to put a down payment on a cabin of your own. *You need a place of your own, Janie.* Your mom is great, but... I think you've reached a natural conclusion to life in your childhood bedroom. What changed your mind? You were so sure."

I shrug. "I don't know. I'm starting to think I should save it for someone special again." If I had my choice, that someone special would be Huck, but I promised myself yesterday that I was done with thoughts about him. I'm turning a new leaf.

"Did you meet someone?" Ann twists her golden hair around her index finger.

I close my eyes and shake my head. "No. I'm just being hopeful, I guess. Either way, I'm probably roped into it. The listing expires in five minutes and truthfully, the money will be good for everyone involved. I know my mom needs a few things fixed around the house and I have college to pay for and yes... a cabin of my own would be nice."

"Plus," Kate sets her coffee mug onto the counter, "you get to take control. You're not waiting around for some guy. You're in the driver's seat. Where do you meet the lucky winner, anyway?"

"Mountain View Lodge. The same place as the Christmas Eve party tonight." I roll my eyes. "It's weird, but also kind of good. Everyone in town will be there so if anything goes wrong, there will be a load of witnesses. Plus, I asked Bo to watch out for me."

"Bo, the seven-foot lumberjack who doesn't talk to anyone?" Ann laughs. "What did you tell him? Does he know about the website?"

I shake my head. "God no! I told him I had a blind date. I offered him money, but he insisted he'd do it for a dozen of my mom's sugar cookies. He's going to stand on the street near the hotel and wait for my messages. I'm sure everything will be fine. I mean the guy is vetted through the website, but just in case."

"That's cool. So, you hired a pimp for your cherry popping with a canister of your mom's Christmas cookies. That couldn't be more poetic." Ann laughs. "'Tis the season!"

"Maybe he's some billionaire who gets off on deflowering virgins." Ann twists her cup in circles gently, aerating the sweet scent of whatever latte she's been sipping.

"Well, he obviously gets off on the deflowering thing, billionaire or not," I retort, swallowing down the anxiety this conversation is causing.

"Maybe he'll tie you up or make you run so he can chase you." Kate runs her hands through her chocolate brown hair. "That's what rich people like, right? Something kinky and exciting?"

"Well, he's going to be severely disappointed then. I don't even know what to do with my body. I mean, I've seen people online and stuff but I don't know... I feel like I'm going to freak out and do something stupid and he'll want his money back."

Kate shakes her head and swallows down another hard sip of her coffee. "Nope. Sorry... no refunds. You pay to play, the end. What's your bidding up to now?"

I look down at my phone and my chest tightens. "One minute left, and someone called LochNessCock is in first place."

Ann bursts into laughter. "LochNessCock? What the hell does that mean? Is his cock magical? Does it disappear? Has no one ever seen it in real life? Has it been photographed by Scottish tourists and debunked by internet skeptics? Is it huge and crooked? Are you going to have to drain the pond to see it?"

I can't help but laugh. I love the way Ann can make the most serious things light. "It doesn't matter. I'm not meeting LochNessCock. I'm meeting Mr. Claus. Well, as long as he transfers half the money into my account before tonight."

"Mr. Claus?" Ann laughs. "That's even worse. Does he show up with a big red sack? Is he going to make you clean out his chimney? Is he going to fill your stockings with care?"

I don't laugh as hard this time. Instead, I hold my hand over my stomach, willing the acid to stay put. The only man I want touching me can never touch me again. Maybe this is the first step to moving on. Or maybe, this is the biggest mistake I'll ever make. Either way, *The Virgin Mary*, is about to lose her lunch.

Chapter Eight

Huck

My family has had this old truck for generations, and I always thought it would be hell selling it. But as I transfer the last of the money into Janie's account a bit of relief washes over me. She's safe from LochNessCock and I'm happy knowing she'll have the money she needs to finish college. Also, the rest of the money left over will be useful to fix this old cabin of mine. The roof has needed redoing for a few years now and I could finally get that electric fencing installed outback. Truly, it's a win overall. The only thing I'm not sure of is how to manage what happens tonight. There's no way I'm actually buying her virginity, and I'm not sure I want her to know I've even done such a thing. Still, I can't stop searching for excuses to see her again. Excuses to take her to the Christmas Eve ball, excuses to touch her, excuses to romance her like she deserves to be romanced.

Slow, heavy footsteps stomp down the wood staircase and Mark ducks into the kitchen. His hair is a wild mess from sleeping and his expression is still less than amused.

My stomach tightens with concern that I'll never be able to fix what I've broken.

I pour him a cup of coffee and settle it onto the butcher block island in front of him, hoping he's woken up with a new frame of mind.

"So is Janie going to be my new mommy or something?" His tone is crass and annoyed. I guess sleep didn't help.

"I know this is hard for you, and I hate that I feel the way I do, but if I'm honest, I don't know how to stop feeling what I do for Janie."

Mark sips his coffee and stares back at me like I've lost my ever-loving mind. It's not as terrible as the stare from last night where I could see he was on the edge of clobbering me with whatever heavy object was nearby. Today, it's a darker stare. A cold closed off stare. One that tells me he has no intention of forgiving.

His eyebrows crinkle. "Look, I just came down for coffee, not a love story."

I tip my head back and forth before taking a sip from the steaming cup of coffee in front of me. "Okay then. You going to the Christmas Eve dance tonight?"

"I don't know what I'm doing." He grabs his cup off the counter and turns back toward the stairs. I hate that this happened like this. I don't get to see Mark very often now that he's in the city for college. That's why I pushed the phone job at the tattoo shop. I was hoping it would bring us closer together when he was home.

"Mark... it's tradition. We always go down there and share cookies with everyone in town. Don't you remember that little—"

"I don't know what I'm doing tonight, Dad. I'll let you know." He spins away from the counter and jogs back upstairs coffee in hand and every thought I've ever had about Janie slices through my brain with disfunction and self-ridicule.

I'm a fuck up. Who the hell does this shit? Who the hell wrecks their family so selfishly?

The worst part of the whole thing is when it comes to Janie, I don't think. I've become a caveman driven on feeling and emotion. I act on urges and cravings so instinctively that my brain is superseded by some internal need that's nearly impossible to control. Like right now for instance. Despite the fact that I know I'm a fuck up, I can't stop wanting Janie. I can't stop thinking about her wild hair in my hands or her soft skin against my face, or the way her thighs shook when I bandaged her up. She's precious and perfect and I'm desperate to hold her and keep her safe from everything and anything.

Fucking hell. I pour my coffee into the sink and head out back to the woodpile, stacking piece after piece on the chopping block before throwing the axe into the center. The motion and sound of the wood cracking in two relaxes me. The winter we moved up here, I spent every day chopping wood. So much wood that I had enough to last the following three winters.

At the time I was releasing aggression that I had toward Mark's mom for refusing to fight for him. I raised him up fine, and I knew when we came up here I could do it, but a boy needs the softness of his mother. Not that his mother was ever soft. I got lucky that a few older women in town helped me with some of that. It really took a village with that boy.

I slam into another piece of wood. The crack echoes through the forest and I lose myself somewhere between the sound and the scent of pine as the sun sinks low in the sky. Who knows how long I've been out here... numb, cold, struggling with myself? This may be the lowest I've ever been.

It was one thing knowing that Janie was out there somewhere without me. Sure, we weren't together, and I was longing for her, but we had distance between us. Enough that nothing real ever happened. I could convince myself that this feeling was all in my head. But now, having touched her, having felt her against me, having watched her lips move, having seen her emotion, *having her*... what do I do with that? How do I recover from a pull that strong?

My cell buzzes in my pocket and the jolt pulls me from the downswing of another block of wood.

Maddox: You coming to the ball?

Truthfully, I'd talked myself out of the dance. If I can't take Janie, and Mark isn't going, I don't see the point. But it's hard to say no to Maddox. He's probably the best buddy I have up here. He's also my boss and the guy who runs the whole thing. Besides that, it would be weird if I didn't show up after being there religiously for the past fifteen years.

Me: I'll be there soon.

When the text is sent, I let out a heavy, labored sigh and lay my axe into the last piece of wood. I bend down to toss the split pieces into the woodpile. I'm not sure how much I chopped today, but judging by the size of the heap, I'm guessing I have enough wood for next winter, after it all dries. Trouble is, I don't give a fuck about next winter.

My life has gone to hell.

My son hates me and I'm sure won't look at me the same ever again. And the only chance I have at a real love has blown away before it's even had a chance to ignite.

Chapter Nine

Janie

When I see Huck's truck parked outside the hotel, a streak of excitement washes through me. I don't want him to risk his relationship with Mark, but I've been dying to see Huck since he left yesterday. And truthfully, I'd be on the bible lying if I said I hadn't had fantasies where he sweeps me up from my bed and we disappear to some cabin in Whiskey Falls behind the ridge where barely anyone goes. The weather is too bad up there for most people to stand, but we'd be fine tucked away with each other by a fire.

That, however, is one hundred percent not going to happen. Just like this date I'd planned for. I got the final deposit ten minutes ago with a message wishing me a *'Merry Christmas'* and letting me know that I should keep the money but give myself to someone who's earned it.

I can't even sell this virginity away, and I don't feel good about keeping the money. Who knows where it came from, or who it was that sent it. This whole thing is a mess.

Music from the Christmas ball echoes through the corridors of the lodge and I tempt myself with going down for dinner and having a chat with my mom, who I'm sure is wandering around. She's helped Maddox and his wife, Emma, run the Christmas ball in Rugged Mountain since we moved down here from The Springs when my dad died. Plus, I'm already dressed to impress in a satin red dress. I shouldn't let it go to waste. Who knows the next time I'll be this fancy again?

The lodge overlooks the best views of Main Street. Tall, white-capped mountains and jagged rocky paths, all surrounded by dark green pine and cedar. Tonight, though, the scene is much different. With the mountains under the veil of darkness, the only view is the hundred or so trees decorated with twinkling white lights in the field outside the picture windows.

Inside, the décor is much more elaborate with a three-story tree decorated with hundreds of white lights and green and red vintage ornaments. The star on top has been handed down through Rugged Mountain's history and it's said that it originally belonged to Maddox's grandfather. A man whose lore in the mountains lives on to this day. His picture sits above the fireplace in the lodge and every Christmas, Maddox tells stories about his very first Christmas up in the mountains. The resemblance between Maddox and his grandfather is eerie, like one of those click bate articles on the internet where they show Cleopatra's twin living in the current day. Maddox's grandpa has the same long gray beard and kind dark eyes.

My mom waves from the back corner of the room where she's socializing with Mrs. Robinson—the town gossip. They're both dressed in fancy holiday clothes and bright red lipstick, like it's a requirement of the season. I intend to say hi, but I get distracted by the bartender and a big, dark bottle of whiskey sitting behind him. I could use the warm-up, and the distraction.

"Double shot of whiskey," I say, leaning forward against the bar.

I've seen the bartender around town here and there, but not enough to know his name. He's a tall guy with dark hair and a piercing in his septum. He cocks a heavy eyebrow. "Double shot? Are you here by force?" he laughs.

I contemplate spilling all my tea out on the counter for him to drink, but the day has been traumatic enough. What I need is this shot and some of those mozzarella sticks on the table behind me. After I've acquired the best Christmas has to offer, I'll retreat to my room for a long, sappy Christmas movie that will make me regret every life decision in slow painful mockery. And when I fall asleep, virginity still intact, hopefully I'll dream about Huck and the life that we'll never have.

"Kind of," I joke, taking the double shot he slides toward me. I don't drink it all at once. I sip the liquid slowly and take another glance around the room, studying all the happy couples and smiling faces of Rugged Mountain, searching inadvertently for a glimpse of Huck. I'm not looking for long before I see him. He's standing next to the Christmas tree alone, his hand tucked into one pocket of his jeans while he stares up at the tree.

My heart pinches in pain and blood rushes from my head into my toes, prompting me to leave the bar.

The bartender's talking, but I don't turn back. It was a mistake to come down here. I thought I wanted a glimpse of Huck, but it's too hard to see him. If he were to see me too, I would be humiliated. *What would we say? How would we say it?* I move through the small crowd of people toward the front door, desperate for some fresh air, but what greets me is anything but freshness. It's Mark, and he looks like he's about to steal what's left of Christmas.

"Janie." He says my name like we're business professionals passing each other in a boardroom, not like the guy who's been my best friend for years. Not like the guy who talked me off a ledge at least four times our senior year of high school because I tore my dress in the bathroom at senior prom and had to waddle out of the school with Mark's suit coat tied around my waist. Pictures still circulate to this day.

"Mark, wait." I twist toward him. "Please talk to me."

He shakes his head. "I don't even know why I'm here. Truthfully, I wouldn't be if it weren't Christmas."

"You're here because you're my best friend, and I know deep down you're hoping we can fix this." I reach for his hand, and thankfully, he doesn't pull away. "I should've told you I had feelings for your dad. It's so fucked up."

"Yeah," he sighs, "kind of. Why are you here alone, anyway? Don't you have your cherry popping event going on?"

"The guy never showed, but he still paid. I don't know what's going on. I think I have to contact the company and figure out what to do next."

Mark's brows turn inward. "What was his handle?"

"Don't laugh. It's so stupid."

He nods.

"Mr. Claus."

He lets down his shoulders. "I think my dad sold his truck last night to pay for your virginity."

"What? No. He didn't. His truck is right outside and like I said, whoever did this didn't show up. Your dad wouldn't do that. He didn't even know I put the listing up. It's not—"

"He knew. We talked about it last night. And I just ran into Bo outside. He was climbing up into Dad's truck, so I asked him what was up, and he told me that he bought it this morning. What else would Dad have used that kind of money for?"

I turn back toward the tree, and see Huck is still standing there, now with a bottle of beer in his hand.

"You don't really think he'd do that, do you? He loved that truck."

"Sure did," he sighs. "Can I be honest with you?"

I nod, swallowing down the lump that's growing in my throat. I don't know if a good conversation ever started with *can I be honest with you.*

"I've seen the way he looks at you. I've seen it for years. He'd be happier when you were around, and I guess I always knew in the back of my head he was thinking about you." His face crinkles up. "It's gross, but I see it." He shakes his head as though cooties have just crawled all over him. "What I'm trying to say is... if he sold his truck to keep you safe, he must like you a lot more than I could imagine. You guys should talk."

My head spins with a cocktail of whiskey and a hormone shift that I'm not accustomed to. "What do you mean?"

Mark rolls his eyes. "I'll go talk to him."

"Wait." I grab his arm and pull him back. "What's going on? You hated that we were talking. You never wanted to see me again."

"It's going to be weird at first," he shrugs, "but I don't know... I wouldn't want someone holding me back from somebody I was willing to trade my most valued possession for. Just don't tell me all the weird details... okay?"

My cheeks turn pink, and my stomach tightens. "Yeah. Of course. I wouldn't."

He nods and wraps me in his arms before whispering, "Also, I think we have to set Bo up with someone. He just had a thirty-minute conversation with me about cutting down the whole forest around his home to keep busy. I think he's losing his mind."

I smile and hold Mark tight. "We'll have to brainstorm who we can send his way."

He squeezes my hand and I watch as he walks toward Huck who's talking to Maddox.

As much as I want to be a fly on the wall for his conversation, I don't have it in me. My head is spinning about how I'll get Huck's truck back for him. Then, there's the truth that Mark being okay with this doesn't change how weird this whole situation is. Maybe Huck has realized that too. Maybe this isn't the beginning of something great. Maybe this is the end of something that never was.

Chapter Ten

Huck

I tap three heavy knocks on Janie's hotel room door. There's a lump in my throat and my stomach is tied like a honda knot, but I have to see her. I have to know if she feels the same way for me, if she sees this as something she wants forever.

The door opens slowly. "*Huck?* How'd you get my room number?"

I grin the second I see her in the tight red dress. Her breasts round, her nipples hard. "I know the woman at the front desk well. I told her I had a gift for you." I pull a small box from behind my back and hand it toward Janie. "I could've mailed it, but I figured it would be better to give you in person."

She looks up at me with wide blue eyes then sits back on the queen-sized bed that's draped in a white and red quilt. "You didn't need to get me anything, Huck. I know you sold your truck for me. You need to get it back from Bo. I can give you the money. I—"

"No." I sit beside her, holding her shoulders in my palms. "Mark told you, didn't he?"

She nods and stares down at the green velvet box before looking back up at me. "Why did you do that? You love that truck. And you—"

"I love you, Janie. It took our time together this week for me to realize I've loved you for years. I've loved you from afar, over countless sleepless nights, and I love you more now. That truck is a piece of metal. Your virginity is something you can never get back. I couldn't let you give it away like that."

"But you could've talked to me. I don't need your money, Huck."

My hand goes to her face. "I want you to have the money for school."

"I don't need thirty thousand dollars for school, Huck. I have loans to cover the rest."

"And you'll pay off the loans." My hand slowly combs the hair on her shoulder. "You don't owe anyone your virginity for the hard work you've done, Janie. You're beautiful. You should give yourself to the right person when it's time."

"I can't take it," she says. "You have to get your truck back. It's too much."

My hands wrap around hers, the velvet box still in her palms. "Open your gift. I want you to see something."

She looks down at the box and pulls at a bright red string, then lifts the top slowly, her eyes brightening when she sees the bracelet that she'd lost that day we were putting in the seats.

"Where did you find this?" Janie gasps, tears welling in her eyes as she looks toward me. "I thought it was gone forever."

"I was cleaning out the truck for the sale, and I lifted the passenger side rail where the seats connect. It was hooked on the bar. That's why we couldn't find it." I squeeze her hand. "It was the sign I needed to know I was doing the right thing, honey. I can't quit you. I won't. I knew it the second I touched your skin last night."

She slides the bracelet onto her wrist and twists toward me with more pause in her throat than I'd prefer.

"What's wrong, honey?"

Tears drip from her cheeks. "Everything. I mean, Mark is okay with this now, but what happens when he's not? What happens when reality sets in and we're living together and we think everything is good, then all of the sudden, he realizes how weird this whole thing is. *Then what?* Do we stay together? Do we separate? Because I can't hurt him, Huck. The past few days have been hell."

Seeing Janie in pain is like sticking knives in my eyes, but I don't know what to say.

"Yeah," I brush my hand against her cheek, "and what if you and I create a world so happy that Mark aspires to have the same? What if you're the realest thing that's ever been? What if there's nothing else? What if we were meant to be?"

She stares back at me, her chest rising and falling quickly as her head dips onto my shoulder. I wrap her up in comfort and hold her close, feeling the wave of her emotions as they crash onto the shore. Love isn't enough. Love could get us here, but it can't keep us. She needs security, and I can't give that to her. The worry of what we've created will sit with her for a lifetime, taunting every memory, every happy day, every second, like a bomb waiting to go off.

"I'm sorry, Huck. You should probably go. I'll make sure you get your money. I—"

"I don't want the money." I stand from the bed and hold her against my chest. "I want you, Janie. Now, forever, and always." I kiss the top of her head and hold her tight.

"It's hormones." Tears drip from her eyes. "None of this is real. We're just fueled by all this chemistry. It will wear off. Then we'll wake up and realize we've made a terrible mistake."

I shake my head and swipe a strand of her hair out of her face. "You will never be a mistake to me, Janie. *Never.* Everything I feel for you is real. It's you that's woken me up. It's you that makes me feel alive. No one else has done this. No one else can."

She sucks in a deep breath and lets it out slowly, wicking away her tears as they fall off her cheeks. "Then we should do this tonight. We should have sex, get it out of the way, and then see if what we have left is real, not an accumulation of desire and dopamine."

I paint her cheeks with my fingers and stare down at her sweet face. "I'll never fuck you like you're not something I need forever. And you will always be more than desire and dopamine. You're my heart, Janie. And when we make love, it's because this is forever. You're mine, I'm yours, and our future is each other."

A deep breath staggers in through her lungs and she looks up toward me. "Then do it, Huck. Make love to me. Touch me like you did last night." Her voice is shaking. "Like it was always you I was saving myself for."

Fucking hell. The sound of those sweet words slipping from her lips has my cock rock hard. I've never felt more important, more cherished, and I want nothing more than to take her up on the offer. But I can't take her virginity tonight, not on the weird premise that I've just paid for it.

"We should wait. Besides, I don't have protection."

She steps toward me and backs me onto the bed, tucking her curved frame between my legs as she looks down at me with dreamy eyes and a stare that would kill any man within a ten-mile radius. "I'm not worried about protection, Huck. And I'm in love with you. You didn't buy my virginity. I'm giving it to you." Her mouth twists, and she turns around, lifting her hair to make room for my hands to unzip her dress.

Nothing could ever prepare me for the way it feels to unzip her and soon the scene unfolds like an out-of-body experience. I'm lost in her smooth skin as she exposes herself slowly. Inch by inch I unwrap her, then all at once the dress slips to the ground. She's bare beneath the fabric except for the tape holding up her breasts and the small white underwear that her ass has swallowed.

"Don't hold back with me, Huck. I want you to take me untethered. I'm not a flower. Be rough." She swallows hard and looks toward me. "I've always liked that you're a little rough."

Fuck.

There's longing on her innocent face that I don't trust myself with. If I let go, I'm going to ravage her. I'm going to claim this sweet angel for myself and I'm never going to let her go. I've denied myself so long, it's surreal that I'm here, in this moment.

Janie bends down in front of me and unzips my jeans, tugging them to the floor. Her pink lips part and she stares up at me with imploring eyes. The tip of her nose rubs against my cock playfully and then her cheek.

I'm a bad man. I don't want her on her knees, but when her lips touch the tip of my cock, it's a free fall. A frenzy of insatiable desire I can't stop.

She moans against my cock and takes me in deep, sucking and pumping her lips faster and faster. I need her. I need her taste, her touch, her heart. I need it all. She's a part of me.

I hold the back of her head as she works, giving me more and more until the tension rises and I have to pull her away.

"Stand up for me, honey." I growl out the words, but she stays in place, sucking harder.

Oh, she's a tease.

I like it... *too much.*

All at once, she pops off my cock with a sound that drags me back to reality, a sweet grin on her face as she stares up at me.

I'm not going to last.

I grip the back of her neck and pull her into me, licking the inside of her mouth. "You're mine, okay?"

She nods and kisses me back. "Always."

Even with the approval of my son, this still feels wrong. She's so young, so innocent. And the excitement I have over sinking into her tight little pussy is probably a mental illness.

My hand slides over her hips and trace toward her core. She's damp and swollen. I lift her thigh to my hip and slide two fingers inside of her, thrusting into her deep, slick pussy. My free hand holds her back and my lips suck at her breasts.

She whimpers and her head dips back. "Oh my god. That feels incredible."

"You're soaking wet for me, honey." My voice is deep and nearly growling. I swirl my tongue around her nipples and let my fingers search her insides, paying close attention to every breath she takes.

She's tight. Even with my fingers, I'm pushing her body's limits.

"Harder," she pants. "I need your cock, Huck. Please!" There's need in her tone that humbles me. Her teeth sink into my chest, and she groans as I thrust my fingers back and forth, circling her clit with my thumb.

"Fuck. I've dreamt about this for years," I groan in her ear. "Do you know how fucking insatiable I was every time you left the house? I wanted to grab you by the waist, pull you back into the cabin, and make you mine. I spent night after night fantasizing about it... about this."

She swallows hard and slides her hand down over my beard, staring up at me with hooded eyes that send a carnal signal straight through to my dick.

A growl leaves my throat and red flashes in front of me like a signal from some evolutionary DNA tucked deep within me. The room spins and everything is blurry except for the woman I love, the woman I've waited a lifetime for.

Janie sees the shift, and she grins coyly. "Take me, Huck. Fuck me hard. Please!"

I suck her nipples into my mouth and run my tongue over the hard spears that've formed. Another growl rumbles through me as my fingers pull from her sticky, sweet core. Two at a time, I lick them clean, tasting her sweet scent against my tongue as I look her in the eye.

Fuck.

Janie leans back on the mattress and I kneel before her, scraping the head of my cock against her slippery entrance. I lift her leg up to my shoulder and close the distance between us. "It's going to hurt, honey. Are you sure you're ready?"

She nods and swallows hard as my cock slides into her tight core further.

Sigh after sigh. Moan after moan. It's all pleasure until she squeaks. "Oh fuck... that's big."

I'm bent over her frame, holding her close, staring into her eyes as I thump against her. "You're okay, honey. Do you want me to stop?"

She shakes her head, but I know she's struggling. I can see it on her face, and I can feel it on my cock. She's strangling me. She's so tight. So fucking tight. I move slow, trying not to hurt my sweet angel, but I'm not sure I can get much deeper without pain.

"Are you okay?"

She nods again, panting and needy. "Go deeper, Huck. I can handle it."

Blind with heat, I push in a bit more, digging into her tight core until I meet resistance and she's whimpering beneath me.

"Good girl." I kiss her forehead and swipe a finger down over her cheek and onto her bottom lip. "I'm going to speed up. Are you ready?"

She nods, and I don't waste time, thumping into her harder and harder as I circle her clit with my thumb. Her curved body shudders beneath me. Jumping. Thrashing. Tightening.

Fuck. I can't hold on much longer. Between the tight grip she has on my cock and the erratic movements, I'm a dead man walking.

Janie bites her bottom lip and her cheeks turn pink. "I'm going to come, Huck. Go harder. I need you."

She's been forbidden so long that her words send a shiver of excitement through me.

The bed squeaks and the salty smell of sex surrounds us in the heat of the room. She's elemental. Her pussy clamps down on my cock and her fingers fly through her long hair in a manic fashion.

My hips slam against her with desperation. "Tell me you need it, Janie. Tell me you need my come."

"I need your come, Huck. Come for me!" She cries the words out with desperation until she releases, spreading her silky come all over my cock.

Within seconds of hearing that, I release a flood of hot pleasure inside of her. My pulse races against my neck and the room spins around me. I pull her into my arms and hold her close, collapsing beside her in the bed.

"Tell me again you're mine, Janie."

She sighs sweetly, then rolls into me, running her fingers through the hair on my chest. "I'm yours, Huck. Now and forever."

"Forever," I repeat. "Forever."

Epilogue

Janie

S ix Months Later

I dip my sponge into a bucket and scrub at the mud on Huck's old truck. We took it up onto the ridge last night and it's been covered ever since.

"See... aren't you glad I got this back for you?"

He grins wide and makes his way toward me, sponge in hand.

Why do I have a feeling this isn't going to be good?

"What I think is incredible is that you got him to reverse the sale with a tin of your mom's Christmas cookies. I'm not sure anyone has that power, but you."

She laughs. "Not true. Bo's a good guy. Aren't you a little curious about what he's been up to lately?"

Huck shakes his head and grips me in his soapy hands. "If you talk to three different people, they'll all tell you a different story about what he's doing back there in the woods." Huck kisses my cheek. "I'm going to mind my own business and stay focused on what I have here."

Staying focused on our own family is a good thought, and I'm all for it, but I'm still curious why Bo is so enthralled with his new project. Maybe I'll send Kate or Ann up there to check on him.

Huck leans into my lips and kisses me again, this time harder.

Okay, I can forget everything else.

"Get a room!" Mark shouts from the front porch. "You two are gross. We had a deal. No kissing or touching in front of me."

Huck laughs and kisses my neck playfully. "Last one... *this minute.*"

Mark rolls his eyes and steps off the front porch toward me. "Shouldn't you be resting?" His gaze drops to my expanding stomach and up again.

I won't lie, this has been awkward at times. The wedding, moving in, telling Mark about the baby. But he's been supportive as hell... with a sarcastic comment or two here and there. We laugh it off and truthfully, it adds levity to a weird situation.

"He's right," Huck seconds, kissing my forehead. "You should be resting. Why don't you head inside, and I'll come fix you dinner in a few."

"Basically, he's sending you away because he knows I'm going to bust his chops again for being the oldest father on this mountain."

Huck laughs. "Now I know you've been missing class. There are at least half a dozen men on this mountain older than me with young babies." He gives Mark a playfully sinister smile. "Plus, I needed another chance at getting the son I always wanted."

As I watch those two tussle in the driveway, I realize I'll never understand a dad and his son's relationship. They say the meanest stuff to each other and then laugh as they wrestle it out.

I shake my head and make my way into the cabin. Just watching them go at it is exhausting.

The last six months have flown by and sometimes I look up and wonder where all the time has gone. I suppose that's what happens when you're having fun.

When I'm in the cabin, I head to the back room where baby Clay will sleep and sit down in the rocking chair that Maddox gifted to us. It's handmade from wood from our forest and has been used to rock many children on the mountain to sleep. It's here that I feel a part of something. In this home with Huck. In this rocking chair with my baby boy kicking inside of me. In this crack of the universe where fantasy has become reality and true love is allowed to exist.

Lumberjack

Chapter One

"**I**'m innocent!"

The words come from the lips of a sweet-looking woman with big dark eyes staring at me through the tree line. She wears a tight orange jumpsuit, and her dark hair is tied into a low ponytail. It's not common to come across someone on my property. It's even less likely to come across someone in a prison uniform, but I suppose there's a first time for everything.

"Okay," I holler back, balancing my axe on my shoulder. I was out chopping wood before she popped out of nowhere. "What are you innocent of?"

Her eyes dart from left to right before she shakes her head and leans forward slightly, as though she's going to whisper to me from thirty feet away. "I can't say that out here."

I nod slowly, staring toward her short, curvy frame, wondering what the hell this woman could ever have done to earn the traffic cone she's wearing. From this distance, she doesn't look like she'd have the capacity to physically harm anyone. Though, I guess she could be carrying pure muscle around under that suit. Also, I guess crimes aren't all physical. She could be innocent of tax evasion or something even more boring.

"Can you help me?" she scream-whispers so loud she may as well speak.

"Help you what?" I shift backward and drive my axe into the tree stump next to me. "Last I checked, it was illegal to harbor a fugitive. I'm not looking for trouble."

She rolls her eyes and crosses her arms in front of her chest as though I'm the problem.

Makes sense. I'm the one refusing to shelter her from the cops I hear rustling up the path.

Dogs bark and a voice echoes, "We know you're out here, Rose. The dogs will bring us straight to you. You're better off coming out on your own."

Rose. A sweet name for such a strange woman. Her arms fly into the air, and she stares toward me. "Please!" she mouths, pressing her palms together firmly as though she's begging.

Fuck me.

The dogs bark again, closer this time. I'd guess they're less than a few hundred feet from the cabin. I'm not even sure I have time to hide her if I wanted to. I'm also not sure if I can just leave her there.

What if she is innocent? I've known the law to be a bit jaded from time to time. And a woman like her, with all these exaggerated hand movements and loud whispers, can't be faring well in jail.

I huff out a heavy sigh and wave her forward, twisting away before she can catch up. I'm not sure what I'm doing yet, but I know we aren't going to talk pleasantries while I do it.

"If the cops catch up, I'm telling them you followed me, and held me hostage."

A soft giggle bubbles behind me. "Forgive me, but I think the cops would find that less believable than what I've already told them. You're a giant... and look at me."

I glance back to see she stands no taller than five foot six inches. Up close, you can really see the height difference. No one would believe a story about her holding me hostage. I mean, she'd have to stand on her toes just to be eye level with my chest.

The dogs bark again.

"They're gaining on us. How far is your cabin?" Her voice is still soft and sweet, despite the fear I'm sure she's feeling.

"They've changed directions. You're lucky it snowed last night. It's harder to keep a scent track in this weather. I guess it bought you fifteen minutes or so. Are you covering your tracks?"

"Yes." Her tone is sarcastic, as though she's insulted that I'd ask.

"Okay then, we should be back before they catch wind of you again."

She expresses an audible sigh of relief as we walk quickly through the pine forest and into the clearing toward my little cabin on the edge of the mountain. I've lived here nearly all my adult life and I have the terrain memorized. Every dip in the landscape, every blade of grass, every patch of moss, every pine tree, every stream. It's all mapped out in my head, so when I step over the spring trap I have set, I do it automatically, like I've done a thousand times before. It isn't until a shrill yelp echoes in my ears that I'm reminded of my stupidity.

Fuck.

I twist toward Rose. She's on the ground, holding her ankle, biting her fist as though she's trying to stay calm, despite the pain. I bet it hurts too. Those spring traps bite right into the tendons.

Damn it. Now, there's an obligation to help her. My idiocy let her walk straight into my trap.

I bend down to her side, releasing the spring. I'm not sure what I'd seen from a distance earlier, but up close, she's indescribably gorgeous. I'm at a loss for words.

"I don't think I can walk." Her whispers shake me out of the trance I'm in.

"Yeah, of course." My hand grazes her already purple and swollen ankle. "You did some damage. We'll have to look at it closer when we get inside. Can I lift you?"

She shrugs. "I don't know, *can you?* I'm not light as a feather."

Fifteen minutes isn't long enough to have a debate on whether or not I can lift her, so I act. Bending quickly, I pick her up from the ground and carry her in my arms toward the cabin fifty feet from where we stand.

"You're strong." She looks up at me with big round eyes that speak more than I'm ready to comprehend. There's pain behind them... fear. It's more than the injury or the cops chasing her.

Then again, maybe I'm wrong. I've never been the best at picking up on facial expressions or emotions in general. My sister was going into labor next to me in the truck on our way to The Springs and I'd have totally missed it had she not turned to me and said, *'Bo... I'm in labor.'* I thought she had to use the bathroom the way she was clenching her stomach.

"This is me." I kick open the door with Rose still in my arms and settle her onto the couch, then lock up the cabin door.

"Is this a reverse hostage situation now?" the woman jokes. "You lead me into one of your traps, then lock me in with all those deadbolts until I become your baby making slave?" She clears her throat and presses her palms into the sofa to readjust herself. "You have no idea what I did to the last man that tried shit with me." She laughs, but I wonder if that was a small dose of truth. There's a reason she's been behind bars.

"I could unlock the doors if you'd like. No skin off my back if the cops come looking for you." I run my hand back through my hair. "And I have no desire to parent a child, so you're good at the baby-making thing."

She balks. "A big man like you? So virile and strong? You have no desire to keep your blood line going? I think you're letting down a generation of Vikings."

"Maybe in my younger days. Now, I'm too old for that shit. Can you imagine me chasing a toddler around here?"

"I guess that's true. You were a little out of breath carrying me in."

My brows narrow at her comment. "How so? I've been having a full conversation with you since I picked you up."

"In fairness, it's probably my size. Even in prison, I can't seem to slim down. You know those prison meals aren't half as bad as people say they are. The cornbread and chili are really some of the best I've ever had."

Staring back at her, I'm unsure of what to say. She's mentioned her size twice now, but I don't see the problem. In fact, I see just the opposite. She's perfect. Does she really believe that she's not?

"Ah, you're beautiful," I say. "You have to know that already. I'm sure you're complimented all the time."

"I didn't say I wasn't beautiful. I said I was fat. There's a difference." She lifts her leg onto a pillow at the end of the couch and stares back at me like she's pointing a gun straight at my face, waiting for a response.

Why do I like it?

"Fat or not," I say, "you're beautiful, and you should stop talking about it."

"Fair enough. What about you? Do you live out here alone?"

My brows narrow as I grab a bag of ice from the freezer and make my way back to her side, carefully settling the bag onto her swelling ankle. "I don't think you understand how this is going to work. I don't mind giving you a compliment on your looks, but I also see your orange jumpsuit and the broken cuffs you're wearing like bracelets. So, maybe you're going to need to tell me what's going on before we take this conversation any further."

She looks up at me and shrugs. "It won't matter what I say. You're not going to believe me. No one does."

"Why don't you try me?" I exhale a heavy breath, seeing this isn't going to be the easy walk I was hoping for.

Snow falls outside and a heavy wind picks up. It's good news for her. The wind will distort the scent, sending the dogs off the trail, and the snow is going to further that prayer.

"Trust me, I've talked to a thousand people like you. None of them believe a word I say." She chews at the inside of her cheek and stares down at her purple toes. Trouble is, I can see that heartache in her eyes again... and I know it's not her injury.

Fucking hell. Why do I want to fix it? I've been out here alone too long. That's the reason.

"Are you really going to make me go through the Rolodex of crimes until you tell me what you did?"

She looks up at the ceiling and sighs before drawing her gaze toward me again. "Trust me, you wouldn't understand. It's better if I let my ankle heal, then get back out there on my own. How long do you think before this thing is workable again?"

"Weeks," I huff. "The joint is dark purple and swollen to twice its size. You need to stay off it and give yourself some time to heal. Even then, where are you going to go? Have you been up here before? This is the most rugged terrain in the west. It's almost all undeveloped land. You'd be food for wolves or God knows what else."

"What do you care? You don't owe me anything. I could be a murderer for all you know."

"Are you?"

She shakes her head and bites the inside of her lip. "No."

"Well then, at least we know that much."

Wind whips against the side of the cabin and a gust of cool air filters in through the crack in the windowsill. I've been meaning to fix that all winter, but something else always came up. Now, seeing I have a guest, it seems like a priority.

"Why don't you rest? I'll get you a cup of tea, put a log on the fire, then I'm going to head out and caulk up that leak in the window." I stand from the bed to head toward the kitchen just five feet away, but she reaches out and grips my hand in hers.

"No. Please don't go."

In mine, her hand is small and fragile. "I'm right here. I'm just going to make some tea and—"

"I know," she whispers, "but could you just sit here with me for a few minutes?"

As I stare back at her innocent face, the instincts I'd felt carrying her in flood back. Prior to today, I'd only ever felt this way over my nieces and even then, it wasn't this strong. This is primal, raw, and overwhelmingly intense. I need to know how Rose ended up in that jumpsuit. Then I need to find a way to protect her.

Chapter Two

Rose

T his guy can't be for real.

He's easily the tallest person I've ever seen, and his body is built like one of those bulls I've seen at the rodeo. I wonder if that's why he lives out here. He'd be out-of-place anywhere but alone in the woods.

Maybe I tripped and fell somewhere in the forest, and this is my coma dream. A fantasy about a big, burly woodsman who carries me to safety and keeps me hidden from the rest of the world. He does check all the boxes.

Beard... check.

Tall... double check.

Dark, mysterious eyes... can't miss them.

Smells like a forest of pine and some manly musk I can't identify... affirmative.

Black ink covering his arms, shoulders, and hands... triple check.

He has it all, including the kind of personality that didn't mind holding my hand for at least an hour last night while I came down from a panic attack. There has to be something I'm missing. Why would a seemingly perfect man be living out in the middle of nowhere alone? Maybe he's a criminal. Maybe he's evading the law. He did pick me up pretty quick yesterday, and that yard is like a minefield. Who knows what this guy's done?

I breathe in deep, centering myself before lifting the flannel blanket he tossed over me in the night. The fire is still roaring, too. He kept it going. Truthfully, it's the best night's sleep I've had in months. Even before prison, I was having nightmares daily. Inside, the terrors only got worse.

"Morning." His voice is deep and graveled. He's already dressed in jeans and a red flannel shirt that hangs loose. The sleeves are rolled and cuffed, showing off the ink on his strong forearms.

I need to get out of here before I start making more terrible life decisions. Though, I suppose one could argue that getting mixed up with a big mountain man might not be the worst decision I could make.

"Morning," I say, lifting my leg up and off the couch. "Thanks for keeping the place warm last night. I'm sure you don't mess with that when it's just you. Also, thanks for holding my hand 'til I fell asleep. I... you... that was above and beyond. Thank you."

He nods, accepting my thanks, as he stoically watches me try to lift myself from the couch. "Going somewhere?"

"Yeah. I was hoping you'd let me take a shower, then I'd head out. I want to get ahead of the police. The snow has slowed, so I assume they'll be after me soon."

He grins coyly, then pours himself a cup of coffee, filling a Harry Potter travel sized mug to the brim. "You're not going anywhere. Your ankle is still beat to shit. A shower on your own sounds like a terrible idea and there's more snow coming this afternoon. I doubt anyone will resume searching until late tomorrow when the storm passes."

"Okay... well, I think I'll still try and get moving. At least get a few more miles on them."

He looks toward me and nods before popping two slices of bread into the toaster. "And where are you staying? During the storm, I mean?"

"I'm sure there's a tree, hunting cabin, or something I can cuddle up in."

"And you don't think the cops will be looking in hunting cabins?"

"They haven't looked here yet."

"Because of the storm. When it passes, cabins will be the first place they look."

"And they'll find me here too."

He shakes his head and pulls a stick of butter from the pantry. "No one will find you here. Trust me."

I laugh. "As big a fan as I am of blind trust, I'm not sure I have the capacity for it at this time."

The toaster jumps and he pulls a slice of toast from the machine one at a time, buttering each piece generously before stacking them on top of one another and handing me the plate. His eyes are on me, then on the ground. He lifts a scatter rug and presses it sideways on a floorboard with his boot, opening an underground space. His gaze meets mine again. "You'll go in here if anyone comes. It's built smart. You'd be safe."

I'm tempted to ask him why he has it, but the Harry Potter mug he has in his hand is bothering me more than anything. *How is this big, burly guy, with a secret, into Harry Potter?*

"What's with the mug?"

He looks toward the cup that has a snake on the front and the word Slytherin beneath it.

"It was a gift." He says the words hard and solid, as though he won't entertain more questions, but I press anyway.

"A gift? So, you don't know what a Slytherin is?"

He shakes his head and lowers the bunker closed. "No, and I'm surprised that's what we're focusing on here. I was showing you the fallout shelter."

I grin. Maybe razzing him could be my new pastime. "Like in case the cops are after you?"

"After me?" He recoils. "You're the one in an orange jumpsuit, so I think you're going to have to do the explaining."

I want to keep arguing, but my stomach is rumbling, and the bread looks fresh, like he made it himself. *Would a Slytherin bake their own bread?* In Harry Potter, I think the Slytherins are the jerks. So I guess maybe they would if they thought no one else could do it as well.

"Speaking of the orange jumper," I start, "I was hoping maybe you'd have something I could wear. This thing stands out like you wouldn't believe." I laugh, trying to lighten the mood, but he doesn't laugh back. Maybe I've pushed the mockery too far.

"I'm three times your size. I don't think I have anything for you, no. Well," he swipes a slab of butter across his toast and looks back at me, "my buddy Waylon was supposed to stop by tomorrow. He has a daughter that might be about your size. I could have her bring some clothes."

"What?" I try to stand, but the blood rushing to my ankle has other plans. "No! You have to tell them they can't come. If they see me, they'll turn me in."

His eyebrows wrinkle and he takes another sip of his coffee. That damn mug is pissing me off. Why won't he admit he likes Harry Potter?

"We don't have to tell them you're a criminal. You can wear one of my shirts. I'll tell them you got lost hiking and you needed some help."

"And when they see me on TV? When they hear that a lost convict is running around in the woods? Then what?"

Maybe he isn't a criminal. This is basic stuff. If he talks about me with his friend, or with anyone, this guy is going to know what I did. Maybe I should tell him, clear the air, and get things out before he has a chance to form an opinion of me.

"Never mind." I slide back into the blanket and lift my leg back onto the pillow. "I'll rest for another few hours, then I'll wear my jumpsuit out."

He laughs under his breath, then busies himself with clanking dishes in the kitchen before turning toward me with another cold bag of ice. Pulling a stool from the corner, he sits next to me like he had last night, his big firm hand on my sore ankle. Carefully, he presses down on the swelling, noting the amount of fluid still trapped, then grunts disapprovingly before putting the ice in place.

"What?" I stare toward him with a racing heart. "What was the grunt for?"

"Grunt?"

"Yeah, you grunted. What does that mean?"

He glances up at me, holding his stare for a long minute before standing from the stool and sliding it back into the corner. "You're not going anywhere."

I scratch my forehead and look toward the big man standing in front of me. "I think it's time you tell me what you did, princess."

"*Princess?* Gross. When was the last time you saw a princess in an orange jumpsuit?"

He chuckles. "Today, I reckon."

My heart slams against my chest and goosebumps lift onto my arms. "No. Not until you tell me what you did."

He leans against the kitchen counter and stares toward me, lifting his Slytherin cup to his lips. "What makes you think I have something to hide? You're the one running from the cops."

I stare back at his handsome face, watching as his large hand scrubs over his beard. I've been staring at criminals for six months now. I thought when I went in, I'd be able to tell the difference between a person who committed a crime and me. But the truth is, criminals don't have wild in their eyes like the Disney movies I used to watch. There's no horn on their head either. They're just people. We're all just people... capable of anything.

"At least tell me your name." I stare toward him, taking in his big solid body as he leans against the kitchen counter.

"Bo." He takes a sip of his coffee.

"Okay, Bo. It would be nice to hear your story, but I guess you don't owe it to me."

He laughs. "But you do owe me yours. I brought you into my home. I'm giving you a place to stay and I'm harboring you from an active man hunt. I need *something*."

I suck in a deep breath and let it drain slowly. He's kind of right and I hate it. "I already told you… you're not going to believe me, anyway."

He pulls the stool back out and lowers himself onto it slowly. "Maybe not, but if you want my help, you're going to have to tell me what I'm dealing with first."

I'm not sure I need his help. I could make it on my own. I managed my way off a prison bus, broke my cuffs, evaded a police chase on foot for three miles, and I never in a million years would've thought I could do that. I could find the strength again.

I lift my head and stare out the back of the cabin. The snow is falling harder now. The tree that I'd been admiring this morning has disappeared and all I see is white.

Okay, maybe I wouldn't make it on my own. Truthfully, I'd probably freeze to death or fall down a cliff. I'm not used to this terrain, and there are drop-offs everywhere. Not to mention the hunting traps I'm sure I'd run into.

I bite the inside of my cheek and turn toward the massive man in front of me.

Why is he so hot?

I wish he'd found me under different circumstances. Maybe one where I'm wearing a color other than orange and I don't have metal cuffs for bracelets.

"Okay," I sigh, "I'll tell you, but you might want to get more comfortable because this is a doozy."

Chapter Three

BO

"Where are you from?" I stare at Rose and watch her carefully. I spent nearly fifteen years in the military working interrogations and I've carried out over seven hundred successful missions with a near perfect record. The thing is... most people are insanely predictable. They *think* they're slick, every single one. The problem is, we all have a tell. For some, it's exaggerated and obvious, like a nose scratch or a hair flip. For others, it's miniscule, like an extra blink or an elongated swallow. A good interrogator will know that there's no one size fits all when it comes to tells. Everyone has their own, and even then... tells change.

Rose looks down at her hands, fumbling them back and forth over one another. They're delicate and soft, but I ignore that. I'm looking for jittery or anxious movements, something that tells me what her baseline is.

"Cheyenne."

"How long did you live out there?"

Her brows raise and she turns toward me. "All my life. You're not from the area, but there's this trailer park about a mile outside of town in a place called Pine Bluffs. Have you ever heard of it?"

I nod. "I drove through Cheyenne a lot when I was doing work for Waylon's ranch. The family used to run a rodeo up there before they moved to Rugged Mountain."

"You ride?"

I nod again. "Used to when I could find time. Got bucked a few years back though, ended up with a tailbone injury. Couldn't find the fun after that."

She bites the inside of her lip. "That sounds pretty bad. My mom used to take us to that rodeo every year as kids. Some of those falls looked awful."

"Does your mom know what you did?"

She looks up and away before running her small hand through her long, dark hair. "My mom knows I'm in prison, if that's what you're asking."

"Does she believe you?"

Rose shakes her head and glances at me again. "No one believes me."

"What did you do?"

She lets out a long, heavy sigh and chews at the inside of her cheek. Her shoulders rise and fall as she rolls them in circles, trying to calm herself before blowing out a breath. "I was dating this guy. We'd been together for five years. He worked for a steel factory in Cheyenne and he'd commute back to Pine Bluffs every night. Not without stopping by the bar first, though." She looks out the front window, stretches her neck back, and then looks down at her hands again. "Most nights he came home with this attitude like he'd worked his ass off and I did nothing. I'd listen to it and keep my mouth shut, hoping he'd pass out in the chair before things got too crazy. But some nights, I couldn't take it and I'd snap."

"You'd snap?"

She nods. "I'd holler and scream. I'd go nuts. I mean, I was working too. I was on my feet all day long at the Dollar General helping customers, unpacking boxes, cleaning up spills. It's not easy work."

"So, you'd get mad at him. What would he do?"

"So, he'd come home drunk, start talking shit, I'd get upset, and I'd start yelling back. I'd tell him what I thought of him. I'd tell him he was a dirty drunk who didn't deserve me." She looks up and away again, a quiver starting to shake her lower lip, but she bites down on it. "I knew I shouldn't have talked back to him because every time I did, it was met with a shove, or a push, or some kind of physical altercation, but it was so hard to sit there and take whatever he was saying."

Fire bubbles under my skin and a rage I've never felt begins to eat away at me. I have to suppress it if I'm going to check her honesty, but right now, all I want to do is find this fucker and put him in the ground. Then again, maybe she already did. The story isn't over.

"What happened after that?"

Her breath hitches, and she fumbles with the end of the blanket. "For years I just let him do it. He'd push me and I'd lay there. He'd hit me and I'd lay there... *crying.* He'd blame me for instigating him and he'd roll off to bed, leaving me there on the floor." She shakes her head, and her teeth grind against one another as her gaze draws to mine. "But that night, I didn't. I didn't let him get the last—"

A heavy rap hits the door. "Just me, buddy."

Rose's eyes go wide. "Who is it?"

I stand from the stool and peek behind the curtain. "It's Waylon, the rodeo guy I was telling you about. He's got a girl with him." I stretch further, trying to see in the blizzard, but all I can make out is her black jacket and blonde hair.

Fuck. If Rose did what I think she was about to tell me, we're in deep shit. The news is for sure reporting on her, probably as extremely dangerous.

"I have to answer it. It's not like them to be driving through a storm like this. Let's get you into the bunker."

The door knocks again, then swings open, a cold breeze blowing in behind it. Up here, it's not uncommon that folks will let themselves in after the first knock, especially close friends and family.

"Coming in, man." Waylon ducks as he steps inside the cabin, knocking his boots on the doorway before finally looking up to see me standing next to the window. His eyes dart to Rose, whose face has turned a shade of white I'm not sure I've ever seen. "Fuck. Sorry about that. I didn't realize you had company." He looks toward Rose for too long, taking off his Stetson to nod. Ann follows in behind him.

"Hey y'all." Her smile is wide and bright despite the weather. Though, for the most part, Ann is usually smiling.

"No worries." I shake my head and stand to greet them. "Is everything okay? I'm surprised to see you guys out in a storm this bad." Truthfully, I'm shocked to see Waylon and Ann together. I didn't realize they knew each other. Ann works at the library and Waylon is a rancher and rodeo mogul. I can't imagine those circles overlap often.

Waylon nods. "I was up here looking for a horse that got loose when I saw Ann here had gone off the road on Preacher's Pike when the storm hit. I was already close to your cabin, so I thought we'd wait it out here since I was supposed to be stopping by anyway, but I see you've got company." He looks toward Rose and reaches out his hand. "I don't think we've met. Ranger Waylon. Everyone calls me Waylon."

Rose glances up at me, then smiles toward my friend, keeping her bracelets tucked beneath the quilt she's covering herself with. "Great to meet you. Sorry I can't give you a proper hello. I busted my ankle up pretty good yesterday."

Waylon glances down at Rose's swollen ankle. "Bad time for that. You sure you didn't break it?"

She nods. "Bo checked me out pretty good, so I think I'll be okay after a little rest."

Waylon nods. "You wandered toward the right cabin. Bo has some experience with the wounded. He worked interrogation for the military for years. Got himself an award for keeping some folks alive after a bomb exploded, too."

Fuck me. It wasn't *my* secrets I thought would be brought to light here.

Rose glances toward me, nodding as though she's making sense of something I can't figure. Though, something tells me she's going to be less likely to tell the rest of her story now that she knows I'm a human lie detector test.

"You're making too big a deal out of it," I say. "Can I get you a cup of coffee? Maybe a piece of fresh bread. I picked it up at the bakery yesterday." I'm hoping he says yes. The more food that's in his mouth, the less time he has to answer questions. "What about you, Ann?"

Ann shakes her head and hangs her coat on the hook next to the door before shuffling toward the fireplace. "I'm good. Right now, I need the heat."

"How are things at the library, Ann?" I'm still trying to avoid any topic but me, or any probing that might make Rose uncomfortable.

"Good." She smiles, flipping her long hair to the side. "Did you finish the Harry Potter I sent you home with? There are three more for you when you're ready."

Bloody fucking hell.

"So, you do read Harry Potter!" Rose grins, and looks toward Ann. "I was trying to nail him to it when I saw the mug, but... this man is full of surprises."

Ann gasps, playfully placing her hand over her chest. "You're denying your Slytherin heritage? What kind of Potter fan are you?"

"On that note," I say, tightening my belt, "I think Waylon and I will head outside. I need to pick his brain about a snowmobile that won't start. You two ladies sound like you'll be okay in here for a while." I glance toward Rose playfully with narrowed brows. A silent punishment for the Potter jokes.

Rose picks up on it right away and grins wide like she's not covered to the neck trying to hide who she is.

Maybe that's what's so intriguing about her. It's not the blanket hiding who she is. It's the orange jumpsuit.

Rose is more than whatever put her prison, and I'm going to make damn sure she knows it.

Chapter Four

Rose

"Where were you hiking to?"

I'm sure Ann's question is harmless enough, but it hits me straight in the gut. Mostly because I don't know the terrain enough to answer her.

"Oh, just out for a walk and I wandered too far. You know how it is."

She laughs. "Nope! I don't. This is the furthest I've been from Main Street since I moved up here a few years ago. Never again. Next year, I'm going to mail my friend Kate's birthday gift to her. I'm thankful I ran into her dad up here or I'd be stuck on the side of the road, probably freezing to death."

"I know the feeling. I was pretty lucky when Bo found me stuck in that trap."

"He's a pretty great guy, even if he did denounce his love for Harry Potter." She laughs and runs her hand over her long, braided hair. "Do you read the books?"

I shake my head. "No, I've heard enough pop culture to soak a lot of it in, but I'm one of those romance junkies. I can't get enough."

She laughs. "Do they all have a shirtless man with the body of a god on the cover? We loan those out a lot. I'm a little obsessed myself. I don't even know why. Most of them are so cheesy. It's like... how could someone fall in love in two seconds?"

"I know," I giggle. "They meet, they almost have sex, they fall in love, they have sex, they get married, the end. Oh, don't forget the ten kids they magically have with no problems and the family and friends who all accept them undoubtedly."

She sighs and rubs her hands together over the woodstove's heat. "Still though, it's a nice fantasy. Especially when you live up here. Sometimes I think I might never meet a good man. What about you? Do you live on the mountain?"

"No." I shake my head, tucking the quilt up higher on my neck. "Just visiting."

Ann presses her lips together and looks toward me with a grin that looks like trouble. "What if you and Bo are like a romance novel? What if while you're staying here, healing, you two realize you have undeniable chemistry and one night when he's helping you up off the couch, his lips slip and fall into yours in some dramatic way that leads to a happily ever after?"

"You do read a lot of books, don't you?" I smile.

Ann nods. "I do. It's a problem. Heck, it's probably why I'm alone. Nothing seems to meet the paper standard I'm looking for."

"Not true," I say, sweating to death under this quilt. "You shouldn't settle. Your dream man is out there somewhere."

Waylon knocks on the window behind the fireplace and hollers. "We need your help holding something. Then we should head out while the snow has let up."

"I guess I'm leaving," Ann says, reaching for her coat off the hook by the door. "I like talking to you. If you're heading through town again, stop by the library. I'm always there. Maybe I can hook you on some Potter before you leave town."

I smile and nod. "That sounds great!" I say, knowing that will never happen. Sure, I like talking to Ann. She's everything I've been missing in a conversation with a girlfriend. Light, fun, focused on books and how they connect with the real world. But the second she gets home and turns on the news, she's going to see me differently.

Then what? I'm a sitting duck here, and as much as I like the idea of staying with this interrogating, Harry Potter reading, mountain man, I know I'm only getting him into trouble as well. Who knows what happens when the cops come looking for me? They could haul Bo away too. I can't let that happen. I need to give this ankle another night, then head out in the morning before he gets up.

Late afternoon sun spills across the cabin floor and my eyes become heavy. What is it about sunlight that makes people tired? I thought it was supposed to have the opposite effect and make you bright and energetic. Maybe it's all the people. I haven't had to be *'on'* like that in a while. And even before jail I wasn't the best entertainer. I always preferred a night cuddled up with books on the couch, loosing myself in a romance novel where I could pretend kind men exist.

My eyelids grow heavy and though I'm fighting it, they close. I tell myself I'm just resting my brain from the stress of the day, but within seconds I'm buried in the dark heaviness of sleep and the world goes perfectly quiet.

****

Heat licks at my skin as I stand outside the fire. It's true, flames really are blue. Blue and orange with little red at all. I cover my face with the bottom of my t-shirt and watch as the plastic edge of a lawn chair bends and melts, the corners curling up and dissolving like a marshmallow on a stick. Smoke fills my lungs, my eyes sting, and a sense of panic overwhelms me as I search for a way through the heavy fog, but no matter where I turn the fire encircles me. I'm trapped. I call out for help, but the strain only results in a cough, and then another. Soon, I'm barreled over, clutching my chest as I heave for air. My knees hit the dirt and my vision goes blurry.

This is it. It's over. *I'm* over.

I struggle for the last bit of air I can conjure when a large hand grips my shoulder and begins to shake me. Suddenly, I'm pulled from the flames, through the darkness, and I'm staring at a giant bearded man with kind eyes. *Bo.*

"You're having a nightmare, Rose. Are you okay?" Bo scrubs his hand down over his beard and looks toward me with tired eyes. His free hand is on my arm.

"Oh god," I slap my hand over my face, "was I screaming? I'm sorry. I didn't mean to wake you up."

"It's only nine o'clock. I was just laying down. Why don't you take the bed for the night. You'll sleep better in there." He bends to help me up from the couch, but I resist.

"No. I'm okay out here. This happens all the time, trust me. I haven't slept well in months. It won't matter where I am."

"What's the dream about?"

I sigh. "Fires. It's nothing. I'm sorry to bother you."

"Fires? What kind of fires?"

"Were you really former military?" I sit up from the couch and lower my leg, closing my eyes as the blood rushes back down toward the pain. I want to move it back up right away, but the rest of my thigh is thankful for the change in positions.

He nods. "I don't talk about it because it's obsolete. That, and people have too many questions that I can't answer."

"So you'd know if I were lying then?"

He nods. "Do the nightmares your having have to do with what happened?"

I bite my lower lip, chewing on my flesh as I stare toward him. What is it about his giant body that makes me want to crawl up in his arms and retreat from the world?

"You should finish your story." He pulls up a stool. "Maybe I can help."

Having gone through the court system, I've heard it all. Everyone pretends they care. Everyone acts like they're going to see your side until you give it. Then, they look at you with wide eyes and a gasp as though you're Jeffrey Dahmer. I don't have enough energy left to manage that look on Bo's face. I have too many concurrent fantasies running through my head that include him. If he were to turn away from me too, I don't know what false hope I have left to hold on to.

"How could you help?" I bend forward and rub my sore leg, busying myself with anything other than the oncoming answer.

He shrugs. "I won't know until you tell me what's happened."

I bite the inside of my cheek. His response is fair. And I know I have to finish what I was about to tell him earlier, despite the fact that I know it'll change everything. "Where did I leave off?"

"Your boyfriend was abusive, but one night you were laying on the floor after he'd shoved you and something happened."

"Yeah," I whisper, running my hands back through my hair, "I kind of went crazy after that. I took a couple swigs of his whiskey, and I decided to leave. I packed up my bags, stared at myself in the mirror long and hard, then chopped six inches off my hair." Bo stares at me as though he's deciding whether or not I'm being truthful. It's a soft, but steady look that I'm sure is meant to bring people comfort so they keep talking.

"I'm sure it didn't stop there," he says. "What happened next?"

I swallow hard, twisting my thumbs against each other. "I rolled my suitcase down the hall and grabbed his pack of cigarettes off the counter and the bottle of alcohol I'd been drinking. I don't usually smoke or drink, but I was stressed and feeling crazy. On the way out, I tripped on his boots and dropped the bottle. It cracked and alcohol went everywhere. When I was bending down to sop up the mess, I set my lit cigarette on the windowsill. I was hanging it off the edge so it wouldn't burn the wood, but somehow it caught fire. Flames built faster than a bullet train running through a city at rush hour." My heart races as I look toward Bo, desperate for him to believe me. "I called out to Jake. I screamed, and I hollered until the flames got too much. Then I went around the back of the trailer and banged on the bedroom window. I should've called the firemen right away, but I was shocked, a little drunk, and the whole thing was playing out like some movie."

"Did Jake make it out?"

I nod. "Yeah. No one died, but I was charged with arson. Two more trailers burned down that night." I swallow hard. "It was an accident. You have to believe me." My eyes widen as my truth spills out for yet another person. "It wasn't purposeful!"

The silence in the cabin is only disturbed by the crackling fire.

Ironic.

"How long did they give you?"

"Twenty years! Fifteen with good behavior." A tear falls down my cheek. "I didn't do anything wrong, and my life is over. But Jake is out there, free to do whatever. He turned it all around on me. He hired lawyers and spent money he didn't have. I don't know if he's crazy or if he just wanted to see me suffer. Either way, it worked."

"How did you get away?"

This part I'm guilty of. "I know I shouldn't have run, but my entire life? *Twenty years?* I'll be almost fifty by the time they release me."

"So how'd you do it?" He's still stoic as he looks toward me, and I'm unsure if he believes me or not, but I'm in this deep.

I suck in a ragged breath. "The prison system in Wyoming was transferring me to another facility. Road closures led them to have to drive into Colorado and they made a stop for the bathrooms. I convinced a male guard to get me a tampon, then I slid out the back door and ran into the woods. I didn't stop until I saw you."

"Smart, staying close. Cops always branch out."

Bo stares at me long and hard, his gaze moving over my face, studying me like a wild animal he's not sure how to comprehend. Then all at once, he stands and leans over me, lifting me from the ground like he had when he brought me to safety.

"Where are we going?"

He looks down at me. "You need a good night's sleep. I'm taking you to the bedroom."

"No. I don't want to take your bed. Besides, I feel less alone with the hum of the generator so close to my ear. I can—"

"I'm not going to leave you." He says the words low under his breath.

He's not going to leave me. He's not going to leave me. He's not going to leave me.

I repeat the words over and over again in my head, unsure of how literal to take them. Most likely he means for the night, for the moment, or until I fall asleep.

Does this mean he believes what happened? I have so many questions, but as he settles me onto the queen size bed and lies beside me, they all dissolve in the back of my consciousness until the only thing on my mind is how his giant body feels against me, how his hands hold firm at my waist, and how his breathing takes me back to center.

He's not going to leave me.

Chapter Five

Bo

My mom used to tell me to *'find my lavender.'* To her, lavender was the sweetest scent of all. It was the one flower that she loved. Natural, pure, genuine. She fell in love with the purple buds the second she saw them, and their presence alone brought out a version of her that nothing else could. Not my father, me, her best friend, or even the family dog. It was the lavender that brought her peace, made her smile, and got her through days that seemed insurmountable.

At the time, I thought my mother was Grade-A certifiable. She spent most of her days shut in the attic painting scenes of lives she'd never lived while listening to the music of composers that have long since left the earth. Sometimes, she'd join us for dinner, but for the most part, she ate after we'd gone to bed, and made breakfast for us before we went to school. The morning I left for bootcamp was no different, except that day, she handed me a bundle of dried flowers and reminded me again, *'Find your lavender, Bo. Whatever you do... find her.'* I don't know if she was disappointed that her lavender wasn't my father, or if the slip was Freudian, but it always bothered me for months after I left home.

My mother's been gone for almost ten years, and it's been ages since I've thought about what she said the day I left for bootcamp. But as I hold Rose in my arms and breathe her in, I know without a shadow of a doubt that she's my lavender. She's the woman that I've been waiting for. Rose is telling the truth. I can feel it my bones.

"I really will be okay on the couch," she whispers, rolling onto her back and toward me.

I hold her in my arms, letting the soft hair sweep against my bare shoulders. "You're staying here with me, unless you want me to leave."

"No." Her gaze lifts to mine. I like that you're here. "But I have to ask, why are you being so nice to me?"

"Why did you stay with him? Why did you let him hurt you over and over again?"

She looks toward me and I expect her to call me out for answering a question with a question, but she doesn't. "He wasn't always like that, and I guess I thought things would get better after he settled in at work. I know I was dumb."

"You're not dumb." I kiss her forehead, wondering if I've overstepped a line. "You're human. People want to believe they can fix things. Hell, I wanted to believe I could fix that piece of shit snowmobile out there, but the truth is, it's going to be better as parts."

"So, you believe me? You believe my story?" Her tone rises and falls, and she sits up slightly, looking toward me.

I nod and hold her tighter in my arms.

She looks toward me long and hard, then slowly her lips move toward mine. The kiss is soft and patient... meaningful. Rationally, I know I should leave it there. I don't want to scare her away, but my body has a different response. I pull her in closer and kiss her lips hard, tracing circles on her wrists with my thumb. I need to get these handcuffs off her.

"I'll be back in a second." I jump from the bed and race out to the kitchen drawer where I throw everything. Scissors, screwdrivers, a deck of cards, a stick lighter, and... bobby pins. You have no idea how often something in this house gets latched that shouldn't.

Flicking the bright light on in the bedroom, I reach down for her small wrists and work the metal cuffs. It's been a while since I've been trained on this, but when you've locked the gun cabinet accidentally enough times, and a big buck walks into your front yard, you get plenty of practice.

These newer locks are better than they used to be, but thank God we have all the time in the world. As the locks pop, she grips her wrists and rings her fingers around them. "Oh my god, that's so nice. Thank you."

"I should've done it earlier. Sorry. I've never taken in an escapee before." I sit next to her on the bed. "You were talking about a shower earlier. Do you still want one? I have a bench I could set inside, and I could stay close. Respectfully, of course."

"I would love that." She stares up at me with a hungry stare I'm not expecting. I could rationalize our kiss. It made sense in the moment. But this look in her eye is more than a simple rationalization can justify. It's unfiltered and honest.

I push away the archaic response and lift her again, carrying her to the bathroom. This is going to be more challenging than I'd thought. She still can't put much weight on that ankle and even with a bench, I'm not sure how she's going to get the jumpsuit off and get into the shower without some help.

I set her on the edge of the tub and run back into the closet, grabbing the small stool I use for climbing into the attic. It's not perfect, but it has rubber feet and it'll give her something to sit on instead of trying to balance herself for however long it takes to freshen up.

"Fuck. Sorry," I say, stepping back into the room to see her orange jumpsuit stripped down to her waist.

She doesn't cover her frame. She only looks back at me like she's used to the intrusion. "I assume you've seen a naked woman before?"

"It's been a while."

A grin lifts onto her face. "Sorry. If this is embarrassing for you, I can cover up. I guess I got used to the whole no privacy thing in jail. I haven't had a shower without an audience in almost a year."

I know there are things that should be said right now. Smart things. Kind things. Things that aren't *nice tits* or *fuck me, you're gorgeous*, but those are the only words that come to mind. It must be obvious too, because Rose can't help herself from laughing.

"You're really staring. When was the last time you were with a woman?"

"Sorry, it's been years. Maybe ten at this point. I lost track after the first few." I adjust my gaze to the knots in the pine behind her, then lean into her naked body to lift her enough that she can push the rest of her jumpsuit to the ground. It's a simple, caring move but my body doesn't see it that way. For a slight second, her hard nipple is pressed up against my bare chest and my cock revolts, standing up straight like a willing soldier.

Fucking hell.

I try to act unruffled and grab a towel from the rack to hold in front of me, hoping she doesn't notice, but she does. The hungry gaze she had on the bed turns wild and needy.

"You must like what you see."

"Be careful, princess. I'm carrying years of sexual tension. I'm not sure how long I can be the gentleman you deserve."

"Is that a promise?" Her tone drops, and she stares toward me as her hand reaches out for mine.

I'm not sure what the hell is happening, but I don't want it to stop. I want to bruise her lips with mine and make her whine for my touch, but there are about ten thousand things wrong with that thought. The first being our obvious age gap. I'd guess she's pushing twenty-five. I'm about double that. The second being her current situation. I'm not interested in fucking her once and letting her go free in the forest to fend for herself. Maybe she wants to run. What would I do if I let myself get close to her and she left? A one-night stand is good for some, but not for me. It never has been.

"What's wrong?" The steam from the shower fogs the small space as she looks up at me. "I thought you liked what you saw?"

I reach down, laying my hand on her cheek. "I do. I love what I see. I think I've just been on this mountain too long."

"Why's that?"

"Because I'm torn between wanting to do filthy, dirty things to you and wanting to hold you against my chest and cherish you like a fallen fucking angel that I have to protect at all cost."

Her hand rises and her fingers tangle in the hair on my chest. "Can't we do both?" Her gaze holds on mine and a shot of electricity wavers through me like I've grabbed a live wire and I can't let go.

"Will you get in with me?" She looks toward the running shower then back at me, her hand now on my boxers, tugging at them lightly.

Inhibitions weak and my heart thrashing, I push my boxers to the ground and lift her frame from where she's sat, holding her tight against my body as we step into the shower.

What am I doing? A million reasons to stop filter through my head, but I ignore them all and brush my thumb over her slippery nipple before cupping her face and bending into her lips. I draw a line down the center of her throat, kissing every inch of her needy body as she moans in my ear, then warn her again.

"I want to be careful with you, Rose, but I've never felt more unguarded."

She leans her head against my chest and kisses my shoulder, then looks up at me through the falling water. Her pink lips are wet and eager. "I don't want you to be careful with me, Bo. I want you to take me like the animal I know you are. I want you to be free with me. I want to let go together."

I grab her hips and kiss her lips again. Harder this time. My hand grips the back of her neck and my cock presses into her stomach.

She groans under her breath and reaches up to grip my length, pumping her small hand over and over as her eyes bore into mine.

Fuck. Heat washes over me and I lower her onto the bench behind us, then kneel before her, desperate to taste her sins and swallow her truth. Her fingers slide through my hair and tug as I lick her seam and draw my tongue inward, circling her clit. Thick thighs press against my cheeks and my cock grows harder.

"You taste so fucking good," I groan into her, sucking in the scent of her sweet musk as I devour her folds and pull up a suction at her most sensitive area.

Moan after moan echoes through the small bathroom as hot water beats on my back. Her hips thrust forward and her pussy grinds against my beard.

I love it. I want to eat every last drop of her and swipe my beard over her come like a maxed-out credit card, desperate for one last shopping trip.

One by one, I slide two fingers into her core. She's hot and slick, wide and pleading.

"You have no idea how bad I need you, Bo." Her fingers dig into the back of my shoulders as she rocks against my beard, thrusting my fingers further inside her swollen pink pussy.

"Do you want me, Bo? Do you need this tight little pussy on your cock? Have you been thinking about it since you picked me up?" There's arousal in her tone as she chokes out the words.

My jaw tightens and my teeth graze her clit. I expect her to jump away, but she leans into it and thrusts harder.

She giggles. "Is that a, yes?" Her entire body rocks and moves against me. When I look up the hills and valleys of her chest are heaving and she's flicking her own nipples hard.

Fucking hell. I could come right here. I could stand her up and thrust myself inside while I bury my face in the nape of her neck. I could torment her clit with my tongue until she's almost come, then stop, watching her squirm against my cock would be worth the madness I'd cause.

With one hand, she tangles her fingers in my hair and tugs. "Fuck me. Fuck me, Bo!" Fluid drips from within her and spoils me like a kid in a candy store as I lick up the creamy center I've been working for.

Rose squirms beneath my touch, but I don't stop. I hold her thighs in place and keep eating. Desperate and hard. She's a drug and I'm an addict. I can't get enough of her.

"Okay..." She tries to stop me, but I go for another minute before pulling away from her. My cheeks are wet, her musk all over me, and the shower is cooler than I remember.

My cock thumps and hardens, desperate to press into her slippery core, but we don't have protection, and I can't in right mind put a baby inside of her knowing what her future could be in prison.

She grips my cock in her hand and pumps again, this time sliding me into her mouth. Pumping, sucking, twisting, gripping. Harder and harder she works my dick as I hold her head in place, twisting the silky-damp strands against my fingertips. There's no turning back. I'm about to come. I'm about to be boneless at her will and nothing can stop it.

"Good girl, princess," I growl. "Don't stop."

She works me harder and harder until my body goes hollow, and the orgasm I've been desperate for, is on the edge of release. I'm blank. An empty slate. The devil could take my soul and I'd let him. She's an angel with her lips and that tongue is like heaven against my skin. Then all at once, she pulls away.

"Do you hear that?"

I refocus on the room, on the water beating against my back, on the dogs barking in the distance.

Dogs. Dogs barking in the distance.

I don't live close enough to neighbors for there to be dogs barking this late at night. The cops are back again, and I have a feeling, they're headed straight this way.

Chapter Six

Rose

Is it bad that I'm more worried about the orgasm Bo didn't get to have, than the cops that are knocking on the door?

Probably.

Bo's done so much for me. I want to please him. I want to relax him. I want to make him feel as good as he's made me feel. And holy hell do I feel good. The way he spun his tongue around my clit was like nothing I've ever felt before. My evil, awful, drunken ex had an aversion to oral sex. Well, all sex really. In a year, we tried at least once a month, but he always had trouble getting it up. I don't know if it was drinking, or if I was that repulsive. Either way, he never got it in, and so we never really did anything.

Looking back, I can't believe I was set to live a life without sex. It's funny the things you convince yourself of while in a relationship. You can convince yourself that someone loves you when they clearly don't. You can convince yourself that you don't need a specific emotion, or act, or anything really. As long as that person is there with you, everything will be fine.

What a lie that is.

Footsteps knock across the floorboards of the cabin, too many to count. Bo's fallout shelter is interesting and all, but I'm not sure it's fool proof. At any point, a Wyoming state sheriff could lift the blue and white scatter rug, step on the wrong floorboard, and my entire cover would be blown.

I should turn myself in. I should save Bo from ever being caught. I know that's the right thing to do. But right now, I'm not sure I'd be able to explain why I was wearing a towel and how I was able to slip my cuffs without help.

God, I hope he remembers they're still sitting on the bed before they go back there.

If I'm found here now, it'll be obvious that Bo was hiding me. They'll charge him.

What's the punishment for harboring a criminal?

The floor creaks and heavy footsteps hover above me. Deep voices rumble back and forth but it's too muffled to hear what anyone is saying.

Why would the cops be out this late?

Maybe there's a break in the snow.

Maybe Ann or Waylon called them after seeing me here.

Oh god, what would that mean?

My heart thuds against my ribcage as I back up against the rough dirt wall. Everything is dark. I can barely see my hand in front of my face unless I step into a sliver of dim light shining from a crack in the floorboards to the left. But I refuse to go there on the off chance that the dog can smell me. If I'm covered in dirt, there's less chance he'll pick up my scent. I'm not sure the same can be said for the rest of the house. My scent is all over the place. I'm surprised the dog isn't barking yet.

My ankle throbs as I chew at my fingernail, lean my head against the cold dirt, and stare up into the darkness listening to the low rumble of voices, all of them deciding my fate.

How did this happen? How did I end up here? Why did I think it was a good idea to run? Better yet, why did I ever think staying with Jake was a good idea? I could've left him a thousand times over and been in the right. I could've turned him into the cops for assault.

I didn't.

Look where that got me.

Heavy footsteps move toward the back of the cabin. I hold my breath and my heart thumps in my ears.

Woosh. Woosh. Woosh.

The heavy stomping returns overhead and the cabin door creaks open, then closes all at once.

I stay quiet, waiting for Bo's response but he doesn't come after me. Instead, the cabin is silent.

Did he leave with them? Did they arrest him on the spot for hiding me? Do they know where I am? Are they waiting to pull me out?

The torture is unbearable. I suck in a deep breath and let it out slowly, trying to reason with my heartbeat, but nothing helps. I made a mistake letting Bo help me. Now, I have to make it right.

****

Light filters through the floorboards as Bo lifts the hatch and reaches his hand down toward me. I don't know how long it's been, but if I had to guess, I'd say it's been at least two hours.

"Sorry." He pulls me into his frame, dirt and all. "I didn't want to talk or lift the hatch until I was sure they were gone."

"What happened?" My breath is still ragged from the stress of the moment. "Did they see my things in the bathroom and your bed? The quilt! I'm sure the dogs smelled the quilt."

"I told them I was allergic, and the dogs stayed outdoors. Thankfully, the one cop only skimmed the house. Considering I didn't have to let him in, he was polite enough. I called Waylon."

My jaw drops. "Was he the one that tipped the cops off?"

Bo shakes his head and runs his hand through his beard. "No, but I told him what happened. He owes me a favor, and he knows a few guys. More than one of the rodeo hands he's hired have come from dark places. He's given them a fresh start."

"What does that mean?"

"It means... he's calling a guy to build you a new identity. I asked him to put a rush on it. The paperwork should be ready by tomorrow morning."

"And then what, Bo? I can't stay here. I can't put you at risk."

Bo's eyes go dark and close the gap between us. "I decide what works for me. Do you understand?"

I shake my head. "No... because you're deciding all wrong. This started with a mistake, but now I'm continuing to make them, never learning. I don't want to be that girl. I want to run and live a quiet life in the middle of nowhere alone, where I can't hurt anyone, and no one can find me."

He narrows his gaze. "You're what... twenty-four years old? And how many survival skills do you have? Let's be real, Rose. You'd be dead in a week out there, if not sooner. I can fix this, but you have to be willing to roll with the punches. You can't fight me at every juncture."

I stare down at the ground, then back up again. Bo's normal scent is covered and obscured by the iron in the soil covering me from head to toe. "What does this mean for you?"

"This isn't about me. This is about you finding freedom from a crime you didn't commit. Do you think you're going to get that with a good lawyer?" He grips my hand in his, swallowing me up. "They're going to tack time on now for your escape, Rose. This is the only chance you have at a life. Don't you want to take that chance?"

I do. I want to take that chance more than anything. "But will you be tied to me? Will you get in trouble?"

He shrugs. "I don't see how. As far as I would know, you're a hiker named Sky Tate who wandered in from the outside and asked for my help. You'll color your hair, you'll have new identification, and you'll live up here with me. Quiet. Undisturbed. Peaceful."

When he talks, the answers all seem clear as day. There's no way this can go wrong.

Bo leans his head against mine and holds me close. "I'm not going to let them get to you princess. You have to trust me."

I stare up at him, letting the calm in his gaze bathe me in an assuredness I don't yet have for myself. Since Jake, I never imagined letting another man in, let alone trusting one to call me princess. But Bo is different. *Bo isn't Jake.* Bo is strong, stoic, and kind... which is exactly why I can't let him take care of me. He deserves better than some girl on the run... and leaving might be the only way I get to thank him for what he's done for me.

Chapter Seven

Bo

When I wake up in the morning, Rose is gone. The bed is empty, her jumpsuit picked out of the trash, and my heavy flannel missing.

I can't do more than just shake my head. Does she really think that's warm enough for this climate? Last night, the temps were in the single digits.

I grab my rifle, toss on my boots, and pull on my coat before heading out the front door. It snowed last night, so her tracks are covered.

Just fucking great.

Why does it feel like I've lost a limb? Like there's a hole in the pit of my stomach with a chicken inside pecking its way out? I have to know she's okay. I have to hold her and tell her that I need her just as badly as she needs me. I didn't realize how empty my life has been until she showed up.

The snowmobile is shot, so I jump on the four-wheeler. I know the truck won't make it through the back country and part of me doubts the ATV will go everywhere I need it to, but it'll save me some walking. If I'm lucky, I can catch up to her faster. Granted, I have no idea which way she went. South is town, which would make sense if she were going to find Waylon and pick up her new ID's before taking off. There's less risk of injury that way because there's a road she could follow. But most of me doubts she'd take the risk of a main road since the police are still looking for her. North, is backcountry and every part of my body aches thinking Rose went that way. There are drop-offs, wild animals, hunters, traps, sub-zero temperatures, and rugged terrain that she couldn't navigate with an ankle so swollen. Hell, I'm not sure I could scale these mountains on foot, and I've lived up here all my life.

The ATV presses through the snow slowly at first but picks up speed as it gains momentum over the heavy snowfall. I scan the early morning landscape for anything that might give me some direction, but it's like she's disappeared. I check my phone for the time and consider calling Waylon for reinforcements but I'm already too far into the woods and I've lost reception.

Fuck! My stomach tightens as I push forward, scanning the landscape for anything that could give me direction, but there's only white. White with blankets of green overhead. I skid into their shelter and weave between them, slowly, carefully. The ATV tires sponge on fallen pine and squirrels rush from tree to tree, avoiding my disturbance. In the distance, a red dot catches my eye and I press toward it before I'm blocked by a fell tree. I'm going to have to walk from here.

Fifty feet ahead, the red becomes clearer. Rose wore my red flannel out, but this is rural Colorado. Red flannel isn't exactly a signature look.

I holler out, "Anyone there?"

No answer.

I holler again, "Are you hurt?" I figure this applies to whoever is ahead, though as I say the words out loud the realization hits me that someone else could have found Rose. Another woodsman. Not everyone is as welcoming as I am. A lot of men up here never leave the mountain, and it's been years since they've seen a woman. God knows what they'd do to Rose if they found her.

My heart constricts and my pulse goes wild as I jog forward, my rifle tapping against my shoulder as I move.

"Bo?" Her voice is soft and sweet. She's alive! She's huddled next to a tree shivering and cold, with her ankle propped up against a rock... but she's alive.

I rush toward Rose and run my fingers back through her wavy hair before pulling her close. "What are you doing out here? I thought we decided to go to Waylon?"

She buries her face against my chest. "I didn't want to burden you. You've been so nice to me. No one's ever been this nice." She sniffles and wraps her arms around me. "I'm sorry. I thought I'd get further. You shouldn't have come."

I hold her so tight that I have to remind myself to loosen my grip. "You shouldn't have left in the night. Anything could've happened to you out here."

She doesn't speak. She stays against my chest, and we sit like that for some time, holding each other, silent, as though we're soaking in the warmth of each other's existence.

"I missed you," I continue. "I missed your smell, your touch, the sound of your voice in the cabin. Hell, I even missed all the Slytherin talk."

She bites her lower lip and stares up at me through the mid-morning light that's filtered by pines surrounding us. "I missed you, Bo, but I'm going to ruin your life."

"If what I've been sharing with you is ruining my life, then ruin it Rose. Ruin every single day for the rest of eternity. I want it." My hand slides against her cheek. "I want you."

Her lips crash into mine without hesitation and my chest cracks open with relief and warmth and love. *Love.* I'm not sure I can go another second without telling her, without my hands on her bare skin, without her laid out beneath me, without her desperate to be devoured like she was in the shower. I lift her from the ground and carry her toward the ATV.

Rose cuddles into my chest and leans against me as though that's where she's meant to be. "Bo..." I'm not sure my name has ever been said as sweet.

"Yeah, princess."

"Princess?" she smiles. "You're really not quitting with that, huh?"

"Never," I chuckle. "What's up?"

"Will you take me home and let me do things to you?"

"What things?" My cock stiffens at the thought of what she might be saying.

"The things we started yesterday," she whispers, spreading warmth along my earlobe. "I want to thank you for coming out here and for taking care of me."

The thought of her thanks all over my body sounds like fucking heaven. "You don't owe me anything, princess. I want to take care of you."

She kisses the lobe of my ear before I set her down on the ATV, then looks up at me so sweetly that I worry I might burst here and now in the pine forest of squirrels and cardinals. "I know, but I want to." Her hand drags down the center of my coat. "I want to take care of you in *every* way."

Oh, I want that too, princess. Trust me.

"I do have to tell you something, though." She squints her eyes as she talks, and I worry there's another shoe she hasn't dropped about her escape.

"What is it?" I grip her hand in my palms and sit next to her, warming her freezing body against my heat.

Her gentle gaze meets mine. "I was with Jake for a year, and we did things but... we never actually did *the* thing."

"The thing?" I'm confused.

"Yeah, like, we messed around with oral and stuff, but he couldn't," she bites her bottom lip, "get it fully up. So, we never really... actually... had sex."

Oh fuck. She's a virgin. I shouldn't be immediately aroused, but I am. The thought of pressing into her innocent body has me weak with anticipation.

"Okay." I stare toward her like a deer in headlights. "Well... I guess we'll take it a step at a time then."

"You don't have to with me. I know what I like. I know what I want. I just wanted you to know what you were getting into."

I nod, unsure of what to say. I can't tell her how excited I am to be her first. I can't tell her how wrong it feels that I'm twice her age and taking something so precious makes me feel like a criminal. So instead, I unzip my jacket and wrap it around her shoulders, then zip it to her neck. "It's going to be a cold ride back."

"And you'll freeze," she says, as I tuck in behind her.

"I'll be fine. You've got me all warmed up with your talk, anyway." I lean into her ear and start up the engine. "You keep thinking about what happens when we get back to the cabin, because I have plans for you."

Her small frame presses into me and her neck cranes up until she's whispering in my ear with a grin, "So you *do* want to trap me inside and keep me as a baby making slave. I knew it!"

My cock hardens and for the first time in my life I want nothing more than a house full of babies with the woman I love. "Is that going to be a problem?"

She kisses my beard and lifts her hand back to hold my face. "No. That's not a problem at all."

I growl low in her ear, "Hang on, princess. I have to get you back before you change your mind."

Chapter Eight

Rose

By the time we make it back to the cabin, I'm wet, slick, aching, and Bo's eyes have the intensity of an eagle about to claim his prey.

I love it. It's the same look he had in the shower the other night and it drives me wild. I've never had a man look at me like this before. His face is tough, his teeth bared, and his stance wide. He carries me into the cabin and tosses me onto the bed. He's a giant. A huge man with broad shoulders, that ducks to enter every room. His hands are big, rough, and scale me like a monster climbs a building.

"Do you like the name Sky?" he groans between the rough kisses he plants on my collarbone.

I moan in approval, and he grips the back of my neck, tight and rough... like he owns me.

"Waylon left your documents at the door with a box of hair color. What do you think about blonde?" He lifts his flannel off my skin then unzips the jumpsuit, yanking it to the ground with fury.

"I've always wanted to try blonde," I pant, unbuckling his belt, desperate to see the thick cock that I'd sucked yesterday. I don't have much experience with men, but I know when something is big, and Bo's dick is enormous. He's thick and long, and I know without a shadow of a doubt that he's going to hurt sliding in, but I want it. I want all of him.

My ankle was throbbing all night while I walked, but now it's barely a thought as every other nerve in my body comes to life.

"I don't have protection," Bo groans, rubbing my clit with this thumb.

"I thought we were starting a troop of our own." I scrape my teeth against his shoulder, panting. "I want your babies, Bo. I want all of you."

He grips my hip, and exhales against my neck, sucking and licking his way up to the lobe of my ear. "It's going to hurt, princess. You with that tight little pussy, and this cock."

"I know," I squeak, "but I want you." My hips rock back and forth kneading against his naked thigh.

His hand cups my face and his lips land on mine with fire. The kiss deepens, and he growls deep, sending a vibration through my body. Slowly, he drags a finger from beneath my chin to my collarbone and onto my breasts. His tongue follows his touch, and he latches onto my nipple, sucking, licking, tasting my skin as he rocks into my hips, poking me with the star of the show.

I grip his cock in my hand and pump my small fist around its girth, but the longing is too much. My body aches for him inside of me. "I need you, Bo. I need to ride your cock. I need your come."

He growls and cups my neck in his large hand, guiding me gently toward him as he sits on the edge of the bed. "Don't force yourself on. Go slowly. I don't want you getting hurt."

I climb up onto his lap and hook my arm around his neck. Next to him, I'm small and fragile.

He grips my waist and holds me firmly as I sink onto his cock slowly. Inch by inch, I take him in, looking into his eyes as I lower. His brows narrow as my wetness swallows him up. "Fuck, Rose. You're tight."

I die on the spot, lifelessly morphing over his thick cock, desperate to take more and more of him in. I want him to groan my name and tell me what a good little princess I am for taking every thick inch of him.

"Tell me you need my pussy, Bo."

He groans and grips my jaw in his hand. Our eyes meet. "I need that pussy, Rose. I need all of it. Milk my cock and take my seed."

Good lord.

He bends into my neck and sucks at my flesh while I bounce on his lap. His tip is hitting the back of my cervix, but I know he has more left. He's huge, all of him.

My nipples brush against his chest as I ride him, bouncing, twisting, moaning.

He thrusts upward, knocking the air from my lungs as he stares into my eyes. "Tell me your mine, Rose. Say it loud."

My fingers weave through his dark beard and onto his face. "I'm yours, Bo. Come inside of me." I'm panting, breathless.

His thumb presses between us and he circles my clit as I slam up and down on his cock. I rock and grind against this giant, as my nipples brush against the hair of his chest and his dark eyes sit linked with mine. I'm full. Full of him, full of life, full of desperation.

"You're close, princess," He groans in my ear. "You're going to come." I have no idea how he knows, but the sound of his graveled voice in my ear takes me over the edge.

I clamp down on his cock, and though I want to thrust faster, my body revolts and spasms on top of him.

Bo picks up the slack and pushes into me harder, bouncing me against his massive body like a rag doll as I come. Groaning, he holds my hips firm, and slides into me one last time before he growls out his own release.

My ears go warm as he thrusts his seed inside of me. I'm ruined. I know that now. Ruined for all other men. Ruined for a life alone. Nothing will ever be as good as life with him. These two days have shown me that, and this moment is the cherry on top.

He presses a kiss onto my shoulder and collapses against me, his big body holding me like a tiny prize as he catches his breath. "What the hell did I ever do in life to deserve that?" We're hot and sticky together, and I love it. Every filthy bit.

"I was just asking myself the same thing," I sigh, holding him close. "When I think of all that had to happen for me to find you, it's surreal. I mean, what would my life have been if I weren't here right now?"

Bo spills backward on the bed and pulls me into his orbit, scrolling his rough hands over my smooth skin with care. "You're here now. That's all that matters. I'll keep you safe. I'm not going to leave you, Rose."

I nod and close my eyes as I take in the musky scent of his chest.

He's not going to leave me... and I believe him.

Epilogue

Bo

One Year Later

The library is decorated to the nines for winter. Balsam wreaths with fresh cranberries, and holly strung from pine boughs over arches. The building itself is one of the oldest standing homes in Rugged Mountain but was converted to a library years ago to avoid destruction. Ann and a few others in town do an incredible job keeping the place alive. In a town this small, that isn't easy.

"Thanks for having us over." Rose holds our baby girl on her hip as she leans in to say hello to Ann. "We love parties. Don't we Mable?"

Ann grins and reaches out for Mable's small hand. "I'm the lucky one. I get to see your cute little face! I wonder if you'll be a Slytherin like your dad or a Hufflepuff like your mom?"

"I think we're hoping for Hufflepuff," I laugh, holding Rose in my arms.

"I don't know," Rose looks up toward me, "I think a Slytherin has some useful qualities. I mean, you've gotten us out of some hairy situations."

I kiss Rose's head. "Not true."

"Okay," Ann revolts, "you guys are too cute. You're going to have to stop or I'll go home tonight and cry myself to sleep."

"Come on!" Rose nudges Ann playfully. "You're starting that new job, right? That's something to look forward to. Maybe Mr. Fields is this super freak who's desperate for a *sexy* nanny?"

Ann laughs and rolls her eyes. "Please, if he is, he called the wrong number. To tell you the truth, I'm not even sure how long I'll last."

"Why?" Rose bounces Mable on her hip softly as she listens to Ann.

She shrugs. "He can't keep anyone there. I'm the next in a long line of women who have tried. Apparently, no one in town wants anything to do with his father."

Rose looks up at me. "Your friends with him, right? He was at our wedding."

I nod. "Friends is a stretch, but I've traded him wood for materials over the years. He's a good guy, down to earth, and a shrewd businessman, but most of the ranchers up here are. I'll put in a good word for you."

Ann's face turns red. "God, no! Don't say anything about me. Please. I'm just watching an old man. Nothing is going to happen between us." She looks away then back again as though I've tried to unleash the devil from a magic lamp. "He's my boss!"

Rose and Ann keep talking, but I see Waylon from across the room and excuse myself to say hello.

"Small town events keep us humble, don't they?" Waylon's voice echoes through the small library, quieting the room for a moment.

I nod. "We come down to the library a lot, so we figured we'd support Ann's open house tonight. I'm surprised to see you here."

"Like I said, it's good to support the community. I see you and your lady are doing fine."

"Not a drip of trouble. You heard anything?"

Waylon shakes his head. "Nothing since the cops called off their search. They figured she was dead after we led the dogs to her jumpsuit out on the ridge. Wolves they reckon. Ann and I are the only ones who know, and as long as I'm around, it'll stay that way."

Waylon's not the hugging type of guy, but if he were, I'd squeeze him breathless to show my gratitude for all he's done for my family.

"Anyway," he kicks his boot against the wood floor and holds out his hand, shaking mine firmly, "you take care. I need to get back up to the ranch and make sure these folks are doing what they're supposed to be. Too many people are counting on this rodeo in town. Looks like your girl is headed back this way anyway." Rose passes Waylon on her way toward me. He pauses for a moment to greet them then continues on his path.

"What do you say we get out of here?" I kiss the nape of her neck and pull her close. "I'm thinking we go home, sit by the fire, and—"

"Read?" She holds up a stack of books. The first in line is *Harry Potter and the Half-Blood Prince*. "Ann says it's next in the series. We can't miss it! Apparently, there're lots of Slytherins in this one so you'll really connect to the characters." She grins and stares up with those big bright eyes that continue to enchant me.

"I don't know." I take baby Mable into my arms and slide my hand over the top of Rose's. "I think you girls have turned me to a Hufflepuff."

Rose narrows her gaze and kisses my lips softly. "I'll love you as a Slytherin, a lumberjack, a giant, or a sweet Hufflepuff. As long as I get all of you."

And that's why I love this woman, and why I'm never letting her go.

Bookworm

Chapter One

Ann

J ust look at him. I can't keep myself from staring at the man in the window.

He's tall. Probably six and a half feet. Tall and inked. His tattoos strategically placed to tell a story of mystery and power. Plus, when he walks around the kitchen in his jeans after a long day, he does more than whet my appetite.

So, let's summarize. Tall, inked, mysterious, hot... and totally uninterested in me.

He *must* be my type.

Why do I do this to myself? This isn't some sticky-sweet romance novel. It's real life. The handsome rancher doesn't fall for his curvy caregiver. That's a trope. A trope that I'm not living in. In the *real world* trope, people like me don't end up with sexy men like Holt. People like me, do their job, then quietly disappear to their room at night to read books about love and romance they'll never have. It's reality. And as granny likes to say, *'The sooner I let reality in... the better.'*

She's an eloquent woman.

I check Earl one last time and splash some water on my face in the hall bathroom, then head toward the kitchen for a drink. Usually, I'm at the library part-time, but I've taken a break to help here. Granny says it's a personal favor to her. She knows Earl from her rodeo queen days. I didn't ask questions. She's had more romances than a library, and I'm sure the details would depress me.

"You're up late." Holt's deep voice knots in my stomach as he steps into the room. I've only been here for three nights, but I've tried to be out of his way by the time he comes in, so I haven't seen him much more than a few minutes here and there. "Everything okay?" He takes off his Stetson and hangs it on the hook by the door before kicking off his boots.

What is it about a big, giant of a hard-working man that gets me all hot and bothered? *I need help.*

"Sorry, I was just heading to my room. There's a plate for you in the fridge. I wasn't sure when you'd be in. I can get it for you if you want."

"You're not my maid. You're here for Earl. You didn't even have to fix me dinner. Thank you." His voice is low and graveled, and his big hands pull the cellophane off the fried chicken I made an hour before.

"Sorry. It's probably soggy now. I can fr—"

"You can sit down and keep me company." He pops open the door to the microwave and slides the plate inside. "Dinner smells great. How was Earl today? If he's a pain in the ass, just tell me. I'll put him back in line." His tone is gruffer than it was a moment ago and I wonder what kind of connection the two have. I know a lot of fathers and sons have strained relationships, but Earl is living here, so it can't be that bad. Maybe they had an argument recently.

"He's not a pain at all." I run my fingers back through my hair, suddenly nervous, as Holt pulls the dining room chair out to sit. He's a massive man, but here in the house with normal people utensils, tables and chairs, he looks even bigger. "He's getting around great with his walker. If I were comparing, I'd say he's doing much better than my Granny was after her hip replacement. She was down for weeks."

Holt grunts and bites into the fried chicken with a groan. "Don't give him too much credit. He's a stubborn old man. Stubborn old men can make themselves do just about anything."

There's an awkward silence for a moment where I'm not sure if I should ask what happened between them, or see if he needs another beer, but he beats me to it. "Do you want a glass of wine? I'm sure you need it after dealing with him all day. I should probably double your pay."

"I'm good on the wine." I fumble with a piece of paper on the table, folding the corner into an accordion. "You two really don't get along, huh?"

He takes another bite of chicken and follows it with a gulp of beer. "The man doesn't deserve to be here, let alone having a sweetheart like you taking care of him."

Sweetheart? I try not to take the compliment personally. He's comparing me to the father he hates. I'm sure anyone would be a sweetheart in his head.

"He's really been very kind to me. He even told me a few stories about you. Good ones." I look a glance toward Holt, then down at the paper again, unsure of how he's going to respond.

"Well, I reckon I'm going to have to get you outside for some fresh air tomorrow, cause you're starting to hear things. That man doesn't have a good story in him. I know that for a fact."

I smile. "He did, though. He said when you were young, you taught your horse to side pass."

Holt wipes his hand on a paper towel and chuckles. "Yeah. He tell you what a sissy I was after that? That man hated that I wanted to teach my horses everything, even soft movements. He thought I was dimming the family line of big, strong, mountain men." Holt's arms tense as he puts his beer down. "His way of managing anything was... break something down until it's obedient, run it into the ground, and then discard it when it's no longer useful." He clears his throat. "It was especially bad with the horses."

"I guess he left that part out," I say with a smile, "but I'd like to see all the things your horses can do, though. The only experience I have with horses is in books. I read this one novel that was this love story between two horses." I grip my chest. "It was the most beautiful thing. They were separated by neighboring farms for years and they were depressed and sad when they were apart, but when they were brought back together, it was like magic. They remembered each other."

He laughs. "I'm not sure what to address first. The fact that you live up here and you've never met a horse, or the fact that you read a romance starring two horses."

"Is it that pathetic?" I pinch my lips to the side and look down at the solid oak table that looks like it's been worn over time.

"That's an easy fix. I'll take you riding tomorrow."

I shake my head. "I'll pet one. But riding, that sounds dangerous and I'm not big on taking unnecessary risks with my life." I get the feeling he's going to ignore my apprehension.

"What time does Earl get up in the morning?"

"Seven-thirty. I usually get him breakfast, help him wash up, then play cards with him while we watch you do chores."

Holt laughs and crumples his napkin up on his empty plate. "You're watching me do chores?"

I stand from the table and grab him a cupcake from the glass dome on the counter, then sit back at my chair, and watch as he stares toward me with a softness I haven't seen in him yet.

"Did you make these while you were watching me, too?" He laughs.

My eyes stay on his and energy passes between us. "Something like that. Your dad says you've run the ranch on your own for almost a year now. Aren't you tired?"

He bites into the chocolate-raspberry cupcake and closes his eyes like he's savoring the taste. I'm not sure I've ever felt so appreciated. "Tired is an understatement. More importantly... holy fuck. These are good. I'm starting to think I'm holding you back from some big chef career."

"If following a recipe makes you a chef, I guess I should be going then. Seriously, though, how do you manage everything? You're out there from sunrise until way after sundown."

He crams the rest of the cake in his mouth and dark red crumbs drop down from his lips, into his beard, and over the button up flannel he's wearing. *How is it that he's made wolfing a cupcake sexy?*

"Not trusting anyone helps." He stands from the table and tosses his dishes in the sink. "Meet me out by the barn tomorrow after the old man goes down for his nap. I'll show you around." He steps closer and locks eyes with me. "And don't do these dishes. I'll get them in the morning." He takes a pause, and I wonder if he's seeing his gaze is melting me into the floor. "Dinner was incredible, but you don't owe me a meal. You're here for Earl." He nods toward me and turns down the hall, disappearing into the dark, while I sit in the kitchen wondering what the hell just happened.

Chapter Two

Holt

I shouldn't be thinking about Ann for many reasons. First, she's at least twenty years younger than me. Going after younger women is my father's thing. Second, she's working here. Sure, my father hired her, but technically, it's me cutting the check for her service. Boss-employee relations aren't professional. I think there's a rule book about that somewhere. Third, I've got enough to deal with without throwing a taboo romance into the mix. So, leaving the kitchen as quickly as possible was in both our interests. I don't even know why I invited her to the barn. It's been so damn long since I've noticed a woman. Why do I have to notice this one?

The shower runs cold, and I reach for my towel on the rack behind the door, noticing my phone is flashing with a missed call.

Fucking hell. It's ten o'clock at night. This shit never ends. I could ignore it, but the call is from Waylon. He owns one of the biggest ranches on the mountain range and runs the rodeo in town. He's quickly become one of the biggest deals in the area and the go-to guy for all things ranch related. If I'm short on hay, he's got some to sell. If I need an extra hand for the day, he's got a cowboy that he doesn't mind sharing. Truthfully, I probably owe the man more beers than I have time left to buy him. At the very least, I guess that warrants a callback.

"Everything alright?" I let the towel fall to the closet floor and weed through my dresser for a pair of boxers as I talk.

"Not really." He's more somber sounding than usual.

The floors creak outside the door. I snap my boxers into place and peek into the hall, hoping to catch a glimpse of Ann from where I'm standing, but instead get a whiff of my father's terrible cologne. He must have gone to the kitchen. If he's getting around fine, I'm not sure why he thought he needed help. Probably so he could get a little eye candy with his recovery. *God, that man needs help.*

"Jake got bucked off Bruno during the rodeo tonight. He did some pretty bad damage to his neck. Doctor says he's gonna need a few months of recovery time."

"Okay..." I stand in the hallway beside my bedroom door, waiting for Earl to head back to his room. I don't know why, but it's good to know he's in his bed before I go to sleep.

Maybe it's because I don't want to trip on him as I work through the pitch-black house on my way to the barn in the morning. "How can I help with that?"

"Well," Waylon's voice rises an octave or two, "I was hopin' you'd take over for him. At least until he's healed up. There's a good pay package if yo—"

"I'd love to help you, man," I rub my hand against the back of my neck, trying to loosen the muscles that have bundled, "but I've got my hands full here. With the ranch and Earl, I'm barely keeping the training sessions straight. Two of these horses are supposed to go to the Baxter farm for their grandkids, and I'm not sure they're ready. Besides, I'm an old man, Waylon. I fall off once and I'm done for."

Cups clank against one another in the kitchen and water runs. The old man is getting himself a drink. Can he make any more noise? He's going to wake up Ann, and the last thing that girl needs is no sleep after dealing with him all day.

"Think about it," Waylon argues. "I'll bump the pay up. Two grand a week until Jake's back. Let me know by the end of the week." The call ends and a plate crashes, followed by a series of curse words that remind me of a childhood Sunday morning. The kind where Earl had been up drinking all night and Mom was trying to get him sober enough to head to church, which only resulted in an argument. She deserved better.

"Is everything okay?" Ann questions as her bedroom door opens. "I thought I heard a noise." She steps into the hall, wrapping a thin black robe around her waist tightly. The woman's gorgeous. There's no doubting it. Long, thick curls bounce on her shoulders and her plump lips part. She looks toward me, scanning me up and down before her cheeks turn pink, and she looks away.

"Fuck. Sorry." I'm still in my boxers. I tip back into the bedroom and grab a pair of sweatpants from the drawer. "I was getting out of the shower when I heard the noise, then I had a phone call, and—"

"No. It's your home. You're okay. I'm going to see if your dad needs help."

I reach for her arm. "No, I've got it. You're not on call twenty-four seven. He's a handful and you need your rest."

"Actually, I am. Your dad hired me for round-the-clock care." She sets the paperback she's carrying on the dresser inside her room, then rushes down the hall. Her voice is sharp as she sees him. "Earl, you're bleeding!"

Bleeding. Of course, he's bleeding.

I follow behind Ann and make my way into the kitchen, where she's rinsing the old man's hand off in the sink. "It's just a small cut. A Band-Aid will do him fine." I hate that she's up taking care of him. She should be asleep, or resting, or reading, or doing whatever it was she was doing before she was interrupted by his idiocrasy.

When she has the Band-Aid in place, she bends over to pick shards of glass with me. Earl stays leaned against the back counter, his hands shaking. That's new.

"I've got this," I say, standing quick to grab the hand sweep in the pantry. "Why don't you head back to bed? I can get him to his room."

We're kneeling together, eye to eye, our breath mingling like a late summer storm about to take hold of the farm. I need to get out of the same space, or my imagination is going to take over.

"Are you sure?" Her lips move softly, remaining gently parted.

I nod. "I want to talk to him for a few minutes, anyway."

"Okay." She stands from the floor and smiles gently toward me, then my father, squeezing his hand as she walks past. "I'll see you in the morning."

I roll my eyes and finish sweeping the smallest of the shards. He wants that squeeze. He likes it. I need to have a talk with him and let him know she's off limits.

Footsteps creak down the hall and the heavy wood door to Ann's bedroom closes gently. I turn toward my father, pressing the pad to the trashcan to empty the glass from the dustpan. "What are you doing out here?"

"Being self-sufficient." My father turns and reaches for another cup from the cupboard, lowering it to the counter before opening the fridge for the pitcher of orange juice. "I figured Ann needed her sleep and God knows I can't ask you for anything."

"Please. I've been dragging your dead weight around since I was a kid. You could've asked me for a drink."

He successfully pours his orange juice and shrugs. "Well, I didn't... so sue me." He grabs his glass off the counter and carries it toward the hallway, without another word.

"Woah, woah, woah." I circle to the front of him and stare down at my father. We live together, but it's been at least a few weeks since we've had a real conversation. For the most part, I avoid dinner, and stay in the barn until early morning—by choice. This close, it's startling how much he's aged. His face is long and wrinkled, dyed by the sun, and the rim of his hair is silver where his hat used to sit. This man isn't my father. He's a version of the man that was supposed to be my father.

"What do you need?" he snaps, clearing his throat. "My shows are about to start."

His shows? I remember how this man preached every time he saw me watching TV, laying into me with stories about how it would rot my brains, and then find a new chore that immediately needed to be done.

"What were you thinking hiring that girl?"

He narrows his thick brows. "I was thinking the first five women I've had all quit. This one seemed to have some stamina. What's it to you?"

He's playing coy, as usual, and it's pissing me off.

"Ann is sweet. Don't do anything stupid."

He shakes his head and grins. "And what does that mean, son? Is that another dig at me for your mother? It wasn't my fault she got sick."

"It was one hundred percent because of you, but that's beside the point. Ann is off limits. Do you hear me? No lingering looks, no ass grabs, no flirty comments. Leave her be."

"You like her." He grins wider, as though he's just figured me out.

He hasn't.

"No! She's a young girl. Hell... how old is she? Twenty? I could be her—"

"Twenty-four. She's a part-time librarian, and in school for teaching, I believe. You should talk to her, she's a nice gi—"

"She's here until you're getting around better. Which, by the looks of things, seems to be any day now. So, I'm not sure there's a need for us to talk."

I don't mention that I'm meeting her at the barn in the morning. He doesn't need to know everything. Besides, he'll blow it out of proportion.

"Right." Dad smirks and walks slowly down the hallway. "Well, you should get some sleep, son. You've got a big day tomorrow with all the *chores* and all." The way he says chores makes me wonder what he thinks I do out there all day.

If it were up to me, the man would be in a nursing home an hour away thinking about all the shit decisions he's made in his life, but it's not up to me. He took that choice away when he spent the rest of our damn money.

I swallow hard and head back into the bedroom, passing by Ann's door slowly. I'm not sure why. I'm only torturing myself. She's listening to a soft bluegrass instrumental, maybe twisting a single curl around her index finger while she imagines the romantic scenes playing out in her book. The thought of her only a wall a way sends a shock of electricity straight to my dick.

Fucking hell. I can't turn into the old man.

Chapter Three

Ann

T he beds at Misty Oak Ranch are exceptionally comfortable. A firm mattress with thick, luxurious bedding, and the temperature in the house is set low, perfect for sleeping. So then, it makes no sense why I was up all night long twisting my brain in circles, wondering why Holt held eye contact with me so long in the kitchen.

Maybe he hates me. Maybe he hates having someone else around the house. Maybe that's why he stays out in the barn so late. Maybe *'tour of the ranch'* really means Holt is going to fire me or persuade me to leave. He did leave the kitchen exceptionally fast after he'd finished eating, then kicked me out last night after Earl fell.

I pour Earl another cup of coffee and fiddle with the sugar jar in the center of the table. It's an old, teal-stained mason jar that looks to be older than the house itself, but it's charming. I love old houses like this. Ever since Granny and I moved to Rugged Mountain, I've fantasized about owning an old farmhouse with chipping white paint and an American flag flying out front.

"What's bugging you this morning, dear?"

I stare at Earl. He has the same eyes as Holt. Brown with flecks of green. Though, Earl's eyes are surrounded by dark circles and the lines of a life well lived. He reminds me of Clint Eastwood. Older, but still attractive in his own right.

"Oh, nothing." I redirect my gaze toward him. "Can I get you another biscuit? You didn't eat much for breakfast."

He shakes his head. "You know, I've lived a lot of years. I probably have advice for you, whatever your dilemma." His tenacity reminds me of my granny. She's been known to plunk herself down in the kitchen with a pot of applesauce stewing on the stove behind her, a bushel of apples in front of her, and then demand to know all your secrets. There's no sugar coating to her. She's intense. I'm sure by modern standards, people would say it's borderline mean, but everyone in the family opened up to her. And to her credit, she always has the best advice, no matter what your problem.

But Earl isn't my granny. He's Holt's father, and I'm working for him. I don't think he'd find pleasure in knowing I thought about his son all night long, tossing and turning to fantasies of his hands all over me.

Nope. That's weird.

"Thank you," I finally say, "but I'm fine. It was a busy night for you. I'm sure you're excited for your nap today."

"A little." He yawns and lifts his coffee cup to his lips. "When you get old like me, the caffeine stops working."

"I don't think you have to be old for that to happen," I say, standing from the oak table to help him from his chair. I know he doesn't need the help. He's getting around pretty well on his own for just having surgery five weeks ago, but still, I offer it. "I drink two cups in the morning and I'm still yawning all day. What does that mean?"

"It means you needed three cups." He laughs, and we make our way down the hall toward his bedroom, which is more like a little apartment. There's a sitting room inside, fitted with a couch, and a wall mounted TV. There's a separate bathroom and a bedroom just off that. In its heyday, I'd bet the house was the fanciest on this side of the mountain. "You should go out and see Holt if you're not napping. I'd bet he'll show you around the farm if you're interested."

"Oh! He invited me out there already. I thought I'd head on down after I settled you in."

Earl looks back at me and raises his thick brows in the air. "Well, I'm settled. Go down there and let him show you the ropes. The man is impatient." He glances out the window and down toward the red barn ranch that sits on the bottom of a hill. Holt is on the phone, pacing back and forth.

"He looks busy. Maybe I'll wait for a bit."

"No." Earl scoots himself into bed and lifts his good leg before slowly raising the other. "He will stay busy if you let him. You're helping his mental health. Go say hello."

"We'll see," I say, pulling Earl's blanket up over him. "I'll be back in a few hours. You rest well, okay?"

"I'll rest better knowing you're down there getting him out of trouble." He grips my arm in his and looks up at me with a pleading gaze. "Holt is a good guy, but he's terrible at people. It would mean a lot to me if you could get him out of his head for a bit."

Wow. No pressure.

"I'll see what I can do." I smile kindly, then make my way out of the room before Earl can make any more demands. If anything, I feel like Holt needs to know that his dad truly does have good intentions with him, but it's not my place. It's also not my place to interrupt his call. Who knows what business he's working on? The man trains troubled horses that go to ranches all over the country. I'm sure whatever his phone call is about, it's more important than me.

Then again, he did invite me, and he has an idea when his dad takes his nap. Maybe he's just killing time until he sees me leave the house. I pull back the sheer white curtain in the kitchen and look out at Holt, still talking. He's standing right by the barn door, and he does keep looking up, as though he's expecting me. Maybe I should go outside.

I chew at the end of my thumb and pace back and forth in the kitchen, my heart thumping wildly against my rib cage.

I'm going to go, right? I should go. I'm going to go.

I grab my coat off the hook and check my hair in the mirror, ruffling it back, then to the side, then back again before opening the front door.

What's the worst that can happen? He says he's busy? I'm just doing what he's asked. I'm showing up on time. I'm punctual. That's a positive thing.

Stepping across the gravel driveway, I make my way toward the barn at the bottom of the hill. It's snowed the last few days and there's a heavy blanket of white on either side of the path, but I step where Holt had stepped earlier, avoiding as much cold as possible. I have no idea how many acres this place is, but the land seemingly goes on for miles with stockade fences bordering different pastures and a crimson red barn sitting at the front of it all.

Holt's giant body leans against the open barn door. He waves when he sees me.

Thank God! My shoulders relax. He does want to see me. He's been waiting in the doorway the whole time.

"I'm hurrying," a female voice says from behind me.

My head snaps back and my stomach falls to the ground.

Oh God. Holt wasn't waving at me. He wasn't waiting for *me*. He was waiting for the gorgeous girl making her way toward him.

In fact, from this angle, I bet he hadn't even seen me coming.

"Hey." The woman's voice is soft and sweet. "You must be Ann. Earl has told me all about you."

My brows wrinkle unintentionally as I try to gather what's happening. I want to hit her with a *'really, cause I've heard nothing about you,'* but I choose the high road, and reach out my hand. "Great to meet you! I love caring for Earl. I was just heading down to see if Holt needed anything for lunch."

"Oh, I didn't realize a caregiver took care of everyone in the house." She flips her long hair back and smiles sweetly. I hate her.

"It's not a requirement. I'm just being polite." My words are curt and probably too short. I should think of something else to say. What if she's Holt's girlfriend? I don't want to make any more of an ass of myself than I already have.

Of course, he has a girlfriend. He's a massive, handsome rancher. Men like that don't last long around here.

"Dakota, this is Ann." Holt clears his throat. "Have you two had a chance to meet?"

I nod, and Dakota hands a folder of paperwork to Holt. "I won't keep you long. I just wanted to hand this off to you. My uncle says he needs the final papers signed by the end of the week, if you're interested."

"I just got off the phone with him. He's going for a hard sell."

The pretty blonde nods and winks. "He knows how good you are. I'll be back to pick up the paperwork on Friday. That is unless you don't sign. But... we both know you're going to sign." She grins wide, showing off perfectly white teeth before heading back down the driveway.

It doesn't seem like they're dating. I guess that's a relief. Though, if Holt is hanging around women this beautiful and not dating them, what are his standards like? I'm overthinking this.

"You ready for that tour?" His thumb is hooked into his belt loop, and he nods toward the interior of the barn as a horse whinnies. "They've been waiting all day to meet you."

I step into the barn, my heart sandwiched somewhere between my throat and my stomach as Holt opens a stall and lets a black and white beauty out. I have no idea what kind of horse she is, but she's gorgeous. She's already wearing a saddle.

I look her up and down for any imperfections. She seems sturdy enough. Maybe this won't be so bad. That is... until I see the ominous name above her stall.

"I'm not riding a horse named Lady Lightning." I wave my hands back and forth dramatically, biting back the nervous grin that's formed.

Holt laughs.

"You know, if I get thrown off, you're going to be the one taking care of your dad."

"Ah." He grins. "Old Earl will have to take care of himself, or we'd end up duking it out like a couple a country boys fighting over a property line. Come on now. I'll boost ya up."

As much as my body wants to repel the gorgeous animal clomping and hawing in front of me, my heart wants Holt to boost me up even more.

I reach toward the horse and hold firm on the nose of the saddle like I've seen cowboys do on TV.

"Shit! You're a professional." He grips my waist as I hook my toe into the stirrup. My entire body vibrates with excitement. His hands are big and warm, and I'm desperate for more.

God, I'm pathetic.

"Good girl," he says, running his hand down over Lady Lightning. At first, I think he's talking to the horse. She's stayed still long enough to allow me to climb on. But when I see Holt's eyes on mine, I can't help but wonder if the praise was meant for me.

Chapter Four

Holt

Ann is a natural. Most folks pull too hard on the reins, but she holds them loose and lets Lightning do the work.

"You're staring! Am I doing something wrong?"

"Quite the opposite," I say, leading the way down into the open pasture. "I figure we'll trot down there and have a snack by the river while the horses get a drink of water. Unless the cold is too much for ya?"

She shakes her head and glances toward me quickly before looking out at the pasture again. "I'm good. It does look like it's going to snow again, though. I'm not sure how much more we can handle. I think the roads were just cleared from the last storm a few hours ago."

"Isn't that the truth? When it stays bad like this, you struggle to keep up. The second you finish checking all the batteries on the farm and making sure they're all turning over, you start worrying about the snow that's accumulating on the roof. There's no shortage of work when the weather cooperates. When it doesn't, mother nature makes sure you give her all you've got each day before you go to bed. The good thing is I have a couple of horses going out this week that have been a handful and that will free up some time. How's Dad doing this morning?"

"*Dad?* You didn't call him old man, or Earl. Last night must have been the bonding conversation you both needed."

"It wasn't. I don't know how you stand him."

"He's kind. He talked about you again this morning, actually. I think he wanted me to come out and keep you company. He worries about you working all these long hours."

"Well, he had ten people working the ranch with him. I take care of everything myself." I tilt my head back and forth. "Granted, I occasionally get a cowboy or two from up at the Waylon Family Ranch. Have you been up there? The place is insane."

She shakes her head. "I hear a lot of folks talking about it now that the rodeo is in town, but I've never been up there."

"I'll have to take you over there one day. It's massive, just under two thousand acres. If you appreciate open land, you can't miss some of the views he has."

"You've got some pretty great views right here. Have you been out at this ranch your whole life?"

I nod. "Born and raised. Rode the rodeo whenever it came to town. Waylon asked if I'd be interested in riding again. I guess I'd be filling in for a guy who's out with an injury. That's why Dakota stopped by. She brought all the disclaimers to sign."

"That sounds dangerous. My granny was rodeo queen, two years running back in the fifties. She still talks about all the injuries people had riding."

I reach out for Ann and run my hand down over her curved frame as she swings her long leg over Lightning and hops to the ground. "Dad got himself into some heavy debt back when he was running the ranch. I've been struggling to keep things afloat since I took over. Waylon's offering to pay me top dollar to ride for him. Enough that I could pay off the rest of the debt in three months of riding. If it weren't for this old body, I'd jump right back up there. But damn," I laugh, "I'm old. My body doesn't recover the same."

We crunch in the snow toward the edge of the river where there's an old picnic table set out in the sun.

"You shouldn't mess with your body. What would happen if you ended up getting hurt? You'd have to hire people to take on work and then you'd be even further behind the eight ball. Besides, I'm not sure how I'd care for two stubborn men." She smiles.

"So, you'd take care of me, too? I'm not sure that's in your job description." A breeze blows between us as we stand at the edge of the river, face to face. The horses are a hundred feet away drinking and for all intents and purposes, we're alone. I can't remember the last time I was alone with a woman like this. Maybe a decade ago, probably longer. Before the ranch, I was focused on the rodeo. And I'm not so sure I can say I've ever been alone with a woman who said she'd take care of me if I were hurt.

"Of course, I'd take care of you too," she nudges my shoulder playfully, "but I hope it doesn't come to that." She smiles and looks down at the river, pushing back her long locks before glancing up toward me again. "What happened between you and your dad, anyway? If you don't mind me asking."

I suck in a deep breath and blow it out hard as I stare toward the river. "How long do you have? The man is a narcissist to say the least. I know he seems all sweet and kind now, but he cheated on my mom every chance he got, spent money he didn't have, and couldn't find the time of day to spend with my brother and I when we were young. Now, he's all old and pathetic and he wants sympathy, but I don't have any for him. Ya know what I mean?"

"That must have been rough for you all."

"I managed, but my brother and mom weren't so lucky. My brother left for the military the second he got old enough. He had a lot of anger to work out. He lives in Ohio now outside the Air Force base. He's got his life turned around, even has a couple kids." I chuckle a little under my breath. "Since he left, he's never looked back. I guess it's just easier for him. He knows I love him, but that's enough. Every time we talk, I know he comes right back to his time on this ranch, and it pains him all over again."

"You said something about your mom. I've been too anxious to ask where she was." Ann shifts her gait as though she's afraid she's pushed too far.

"Mom passed away a few years back. She was old school. No matter what Dad did, he was her husband, and she forgave him." I shake my head. "I struggled with it for years, but she would always smile and tell me she knew what she was doing." I catch myself laughing. "That was my mom. She loved with her whole heart. It never mattered to her if the other person deserved it or not."

As we stand in the cold breeze, I can't help but feel I've overshared. She asked me if I got along with my dad as some sort of positive, and then I dragged her through our family drama. Nice going, Holt.

Ann gives me the warmest smile. "She sounds lovely. There are worse things in this world than being too kind or forgiving." She brushes a strand of hair behind her ear. "I can relate to your story. My dad left when I was young. He didn't do anything wrong. He just left my mom to do everything that wasn't children." She laughs. "Until he met another woman and then, poof, just like magic, he had all the desire in the world to raise a whole litter. I'm not sure I'd be the same forgiving saint as your mom if he tried to come back into my life after all these years. It would feel like a betrayal to my mother. She's been gone so many years now. I couldn't do it." There's pain behind her eyes when she talks, and a need passes through me. It's carnal and savage, like nothing I've ever experienced before in my life. I hate that anyone has hurt Ann, and every part of my body aches to protect her.

"Where is he now?" My tone is deep and suspended.

She shrugs. "No clue. He tried getting in touch a few years back with this weird Christmas card. He signed it with love from his new family." She shakes her head. "I have no idea what that was about, but I didn't respond. Maybe he wanted to rub it in my face that he was happy with his new children. I don't know. It's strange to think I have half siblings I've never met, though. I mean, my mom never had more kids so my father's children would be the only family I have left outside of Granny."

Shit.

How do I make all this better for her? How do I make up for years of heartbreak and childhood pain? How do I tell her that I want to keep her safe and somehow also do the dirtiest, filthiest things to her? How do I get a grip before I make a fucking idiot of myself? I'm a sick man. She's twenty-four years old. I'm forty-five. I shouldn't want to touch her the way I do. I shouldn't want to hold her and care for her the way I do. I should be able to control myself.

I whistle toward the horses.

Ann looks up at me with a big, round, innocent gaze, that just about kills me.

Fuck. I want to take her pain away... now! I can be her family and kiss her until she feels better. I can lay with her in bed next to her soft curves, long hair, gentle hands, enormous tits, and tell her all the things it would take for her to never want for anything ever again.

I'm sure she's confused as to why I'm ending the tour early, but I made a mistake inviting her out here. I need to get the hell out of this pasture before I say something stupid and make a god damn fool of myself.

Chapter Five

Ann

I sit at the edge of the bed and stare down at the line of selfies I've just taken, then send two of them to my friend Morgan. We've been best friends since high school and she's the best at talking sense into me.

Me: <selfie>

Me: Does this look casual enough that I don't look like I'm trying, but nice enough that if I were to see a certain someone, I'd look hot?

Morgan: Girl... you're hot as hell.

Me: Also a little trashy, right?

Morgan: Ha! That's not what you're going for?

Me: No! I was going for casual sexy. Like... just got off work, hair in a loose bun, kind of vibe.

Morgan: Tie that t-shirt up a little, or *accidentally* tuck it into the back of your panties. That will really get him going. Is this for that old man you're caring for? If so, we should talk.

Me: No! God! What do you take me for?

Morgan: Well, who's it for then? Does he have a sexy nurse you're trying to persuade?

I realize quickly that Morgan may think Holt is old. If I were guessing, I'd think he were in his mid-forties. To most in their early twenties, that's ancient.

Me: Something like that. I don't know what I'm doing! HELP! I'm not even sure he likes me. He keeps ending our conversations early, but we have this weird connection that I can't explain.

Morgan: He likes you.

Me: How do you know?

Morgan: Cowboys are like that. They get all bottled up with their feelings and over-complicate everything. You have to lay it on thick, so he knows he isn't going to get himself hurt. Wear a long t-shirt, casually get a drink, lift your arms when he's looking, give him full ass, and he won't be able to resist.

Me: You think?

Morgan: You must really like this guy. You're usually not this... free.

Not this free? Am I being free? I guess I'm about to pretend I don't hear him out there and prance around in a short band t-shirt while reaching for a glass on the highest cupboard, so he gets a glimpse of my panties, and hopefully ravages me right there in the kitchen.

I laugh at myself. This plan is ridiculous.

Maybe I'm less free, and more desperate.

Thing is, there's something about Holt that makes me wild with urges I've never felt. Not firsthand, anyway. I want him to know I'm interested, but maybe this is too far. Maybe I should just wander into the kitchen in my flannel sleep pants and see what happens.

Me: You're right. I'll scale back.

Morgan: No! That's not what I said. Go for it! You're there, you like him, so let your freak flag fly. Just text me right after and tell me every detail, including more about who this guy is. And if I don't hear from you until morning, I'll know you're a dirty slut.

I text her back a heart and take another look at myself in the mirror, before sucking up the rest of the confidence I have, open the bedroom door, and make my way down the hall toward the kitchen. If he rejects me, that's fine. I can leave Rugged Mountain and start a new life on the other side of the world.

I'm sure Russia needs teachers.

God, what am I thinking? This t-shirt is barely hanging on. What kind of respectable woman pulls this kind of thing?

I try to remember Morgan's pep talk, but I'm interrupted by a deep voice.

"You're up late." Holt clears his throat and stares down at his plate before glancing up at me again.

Oh God. The *thought* of doing this, and the *reality* of doing it, are two completely different events. I cover myself up as best I can. "I'm sorry. I didn't realize anyone was out here."

Lies! What kind of monster am I? No. I have to own this. What would a romance heroine do? Would she cower, or would she take the man she wants?

"Don't be sorry." Holt pulls out a chair beside him. "Sit and keep me company. I'm driving myself crazy with indecision about this rodeo thing. I need to get out of my head. By the way, thank you for dinner. It's delicious. I don't know what I'm going to do when you go back to your real life. I'm getting used to these fancy meals."

"It's just crock pot stew. You don't need to get excited... but thank you. Your cabin really feels like a home to me." I trace my finger along the edge of the sugar container still in the center of the table and stare toward Holt. Do people have *security objects?* If they do, I call sugar container.

His eyes gaze toward mine as he bites into the apple hand pie that I wrapped for him. "Well, I have to say, it hasn't felt like a home in a long time. I think it might be you making it feel that way."

My heart swells and warms. I'd do anything to be that hand pie right now. Wrapped up warm in his big, calloused hand as he angles me into his mouth. My clit throbs, and my nipples harden at the thought of it.

Why does he have to be so handsome? He's not built like he spends hours in the gym. He has the body of a working man. Strong shoulders and bulking biceps from hauling feed bags and bales of hay. I wouldn't mind being either of those as he tosses me across the mattress and has his way with me.

I laugh to myself at the thought. I really need to get a grip. He's clearly complimenting my food, not my eyes or the shoulder I have hanging out.

"I saw you reading a book last night." His voice is low and graveled, and the sound alone sends a shock of arousal straight through me. "Anything good?"

"It was a romance novel. I swing from everything geeky to everything romantic. It's an obsession. I love being at the library so much. I get to see all the books people choose. Do you do any reading?"

"Does the back of a feed bag count?" He grins and runs his big palm over his beard. "Not much time for reading these days. I'd like to hear more about your book, though." His eyes are on me so intently, that I think they may be burning a hole in my face, but I like the heat and I stare back at him, sparks flying everywhere.

I hope he feels them, too.

Howling winds cut through the eaves of the house and my eyes go to the window of white in the kitchen. The storm picked up. I'd bet we have another foot or two of snow on the horizon, but the storm could be a world away as I focus on Holt's energy.

I inch my hand toward his. It's a subtle move, but one that I figure could double for anything. I could be reaching for his plate to clear it, or I could be getting him a fresh glass of milk. It could be anything... but it's not. It's not anything. I want my hand in his. I want our bodies against one another. *I want him.*

Holt's massive, inked hand rests on top of mine, his gaze still on me hard and heavy. "Did you wear that out here on purpose?" His voice is deep. "Did you want me to see you like this?"

My heart slams against my chest and I nod, biting my lower lip, completely unsure of what I'm getting myself into. His question is so poignant and I'm not sure how he means it. He could be insulted that I'm dressed so scantly in front of him.

He stands from the table, unfolding his body until he's towering over me, reaching for my hand. I've never been this close to him. From here, he smells like cedar and bales of hay.

When I scan his body for the source of his musk, I begin to feel our size difference. I'm not a tiny thing, but standing next to him, I'm dwarfed. It's only now that I realize how strong he must be.

A second goes by, maybe two. He bends down and grips the back of my neck and kisses me hard. His tongue dives into my mouth and he growls out inside of me as though he's an unchained animal taking what he needs.

I love it. I want to be taken. I want to be needed. My panties soak and my clit throbs hard.

He leans me back on the clear end of the table and bends over me, touching my throat, my breasts, my stomach, and my thighs. His touch is heavy and rough, but careful and focused.

"You wanted me to see all this soft, pale skin... didn't you, trouble?" He bends down and pulls my tits from the break in my t-shirt, palming his big hands over each one before bending into run his tongue over the tips.

"Trouble?"

He groans into my neck. "That's what you are, right? A sweet, little ball of trouble? I've been trying to deny whatever it is I'm feeling, but you're out here enticing me, aren't you?"

My clit throbs as his warm, heavy breath tickles my ear. Why do I like being his *trouble?* Why do I want to hear him say it over and over again? Preferably while he's thumping inside of me and spreading me wide.

"Maybe I am." My hips rock against his and for the first time the hard ridge of his cock is apparent. This is real. He's real. He's turned on by me. The hottest man I've ever seen is somehow turned on by me. How does that happen?

Should I touch him? Should I run my hand over his cock? Should I tell him how desperate I am for him?

He groans out and backs away before I get a chance, lifting my bare legs to his shoulders. He kisses the inside of my thighs.

"It's wrong of me to think about all the things I've been wanting to do to you." His rough beard brushes against my legs as he creeps his way up toward my upper thighs.

My eyes shut as tingling pleasure runs through me. "Why is it wrong?"

He groans. "Your age. The fact that I'm your boss. Pick your poison."

"If this were one of my books, you'd push past those thoughts. Right into this tight, virgin pussy."

I don't know who I am right now. I'm delirious, pumped with hormones and emotion. Desperate for him to touch me. Desperate to come. Desperate to feel his big hard cock spread me wide. I'd have to be because I've never in my life talked like this.

"*Virgin?*"

I regret saying it the second he repeats the word.

"It's not a big deal. I just thought you should know before we..."

He stares at me long and hard. This momentary pause makes my heart tighten. I've ruined the moment. He's going to retreat. I've scared him away. *Of course, I have.* What grown man wants to mess around with a woman who has zero experience?

Definitely not a man that looks like this.

"It's okay," I say, sitting up from the table. "I've made things weird. We can just forget this ever happened."

He grins and leans into my lips, his hand between my legs, cupping my mound, as a single finger glides along my panty covered seam. "Do you really want me to stop? If you do, I will."

"No," I squeak. "I never want you to stop, but I thought the virgin thing would be weird for you."

He groans and pauses for a second. "I didn't realize I was such a sick man."

"Sick, how?" I'm panting, losing control of my breath.

"Sick," he groans low into my neck and pushes my cotton panties to the side to pet my bare pussy, "like it turns me on to know I'm the first to touch this sweet, innocent body of yours." Warm breath grazes my neck as he slides his finger inside of me.

My head arches back and I moan again and again. "You're not sick, Holt." I take a deep breath. "I want you," escapes my mouth between groans.

One finger becomes two.

I moan out in approval, and he commends me for my noise.

"That's right." He brushes his hand back through my hair and watches my face as he thrusts his fingers in and out, over and over, sliding through my juices.

The world is hazy and I'm dizzy with heat and a fever I've never felt before. "Fuck me, Holt. Please... fuck me hard. I want to feel you all over me."

A low rumble in his throat emanates as his teeth bare. He bites into my shoulder and kisses my arm, sucking intermittently as he makes his way between my legs. "I will, but first I want a taste of that sweet little cun—"

A loud crash echoes outdoors and our attention is diverted to the sound. A sound that I have a feeling is going to change the trajectory of the night.

Chapter Six

Holt

It's times like these I realize I need a break. A break from farm life, a break from the ranch, a break from responsibility. Though, I can't imagine what I'd have to do to make that a reality. Not now, anyway. I owe too much damn money to the bank, and now with the barn roof half caved, I'm going to be even further in debt.

"I'm so sorry, Holt. Maybe I can call around and see if someone can help you fix it. Everyone in town is always happy to help wherever they can." Her small hand is cupped in mine while we stare at the damage. Thankfully, it's only the back half that collapsed. The front of the barn, where the horses are, still looks stable. Though, I'm going to have to call Waylon tonight and see if he can house them temporarily until I get it fixed. It's not safe for them to stay there overnight and it's too cold to keep them out in this storm.

"I should've been up there shoveling the snow off today. It was accumulating, and I knew this roof wasn't the best. Let's get you inside. I'm going to call Waylon and see if he can get someone to come help me."

Ann glances up toward me with sweetness and a tinge of guilt in her eyes. "Text me Waylon's number. I'll call him and have him send some people over for you. Then I'll get dressed and help you."

For a long second, my brain stalls. *She wants to help? Outside? With the ranch work?* I haven't met a woman yet that would leap into action so quickly, and I know it's not because emptying a horse barn at ten p.m. is her dream. She's doing it because she wants to help me.

"You sure? You don't have to."

She twists her hair to the side of her shoulder and looks up at me in the tiny little t-shirt I was going to tear off a second ago. "I want to help you, Holt. I'm going to help."

I bend down and lift her from the cold ground, realizing she's run out in her bare feet. "You're trouble. Do you know that?"

She grins. "You like it."

Her smart remark has my cock on the rise and for a second I consider the thought that the barn can wait. I need to feel her against my skin again, taste the juices she was working up for me, press into her tight virgin pussy, but the sounds of cracking behind me filters me back to reality.

"You're right." I set her down on the kitchen floor of the ranch house and kiss her forehead. "Grab some of my clothes from the closet. Their warmer than whatever you brought, I'm sure."

Another bright smile lifts onto her face and somehow, the collapsing barn doesn't seem so bad. Though, I'm sure the horses inside would beg to differ.

I run down the path, through the heavy snow and toward the barn, opening each stall quickly as the roof creaks overhead. The horses know well enough to run into the side pasture when they're released and they're intuitive enough to know something isn't right, so they hustle. I'm not sure how long it takes, but I effectively have all the horses away from the barn by the time Ann makes her way from the house. She's dressed in a pair of leggings, an oversized flannel, my work boots, and a smile on her face as wide as Colorado.

"What do you think?" She spins in a circle showing off her attire and I have to hold myself back again from biting at her neck and tackling her in the snow.

"I think I want to take you inside and strip all this off." I lean into her and nuzzle against her warm neck, sucking in the soft scent of lavender in her hair.

Fuck. I need to be alone with her. I need to devour her like the last cookie in the jar.

Headlights and the clanking of horse trailers interrupt my thoughts. It's Waylon and the cavalry.

"That was fast! Does he live close by?"

"Just around the corner. He's probably got ten guys on payroll just waiting for some shit to go down. I owe this man a lot."

Waylon hops from his truck, leaving the engine on and the headlights running. "Fuck, man, that barn has seen better days." He wanders down the path and stares toward the mess. "I can send a few guys over to build you a new one. No charge. We've got old wood up on the ridge and I'd bet Henry has some tin lying around we can use."

Henry's family owns the mountain, but Waylon is second to the crown.

"I can't take anything from anyone. Y'all have your own shit to worry about."

Waylon hammers his hand onto my shoulder and lowers his voice as he says, "You'd help me if I were struggling, right?"

"You know I would, but I'm not taking handouts."

"It's not a handout. It's a gift."

Waylon's a nice guy. One of the nicest. He's also a businessman. A shrewd businessman. The kind of businessman that doesn't run around doing favors for everyone. I'm lucky to have him on my side. I have to bite the bullet and do the rodeo run.

"You still looking for a guy to ride this weekend?"

Waylon nods. "You sure you're up for it? I don't want to guilt you. You don't owe me anything for the barn. I'd still pay you for your time in the ring."

A few weeks of riding won't kill me. Hell, it might be good to get back up on a bull again. "I'll do it for half pay and I'll come train your horses for a month as thanks for the roof. Deal?" I hold out my hand.

"You know you don't have to do any of that." Waylon adjusts his hat.

I pull Ann into my side, and hold her against my waist, rubbing her arm up and down as the wind catches us from the side. Waylon looks toward us, confused at what's happening.

"Who's this? I didn't realize you were seeing anyone."

I glance toward Ann, then back toward Waylon. "This is Ann. She's been helping Earl and well... she makes a damn good apple pie."

Waylon grins. "That'll do it. Does every time."

I'm not sure what to call Ann and I, so I don't put a label on it. Though if it were my choice, I'd call her my wife right here and now. I'm not sure she'd agree.

"Well let's get these horses loaded up. We can talk details in the morning." Waylon unchains the back door on his trailer and lets down the ramp. "This storm is picking up something awful. You're lucky you didn't lose the whole roof."

Luck isn't the word for it. Those horses are like family. I can't stand the thought of losing any of 'em.

"Is that your dad?" Ann's voice contorts with confusion as she turns toward the pasture. Her eyes squint into the darkness.

"Can't be. Why would he be out here in the storm?"

"That's him." Ann takes off into the squall of white, sprinting toward him.

I follow behind.

"We've got this," Waylon shouts. "I'll call you in the morning. Let me know if you need anything else."

I wave back toward Waylon, thankful that one problem is solved. But leave it to my father to amp up the drama. If there's one thing he can be counted on for, it's to do exactly the worst thing at the worst time.

Chapter Seven

Ann

"What am I doing out here?" Earl's voice shakes when he speaks. "Ann, dear, did you bring me out here? You've forgotten my shoes."

I look down at Earl's crimson red feet and a shot of panic streaks through me before glancing back toward Holt. "He's going to need help getting back into the house. Can you lift him?" Deep down, I'm sure Holt loves his father, but right now I'm sure this isn't what he wanted to deal with. It's been a long day. An insanely long day. A day with more problems than most people have in a month.

Regardless, he bends down and lifts the frail man from the ground and carries him into the house. Calm and stoic, not a word spoken. I imagine in his day, Earl was a big man as well, though now he's flimsy by comparison to his son. A man that could probably lift both of us at once and not break a sweat.

"What's going on with you, Dad? Why are you out here?"

I've seen this behavior before, in my grandad a year or two before he passed. I was too young to remember a lot of details, but he started forgetting things, and wandering off without remembering where he was going to. The doctors never diagnosed him with dementia because he never went to see a doctor. Most people up here repel the thought of modern miracles. They prefer a simpler way. Pops believed forgetting was a part of old age and started wearing a bell around his wrist, so we'd know when he was up and moving. As the years went on, there were bells on the doors and windows too. It worked for us, but for a lot of people, I can't imagine that being the case, especially a busy guy like Holt.

"I was inside, and then I was out," Earl says, his voice shaking.

Holt kicks open the back door and carries his father inside, wrapping him up in a blanket on the bed while I put another log in the fire. "You have to stay in the house at night. You could freeze to death out there. Understand?"

Earl nods and a pang of guilt hits me in the chest as he looks up at his son. I know they've had their differences, but there's pain in Earl's eyes to make up for those years. Sure, maybe he doesn't deserve mercy, *but do any of us?*

"We're going to head back to our rooms. You call us if you need anything."

Earl reaches for Holt, gripping his shoulder. "I have something to give you, son. Can you sit for a minute?"

Holt looks back at me, his jaw clenched. He's frustrated, rightfully so. His barn just collapsed, he found his dad wandering in the snow, and he was busy with day-to-day chores until well after nine. It's a little much to ask for a conversation after all that.

Holt sits anyway, staring at his father from the edge of the bed. I'm not sure what kind of stare it is, but if I were to guess, I'd say it's something along the lines of... obligation.

"I'll go get some tea—"

"Stay." Holt reaches for my hand and looks toward me. "Please."

"Yes, dear," Earl says, opening his side drawer. "You should hear this, too."

As he sighs and opens his mouth, I dread what's going to come out. Something tells me Earl's about to ramble on with words that don't make much sense at all. I wonder how I can convince him to see a doctor in the morning.

"Open it, son." He hands Holt a crisp white envelope.

Thick lines form on Holt's forehead as he pries open the letter. Inside, is a blue and white check. Holt's gaze darts back to his father. "What's this?"

"It's a check with your name on it."

"I see that. Why? How? I've been fighting off debtors for almost a year now. Where did you get this money?"

"When your mother was alive, God rest her soul, she was my angel. I did everything I could to drive her away, but she wouldn't leave my side. She was the best person I've ever met and saw things in me even when I was lost. She believed in me no matter whatever piece of shit mess I got into, and I owe her."

Holt looks back with a blank expression. "So, you're buying her forgiveness?"

"Far from it, son. I can't atone for what I've done. I know that. But when I was out making a mess of our lives, she squirreled away bonds with any excess money. It was her way of keeping anything extra from going into a bottle or worse."

Holt sits in silence. He looks over at me periodically as to ask if he's dreaming or not.

"So, imagine my surprise when she shows me them all on her deathbed. The day that the Lord took her home, she looked me dead in the eyes, and told me it was for you boys." A tear starts to roll down his cheek. "Son, I held the bonds in my hands so many times over the years, eager to change... anything. I lost my angel, and I wanted to feel good, but I couldn't let her down like that. I wouldn't."

Holt waves the check back toward me with wide eyes. "It's eight hundred thousand dollars." He looks back at his father. "Even with just my half, I could pay off our debts, fix everything, and maybe hire some people to help me out around here."

"Or you could sell everything and start fresh," Earl says.

Holt places his big hand on his father's shoulder. "See, that's the thing. The thought has never crossed my mind. No matter what happened, this is the place I belong. I've met plenty of folks who chase money at the expense of their happiness, and I'm not going to be one of 'em. Ranching, and the work involved, makes me happy."

Holt glances down at the check again. "She really was a saint. But I gotta ask, if you were sitting on this, why didn't you help me out sooner? I've been struggling with—"

"Truthfully, I always saw too much of me in you. Every morning, you come around the corner of the kitchen, angry as a hornet, and I thought you were just like me. Nothing was ever good enough and you took for granted anything good in your life." Earl's eyes reach out to mine. "That is until I saw you with her. That's when I realized you weren't me. You showed the kindness and attention that I wish I had given your mother all those years. So, I got right on the phone and the lawyer brought a check while you all were out on them horses."

Holt looks toward me and squeezes my hand. His shoulders relax as he looks toward his father, then down at the check in his hands. "I don't know what to say."

"You don't have to say anything," Earl says. "All I want to hear is that you'll take that woman behind you out for a nice dinner."

Holt turns back and swallows my hand in his. "I think I can make that happen."

My heart warms, and for a second, I picture my life in this farmhouse. I imagine taking care of Earl, baking cupcakes and apple pies, helping Holt out in the barn, chasing children around, and dragging in fresh cut Christmas trees. I imagine casseroles on the stove cooling while I watch through a snowstorm for Holt's giant frame to appear as he makes his way in after a long day's work. And I imagine the two of us cuddled up in bed every night whispering sweet things and tickling each other slowly until he's pressed me into the mattress with his heavy weight and soft kisses. It's a fantasy, I know, but it's one I can't get out of my head. I can only hope Holt feels the same way.

Chapter Eight

- -

Holt

B y the time I get cleaned up, Ann is already curled up in my bed, her body hugging my pillow as though she's searching for my scent.

Why is this the hottest sight I've ever seen? A sweet, innocent woman naked against my pillow, in my bed, wiggling her ass back toward me as I make my way under the sheet.

"You're finally here," she groans as though she's sleepy. "I was starting to think you had another barn emergency."

"No more emergencies tonight, baby. Just you and me." My hand runs up and over her bare shoulder. She's soft, pale, and perfect. My balls tighten and my cock strikes hard against my boxers at the sound of her voice. She's so fucking precious.

"You and me, huh?" She rolls over, her nipples firm and erect against the cool air in the room. She brushes my chest and the hard tip of her breast hits me again and again, thumping my cock harder and harder.

I'm going to have to leave the room or ask her to marry me. I'm not sure which makes more sense right now. It's been a long, crazy-ass day, so I'm thinking I could get away with the latter, but I don't dare press my luck.

"You and me," I repeat. "What do you think about that big old check the old man just threw in my lap? Concerning or kind?"

I already know her answer. "Kind. People change, Holt. He's changed. He wants to make amends with you. He wants to do the right thing."

I look toward Ann, so innocent with her words. So kind, so understanding. If she listened long enough, I'm sure she'd find a way to forgive a bank robber. That's the good in her, though. It's why I'm falling for her. She sees people in a way I can't. She finds the pieces of grace and she lets that person shine.

"I'll take the old man to breakfast in the morning and maybe I can get Jimmy on the line. I'm sure we could all use a good old-fashioned talk."

"I like that for you." She smiles and nuzzles into my chest, running her fingers through the hair on my stomach.

"And how do we fix *your* childhood? If anyone deserves a bag of money, it's you."

She narrows her gaze and lifts on top of me, straddling my waist. Her large breasts fall and sway with her movement. "Fix my childhood? What's there to fix? I was loved, I had everything I needed, and I became a perfectly well-rounded, cutie-pie, that you can't keep your hands off." A playful grin lifts her face.

I smell her arousal, a scent that has me salivating like a fucking dog. My palms lift to cup her breasts and my cock goes harder.

"You cause trouble like this," I growl, "and I'm going to have to teach you a lesson."

She giggles and digs her hips into me further. "Oh! I like lessons! What have ya got?"

Why does her sweet banter get me so fucking hard? She's innocent and bubbly. Sweet and kind.

"Are you going to come for me tonight?" I lick and suck the tips of her nipples, taking my time with each one as she squirms on top of me.

She nods. "I'm going to come so hard for you."

Hearing those filthy words slip from her sweet lips is an out of this world experience.

Her small hand reaches beneath the sheet and grips my cock. She pumps my girth fast in her hand as she slides back slowly. I'm not sure where she's going at first, then her head angles down on my dick. Her soft lips take me in as her tongue swirls haphazardly and her tiny fist pumps.

Fuck.

My hands weave through her thick hair and those sweet lips rock back and forth over the tip again and again.

"That's a good girl. Take my cock."

She whimpers with parted lips, taking me deep into her throat, gagging as I reach the back. It shouldn't turn me on, but it does. The thought of grazing the back of her throat with my cock arouses me like I've never imagined.

I groan as her hollowed cheeks suck me hard.

I'm going to come if she doesn't stop. Fucking hell, I'm going to come.

"Eyes on me," I demand, tipping my index finger under her chin.

With my cock still in her throat, she gazes up at me.

"Do you like this? Do you like having my dick in your mouth? Does it turn you on?"

She nods, and sighs in agreement.

"Of course, you do. You're trouble." I growl out as she sucks me harder, bobbing her head up and down, over and over. "Okay, stop. I want you up here. Right now."

She doesn't listen at first. She keeps working, stroking my cock just right, sucking with ambition, desperate to taste me, but that's not how we're playing this.

I back away from her grip and she lets out a shiver. "Lean back on the bed."

She wipes her mouth with the back of her hand and does as I've asked, leaning back. She's dripping wet down her thighs, and her little pink mound is swollen and ready.

Fucking hell. I'm going to bust a nut just staring.

I lean into her core and brush my beard against her pussy, licking the tender flesh that surrounds her clit before pulling up a suction. My tongue swirls around the outside as she fists the sheets. Her hips rock upward unintentionally, desperate for relief.

"I need all of you, baby. Give yourself to me. Come in my mouth. Come for me."

She moans with pleasure and tilts her hips in every direction, scratching herself against my beard.

Over and fucking over, that sweet pussy taste spreads against my lips, on my cheeks, in my beard.

Fuck.

There's not a collapsing barn in the world that could stop me from this moment. "Come for me, baby. I need to taste your excitement."

Her small hands thread through my hair and tug gently as I slide a finger in. In less than a second, she's spilling sticky sweetness all over my lips, and I'm lapping her up like a melting fucking ice cream cone.

"I need you," she begs. "Now! No more waiting!"

"Trust me, I don't want to wait either, but I don't have a condom."

Her gaze drifts off to the side for a moment before she looks back. "I don't need a condom. I want you, Holt. I want you so bad."

"You know if I take you tonight, you're mine, right? No going back. I'm going to fill you up, and you belong to me."

"Fill me up, Holt. Fill me up!"

The anticipation of driving into her tight little pussy has my cock harder than it's ever been. I want her body, mind, and soul. I want to give her my babies. I want to marry her. I want to have a life with her on this farm. I want her to have her dreams, and I want us to live happily ever after. I want it all. I want it all with Ann.

I lift her leg onto my shoulder and twist her to the side, sliding my cock in gently through her arousal. "It's going to hurt. Tell me if I'm going too fast."

She nods and I watch her face gasp and contort as I press into her.

I underestimated how tight she'd be. I move slow, stretching her half an inch at a time, until she's more comfortable with the feeling.

"You okay, baby?"

She nods and I land kisses on her forehead. "I'm sorry, honey. It'll be easier next time. You feel so fucking good. Like you were made for me."

Her eyes close and her head leans back. "You can go faster. I want all of you. Stretch me wide, Holt."

The further I go, the tighter she is. She's strangling my cock, and I love it. I love the lavender scent of her hair, the sweet musk of her pleasure on my beard, the soft touch of her skin, the way her sounds vibrate through me, and the way my cock feels thrusting inside of her wet and snug.

"Fuck... I'm not going to last much longer. You're so fucking amazing."

I cup her breast and thrust harder and harder, watching her lips widen as I thrust deeper and deeper. I don't have another second in me. She feels too good.

One last thrust and I orgasm, growling out in pleasure as I release inside of her welcoming womb.

"You're everything," she pants. "I've never felt anything that good."

I lean against her shoulder, sucking gently as I pull from within her tight core. I'm not gone a second before I miss her warmth.

"I'll be right back," I say, before grabbing a cloth from the bathroom. I clean her thighs and kiss them gently before collapsing next to her on the bed, holding her in my arms.

"I don't think I can let you ride in that rodeo now." She twists at the hair on my chest as she talks. "I couldn't bare it if anything happened to you."

"Waylon might be up for a new deal now that I have money. I'll have to talk to him in the morning."

She wraps me up in her arms and holds me close. "I just want you to be safe, Holt. Whatever you do."

There it is again, those words she doesn't have to say. The words I've never heard from another soul. *She wants me to be safe. She cares about me. Not because I've done anything for her, or because she's obligated to. She just cares.*

I kiss her forehead and lean on top of her, swallowing her up. "I think I'm falling in love with you, *trouble*."

She grins wide and bites her bottom lip. "Then I think my plan worked."

Leaning into her lips, I kiss her over and over again. In life, there's never much assurance to anything. The barn could collapse, your dad could be an asshole, you could be handed a million-dollar check, or a snowstorm could leave you stranded for days. But the way I figure, if I've got Ann by my side, I've got everything I need.

Epilogue

Ann

One Year Later

Holt stands at the edge of the pasture with Lady Lightning, and our newborn daughter in his arms. It's unseasonably warm for January, but the baby is still bundled in a snowsuit and a thick wool hat. I have a feeling she's daddy's girl already. The two have been inseparable since we brought her home from the hospital.

"You know," Granny says, bumping against Earl's shoulder, "I didn't see him taking to fatherhood so well, but he's a natural."

"Careful there, Granny. You keep touching him like that and people might get the wrong impression," I say with a smirk.

Earl looks down at Granny and smiles. "Trust me, I would be the lucky one."

"Yes, you would," Granny says. "I'm already keeping him off the street most days and giving you two peace and quiet." She chuckles. "If he wants anything more, he's going to have to earn it."

Earl blows out his lips. "If you're waiting around for me to impress you, I fear I'll be long gone before that happens."

"What are these two arguing about now?" Holt meets us at the top of the hill, Blossom peacefully sleeping in his arms. She's only six pounds, but she looks even smaller against his giant frame.

"Nothing," Granny says, leaning into him for a hug. "We're just heading out. I see Waylon just pulled up, though. You owe him another rodeo tour?"

Holt rubs his back. "Nah, the last one was good enough for me. I was lucky I didn't do any permanent damage. I'm not sure what he wants."

Earl kisses baby Blossom on her head and turns toward the truck. "We'll see you two soon. Don't wait up." Granny rolls her eyes and grabs Earl by the arm to walk him away.

Before they get too far, Holt pulls Earl in for a hug. "See you later, Dad. Stay out of trouble."

It's only the second time I've heard him call Earl 'dad' and the first time I've seen them hug. Even at our wedding, they only waved goodbye to each other.

"Don't read into it," Holt says, glancing toward me.

I grin. "I already have."

Waylon parks at the end of the driveway and walks up slowly, taking a survey of the property as he moves. He's a tall man, covered in ink, with a long beard that he keeps trimmed just below his chin. I can't imagine why he hasn't found a woman yet. My friends are always asking about him.

"What do you think he wants?" I reach for Blossom, but she fusses when I touch her. *Okay... you can stay with Daddy.*

"I'm sure it's something about the cattle drive. He's been looking for day labor or a few more cowboys. Maybe he's wondering if we know anyone."

Waylon tips his hat and greets Holt and I. "Nice to see you two again... and to meet this little girl. Everyone in town is talking about her. Granny says she's the next rodeo queen."

Holt shakes his head. "Not if I can help it. I plan to keep her locked up until she's at least thirty. Even then, we'll screen all her visitors. What's going on with you? Everything okay?"

Waylon nods. "We're all good here. I'm just hoping you could help a man out."

Holt and I look toward each other with a narrowed gaze. Waylon is usually a straight-shooting man. When he wants feed, he asks for feed. When he needs help with a tractor, he asks for it. This cryptic conversation is new.

"What's going on? We're always here to help." Holt shifts and readjusts Blossom in his arms as a cool wind blows across the driveway.

"Well," Waylon stalls, "I need help with a girl."

"Interesting, you old dog." Holt nudges Waylon and grins wide. "Who's the lucky lady?"

"That's the thing," he groans. "It's a little messy."

"Okay." I'm desperate to tell him to spit it out, but the man is still a business contact, and I'm beyond curious why he made a special trip over here to tell us he's met someone. "What's the problem."

Waylon rubs his hand over his beard. "She's a friend's daughter."

"Are you serious?" Holt, who has no social decorum, let's his voice slide into a weird criticizing tone that I have to clean up.

"Everyone around here knows everyone. Of course someone you want to date has a family you know."

Holt looks over at me. "Baby, it's because she's also young."

I look back and forth between the two bulls and you can see the air has changed. "We have a gap in *our* age. That isn't a huge deal."

"How bad is it, Waylon?" Holt rubs Blossom's back gently as she coos. "I just got finished saying that I was locking this one up. If you're telling me you're here to take her, I would start running before I can draw."

Waylon laughs, but I think Holt's made his point.

"She's not that young, and she needs my help. She's got this shitty ex who won't stop harassing her and I can't help thinking I need to step in." Waylon nods his head, as to justify what he's feeling and what he wants to do.

"Well, I think it's lovely, Waylon. You've been a good person to us always and to this town. If someone is lucky enough to catch your eye, I say give it a shot." I reach forward and give him a hug. "I know you're not the kind of guy who would screw over anyone."

Waylon nods toward us, his massive shoulders widening before they relax. "Thank y'all for listening. I know this will be messy, but I need to find out what this could be." He smiles at us both and then rubs the top of Blossom's head. "I'll leave you be with your little one." He turns and heads back down the driveway. "Oh, and I've got another rodeo run for you if you're interested."

"He's good," I shout. "We'll be at Saturday's show, though. I hear Jake is up and riding again. I can't wait to see his comeback."

Waylon smiles and takes off toward his truck, but I can tell the smile is strained. Maybe we should've invited him in and let him talk about his dilemma more.

"He knows what he's doing. On paper, we aren't that much different." I place my hand on Holt's arm.

"Yeah, but a friend's kid?"

I laugh and shrug my shoulders. "Please, that isn't even the most taboo thing I've heard all week."

Holt gives me a look like I better talk fast.

I laugh out loud. "You see, I'm reading this book about a woman who falls in love with three men at one time."

Holt rolls his eyes. "Well, by those standards, Waylon's basically a saint." He smiles and leans into my neck, nuzzling me gently.

"Just be careful, mister. I've been known to cause a little trouble from time to time."

Thank you for Reading!
Love Rugged Mountain's Rough Alpha's?
Keep Reading for a preview of Protector Cowboy!

About

Khloe Summers is the author of over one hundred short and steamy romance titles. Her books are written in many different tropes, but always contain growly older alphas, curvy women, and lots of steam.

Khloe lives with her husband, (who she affectionately calls Daddy) in sunny Florida. They spend most of their free time sinking their toes in the sand, eating too many pizzas, and hollering obscenities at the TV on football Sunday. (At least he does. She sits on the sidelines and quietly orders nonsense off Amazon.)

Before this life is over, Khloe would like to check everything off her sexy bucket list and visit South Africa to wrestle evil poachers into submission. (And maybe see some baby elephants.)

HEA Guaranteed.

Read Bonus Scenes

at

www.authorkhloesummers.com

Protector Cowboy

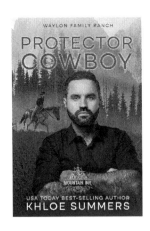

Chapter One

Penelope

I've read every romance novel I can get my hands on. The long ones with the angsty, drawn out love that takes forever and a day to establish. The short ones with an instant attraction that seems too unreal to be true. And the super toxic stories, where the couple fall for one another despite one partner's penchant for murder. They're all good one way or the other, and I've related to them all at different points in my life. The toxic stories, less. But still, the happily ever after that infuses my blood with dopamine is enough to get me through the week.

They're addicting, though. You get a high from the characters love, and when that wears off, your back like a junky, desperate for more. Wishing, hoping, praying, that one night you'll be lying in bed and a six-foot five Prince Charming will break into your house, admit his terrible fondness for robbery, and you'll fall in love with his dark brown eyes, massive muscles, and the giant cock that he can't even hide through a pair of jeans.

My love story went a little differently. I have the one where the girl misjudged a guy when she was naïve and doomed herself to a life of regret and disappointment. I say doomed with a sense of self-loathing because that's where I am right now.

Self-loathing, USA. It's a cute little spot by the river where white and gray ducks chase each other in a murky green pond. People gather round its edge to contemplate their life choices. I give it... four out of five stars.

There's the elderly man who sits slumped over the bench to the right of an oak tree. His frame is hunched over as he tosses tiny pieces of bread to the shameless ducks to rush out after. I bet he's lost someone. I imagine he and his wife came out to this same spot on Sundays. *No,* they went somewhere nicer, like the lake. The lake up near Whiskey Falls. He can't bear the thought of returning, so he sits here now, reliving their sweet ritual to the hum of strangers' tears.

Poetic.

To my left is a woman. I'd guess she's in her late forties. Her hair is tied back in a loose bun and her gaze is set on the mountain range in the distance. She couldn't care less about me, or the ducks, or the pond, or anything else going on around her. She's focused on whatever's in her head. Given enough time, I could make up a story for her as well, but I see David in the distance, and my stomach turns.

It's funny the things you give passes for when you think you're in love. *Robbery doesn't count. Look at Aladdin.*

David's faults are much more nefarious.

I was never truly attracted to David, but I thought his sense of humor made up for it. Now, everything he says is like nails on a chalkboard, and the humor I once thought was hilarious, grates on my every nerve. How could I laugh with him after all the hurt he's put me through?

I glance back at the pond and stand from the bench, making my way up the gravel ravine toward my car, parked on the west end of the lot. I should've parked closer. The last thing I want is a confrontation with him. I have what my best friend Kate calls co-dependency. Apparently, that means I rely on others too much. And David is the one I've relied on the most. I'd probably need years of therapy to debunk all the lifelong trauma that put me in that place, but I don't have time for that. I need to be strong right now.

"You're running from me again, Pen. We need to talk."

Talk. I laugh to myself at the concept. I tried *'talking'* to the man for months and he dismissed every thought I had with defense and criticism.

I keep walking.

"Seriously?" His voice gets louder, like he's jogging toward me. "You owe me a few minutes, at least."

I have so many things I could say to that, but I've read enough about co-dependency to know that turning around will only make things worse.

I'll state my case, he'll state his, and none of it will lead to the happily ever after I need to get high.

I pull my keys from the pocket of my jacket and press the fob to unlock the door, but his fingers grip the back of my wrist and pull me back.

"Come on, Pen. Talk to me."

If he didn't have a history of violence, I wouldn't overthink the touch. I've grabbed Kate's arm a hundred times and pulled her back from lots of things. *Another shot of whiskey, a date that didn't feel right, a mustard-colored dress that would undoubtedly invite ants.*

But when David looks at me, I know this touch is different. His jaw is clenched, his eyes are narrowed, and the flex of his fingers around my arm tighten.

"You owe this to me, Penelope."

I know it's not advantageous for me to laugh, but I can't help myself. The thought of me *'owing'* anything to a man that cornered me in a hallway last week to remind me how I ruined his life for the thousandth time is just funny, I guess.

"I don't think so." I chuckle and flinch from his grip, walking the last two feet to my car, but he grabs me again. This time, harder.

"It's your fault this shit is happening in the first place. *You* did this to us." There's darkness in his tone. Malice.

I don't answer. Answering only gets me in trouble. I'm proud of myself for staying, but he proves me wrong every time.

Turns out, silence gets me in trouble, too. He backs me up against the car door, his lanky frame hovering over me as his jaw tightens, and his teeth bare. I read about this in romance novels too, but it was never like this. Never with hate.

"Give me the keys," he grunts. "Now!"

"Penelope?" a deep voice interrupts from a distance. I've heard the tone before, but I can't place the man's face until David steps away and the man comes into frame.

Humiliation washes over me like a red-hot fever. It's my dad's best friend, Waylon. If I had to guess, the man is in his late forties, but he's ungodly attractive. I say *'but'* because I'm way too young to be ogling a man in his forties. Though, this guy is six foot six, covered in tattoos, wears a cowboy hat, and talks in a baritone that makes my pussy rumble.

"Hey." I wave toward him as though David wasn't just hunched over me threatening to take away my choice.

"Everything okay here? It looked pretty heated from where I was standing." Waylon glances toward David, then back at me, his gaze turned down as though he already knew what was going on. Of course, he does. He's not stupid. He runs one of the biggest ranches in Rugged Mountain. He employs nearly half the people in town between the ranch and his rodeo. You don't get to be that man without knowing how to read people.

"I'm fine," I lie, my hands still shaking. "David was just leaving."

Waylon looks toward David and his shoulders widen.

"We'll finish this later, Pen." David runs off to his truck like a scared little puppy with this tail between his legs.

We really do live in the animal kingdom, don't we?

I suck in a deep breath and twist back toward Waylon, my face still burning. "Wow. That was... embarrassing."

He shakes his head and steps toward me, his large hand landing on my arm like a giant blanket of warmth. I try not to find comfort in it, but I do.

"Who's that guy?"

I sigh and fidget with the hem of my cable-knit sweater. "My very recent ex, who apparently thinks we have unfinished business."

"Do you?" Waylon's gaze is directly on me, like he's looking for the parts I won't speak about.

"No," I laugh, "I don't. But he won't take no for an answer. I broke it off last week and he's been showing up at my house, at the park, wherever I go. I turn around, and there he is. It's insane."

Waylon looks up toward the west end of the lot, where David walked off. His truck is gone. "Tell me where he lives, and I'll go teach him a lesson."

It shouldn't feel so good to want David to pay for what he's done to me, but it does. Waylon's words fill into the cracks that have split open my heart, and somehow, make me feel important. That said, I say, "No, thank you. I couldn't let you do that. Besides, I think he's harmless enough."

That's a lie. *I know it's a lie. Waylon knows it's a lie.* Hell, I think the man throwing bread to the ducks by the pond, who hasn't listened to a word of our conversation, knows it's a lie. Nonetheless, I stare back at Waylon as though it's the honest to heaven truth.

He tips his head to the side and stares at me, his hand still on my arm, now moving up and down comfortingly. "He had you pinned against the car. You looked terrified, Penny. I couldn't go back to the ranch, look your dad in the eye, and not do anything about this."

"Oh, you can't tell my dad." My eyes widen, and I flatten my body toward him, my face more serious than it had been.

"Why?"

Waylon and my father have been best friends for as long as I can remember. My dad is Waylon's second in command on the ranch and they run in all the same circles through the rodeo in town. It's not going to be easy to ask him to keep this a secret, especially one that involves the safety of his best friend's daughter.

"First off, there's nothing to tell," I lie again. "David is an ass, but he wouldn't hurt a fly. Besides, you know how my dad is. He'll go all caveman, wind up hurting David, get himself in trouble, pull me from my apprenticeship at the tattoo shop, and I'll be destined to work at the diner or the ranch like everyone else in town. And no offense... but neither of those are my thing."

"Why would he make you quit the tattoo shop? David doesn't work there."

"No, but I met David there. He seems to think that hanging around people who cover themselves in ink is asking for a life of a degenerate."

Waylon looks down at his arms and then toward me. "I'm covered. And I've known the man for eons. He's never said a thing to me."

I cock my head to the side.

"*What?*" he probes.

I shake my head. "Nothing."

"It's not nothing. You were going to say something, but you held back."

I stare at him. "It's nothing. Just... Dad always said that's why you... why you're single."

He laughs. "Did he? Because of my tattoos? There are plenty of guys in town with tattoos and nice families. And what's his excuse?"

I shrug. "Anyway, you can see how irrational the man is. I don't want to stir things up with him. I'm begging you. If I thought I couldn't handle myself, I'd reach out to someone, but I can."

"And when the asshole comes back later? What then?"

"Then I handle him like I always have, and he leaves."

Waylon looks toward me with a wary gaze, as though he's trying to find the balance between respecting my wishes and safeguarding himself against possible fault. It's a beautiful gaze, one that I'd like to paint and hang on my wall as the only man that ever took my wishes into consideration before acting.

"Fine," he groans. "I'll keep your secret," he hands me his card, "but you check in with me every day, and you let me install a security system at your cabin."

I consider his offer. A security system isn't such a bad idea. I'm not sure why I didn't think of it sooner. Not only does it keep me safe from the asshole known as David, but it would also be nice to know when a bear is snooping around out back. I walked straight into one last week just making my way to the car for work.

"Okay," I sigh, losing myself in his big, rough palm. "Sounds like a plan. I'll text you my address."

He nods and opens my car door, helping me inside carefully. My body lights. It shouldn't be lit. If anything, this is only proof that I've read one too many books.

"Text me when you get home safe. I know a guy that can install the cameras quickly. I'll have him stop by tomorrow morning. If I'm not with him, don't open the door. Do you understand?"

I nod and stare up toward Waylon as though he has all the answers, like he's Prince Charming, and I'm the girl whose panties are way too wet for chapter one.

Keep <u>Reading Protector</u> Cowboy on Amazon

Made in the USA
Columbia, SC
16 February 2024